IF
I
SHOULD
DIE

IF
I
SHOULD
DIE

•

Judith Kelman

BANTAM BOOKS
NEW YORK • TORONTO • LONDON • SYDNEY • AUCKLAND

IF I SHOULD DIE
A Bantam Book

ISBN 0-553-29102-5

For Kathé and Rolly Allen,
miles and centuries better
than the chicken pox

ACKNOWLEDGMENTS

Many thanks to Dr. Manuel Zane, Doreen Powell, and all the staff and patients at the White Plains phobia clinic who allowed me to share their courageous journeys.

As always, I am grateful to my amazing agent, Peter Lampack, and my most excellent editor, Kate Miciak, for their skillful support and encouragement.

"The better is always the enemy of the good."
Sigmund Freud

IF

I

SHOULD

DIE

CHAPTER

1

He waited for the fear.

A dozen paces from the bridge, Theodore Macklin paused and scanned the sullen sky. Grim clouds huddled against a deep flannel canvas. A few intrepid stars bled their hazy shimmer through the gloom.

From below came the rhythmic lapping of the currents. Peering down, Macklin eyed the darkened string of homes rimming the scalloped Rhode Island shoreline. Closer was a scatter of small islands. One, half the distance to a sprawling waterside hotel, boasted a blinking lighthouse. The soothing cadence of the flash seeped into Macklin's mind. Inhaling the bay's briny essence, he felt a startling surge of exhilaration.

Chancing another stride, he braced for the expected jolt of terror. When none came, he trained his reluctant focus on the bridge: the soaring beige towers, the draping suspender cables, the pale green stiffening trusses fencing the sides. Along the span, gangly pole lamps leaked ragged pools of light.

Tacked to the nearest post was a dented blue sign that read: LONELY, DEPRESSED, CONFUSED, SUICIDAL? Underneath was the name and eight-hundred number of a suicide-prevention hotline. Not a phone in sight. He sniffed at the dark irony and searched his pockets for a cigarette.

Macklin was a large man rendered in broad-brushed squares. For years he had capitalized on his commanding presence: the earthy rumble of his voice; the harsh, chiseled features; the intimidating stare. The bulk and gruff demeanor were perfect camouflage for the timorous little boy who cowered inside.

Few who knew or even saw the man would have suspected the truth. All his life, Macklin had been bullied by a strident crowd of fears. The fears had dictated his every move, consumed his consciousness, reduced the scope of his existence to a suffocating cell. Now, balanced high above the water, the catalog of terrors reeled through his head in a taunting loop: bugs, dead animals, lightning, elevators, bridges.

Bridges.

The word evoked the typhoon of visceral horrors he now anticipated with a curious, electric dread. Macklin could imagine his heart thundering like wild hoofbeats, his throat locked in vicious spasm. He conjured the dislocating swirl of unreality that would overtake him without warning, buffeting him like a leaf in a violent storm.

The fear was unbearable; the waiting was worse.

He drew closer until his shadow slithered onto the concrete floor of the span. Nearer still, he extended an arm and ran his fingers over the curve of the side railing. It was slick, chill, strangely soothing. Clutching the metal tube, he drew a hard breath and ventured onto the forbidding body of the bridge.

The lady shrink at the phobia clinic had advised him to expect the fear. *Accept it.* She'd urged him to surrender his futile resistance: *Ride the terror through. It will only last a minute or two,* she had blithely assured. *No permanent harm will be done.* She'd sworn that panic had no power to harm or maim or kill despite the mind's screaming certainty that it would.

Desperate for relief and a measure of freedom, Macklin had struggled to believe her. He'd placed himself in her reputedly capable hands, though she had been far too young and desirable to serve him as anything near a figure of succor or authority.

In fact, she'd reminded him of the one he'd worked decades to forget. Same eyes: green marbles shot with amber flecks. And she'd had the same power to fill him with hot squeezing waves of lust.

During their sessions, he'd found his attention veering constantly to the ripe swell of her breasts, the suggestive curve of her upper calf, the inviting hollow of her lap. Lying on the leather couch in her office, confessing his humiliating fears and weaknesses, he'd pictured her kneeling over him. Straddling him. Taking him in her mouth.

That's how Macklin had ached to employ that particular doctor. But he knew how crucial it was to control the lethal longing. An instant's lapse, and it could turn out like the last time. Events gathering speed, spinning out of check, bursting into shards of bloody horror.

Remembering, Macklin had battled the desire. He'd forced himself to listen to the doctor's canned advice and neat theories. And he'd endured the humiliating therapy program, though none of the foolish tricks or tools or exercises had seemed to make a bit of difference. After ten days, he'd left the clinic's intensive course with nothing to show for his efforts but the bill.

Or so he'd thought.

But now, instead of panic or even a twinge of apprehension, he felt oddly at ease. His breathing was slow and regular, his heart the vague flutter of a hovering moth. His muscles felt lithe and easy. No vertigo. No hot currents coursing through his veins.

Moving with unaccustomed grace, he started across the span at a brisk walk. In moments, his pace quickened to a jog and then a buoyant run that took him across the bridge and rapidly back again to his starting point. His senses were superkeen, his mind charged with elation.

"Yes!"

His voice was a trumpet blare of euphoria. He caressed the rail and shivered with the thrill of the conquest. Playing the uprights like a xylophone, he strode to the center of the bridge and peered overhead at the lofty steeple-shaped tower. No adverse affects. Not a trace of dizzy dislocation. Not a pinch of fright. He imagined himself a magnificent bird perched on that celestial peak. Flaring his wings and soaring unbound toward infinity.

Macklin slipped off his custom-made black wing tips

and navy silk socks. He wrestled off his silk tie and wrenched open the starched collar of his shirt. Shrugging off his suit coat, he hefted himself onto the railing. There he sat for a moment, staring at the inscrutable black depths below.

He was one with the stillness. Whole and wholly free for the first time in his life. Everything but this vivid scene melted to irrelevance, everything including the dark troubles of the past week. They had discovered him, and now he was poised to face the unthinkable consequences: indictment, trial, public humiliation, prison. The only chance he'd seen was this hopeless, terror-filled flight.

But now, he was overwhelmed by a melting wash of well-being. Strange.

Lovely.

Hefting himself onto the railing, he deftly found his center. Arms akimbo, he began treading toward the distant end of the span.

A gentle breeze urged his progress, ruffling his hair. His step took on a jaunty spring. He was a clown-faced acrobat on the high wire, wielding a whimsical parasol, dazzling the gaping throng with his feats of nimble daring.

Ladies and gentlemen, I direct your attention to the center ring where the world-famous Magnificent Macklin will perform incredible feats of death-defying courage on the high wire. Please, no sudden noises.

Whistling his own accompaniment, he executed a pair of swift, bold pirouettes and landed on the balls of his feet.

"Ta-da!"

He proceeded at a wanton clip, leaping and turning, infused with joy, until he reached the center of the far suspender cable. Only a short way to the roadway beyond.

Winded, Macklin gazed over his shoulder at the conquered span behind him. He cast a bold eye at the heavens and raised an exultant fist. Then, glancing down, he spied the stolid face of the silent bay two hundred feet below him.

Suddenly, a tidal wash of dizziness assailed him. The

walls of the world began to tremble and fall apart. Reaching out, he groped frantically for solid purchase. But all he caught were teasing crumbs of the disintegrating sky.

He worked his bare feet in a desperate dance. *Where was the railing?* There, he felt the hard metal bite under his left heel.

Macklin calculated the way to bring his right foot in safe alignment. Probing with his toes, he sought the safety of the rail. But he kept stepping down in the emptiness.

Thrashing wildly, he felt the tightening grip of a blind panic. His heart stammered, and his throat slammed like a triggered trap. The world shattered in a reeling kaleidoscope as he tried to wrench a strand of reason from the tangle of horror.

At the last second, he clung desperately to the doctor's words. *The panic will be over quickly,* she'd told him. *Only a minute or two.*

But it was time he did not have.

CHAPTER

2

No time to worry about it now.

Tossing the troubling note in her desk drawer, Maggie Lyons swiftly donned her lab coat, traded her running shoes for a pair of pumps, and headed to the fire stairs linking East End Hospital's second-floor psychiatric service to the medical wing on three west. A smooth-cheeked resident brandishing a chart greeted her with a scowl.

"She's in there, Dr. Lyons. And frankly, you're welcome to her."

The young doctor, whose badge identified him as Mitchell Goldberg, stabbed a finger toward the semiprivate room opposite the nurses' station. Goldberg's baby face was pinched with disdain.

"Woman's completely off the wall," he said. "Wacko. Don't know why EMS didn't bring her up to the cracker factory in the first place."

Struggling to ignore him, Maggie started toward the room, but Goldberg stalled her with a continuing litany of complaints.

"We had to move the roommate in the middle of the night. Poor old lady couldn't handle the commotion. Got a migraine from all the carrying on. Every time we think she's finally given up, she starts in again. Would you believe four doses of Valium, and she's still putting up a fuss?"

Maggie flipped through the chart and frowned. The patient had been shot full of enough tranquilizers to fell an

6

elephant. "Says here she was admitted at two A.M. Why didn't you call me earlier?"

Goldberg shrugged. He had the wide eyes and curly locks of a baby lamb, and his white coat was long in the sleeves. Gave him the look of a kid playing doctor. Then, maybe he was.

"Thought I'd let you sleep and wait for a decent hour. Figured she'd keep."

Maggie held her tongue. An appalling number of her fellow physicians viewed the patient's mind as a largely vestigial organ. Psychic distress had a way of paling beside the grand drama of physical disease, she supposed. After all, the mind didn't bleed. It didn't rupture or fracture or yield startling lab results. The mind wasn't amenable to high-tech treatments or the sort of sensational research that caught the eye of prize committees. And it was not, in the grand budgetary scheme of things, all that terrific a profit center, either.

Since hiring on to run East End's new phobia clinic three years earlier, Maggie had stubbornly endeavored to lead her more prehistoric colleagues to the light. No medicine was as potent as psychic well-being. Loneliness, despair, and self-loathing could be far deadlier than excessive cholesterol or inadequate exercise. People were considerably greater than the sum of their bruised or degenerating parts.

To Maggie, fledglings like Goldberg were the most crucial converts. And with her typical fierce optimism, she decided there was some hope for this one. True, the little twit had subjected the patient to hours of unnecessary anguish. But at least he'd finally conceded the need for psychiatric intervention.

"I'm sure you were trying to be thoughtful, Doctor," she said in the most neutral tone she could muster. "But I never mind being called in an emergency."

"Didn't think it was." Goldberg shrugged and strode away. Noting his supercilious swagger, Maggie resolved to get to work on him as soon as possible. The guy had certain incipient jerk tendencies that could easily turn chronic.

Maggie knocked at the patient's door, waited a decent interval, then entered. At first glance, the room appeared ransacked and abandoned. The blinds were drawn, webbing the space with shadows. The sheets had been wrenched off, exposing the stained flannel pad and striped ticking underneath. There was a gaping wound in the thin cotton spread and several parallel rips in the pillowcase suggestive of cats' claws. Beside the boxed radiator, the metal nightstand lay upended. It was framed by a scatter of spilled juice, sliced bananas, and dry cereal from a toppled breakfast tray.

Could the woman have walked out?

Crossing toward the window, Maggie recalled Goldberg's dispassionate recital on the phone. "I've got a forty-two-year-old white female admitted for possible smoke inhalation after a house fire. Name's Daisy Tyler, and I'd say Daisy's more than half crazy. So, I figured I'd better give you a call."

By Goldberg's account, the woman had spent the night alternating between fits of hysteria and periods of mute, almost catatonic, withdrawal. No one and nothing, including the outrageous overabundance of medication, had been able to calm her or elicit rational responses.

"Why don't you stop by and have a look when you get a chance?" he'd said offhandedly at the end. He might have been asking her to check a leaky faucet. No big deal.

Rounding the foot of the bed, Maggie caught a breathy whimper from the far corner of the room.

"Miss Tyler?"

As she approached, the cry gained volume and urgency. Maggie paused and spoke in a gentle lilt. "It's okay. My name is Maggie Lyons. I'm a psychiatrist. I know you've been having a terrible time. I'm here to help you."

There was a brittle silence that soon shattered in a burst of agony.

"Take me *home. Please* take me home. I can't stand it!" The voice was scraped raw by hours of desperate shrieking. *"Please!"*

Edging closer, Maggie could see the woman cowering on the floor behind the protective hill of her knees. Her crossed arms fenced her head as if she were braced against incoming enemy rounds. Sinking beside her, Maggie rested her hand on the woman's back. The hospital gown was sweat-soaked. So was the curly gray-brown hair which now drooped in a wriggling wormlike mass. Daisy Tyler exuded a charred smell mingled with the ripe scent of despair.

Maggie worked her palm in soothing circles. Dr. Goldberg's instant assessment aside, this woman was not psychotic. To Maggie, who'd seen many such patients during her ten years as a specialist in anxiety disorders, the problem was obvious. Daisy Tyler suffered from severe agoraphobia, a term whose literal meaning was the fear of open spaces.

Having experienced sudden excruciating attacks of baseless panic, such patients went to great lengths to avoid what they viewed as potentially threatening situations. The condition tended to escalate over time until many agoraphobics were unable to drive or travel freely or even run routine errands. Those most severely plagued felt safe only at home. Some went even further, confining themselves to a single room. There, they remained self-sentenced prisoners, often for life.

"How long since you've been out of the house?"

The woman drew a ragged breath. "Long time."

"Ten years? Twenty?"

"Twenty-two."

Maggie felt a tug of sympathy. This woman had been hiding from her fears for half a lifetime. Suddenly, the only secure place in her universe had been obliterated. As Goldberg told it, the fire had totally gutted the small prewar building on East Seventy-eighth Street where Daisy had passed the last two decades in a three-room apartment. Fortunately or unfortunately, she would not be going back to that particular refuge for some time. Maybe never. It was the worst nightmare imaginable for a person with Daisy Tyler's psychiatric profile.

"Do you have any family? Close friends? Anyone you'd like me to call?"

Daisy shook her head and hunched deeper into the circle of her own protection.

"Nothing is going to happen to you," Maggie soothed. "No matter how bad you feel, you will get through this. We'll help you through it. I promise."

The woman raised her head a timid few inches. Her eyes gleamed with terror and unshed tears. "I can't. Don't you see? You've got to take me *home*. I'll die if I have to stay here."

"No, you won't. You'll be fine. Daisy, they've given you a lot of tranquilizers. A little might have been useful, but the amount you've had is just making it harder for you to get yourself in control. I'm going to help you over to the bed and sit with you until you fall asleep. After the medicine wears off, you'll feel better. Then, we'll start working on getting you well."

"I can't sleep here. I've got to go *home*. Please, *please*!"

"That's not possible, Daisy. You remember about the fire."

She moved to protest, but she couldn't escape the enormity of the truth. "My place is gone," she said dully.

"Yes."

"All my things."

"Yes. But things can be replaced. All that really matters is that you're all right. And you *are*, Daisy. But you need to get some sleep now."

With gentle insistence, Maggie prodded the woman, wobbly from strain and exhaustion, to her feet. Leaning heavily on Maggie, Daisy moved in an inebriated shuffle. Maneuvering around the fallen nightstand, they approached the bed in awkward concert. Maggie smoothed the jumbled sheets with her free hand, eased Daisy down, and pulled the covers to her chin.

"There. Try to rest now."

As soon as Maggie released her, Daisy stiffened and clutched her chest. "My heart's beating so fast. Oh, God, *help* me. I'm having a heart attack!"

The symptom was typical. To be sure, Maggie checked the woman's vitals. "That's just the anxiety, Daisy. When you're afraid, your body pumps extra adrenaline. That's what's making your heart race. It's nothing to worry about. Take a deep breath. Slowly. And another. That's good."

After an hour of steady reassurances, Daisy finally surrendered to a drugged sleep. Maggie decided to sit as she was for a while, not wanting any sudden movement to jolt the woman back to fitful consciousness.

Waiting in the dim silence, she metered her patient's ragged breathing. Daisy's face was puffed with grief, her features still ravaged by the anguish that refused to release her, even in sleep. Thankfully, Maggie thought, there was a way to ease this suffering. The treatment would be long and difficult, but the incinerated ruins of Daisy Tyler's life could be rebuilt, brick by brick.

Then, remembering the note she'd found on her desk that morning, it occurred to her that curing Daisy Tyler might be far from the biggest challenge she faced at the moment.

The memo had been scrawled in Alexander Ivy's flowery hand. The hospital's president wanted to see Maggie in his office promptly at five this afternoon. Command performance. A matter of some urgency, he'd written. Based on her unfortunate experience with the man, she knew there were a number of possible reasons for the summons.

And none of them was good.

CHAPTER

3

Sam Bannister peered through the morgue's viewing window, his eyes blazing fury. Three months they'd spent on the damned case. Three goddamned months, and now that they were finally within sniffing distance of the reward they deserved, the prime suspect had the gall to go out and get himself dead.

The stiff was Macklin. No doubt about it. Even stained the color of wet cement and puffed like a blowfish from his extended soak in Narragansett Bay, there was no mistaking the oversized creep. No matter how he tried, Bannister could not wish away the ax-head chin, the Frankenstein-shaped head, or the truculent mouth.

"Damn you, Macklin," Bannister said. "You spiteful, inconsiderate, ugly son of a bitch. Couldn't you have waited? Would a couple of weeks have goddamned killed you?"

A conciliatory hand settled on his shoulder. "Forget it, Sam. It's over. *He's* over."

Turning, Bannister took in Lenny Price's kindly, beleaguered face. Good old Lenny. No matter how unfair or infuriating the situation, the guy managed to stay cool and philosophical. No steam. No temper.

Made it a cinch to work with him, true. Bannister had teamed up with his old boss from Manhattan South a dozen times since opening his own Boston detective agency five years ago. And Price had never given him an ounce of deliberate trouble. But Bannister dearly wished the guy could work up a little lather over scum like Macklin.

"You're wrong, Lenny. It's not over. Not by a long shot. The prick may be dead, but that no way means I'm finished with him. He's got some nerve, pulling a stunt like this on us."

Price sighed. "Try not to take it personally, Sam. The man didn't off himself to mess up our case, after all."

"That's your opinion."

"Come on. Be reasonable for a change. Macklin's gone. The cops are tagging it a suicide. Nothing we can do about it. Case closed."

Bannister spoke through clenched teeth. "What about the happily-ever-after part? What about our payoff? You know what this does to that big, fat bonus check we were angling for? Makes it fly bye-bye, that's what."

"You knew not to count on that."

"The hell I did. I was going to pay off my national debt with that check. Buy new wheels, maybe. My car's so old, a fill-up is ten bucks worth of embalming fluid."

"What's done's done, Sam. Your problem is you don't know how to let go of things. Lighten up a little. Life's too short."

"*I* don't know how to let go. No one holds on harder than you, Price. You'll follow a lead through a brick wall and back again."

"That's different. I'm talking about knowing it's over when it's over."

"And I'm talking about a fifty-thousand-dollar reward."

"Think of your blood pressure, Sammy. You're getting all red in the face."

Bannister silenced him with a look. Price hitched his shoulders and slumped back into his perpetual slouch. Everything drooped along: eyes, jowls, gut, gray cardigan, worn brown corduroys.

"Try to look on the bright side, Sam. We still get our time and expenses. Mrs. Rafferty told me she was putting a check in the mail this morning. That's something, isn't it?"

Price's flawless good nature finally brought Bannister to a boil. He slammed his frustrations into the wall so hard the plasterboard dimpled. Behind the glass, the horrified coroner's assistant yanked the curtain shut, shielding the corpse from Bannister's unsightly temper.

"Good riddance," Price said with a dismissive swat, and blew his bulbous nose for emphasis. "Forget it. You want my advice? Put it behind you. Take a break, maybe. What's it been, three years since you had a real vacation? It'd do you a world of good to get away. Believe me."

"Yeah, sure." Still staring at the curtained glass, Bannister went grim and silent. His dark eyes narrowed, and his mouth drew in a hard seam. A subtle twist could alter his looks from matinee idol to plain mean.

"I'm serious. You've been pushing yourself too hard. Putting on too much pressure. Better ease up or you could snap, Sam. You don't want to wind up like Macklin."

A beat later, Bannister's expression brightened with a jarring suddenness that made Price take a few involuntary steps in reverse.

"Bless you, Lenny. You just gave me a great idea!"

Price shook his shaggy head. "I know you and your ideas, Sam. Whatever you're thinking, don't."

"Just listen, will you, please? It's like you said. Macklin snapped under the pressure. But it had to take time for him to get desperate enough to take that final dive, right? We've been leaning on him for months and we both know he was starting to come unglued. Meantime, maybe he went for help. Spilled his beans to a shrink or something."

"It's over, Sam. Forget it."

"Don't you see? He might have dumped everything. Made a confession even. I have this feeling that's just what happened—"

"You and your feelings."

"My instincts are impeccable, Price. Admit it."

"Sometimes they're impeccable, and sometimes they're as peckable as the next person's." Price snorted at his own humor.

But Bannister persisted. "We can't give up now, Lenny. Not after all we've put in on this thing."

Price shook his head. His jowels trailed a beat later. "I promised Ruthie no more missions impossible."

"What is it with you? Do you have to get the little woman's okay before you go to the can, or what?"

Price slicked back his fine silver hair and squared his shoulders. "Absolutely not. She gave me blanket permission for our twenty-fifth anniversary."

"Don't those apron strings pinch after a while? I bet you've got dents and everything."

"Tease all you want. So happens Ruthie and I have a good thing going. We love and support each other. And no matter what you think, she doesn't lead me around by the nose."

"By what, then?"

"It's a pity you have such a wrong impression of marriage. You picked a lemon, that's all. Ruthie has never stood in my way."

A naughty glint lit Bannister's eyes. "That's good to hear, Lenny. Because I need you in on this. It's going to take all we've got, partner. But we're going to make it work."

"I said no, Sam. Absolutely not."

Bannister draped an arm across Price's shoulders and propelled him out of the building toward the car. "I've got a really good feeling about this, buddy boy. You watch. Macklin's suicide could turn out to be just the break we were looking for."

Price raised his hands defensively. "Listen to me. When I spoke to Mrs. Rafferty this morning, she was real definite. Now that we've confirmed the floater was Macklin, she's out. No more per diem, no more covering our expenses. I will not let you do me another Schildhauer. That fiasco cost us but good."

Remembering, Bannister flushed with anger. Moe Schildhauer was an oily weasel who'd bilked hundreds of old people out of their life savings with a slick insurance scam. Reacting to a carload of complaints, the state's un-

derstaffed attorney general's office had hired Bannister to
investigate. Bannister had coaxed Price out of retirement
to assist.

The pair had met twenty years earlier in New York City
when Bannister was tapped as a rookie detective to serve
under Price on a special task force investigating the murder of Martha Rafferty.

Polar opposites, the two men complemented each other
perfectly. Bannister was long on nerve and intuition.
Price had an astounding network of willing contacts and a
bottomless well of insight and information. Bannister had
the knack to light Price's long, lazy fuse. Price was an
effective silencer to Bannister's loose cannon. Bannister
took the battering ram approach to a case, while Price's
investigations were slow and methodical and often
detoured in unexpected directions. By the time the state
task force was disbanded, both had recognized they were
doomed to a lifelong friendship.

Even after both left the New York force, they'd continued to find reasons to work together. They'd put in six
months on the Schildhauer case. During their examination of Schildhauer's sleazy operation, Price had discovered that Moe had a stake in a thriving kiddie porn
operation based in Brazil. Stalking that sideline had cost
them critical weeks. By the time they finally had enough
to nail the slime in the local insurance scam, he'd gotten
wise to their interest. He'd moved his entire operation,
damning evidence included, across the border to New
Hampshire.

Given the complexities of dealing with a neighboring
jurisdiction, the authorities had declined to pursue the
matter. The task force was disbanded. But Sam Bannister
was not nearly as practical or conciliatory as the state of
Massachusetts, and his temper was way bigger. So he'd
continued the case on his own.

Bringing Moe Schildhauer to justice nine months later
had been every bit as satisfying as Bannister had expected, but that satisfaction had cost him time, clients,
and a world-class American Express bill. Price, ever the
good-natured schnook, had agreed to foot half the freight.

Still, it was one of those investigations Bannister was happier not remembering.

"That was a matter of principle, Lenny."

"I know, Sam. But neither of us can afford too many of those."

Bannister thumped Price on the back. "Did I say *we* were paying? Mrs. Rafferty will be happy to pony up. She just doesn't know it yet."

"She was real definite. Now that Macklin's dead, she's out."

"That was before I hit her with my incredible powers of persuasion."

"She sounded like it would take something closer to a brick."

Bannister slid behind the wheel of his ancient Camaro. Under the terms of his recent divorce settlement, his ex-wife had gotten the new convertible, the speed boat, the lightly mortgaged house in the Boston suburb of New-town Highlands, and their dream lake cottage in the Berkshires.

Anxious for liberal visitation and wanting to shield Chloe, his thirteen-year-old daughter, from any unnecessary fallout, Bannister had been too damned agreeable. His ex—half Italian, half piranha—had taken full advantage.

"Please don't pull another Schildhauer, Sam. The Price nest is about out of eggs."

"Okay, fine. You want Macklin to have the last laugh, I won't argue with you."

Price sighed. "You know that's not what I'm saying. I was as anxious to see him nailed as anyone. Maybe more, but—"

"So he manages to get away with murder for all those years. No big thing. Guy was a real prince, wasn't he? I especially like how he tried to pin the blame on that retarded kid. Employed the handicapped and all. Maybe we ought to send a nice wreath to the funeral."

This time, Price's sigh thrummed with the sweet sound of surrender.

"All right, Sam. You win. But only if Mrs. Rafferty

agrees. Ruthie keeps reminding me that we could have taken my pension and bought that condo in the Keys five years ago. You have any idea how many rounds I could have played in five years?"

"I hear you, Lenny. You leave Mrs. Rafferty to me. Once I have her say-so, it shouldn't take us more than a couple of weeks. Three tops. And it couldn't be a more perfect time. Things are slow at the agency. Guess it's too nice out for people to feel like chasing stray husbands or sticky-fingered employees. Weather's supposed to hold, too."

"You're getting way ahead of yourself, Sam. We're not making another move on this case until you get Mrs. Rafferty's okay. I'm serious."

"I'll get it. I told you."

Price made a leaky tire sound and stared glumly at the grimy windshield as Bannister backed out of the spot. "I honestly don't see how you're going to convince her. Macklin's dead. The reward she posted was for arrest and conviction."

"So we change her mind. Mrs. R's a reasonable woman. As long as we deliver the goods, how can she object to a little shipping damage?"

Price rolled his eyes. "I have to tell you. I think maybe Macklin's not the only one who's gone head-first off the deep end."

"I'm as sane and steady as I ever was."

"Exactly."

Bannister flipped on the car's wasted radio, which spewed a rhythmic blast of static. Buoyed by the fresh possibilities, he sang along.

"Why the hell do I allow you to get me into these things, Sam?"

"Because life is more than classes and books and socializing and golf. It isn't enough to know everything and everybody in the world. You need a little excitement once in a while. Put a little color in your face."

"Ruthie's right about you. You're cute, but you're trouble."

"That Ruthie. She's such a kidder." Bannister pinched Price's jiggly cheek. "Don't you worry, Lenny boy. We're just going to do exactly what you said. We're going to find the way to put this whole damned case behind us. And then we're going to forget all about it."

CHAPTER

4

Order was everything. Life's essence was precision, endeavors set at scrupulous intervals like garments in a well-kept closet.

Any change in customary routine required cautious preparation. The calls and the news checks had been added with meticulous care a week ago, the day after the parcel was delivered to the midtown Federal Express office. Having dispatched the box by priority overnight service (delivery guaranteed before ten A.M. the following business day), there had been every reason to expect rapid results.

Now, the calls were placed to the man's office each morning at precisely nine twenty-eight, ten minutes after the secretary's customary arrival. The call to the city desk at the local newspaper was at ten to noon, nearly wrap time for the afternoon edition. At four P.M., there was the call to the society editor responsible for obituaries. Four was closing time for paid announcements and classified advertisements.

The trap should have sprung immediately. But so far, there had been nothing out of the ordinary except the man's sudden trip out of town. According to the secretary, the intended victim had departed two days before on a business trip.

Intolerable.

Despite the clear necessity for the calls and the news checks, the disruption of normal procedure was vaguely discomfiting, like eating something at odds with one's digestive system.

Why was it taking so long? According to the scrupulous plan, this first assault should have been successfully completed by now. By this time, the next one should already be in progress. Perhaps even the one after that.

It was inconceivable that the scheme would not work. Animal trials had demonstrated the drug's astonishing effectiveness. Macklin, the first human subject, had received the necessary preparatory dose for several weeks now. After ingesting the massive booster dose, Macklin would be stripped of all normal inhibitions. He would be moved to commit a feat of outlandish daring, probably something bold enough to capture the attention of the media. In the best case, it might prove to be an act of ultimate recklessness: the final act of the subject's useless existence.

Either way, Theodore Macklin was to be the first in a carefully selected string of foolhardy victims. Their inconceivable recklessness would be Dr. Maggie Lyons's undoing. She alone would be held accountable for her patients' unthinkable daring and the accidents and injuries that would inevitably ensue. That prospect was enough to ease the strain of the undertaking. Seeing that woman each day, knowing she was oblivious to the precipice looming before her, was a particular joy.

Dr. Maggie Lyons would pay with her precious clinic first. She would lose her cherished work. Her professional reputation would be destroyed, her future ravaged. Maggie Lyons would suffer ostracism, humiliation, the threat of financial ruin, possibly even criminal penalties. But nothing would be sufficient retribution for all the harm and suffering she had inflicted.

Still, there was the need for order. And order required a suitable end to each beginning. So first, Dr. Lyons must be stripped of everything, left with nothing but despair and confusion. When that was accomplished, it would be time to put the bitch out of her misery.

CHAPTER

5

East End Hospital's executive offices were housed in a five-story brownstone across the street from the block-long medical facility in the Yorkville section of Manhattan. Maggie wound up her four o'clock therapy session, dictated a short note to the patient's file, and left her office.

She was blocked in the hall by Francis Xavier Kennedy, a program aide with flame red hair and a complexion to match. Seeing her, he stood back from the pictures he was straightening. Maggie spotted evidence of F.X.'s compulsive tidying all along the corridor. The plants were in a line reminiscent of the Rockettes. The waiting room magazines had been alphabetized and set in precise rows. The notices had been straightened on the bulletin boards. Compared to Francis Kennedy, even Maggie's fastidious assistant seemed slovenly.

"Hey, Maggie. Hot enough for you?"

"For anyone, F.X. Please excuse me. I'm running late."

He stayed planted firmly in her way. "How about a drink when you wrap things up here? Seven be good?"

"No, thanks. I'm busy tonight."

"You must have time for a quick drink."

Maggie sidestepped him. "Good night, Francis."

Putting the pesty Mr. Kennedy out of her mind, she hurried across the street.

Sweltering city day. Ninety-plus degrees with rain forest humidity. The air hung like saturated towels, rank and heavy. Two minutes outside and she started to wilt. Her shoes pinched, and her beige linen suit took on that crumpled lunch bag look. She reveled in the mighty blast of conditioned air that struck her as she pressed open the ornate front door and quickly entered the brownstone's elegant lobby.

Formerly a private residence, the building and its furnishings had been willed to the hospital two years earlier. The foyer's inlaid marble floor sparkled with pins of light from a Venetian crystal chandelier. Stained Tiffany glass graced the windows. An antique Aubusson runner in shades of peach and turquoise trailed up the imposing staircase.

No time to wait for the cranky old elevator in the rear. Maggie trotted up the stairs and made it to the president's fifth-floor suite at five sharp. Breathless, she smiled at Vivian, the pale, fiftyish fixture behind the desk. The secretary, the office, and the job had all passed from father to son a year ago.

"Hi, Viv. Would you please tell him I'm here?"

Slipping on her rimless bifocals, the secretary tidied the stack of phone messages in front of her, then called inside to announce Maggie's arrival. Hanging up, she flashed an apologetic smile. "Better have a seat, Maggie. Seems he's tied up for a bit."

Maggie was not surprised. Alexander Ivy owned and used every conceivable power tool. He pressed for promptness, so he'd have plenty of time to keep you waiting. Never placed his own calls. Waited three days to return yours, longer or never if you weren't on his critical list.

What did surprise her was the swift and sweeping acceptance Ivy had achieved at East End. Most of the hospital staff seemed willing to overlook the administrator's boorish condescension and hyperactive ego. Or maybe, as Maggie's assistant, Henry, had once theorized, they simply hadn't been treated to that appalling side of the man.

So why was she so lucky?

Maggie eyed her reflection in the glassed photo of Vivian's grandkids on the desk. Same old face. She could still pass for Peter Pan's big sister with the cropped copper hair, large green eyes, and the silly little nose that had refused to grow up with the rest of her. No horns or snaggleteeth or hairy wens. Nothing obvious to inspire the kind of instant animosity she'd aroused in the hospital's new president. And she managed to get along reasonably well with most people.

But young Mr. Ivy was an unfortunate exception. It had been an acute case of loathe at first sight, and things had rolled steadily downhill from there.

Ironically, Alex's father, Lawrence Ivy, had been a valued friend and mentor of Maggie's since their first meeting a decade ago at a professional conference in San Francisco. The elder Ivy had wooed Maggie away from her assistant directorship of the mental health clinic at Johns Hopkins to start an anxiety disorders program at East End. With his encouragement and steady support, Maggie had built one of the premier phobia treatment centers in the country.

But then serious health problems had forced the senior Ivy into retirement, and little Alex had stepped in to fill his father's formidable shoes. The hospital had been founded by Ivy forebears and remained heavily dependent on Ivy Foundation largess. As the only remaining scion of the clan, Alex Ivy was the natural and expected successor to his father's position. The pedigree also gave young Alex the power of the proverbial eight-hundred-pound gorilla. He sat wherever he pleased. And for some reason, he'd chosen to sit on Maggie.

Poison Ivy.

She'd discussed the problem with her friend and assistant, Henry Most. Henry contended jealousy was the culprit. As he saw it, Little Alex envied his father's affection for Maggie, even now when the old man was terminally ill.

But that explanation was too tidy for Maggie's taste. As a seasoned student of human behavior, she knew things were rarely that simple. It was just as likely that she resembled a mean nanny from Alex's childhood or a woman who'd spurned his adolescent advances or some sadistic teacher who'd flunked him in seventh grade math. Whatever the root cause, she was determined not to let the president's animosity undermine her work. The clinic was too important to too many people. Herself included.

The phone issued a Bronx cheer. Vivian answered, listened, and nodded Maggie toward Alex Ivy's office.

Entering, she found the hospital's president hunched over a stout sheaf of computer printouts at his antique Chippendale desk. The office was paneled in burled walnut. A wall's width of glass-fronted shelves showcased first editions and fine porcelains. Brocade drapes in rose and gold tones hung at the windows. Matching fabric swaddled the scatter of settees and chairs. Alex Ivy waved Maggie toward one of them. He did not greet her.

The man was a nineties Napoleon, no taller than Maggie's five four despite the perilous lifts in his crocodile loafers. As usual, his tiny form was packaged in Armani couture and accented by Hermès. His hair, dyed the color of espresso, was scrupulously arranged. So was the shark smile he sported when he finally deigned to meet her eye.

"Thanks for stopping by," he said. "I hope this time wasn't too inconvenient."

"No problem."

He locked her in his steely gaze. "Unfortunately, Doctor, I'm afraid there *is* a problem."

Ivy flipped the mass of computer paper in her direction and pointed at a line of numbers. "The phobia clinic continues to show disappointing results. Frankly, I was hoping to see a significant improvement by now."

Maggie eyed the summary of the program's net revenues. "Ninety percent of our patients report a major improvement in their quality of life after treatment with us, Mr. Ivy. Eighty-five percent have maintained those considerable gains at the two-year follow-up. I'd say those are excellent results."

Ivy blinked slowly. His sapphire contact lenses hopped halfway up the whites before settling back in place. His real eye color, she noted, was cesspool brown. "In these difficult economic times, Dr. Lyons, we can't afford to ignore revenues. We're running a business here, not a crusade."

Maggie resisted an overwhelming desire to grasp his scrawny neck and squeeze. "True, and our business happens to be health care. My department may not be a gold mine, but we provide a valuable, proven service to our patients. And we've done more than our fair share to enhance the hospital's reputation."

Ivy snickered. "If you're referring to your shameless self-promotion, Dr. Lyons, I am frankly not impressed. So you have a good PR firm. So what?"

"I don't have a PR firm, I have a program that relieves serious suffering. The only reason I give interviews is to get the word out to people who need help. But it so happens East End isn't hurt by the positive press."

He waved in dismissal. "I didn't call you in to argue. Bottom line is, the phobia clinic is not pulling its financial weight, and every department must. You have six months to turn it around, or we'll have to make better use of the space. Ambulatory reconstructive is a major moneymaker, and they badly need to expand."

"What specifically do you need to see in six months?" Maggie asked, carefully keeping her voice steady. She wasn't about to debate the critical need for more butt lifts and tummy tucks.

"A twenty percent net increase, minimum. And a viable plan for continued bottom-line growth during the next fiscal year. Give me that, and I'll be willing to keep the clinic doors open. At least, for the time being."

Twenty percent. He might as well have told her she had to run the program on a space station or limit her practice to Buddhist monks with an unreasonable fear of goat cheese. The clinic was already operating at the lowest imaginable overhead, with all the volunteers and donations it could muster. The therapy groups and staff schedules were booked to capacity and beyond. Maggie was already putting in such long hours, she had to pencil in time for frivolities like sleep and nourishment. In fact, she'd been hoping to get the go-ahead to hire some desperately needed extra hands.

How the hell were they going to raise another twenty percent profit? Bake sales? Contract murders? Maggie knew exactly whom she'd like to fit for the first set of cement boots. Size seven, she guessed with a quick glance at his reptile Guccis. Definitely narrow.

"Alex, please, be reasonable. You know there's no way we can squeeze that kind of net increase out of the clinic."

"I'm sure there are ways to reduce your overhead. For starters, you can move up to the old office space we vacated on fifteen. Your program is low volume. No reason to tie up the valuable central footage you've got now. That would cut your space costs considerably."

He was baiting her, but Maggie refused to bite. "You *know* that's impossible. Some of our patients are terrified of heights and many won't ride elevators. We've discussed this before."

"I'm trying to help you out here, Dr. Lyons. You treat grown-ups. If they're afraid of bogeymen, am I supposed to post a bogeyman patrol in the lobby? Coddling those people can't possibly help them get rid of their nonsense. If the clinic moved to fifteen, I'm sure they'd manage somehow. Unless, that is, the clinic isn't as crucial to them as you seem to believe it is."

Maggie didn't bother to argue. True, phobias weren't rational. But they could be as real and debilitating as any illness. Maybe more so.

"We can't move to fifteen. It's impossible. And so are your demands."

Slow, deliberate nod. "Fine, then. I'll announce the program's unfortunate demise immediately. With all your media appearances, I'm sure you'll have no trouble finding another position."

"I didn't mean that." Having started the clinic and nurtured its growth, Maggie had a huge, proprietary stake in its survival. She couldn't imagine folding the place. She *would* not imagine it. "Six months," she said, mostly to herself. "Six months, and you'll have your twenty percent increase."

"I will, or the party's over, Dr. Lyons. Good day, now."

Maggie stormed out, slamming the door shut behind her. A good day, it most definitely was not.

CHAPTER

6

Careful, Jessie!

Watching his little sister through the window, Jason Childs's breath quickened and a rash of terror scaled his spine. Heedless of the skulking dangers, her moves were brisk and breezy, fine hair trailing like a lemon silk scarf. As she paused to poke the bushes, her head was cocked in concentration. Her lips were pursed. Practicing her whistling now that her front teeth were finally coming in, he thought. The way she was going full steam at life, she'd leave him in her dust sooner than he cared to consider. Laugh down at him the way the rest of them did.

He captured her image, held it hard as if she were about to burst like a seed pod and scatter on the wind. Her dress was a shapeless wisp of cotton, tiny flowers strewn across a blush pink ground. It was a year too short, so the hem barely skimmed the tops of her chunky thighs.

Her legs were a patchwork of scrapes and bruises. Especially the knees. Kid was forever trying something new and dangerous: roller skates, scooter board, a two-wheeler. She didn't seem to mind the hazards at all. Or maybe she was too young yet to recognize them.

Jason tried to think back to her age, to imagine himself light and reckless. But it was far too big a stretch over the dark pit of what he had become. Letting go, he was catapulted back to the fearsome present.

Her feet were bare. Sort of pretty. Pink pearl toes and rubber-ball heels. She sidestepped the hot stone path, scuffing instead through the parched brown grass beside it. At intervals, she ducked through the tall hedgerow fronting the house, and he lost sight of her for a breathless second.

Jesus Christ. What if something's back there? Watch out, Jessie! Careful, you little jerk.

There. She was out again. She looked bothered. Hiking the hem of her skirt, she wiped the sweat off her forehead with it. The fabric fell away, streaked with grime.

They were in the grip of a record heat spell, she'd announced that morning in her grating shrill of six-year-old authority. Smart little twerp she was, Jason grudgingly acknowledged. Jess had already absorbed the tacit family tradition of keeping him informed, bringing the world right to him, so he wouldn't have to go out and face his monsters more often than absolutely necessary.

Even looked hot, he thought grimly, pulling his eyes off her for a crucial moment of respite. Watching her was too much like doing it himself. Being out there, open and vulnerable. Risking a run-in with one of *them.*

Shaking off that intolerable notion, he shifted his focus to the shade-dappled front yard. They lived in Bayside, Queens. Less than half an hour from midtown Manhattan, though you'd never guess it from their sleepy circle of a block. Six nice, well-tended houses filled with nice, familiar people. Neat lawns and clipped hedges. Home was enough for him, he'd kept telling them. All he wanted. Why wouldn't they listen? Why wouldn't they stop nagging and pushing and *let him be*?

Usually, Jason enjoyed the neighborhood's rhythms, the comforting routines. Safe behind his window, he passed the time watching the cars as they left for work near dawn and returned each evening. He observed the clumps of kids who gathered to play each afternoon. He watched Mrs. Gavin walking the baby and Mr. Loring delivering the mail. At least once a day the UPS truck trundled up the street to drop off packages from the endless stream of orders Mrs. Hauptmeyer called in to the shopping channel.

At will, he could alter his view to break the sameness. Poised at strategic angles, Jason could catch a stray glimpse of Paul Haskel and Susie Weiss making out on the Weiss's creaky porch swing. He watched the burly Ziegans twins wrestling in their yard, snapping at each other like swamp alligators. Yards away, Dr. and Mrs. Ziegans clinked their martini glasses in front of their living room's bare bay window and fed each other olives speared on frilled toothpicks. Nothing was ever odd or unexpected or vaguely dangerous. But Jason felt an undercurrent of unseen menace. Even here.

Even now.

Right now, one could be out there, lurking in the shadows. Panting. Drooping tail weighted by evil intent.

And they wanted him to walk right into the trap.

There was an ominous stillness to the trees. The air quavered with an oily, unnatural haze. Probably bad for the lungs, Jason thought grimly. Too much ozone or carbon monoxide or some other deadly, invisible poison. Heat like this had to carry an excess of whatever made it so people with heart or lung conditions were warned by the weatherman to stay indoors. Who knew if he had one of those ailments they talked about on the health alerts? Could be he'd contracted one since his last checkup and didn't even know it. They had to let him cancel the stupid appointment.

They had to!

His sister was in front of the garage now, standing on tiptoe to peek through one of the tiny square windows in the roll-up door. His heart squirmed as he imagined a set of cruel eyes glinting back at her from the darkness. Silent. Waiting.

Don't open the door, Jess. For Chrissakes, be careful!

He wanted to fling open the window and shout out to warn her away, but he was frozen in place. Paralyzed.

Jessie crouched and grasped the rusty metal pull. Face scrunched, she hefted the heavy door high over her head. With a nod of self-congratulation, she brushed the effort off her palms and strode inside.

His throat clenched. *Don't let him get you, Jessie! Run for godsakes!*

But the runt acted in no particular hurry, weaving her

insouciant way around the Chevy wagon, tugging open
the hatch, stooping to check under the chassis. Familiar
with the routine, she lifted the lids on the trash cans.
Improbable or no, he could picture one hiding inside.
Ready to pounce!

Peering into the last of the bins, Jessie wrinkled her
cup-hook nose in dramatic distaste. Finished, she turned
toward the house and motioned for Jason to join her. He
read the exaggerated movement of her lips: "Come on,
Jay. It's all clear."

But the fear would not release him. His bowels rumbled, and a fiery pain stabbed his gut. Doubling over, he
knew he could not go through with this. Not today. He
must be getting sick or something. His mother would
have to understand. But then, he felt her standing behind
him in the archway. Turning, he saw the purse slung over
her shoulder. The shopping bag dangled from her wrist.
He tried to take some comfort from the thought of the
doctored watches inside. He'd painted a trace of his magic
formula on the inside of each band. But what the hell
good was that going to do him now?

The keys jangled in his mother's grasp. Her look was
grim and determined.

"Come on, Jason, honey. Don't want to be late for the
first group meeting, do you?"

He shot her a pleading look. "Feel my head, will you? I
think I'm coming down with something." Why were they
making him do this? Didn't they understand? They were
making the terrible things happen.

She frowned at him. "Didn't I hear Jessie go out to
check?"

"Yes, but—"

"Let's go, then. I'll walk right beside you. I promise."

"Not today. It's too hot out. And that guy from Shadow
Traffic on WINS says there's construction on the FDR.
It's tied up for miles in both directions. We probably
won't make it anyway." He heard his voice break.

*Stop this already. You've got to stop before it goes any
further!*

She crossed the room with firm strides and gripped him

by the elbow. "We're not putting it off any longer, Jason. You've got to keep at it like the doctor said. Look. Jessie's waving that it's okay."

"What the hell does she know? She's just a damned baby."

His mother blew an exasperated breath. "All right. I'll go double-check. But then, we're leaving. No two ways about it."

He stood rooted while his mother slammed outside and strode along the walk with Jess skipping behind. She had left the shopping bag in the foyer. Jason chanced a furtive peek at it and turned away.

If they made him go, he would not be responsible for the consequences. Whatever happened would be their fault.

Together his mother and Jessie repeated the ritual, poking behind the shrubbery, scrutinizing the contents of the garage. They peered into corners. Inspected the trash. Jason tried not to think about what would follow. He focused on how they looked side by side. Amazing resemblance. Mom was the obvious source of Jessie's fair hair and high color. Jess had won their mother's stony resilience and steel spirit as well. Little squirt was forever watching what older people did. She took it all in and imitated, him especially. Jessie did everything she could to hurry her way to adult independence. Jason was content to walk in place, avoiding change and challenge at all costs. He'd always favored his father: the mouse.

At six-two, he towered over his mother, and Jessie came no higher than his knees. But Jason knew he was the small one. Useless little nothing. If only he could act near his age and size. Squinting, he tried to imagine himself loping out to the wagon and sliding nonchalantly behind the wheel. He'd drive off for a burger and a beer. Pick up a few other kids on the way.

Maybe even Rina Latham, prettiest girl in the class. Rina had long black hair and eyes the color of pool water. He imagined her coming toward him, hips swinging in a tiny pair of shorts, cantaloupe breasts bobbing under her tank top. He pictured the smile spreading over her luscious lips as if she were thrilled to see him. He flushed and squirmed at the unwelcome quickening in his groin.

Stupid fantasy.

He'd never have Rina or anybody else. He'd never enjoy fun with friends or anything approaching a normal life. He hardly ever even bothered to dream about those things anymore. What was the point? He couldn't even do the basic normal things a six-year-old like his sister could.

He'd been old enough to drive for more than a year now, and he still hadn't mustered the nerve to get his license. The process would require too many trips outside his safety zone. Lessons. Practice sessions. What if one came along when he was behind the wheel? What if one lunged at the windshield? He shivered, imagining the sharp rain of shattered glass and the fanged monster landing on him. Clawing, tearing.

Why the hell couldn't they let it go? Didn't they realize what they were pushing him to do?

His heart squirmed. Jason knew he was getting crazier, more desperate and out of touch. But he was powerless to arrest his own decline. In the month since graduation, all he'd done was hang around the house, staring out the window. Except for his invention, everything seemed a worthless waste. The only feelings he had were the terror and the rage.

Before graduation, his parents had forced him to go to school. Mom had gone out to do the check every morning. Then she'd driven him, left the car running at the curb, and walked him right to the building's entrance.

In class, he'd get busy, and the fear would sometimes slip his mind. He'd been a good student, especially in math and science. In those subjects, he was so advanced the others had taken to calling him Dr. Frankenstein. But Jason had refused to let the teasing get to him. There were far worse things, he knew. At least he was good at something.

There had even been talk of him going to a top school like M.I.T. maybe on a scholarship. But how could he go away to college when he couldn't even get himself from the house to the damned driveway?

His parents kept hoping. Maybe after more treatment, they'd said. Maybe with more time and work . . . Maybe he'd be ready when hell froze, Jason thought bitterly. Or a couple of weeks after that.

Six months of treatment, and he was worse than ever. A few months ago, they'd let him quit. The doctors and aides had stopped coming; they'd left him in blessed peace.

Jason had thought it was a permanent reprieve, but after a couple of weeks, his parents had started in on him again, nagging at him to try attending a group clinic at the hospital. They'd kept at it until he was close to drowning in the flood of words. Finally to shut them up, he'd agreed.

But there was no way he could really go through with it. If he didn't get rid of the doctors and the sessions and the expectations that hung on him like lead weights, he'd lose his mind altogether.

The fear had been a shadow before, a cold looming mass that receded at times, allowing him a merciful glint of relief. But now, he thought about the beasts constantly. Snarling. Dripping beads of rabid saliva. Leaping at his throat. Ripping his flesh to bloody shreds.

At night, wild packs of them slunk into his dreams and circled his defenseless form. He'd wake up screaming from the phantom pain of their ferocious bites and the rank, musky stench of them. It had happened so many times, his parents didn't even hear him anymore. Or they heard, but they didn't bother to squander any more concern.

Only a dog, they'd told him a thousand, million times. Silly little pooch won't hurt you, Jason. Look at him, he's harmless.

Not harmless by a long shot. Someday, they'd see how dangerous. Deadly in fact. But by then, it would be too late for him. Too late for everything.

The door slammed, and he heard his mother's crisp stride followed by Jessie's catch-up hobble.

"Hurry up, Jason. We're running late."

"Hurry, Jay," Jessie echoed. "Can we get a soft pretzel

from one of those pushcart men, Mommy? And a can of soda. Can we, please?"

"Shh. Okay, sweetie. Let's go, Jason."

He was too shaky and weak to protest. Picking up the shopping bag, his mother urged him toward the foyer and out the front door. He wanted to tell her no, but he couldn't find the words. Leave the bag, he wanted to say. For godsakes, stop this before it goes any further. But they were already on the way.

The heat hit him like a sledge as the two of them tugged him toward the garage.

They were in there. No matter who'd checked, Jason knew they were waiting for him. He could hear the guttural growling. Feel the ravenous eyes.

Jason tried to resist. But they were stronger. Even Jessie was stronger. He was a limp balloon. Powerless and insubstantial.

The air bristled with blinding static. Jason strained to see through it. Suddenly, a shadow shifted, and his ears rang with shrill barking. He couldn't move. Couldn't think.

The snarling mass lunged at him. Leaped at his throat. Ripping. Tearing. He was immobile, suffocating under the weight.

"There now. No problem, see, Jason? Put on your seat belt, Jessie."

"I already did, Mommy. Can we listen to lite rock?"

Jason felt his mother's hand on his. Forcing his eyes open, he found her watching him wearily. The motor was running, the wagon shuddering as they backed down the bumpy blue stone drive.

His mother patted his hand and smiled reassuringly. "We're on our way, Jason, honey. You'll see. This program is going to change your life."

CHAPTER

7

Returning to the clinic, Maggie found her assistant rearranging the conference room furniture for the new phobia group. Henry Most had pushed the long veneer table to the window wall and set out sweating pitchers of lemonade and a tray of chocolate chip cookies. Near the door, a table held rows of plastic badges with the names of the group's six young patients.

The meeting room, like the rest of the psychiatric wing, had been done in numbing neutrals: dull army beige and the blue of a listless sky. The furniture was standard institutional fare: molded plastics and mock woods mounted on tubular aluminum frames. Vapid still lifes and seascapes on the walls were intended to pass for art.

The entire floor had been redecorated earlier in the year, but staff input had been scrupulously ignored by the interior design firm hired by Alex Ivy. At first, Maggie had found the decor depressing. But Henry's small, perfect touches had managed to lift the gloom and make the space seem almost cozy.

Bright watercolors from the pediatric art program festooned the bulletin boards and lit the dull corridors. Fresh flowers from Henry's cutting garden further slashed the monotony. Scatter rugs, scavenged on some of his daily rummage runs around the building, hid most of the deadly white-flecked linoleum tile. Other forages had produced the cheerful fabric panels that Henry had transformed with tape and staples into makeshift curtains. Maggie had declined to ask where or how her assistant

had procured the appealing cotton prints. Something told
her she didn't really want to know.

Dear Henry. The man was gentle but fiercely loyal.
Sweet and thoughtful and unfailingly self-deprecating.
Maggie felt a swell of affection as she watched him pass
from chair to chair, making subtle adjustments to suit his
scrupulous eye.

"Looks great, Henry. Thanks."

"Maggie, hi. Didn't hear you come in. Almost ready
here. How was President Ivy?"

"He was himself."

"Too bad. He want to see you about anything in particular?"

"Plenty. I'll fill you in later. We're due to start in a
couple of minutes." She sampled a cookie from the tray.
"Delicious. You make them?"

"No. Gail Weider did."

"I should have guessed. Best chocolate chips in the
universe."

Henry nodded agreement. "She stopped in about an
hour ago. Said the cookies were her contribution to the
new group."

"That's great." Maggie had been concerned about Gail,
a former patient and program aide who'd stopped attending department meetings and self-help sessions a couple
of months ago. Her defection had been sudden and unexpected, and Gail, a guarded and highly sensitive soul, was
not the type to express the reason. Maggie had suspected
she was reacting to some unintentional slight. Hopefully,
the gift of her legendary cookies meant all was forgiven.

Henry adjusted his black-framed glasses, smoothed his
argyle vest, and brushed invisible lint from the leg of his
charcoal trousers. At sixty, he had aged to suit his well-
upholstered frame and mellow features. It was easy to
imagine how he'd been as a little boy, awkward and out of
place. He continued to ready the room while Maggie took
another last-minute look through the intake summaries.

She'd read them over several times and interviewed
most of the group members personally, but she wanted to
set each patient even more firmly in her mind. This was

the first time they'd offered a group restricted to young adults. She knew it was a worthwhile addition to the program. But any adjustment to the clinic's proven operation gave her a mild case of the doubts, especially now.

For the pilot group, she'd restricted enrollment to six. There were four females and two males, the usual skewed ratio for phobia patients. Maggie shared the pervasive suspicion that the disorder struck equal numbers of men and women. But males were generally reluctant to admit to anything as unseemly as being afraid. They resisted treatment until the fear grew strident enough to outshout the stubborn roar of macho pride. Maggie supposed that was why her male patients tended to be among the most seriously afflicted.

She recalled how totally incapacitated Henry had been when he attended her first phobia clinic at East End three years ago. His mother, an indomitable old woman, had convinced Maggie to get involved in the case despite Henry's initial reluctance. By Mrs. Most's report, Henry had not left their Brooklyn neighborhood in the nearly forty years since his graduation from NYU. For almost the last three decades, she said, her son had not ventured beyond their tiny yard.

It had taken two months of home visits by Maggie and the combined efforts of both women to get Henry to the clinic. For most of the group sessions, he'd insisted on his mother's presence in the room. Nearly a year had passed before he made any significant gains. But after that, with constant support from Maggie and an aide, he'd begun to confront and vanquish his terrors. Henry had made steady improvements until he was able to function like a normal adult. Now he traveled freely and attended his own needs. Although Maggie had been concerned, he'd even adjusted well to his mother's sudden death almost a year ago and seemed reasonably secure and comfortable living alone.

Daily, he drove from his house in Brooklyn's Flatbush section to the hospital, where he'd graduated from patient to aide to his current slot as Maggie's chief assistant. Henry could not have been better suited for the job. His excellent management skills balanced her penchant for the haphazard. Scrupulously sensitive and guarded, he tempered her unfortunate tendency to shoot, under fire, from the lip. Henry was mild and mellow and paternalistic, all the things her own father decidedly was not. Maggie hadn't the slightest idea how she'd ever managed to run the program without him, and she wasn't at all interested in attempting to do so again.

"It's six now," he said, eyeing his watch. "Don't want to keep them waiting."

"Go ask them in, then. You're in charge."

"I don't know, Maggie. Are you sure about this?"

"Positive. You'll be wonderful. Now go before I'm forced to start pouring on the compliments and risk swelling that handsome head of yours."

He flushed and averted his gaze. Such a sweetheart, Maggie thought. Having him run a group was long overdue. All of the group clinics were led by former phobics with the oversight of a staff therapist. Despite Henry's characteristic diffidence, he was certainly up to the responsibility. No one had a more intimate understanding of what it took to break the stifling bonds of anxiety. And no one could possibly have a clearer appreciation of how much that break could mean. For the last year, Maggie had made it a point to assign him as the aide to some of her most challenging patients.

"Go on, group leader. Time to start."

He disappeared down the hall and returned in minutes trailing a ragged line of reluctant patients. They stalled outside the door as if the room were on fire. Henry had to urge them inside and direct them to sit. In seconds, the circle of chairs was decimated as several of the newcomers moved predictably closer to the door.

Maggie smiled at the few who chanced eye contact. She'd met all but two of the new patients. There was Tracy, a sallow, skittish twenty-year-old whose social phobia made the group both a particular trial and a critical opportunity. Lauren, a mite with a mass of hair and an ebullient personality, had a terror of insects, real and imagined. Andrea, pert and ponytailed, was terrified of elevators. Melissa, whose prom queen looks belied her reticence, had a dread fear of choking that rendered her incapable of eating in front of anyone else, her family included. The teenager had been forced to drop out of college after a year of trying to subsist on nothing but the crackers and jam she'd kept in her dorm room.

The two young men straggled in last. Other members of the staff had handled their intake interviews, so Maggie didn't know which was which. Looking at them now, she guessed that the sallow, pimpled youth with the shaggy shoulder-length mane was Stephen. An accomplished violinist, he had a morbid fear of storms and all manner of extreme weather conditions. He picked up his name tag, confirming her hunch. So the lanky youth with the pallid complexion and frightened gray eyes had to be Jason Childs, an agoraphobic with a particular dread of dogs.

Jason's parents had brought him to the clinic's attention eight months ago. Because the young man was unwilling to come to the hospital, one of the residents and a staff psychiatrist had volunteered to do the initial evaluation at the Childs's home. The same clinic psychiatrist, a good friend of Maggie's named Pamela Richards, had continued to make house calls to provide weekly therapy. F.X. Kennedy had agreed to act as Jason's aide, traveling to the young man's Queens neighborhood for the necessary practice sessions.

Despite the concentrated effort, however, Jason's progress had been disappointing. Three months ago Maggie and Pam Richards had reviewed the case and concluded that participation in a group might provide the elusive breakthrough. Jason's family had been working on the young man since, urging him to give the clinic a try.

After everyone was settled, Henry quickly distributed a number of sheets and pamphlets from the neat stacks he'd extracted from his briefcase. There was the brochure describing the clinic's brief history, current services, and staff. A pamphlet Maggie had written defined phobias and explained what was known about their causes and cures. There was a preliminary questionnaire that would be compared to a similar survey at the final group meeting in six weeks. The other handouts listed suggested reference works, self-help organizations, and the five basic steps to recovery that would be repeated and reinforced constantly during treatment: acceptance, goal-setting, rehearsal, practice, reinforcement.

Smiling meekly, Henry cleared his throat and clasped his hands behind his back.

"I'm Henry Most, and I'll be leading this group under Dr. Lyons's direction. Three years ago, I came to this room as frightened and uncertain as you are. Maybe more. But Dr. Lyons turned my life around."

"No, Henry. *You* turned your life around. All I did was help you figure out how to go about it."

Henry shook his head. "She may deny it, but Dr. Lyons is responsible for what I am today, for what my life has become. If you're willing to follow her program, you'll be amazed at the changes in yourselves. Every one of you."

Maggie saw the pooled emotion in his eyes. Old Mr. Softie looked ready to break down. But he squared his shoulders and continued.

"Let's start by having each of you explain why you've come to the phobia clinic. The first step in our program is acceptance. We're going to look those fears straight in the eye and learn how to get past them."

Lauren with the big hair volunteered to speak first. She chirped on for fifteen minutes, describing her harrowing run-ins with cockroaches the size of tour buses and diabolical tarantulas who convened nightly to plot her undoing. Lauren was a phobic rarity, able to laugh at herself, fully aware that her fears were baseless and exaggerated. Still, she was powerless to overcome them, and the consequences were sometimes devastating. Earlier that week she'd seen a water bug in the kitchen sink and fled her West Village studio apartment in a panic. Unable to return, she'd spent the next three tormented nights on a bench in Gramercy Park. Junkies and muggers were less intimidating to her than the products of her own imagination.

Andrea spoke next. She eyed the floor as she recounted an adolescence rich in regret and rife with squandered opportunities. No visits to friends in high apartments. No senior prom, since hers had been held in the tower suite of a twenty-eight-story hotel. To her, an elevator was a moving tomb. She imagined suffocating inside, or worse.

Maggie listened as Henry deftly led the young patients through their difficult initial confessions. Acceptance was the first, critical phase. Each had a problem. It was not unique, and there was no reason for shame or denial. The fear could be overcome through a specific plan of treatment and practice.

As usual, after the third group member had spoken, there was a palpable slackening of the tension in the room. Each was beginning to realize they were all in the same leaky boat. Not alone.

Jason Childs spoke last. The teenager's posture was guarded, eyes darting like night creatures facing the hostile unknown. Odd kid, Maggie thought. Nothing said phobics couldn't be every bit as weird as the next person. When Jason finished, Henry fixed him with an expectant look. After an awkward pause, the boy ducked down and retrieved a shopping bag from under his seat.

"Here." He shoved the bag toward Henry. "My dad's insurance firm has a deal with a premium business that makes all kinds of customized stuff. So they cost next to nothing."

Smiling, Henry distributed the contents: T-shirts with *Thursday Night Lyons Club* printed on the back and sport watches with a ring of lions prowling the plastic band.

Henry explained. "When I talked with Jason about coming to the group, he noticed how appropriate your name is, Maggie. Dr. Lyons: queen of the cowardly lions. We thought the club idea might provide some added inspiration. So those are Jason's contributions. And here's a little something from me."

Henry distributed small white boxes. Each held a lion-shaped medallion on a silver chain. For Maggie, there was a special gold version with tiny sapphire eyes. The card read, *"For Maggie. I'll never forget."*

Fastening the chain around her neck, Maggie swallowed a lump of emotion, and she clearly wasn't the only one affected. The group sprouted smiles, and there was a burst of enthusiastic chatter. With the myriad techniques she'd incorporated in the program, she'd never considered the power of good, old-fashioned flattery and tangible rewards. She'd always been an ardent believer in using whatever worked. Looked as if Henry's clever touches weren't limited to accessorizing a room.

The group broke up so the members could meet with their individual aides over refreshments. In addition to the weekly meetings, each patient would complete a series of individually prescribed practice sessions with the help of a specially trained recovered phobic. Henry and Maggie made the introductions.

When they finished, Maggie touched the medallion. "This is so sweet, Henry. Everyone really appreciated the idea."

"Jason thought of it. I just went along."

"Aren't you ever going to take credit for anything?"

His eyes went vague. "There's so much I owe you, Maggie. I can't imagine ever being able to pay you back for all you've done."

She didn't bother to respond. She'd told him dozens of times that he'd been responsible for his own recovery. But Henry persisted in pinning all his abilities and accomplishments on others. It was part of what made him Henry, she supposed. And Maggie was more than willing to accept the package, minor failings included.

"That was a really good first session. Something tells me your group is going to make record strides."

"I hope so. I dearly do. Give you a lift home?"

"No, thanks. I've got a little record keeping to do before I go."

"Take the leftover cookies, will you? I'm trying to lose a few pounds."

"My pleasure." Maggie was a sucker for Gail Weider's masterpiece chocolate chunkers. Good thing the woman only made them once in a while and stubbornly refused to part with the recipe.

Maggie spent the next hour in her office, dictating a

report on the group's initial meeting for her records. Thinking about the six young patients, she smiled. Watching people like those hatch and fly made everything seem worthwhile, even having to put up with Poison Ivy.

Unreasonable creep.

She was definitely not going to let him get in the way of what the clinic was able to accomplish. She'd think of something. Not a doubt in her overconfident mind.

Leaving, Maggie spotted Pamela Richards at her desk in the adjacent office.

"Hey, Pam. I met your prize patient tonight."

"Jason Childs actually showed up? Now there's a medical miracle."

"The miracle will be if we make any headway with him. He didn't exactly seem thrilled to be here."

"The group has to work for that kid, Maggie. I couldn't get anywhere with him and neither could F.X."

Despite the frown, Pam Richards was a picture worth framing. A tall, opal-eyed blonde with aristocratic features and a goddess body, she missed the stock physician image by miles. Though she wore no makeup and sported stern, dark-framed glasses, she was frequently taken for a model or an actress. Strangers would approach with giddy tentative expressions and say, "Didn't I see you in that film with—?" or "Aren't you—?"

Maggie's initial reaction to Pam had been similar awe and an unreasonable pang of envy. The two women had met when both were on the psychiatric service at Johns Hopkins. Though Maggie wasn't by nature a jealous soul, Pam, with her beauty, intelligence, and serene good nature, had instantly been a particular inspiration. Their first few professional encounters had only served to intensify Maggie's irrational resentment. What right did anyone have to look that good and be that affable and brilliant?

But getting to know Pam had evicted the green-eyed monster. Maggie sincerely liked, trusted, and admired the woman. Pam was honest, open, and entirely unassuming. If anything, she was a bit on the shy side. And, while she wasn't unaware of her physical endowments, she was painfully aware of their down side. Men were intimidated by Pam and rarely asked her out. Those who did seek her company tended to do so for unfortunate reasons. The outcomes were similarly unfortunate. Pam's catalog of dating disasters ran to several volumes.

Maggie and Pam had become and remained close friends and compatible colleagues. After signing on to head East End's phobia program, Maggie had convinced Pam to come along and join the staff. Not surprisingly, Dr. Richards was one of the most sought after and effective doctors on the service.

"I hope the group helps, Pam. But if you couldn't get through to Jason, I have to admit I'm not all that optimistic."

"You never know. Look at Henry. No one ever imagined he'd come this far."

Maggie grinned. Pam was the optimist's optimist. The glass might be half full to Maggie, but Pam had it spilling over. The only fault Maggie could honestly find with her friend was how difficult Pam made it to keep up a bout of serious moping.

"I'm starved. You free for dinner?"

"I'd love to, Maggie. But I promised myself I'd catch up on these reports."

"Good idea. I hear the head of the clinic's an absolute bitch about paperwork."

Pam smiled. "That she is. See you tomorrow, boss lady."

No one else was left working on the floor but Dr. Drew Paulson. Paulson was an ardent Freudian who published obsessively and spent so much time in his office that Maggie often wondered why he didn't have himself built in. With his penchant for temper fits, she also wondered why Paulson wasn't spending some time on the other side of the desk. Lunacy was an equal opportunity employer, after all. Psychiatrists were certainly not immune.

As Maggie passed his office, Paulson peered up from the perfectly aligned manuscript he was editing and rubbed his eyes. His skin was the color and texture of old parchment, his hair a patchwork of yellowed cotton wisps.

"Working late again, I see, Dr. Lyons. I hope nothing's amiss."

"Not at all. Everything's going beautifully, in fact. We started the young adult group tonight. Henry ran it. Wonderful first session."

Paulson's dour expression showed no signs of thawing. "Yours is an intriguing system. Effects without causes. Responses without stimuli. Equal treatment for all, regardless of need. Irresponsible, no doubt, but no one would accuse you of being undemocratic."

Maggie smiled sweetly. "I'm flattered to see you've given my program so much thought, Dr. Paulson. Now I'd better run along and let you get back to your groundbreaking research. The world is waiting, after all."

On the way out, she turned off the lights and locked the conference room door. Passing the patient rooms, she stopped to check on Daisy Tyler. The woman was watching the tube through heavy-lidded eyes. She looked drowsy and relaxed. Much better.

"Need anything before I go, Daisy?"

"No, thanks, Dr. Lyons. I'm feeling all right. See you tomorrow."

Exiting the hospital building, Maggie found that the heat had lightened to match her mood. Funny how things could turn around like that, just when you least expected.

CHAPTER

8

Leona Rafferty lived in a harborside duplex on Newport's exclusive Goat Island. Over Price's hefty objections, Bannister drove directly there from the coroner's office in Providence, and they landed on her doorstep unannounced. Waiting for the client to answer her bell, Price kept shifting from leg to leg like a skittish pigeon.

"We should have called first, Sam. I hate busting in on someone like this. Maybe she's not dressed. Maybe she's not even home."

Bannister pressed the doorbell again. He figured they'd already suffered more than their share of obstacles and inconveniences on the Macklin case. The woman simply had to be home and receptive to his plan. He refused to entertain the alternative.

"Really, Sam. I don't like showing up without calling first—"

"Mrs. Rafferty!" Bannister crooned in a muted singsong. "There, I called. Happy now?"

"Actually, no."

Looking himself over, Bannister found all the suck-up essentials in place: paper cone of flowers, affectionate gaze, sycophantic smile.

Given sufficient motivation, Bannister could spew charm like an open hydrant. And right now, he was plenty motivated. Fifty thousand dollars and three months' worth of work were riding on this little visit. So was his gnawing hunger for revenge. The thought of Theodore Macklin sticking his thumb on the scales of justice yet again brought Bannister to frying temperature. That rotten creep's death could not be the final curtain here.

Finally, he heard the trudge of approaching footsteps. The door opened to the limits of the latch chain.

"I told you I was sending a check right out, Mr. Price. By now, I'd think you'd know I pay promptly."

The voice was elderly but firm. Bannister chuckled. "This isn't about the bill, Mrs. Rafferty. Lenny and I just wanted to stop by and say a personal thank-you. Working for you has been a real pleasure."

The door closed. They heard the security chain slip from its casing. The woman reappeared, backlit by the stream of sunshine through the glass terrace doors. Somewhere in her seventies, she had cloudy blue eyes and aristocratic bearing. Wavy white hair framed a strong-featured face softened by melancholy. She wore a navy skirt and a white silk blouse set off by vintage jewelry. Jane Austen's collected works were pressed to her ample bosom, and reading glasses dangled from a chain around her neck. Her gaze skipped from Bannister's face to the flowers he held and back again, and her lips pursed in rebuke.

"What is it you really want, Mr. Bannister? I'm way too old for tap dancing."

Bannister's smile evaporated. "And way too smart."

"True. So if you have something to say, go ahead. But I only speak plain English."

Bannister turned to Price. "I need to talk to Mrs. Rafferty alone, Lenny. Give us half an hour."

"But, Sam—"

"You may as well go, Mr. Price. If I refuse to hear him out now, he'll only nag at me until I give in. You'll find a diner two blocks down on the left. They have excellent pastries."

After Price made his reluctant exit, Leona Rafferty led Bannister through a tasteful living room decorated in blond woods and pastels to a terrace cantilevered over the rippling currents of the bay. Bannister breathed the salted breeze and eyed the lazy line of sailboats floating ghost-like across the horizon.

Felt like he was on his fantasy vacation: Caribbean island-hopping on a chartered yacht. With a bitter frown, he thought this was probably the closest he'd ever come to the real thing, unless you counted his regular cruise on the choppy sea of perpetual debt.

Leona Rafferty's voice shattered his sour reverie. "Coffee?"

"If it's no trouble."

"It is, but I'll get you some anyway."

She directed him to sit on one of the webbed lounge chairs and disappeared inside. In minutes she returned with a flowered porcelain pot, matching cups, and a platter of fruit and Danish.

Bannister sipped awhile, mesmerized by the rocking motion of the tides. The view was so relaxing, he almost forgot the purpose of his call. Almost, but not quite.

"I'll be straight with you, Mrs. Rafferty. I'm here because I'm not ready to give up this case. I don't think Macklin's death has to be the end of the line. In fact, I have a strong feeling we can milk his suicide for some final answers."

"I've already made my decision, Mr. Bannister. It's the end of the line as far as I'm concerned."

"I don't buy that. For twenty years, you've wanted the truth about your daughter's murder. If I can finally prove who killed her, why should it matter whether the guy is dead or alive?"

She sighed. "Because you can't punish a corpse."

"No, but you can settle the score. You can know Macklin was definitely the one. That's got to make it easier to live with."

The woman was silent.

"Give us a couple of weeks," Bannister urged. "Three tops, and I'm sure we'll be able to tie up the ends. I can feel it."

"I'm afraid all good obsessions must come to an end eventually, Mr. Bannister, even one as old and stubborn as mine. At this point, I'm finally willing and able to let it go. I'd advise you to do the same."

Bannister searched her weary face for fine print. He found none.

"Yeah, sure. It was your daughter, after all. If you can forget about her murder, it shouldn't be any problem for me."

She caught him in a hard stare. "That was a cheap shot, Mr. Bannister. I think you'd better leave now."

"Please, Mrs. Rafferty. I can't give up now that I'm this close. It's not my goddamned way."

She blinked. "Pursue it, then. I can't stop you."

"Problem is, you can. Chasing the truth costs money, which I happen not to have. So, if you won't go along, I guess I'll have to drop it. Like it or not."

She stared out at the water. For a moment he thought she had shut down. Then she said: "Chasing the truth can cost considerably more than money. I've found that out the hard way."

Bannister didn't get it. How could she ride this far and slam the brakes on now? He tried to imagine what was simmering inside her. Tried to fathom how he'd feel if the victim had been Chloe.

The thought made him shiver. How could anyone live with a thing like that? Your only child is eighteen. She's a good kid. Sweet, pretty, smart. Plenty of friends, unlimited future. One night she goes to a party in the neighborhood. It's a safe, solid party. The parents are home. You've known all the kids practically from birth.

Your kid leaves the party at twelve-thirty with a pack of friends. Her curfew's one A.M., and she's always been the type to respect the rules. She's the kind of kid who remembers birthdays and gets good marks and sends thank-you notes without nagging and doesn't believe in sex without love. She's the kind who sometimes makes you stop and consider how lucky you are, and the thought makes you nervous as hell.

Half a block from your posh Park Avenue apartment house with the caring neighbors and the watchful doorman, the other kids say good night and peel off. Your daughter has three goddamned buildings to pass. Shouldn't take her more than two minutes to get home along a familiar street. But instead, that innocent little stroll detours through the black belly of hell and lasts for the rest of eternity.

Ten days later Martha Rafferty's nude body was hooked by a sport fisherman angling for blues. She'd been raped, strangled, and dumped in the Long Island Sound. Capricious currents had carried her remains half the distance to Great Neck, New York.

Other capricious currents worked to scuttle the subsequent investigation. From the beginning, the Rafferty case was distinguished by a record number of mistakes. Crucial evidence was lost. Critical interviews were botched. Key information was leaked to the media, generating a spate of confounding false confessions and time-consuming bogus leads.

In the worst of them, an anonymous tipster had fingered a boy from a building two down from the Raffertys'. The investigating officer had failed to locate the kid and deemed him a guilty runaway. It had taken the cops a month to wake up and discover that their principal suspect was severely retarded and living in a residential facility in Queens.

Even the autopsy results had been scuttled when the girl's corpse was accidentally embalmed.

Six months after Martha's death, New York City officials, anxious to atone for the embarrassing mess, had tapped Lenny Price, a seasoned homicide detective with an excellent batting average, to marshall a special task force to breathe some life back into the Rafferty case.

Price had hand-picked his crew, choosing the rookie Sam Bannister in the hope that his youth and looks might give him an edge in gaining the confidence of Martha Rafferty's young friends.

The task force had given the case their best, but there wasn't much left to resuscitate. They'd narrowed the focus to three suspects: a vagrant named Willie Dean known to frequent the neighborhood, a janitor from the building next door to the Raffertys' who'd come forth as an early witness, and Theodore Macklin, a classmate of Martha's who'd lagged behind that night to speak with the girl when the others drifted away on the fateful walk home.

After interrogation and extensive scrutiny, everyone on the task force was convinced Macklin was their perp, but their attempts to prove it hit a series of dead ends and blind alleys. No incontrovertible physical evidence, no witnesses. And the doorman in Macklin's building had corroborated the young man's unshakeable story that he'd arrived home moments after leaving the group without a mark or a drop of blood on him. Six months later, Price was forced to declare the unit out of leads, and the task force was disbanded.

As a last-ditch gesture, a local citizens' group had posted a twenty-thousand-dollar reward for information leading to an arrest and conviction in the Rafferty case. The reward had generated a flurry of renewed interest in the case, but not enough to crack it open. At the time, Mrs. Rafferty had urged her husband to up the ante, but, determined to try to get past the tragedy, he'd refused.

Cut to twenty years later, and the old man dies of pancreatic cancer. Left with nothing but her millions and her hideous memories, Mrs. Rafferty decides to make another attempt to vindicate her daughter's death. She posts a fifty-thousand-dollar reward for information leading to arrest and conviction of Martha's murderer and hires Bannister and Price to take another crack at the old case. By then, both men had relocated to the Boston area, where the principal suspect in the original investigation also happened to reside.

Price jumped at the assignment. Given new forensic techniques, old evidence could be milked for fresh information. Bannister was equally inspired to hire on, though for different reasons. Something about the case had grabbed and held him from the start. In two decades, he'd never been able to get the smell of the unsolved Rafferty murder off his hands.

With Mrs. Rafferty footing the bill, the pair stirred the ashes and followed the yellowed brick road. They sifted through all the ancient evidence, did enough mouth-to-

mouth on friends, neighbors, and relatives to revive mori-
bund memories. Slowly, things started to come together.

Fibers cut at the time of the murder from the carpet of
Teddy Macklin's car were treated with Luminol, a substance that causes even the most minute blood traces to
glow in the dark. Bingo. The traces were analyzed and
found to match Martha Rafferty's blood type, factor for
factor.

It was compelling new evidence, but not enough to
take to a grand jury. As Price pointed out, Martha Rafferty
could have taken a ride with the Macklin boy at any time,
cut her finger or accidentally bitten her lip, and left the
minute amount of blood found on the carpet sample. But
soon, other things started slipping into place.

Both Teddy and Martha had attended the exclusive
Harper School. Several classmates who'd been shocked or
intimidated into silence decades back now recalled
Teddy's obvious crush on the Rafferty girl. They remembered him obsessively scrawling her name on his note-
books, compulsively watching her. More than one alluded
to an ancient rumor linking Macklin to a terrible accident
involving one of Martha Rafferty's boyfriends, Ricky
Bates.

It had happened at the start of Martha's senior year in
high school. Seems the Bates kid was trying to help a
friend navigate his car into a tight parking space in an
outdoor lot. Ricky was standing in the space against the
side of a brick building. When the friend tried to slowly
ease in, the car accelerated wildly. In his struggle to escape, Ricky had fallen and been crushed against the wall.
His knee was shattered, leaving him with a permanent
rolling limp. It took six operations to reconstruct the boy's
face.

When the car was examined, there were signs of tam-
pering. There was no proof against Teddy Macklin, but
everyone was aware of his mechanical bent. Macklin
loved to tinker with engines. In fact, seventeen-year-old
Teddy had rebuilt his own vintage Olds 88 from the
wheels up.

Bannister and Price had managed to track down most

of Martha Rafferty's old friends. When they had compiled a damning but still legally deficient case against Macklin, they decided to confront the bastard. Maybe they could goad him into a confession.

They'd made an appointment to meet with him at his posh offices on Commonwealth Avenue. Teddy Macklin had grown up to be a high-rolling financial advisor. He handled only those clients who had portfolios in excess of a million bucks. Bannister and Price claimed they had plenty to invest and wanted to hear how Macklin would propose to handle it. It was true enough, only they weren't talking dollars.

Confronted with the particulars of the case against him, Macklin had acted every inch the hooked worm. In minutes, he'd gone from mock outrage to angry denial to desperate accusations. Bannister had taken in all the guilt symptoms: dilated pupils, shallow breathing, sweat circles spreading under his arms. But Macklin hadn't cracked.

Leona Rafferty drew a breath, tugging Bannister back to the present and the peace of their perch overlooking the bay. "All I've wanted since Martha died was to see her murderer punished. If Ted Macklin killed my daughter, he killed my chance for final justice as well. You got my hopes up these past months, Mr. Bannister. And that's been far more painful than I ever imagined. My husband was right. I should have left it alone."

Bannister sipped his coffee. It was lukewarm now and bitter. "I can't tell you what to do, Mrs. Rafferty. But if you want the truth, I think we can still get it for you."

Her eyes filled. "Martha was such a delightful child. And so popular. Everyone loved her. But it never went to her head. She remained entirely open and unassuming. Always went out of her way to befriend the children who had trouble fitting in. She managed to find some good in everyone, even a difficult, belligerent boy like Teddy Macklin.

"Teddy had few friends. He put people off. Martha took him under her wing, urged the others to include him as well. Ironic, isn't it, Mr. Bannister? My daughter's own kindness probably killed her."

Sounded like his Chloe, Bannister thought. Kid was a pistol. Charming, smart, caring. She'd inherited the best of her mother and him. Looks, personality. Lucky thing. A different toss of the Darwinian dice and she could have been a vindictive bitch like his ex or a stubborn, hotheaded bastard like her old man. Different roll of fortune's wheel, and she could have been bones and ashes like this poor lady's little girl.

Almost a week now since he'd spoken to his daughter, Bannister thought with a twinge. Last time, Chloe'd been in an adolescent stew over something or other. He'd have to call her later, see how she was doing.

"Kindness didn't kill your daughter, Mrs. Rafferty," he said, and she flinched. "Some sick son of a bitch did that and got away with it. At least, he's gotten away with it so far."

The doorbell rang. Certain it was Price, Bannister went to answer. Lenny had sprouted a powdered sugar goatee, jelly scars, and a satisfied grin. He held up a rumpled brown bag.

"Great doughnuts. I brought a couple for you, Sam. Don't tell Ruthie, will you? She's been after me to watch myself."

"So you'll watch yourself blow up."

Mrs. Rafferty had stepped in from the terrace. With a glance at Price, she proffered a linen napkin. He accepted it as if he were accustomed to having his hygiene supervised. Bannister, watching anxiously, spotted a trace of softening in the old woman's expression. He turned away quickly, before he scared it off.

"Say good-bye, Lenny. It's time we hit the road."

"You needn't run on my account," she said. "Maybe you'd like some coffee, Mr. Price."

Bannister could feel her nibble. Tiny tug on the line. "Thanks anyway, Mrs. R. But we've really got to get going. Anyway, Lenny's trying to cut down. Aren't you, partner?"

He knew to play it nice and steady. Reel her in. Without a beat of hesitation, he steered Price out the door and across the lot to the Camaro. Resisting the urge to look back, he opened his partner's door. As he crossed to the driver's side, he could feel the old woman's eyes on him.

He would not blow it. Under no circumstances would he give her the critical bit of slack. Gritting his teeth, he slid behind the wheel.

"Mr. Bannister?"

He waited, milking the moment. Pretended not to hear her call as he fiddled with his seat belt.

"Mr. Bannister?"

Cupping his ear, he made a casual quarter turn in her direction.

"You'll let me know what you find?"

"Are you saying what I think you're saying, Mrs. Rafferty?"

She motioned for him to come back. Suppressing a smirk, Bannister told Price to sit tight and got out of the car. He'd expected unconditional surrender, but the old shark quickly made it clear she had plenty of fight left.

Returning to the car five minutes later, he set his face in a careful mask of optimism. As soon as he slipped inside, Price hit him with the expected questions.

"So? Did you convince her?"

"It's all set."

"What did she say exactly, Sam? I told you, I will not be party to another Schildhauer."

"You heard me, Lenny. I said it's all set."

"I mean it, Sam. I'm not taking this out of our savings."

Bannister patted his pocket. "You don't have to."

"You saying she gave you an advance?" Price eyed him warily, but his caution yielded slowly to a grudging smile. "You're amazing, Sam. You could charm the pants off Queen Elizabeth, I swear it."

"Liz isn't my type."

"Lucky for her."

Bannister bumped the Camaro out of the condo lot, crossed the Goat Island Bridge, and worked his way through the clotted Newport streets toward the highway. Mrs. Rafferty's parting shot echoed in his mind. If he

proved the case against Macklin to her satisfaction, she
was willing to resurrect the posted reward. But the attempt was strictly on speculation. No guarantee of time,
expenses, or anything else except a giant challenge.

This goddamned thing was not going the way he'd
hoped. But then, almost nothing ever did.

CHAPTER

9

A spike of sunlight prodded Maggie awake. Squinting hard, she looked away and spied the scrawled list on her nightstand. During her training analysis, she'd gotten in the habit of waking sufficiently to jot down her dreams for interpretation. Scanning what she'd written the previous night, she thought about the field day her former therapist, Caroline Grayboys, would have had with this selection.

In one dream, she cut herself shaving. The pain and blood trickling down the shower drain were hers. But the leg was stumpy, heavily muscled, and coated with wiry hair. A male leg. Something was odd about the razor, too. It was antique with a mother-of-pearl handle and a tarnished gold head. Clearly not hers either. Nor was the bathroom. The one in the dream was a stuffy tiled cubicle with a claw-foot tub and a basin freckled with rust. A sable brush and a pot of shaving soap were perched beside it. Both were bloodred and smelled of berries. For some reason, Maggie's unconscious found that hilarious. In the dream, laughter bubbled inside her, and gleeful tears trickled down her cheeks. But when she looked into the tiny warped mirror to catch her giggling image, no one was there.

Another dream had her stumbling through a fog so thick it consumed her extremities as she went. An arm disappeared as she swung it forward, a foot to the knee. She felt the weight of an invisible burden dangling from a leather strap over her shoulder. The bundle grew heavier

59

until the strap tore her flesh. The pain was excruciating, but for some reason she could not let the package go. She struggled on, evaporating in the mist. Crumbling under the pressure.

Maggie shook her head. She certainly didn't need Dr. Grayboys to elucidate the obvious themes: insecurity, fear of failure. Nor did anyone need to tell her that she was more worried about the clinic's future than she cared to admit, even to herself. Alex Ivy, that wretched minimegalomaniac, had even followed her home to sleep.

But the next dream on the list had nothing to do with Poison Ivy or East End, and that one was the most disturbing of all. It was her recurrent nightmare: the window dream. It had been five years or more since she'd last had one of those. Maggie had hoped she was finally done with them.

The scene was always the same. Maggie is a small child in a twin-bedded room with matching flowered spreads and curtains. There is a faded blue rug with a flowered border. Kneeling to say her prayers, Maggie's knees are cushioned by pink cabbage roses and fluffy yellow mums. She twines her fingers tightly and clenches her lids. She hears her own voice say:

> *"Now I lay me down to sleep.*
> *I pray the lord, my soul to keep.*
> *If I should die . . ."*

Music seeps through the wall. The heat is damp and ponderous and has the cloying aroma of overripe fruit.

She rises and slips open the window. It glides like a skillful skater on ice.

Next comes a rush of cold wind and the piercing screech of an angry hawk. Suddenly, she's soaring on the bird's back, flying in dizzy arcs. Struggling to hold on, she clutches fistfuls of feathers. But they come away in her hand. The wings turn to fan blades that raise a blustering squall. She's swept away. Falling. Her screams are swallowed by the wind.

"Lazy bit," she hollers. "LAZY BIT!"

Maggie's heart was racing. She'd spent countless hours trying to decipher the meaning of that awful dream and the screamed nonsense phrase that always jolted her awake, but she still had no idea what any of it might signify.

Crumpling the dream list, she slipped out of bed. She had neither the time nor the energy for such nonsense. Today was for far more pressing business. Her noisy subconscious would just have to take a number. With a burst of resolve, she showered, dressed, and made a pot of killer coffee.

Her ninth-floor apartment, bestowed upon her by her mother after her parents' divorce, was in the Sutton Arms, a pristine prewar building nestled at the juncture of Eighty-first Street and the East River. Maggie's folks had purchased the place at the pinnacle of their marriage, which happened, by fortunate coincidence, to coincide with the collapse of the city's co-op prices in the early seventies. For thirty thousand dollars and change, they'd garnered three bedrooms, two and a half baths, a wraparound veranda complete with built-in redwood seating and planters, and a panoramic view that now featured the sanitarium on Ward's Island across the polluted waterway.

During the growing season, she was treated to a steady feast of revolving color as her mother's annuals and perennials flourished on the terrace in defiance of Maggie's benign neglect and black thumb. In all seasons, Joe, the super, was available for emergency repairs and alterations. A uniformed doorman was always on hand to accept her packages, greet and screen her visitors, and hail cabs for her. With only the meager maintenance to cover, the place cost her next to nothing, at least in dollars.

Maggie's friends were openly envious, especially Pam, who'd been forced to move three times in as many years to flee noisy neighbors, a heat-withholding landlord, and, the last time, her unfortunate proximity to a hospital ambulance route.

But like many alleged blessings, this one was decidedly mixed. The apartment was haunted by the ghosts of her parents' bitter breakup. And, at intervals, these particular

ghosts showed up with their luggage and settled in the
guest room for an extended stay.

More mind clutter. Maggie pushed it aside. Figuring
out how to meet Alex Ivy's outrageous demands was going
to require her complete concentration. That and an indus-
trial-strength miracle.

She spent the next two hours in the spare bedroom
she'd converted to a home office. Reviewing the clinic
budget, item by item, her heart sank. Precious little fat to
trim. The extras were typically contributed by her or
Henry or someone else on staff. The basics were just that.
She couldn't fathom a way to further prune expenditures
for essential materials, equipment, or staff.

Her head throbbed, and the numbers started swimming
on the page. Slipping into shorts and a T-shirt, she decided to take an hour off and try to tone her flabby imagination with a run. Reluctantly, she clipped on her beeper.
This was one of those times when she'd be happy to miss
any stray emergencies.

Pete, the regular day man, was at the door. They exchanged pleasantries. Maggie was tempted to instruct him
to discourage any stray visitors, but she reminded herself
that it was not necessary. Her mother, who now lived in a
one-bedroom apartment in the Gramercy Park section,
was spending the weekend with Aunt Hannah in Stamford, Connecticut. Maggie's father hadn't called since
Monday, which meant a new lady in his life, which meant
he'd be completely preoccupied and out of touch for his
standard relationship run: thirty days. Maggie wasn't even
curious about this latest in his long line of lost-and-found
love objects. She'd come to view the occasional month-
long breaks as a vacation.

By pleasant coincidence, she also happened to be on
one of her regular vacations from Ethan. They'd been a
sometimes couple since sharing a cadaver in first-year
anatomy lab at Cornell Medical School. Ever since, they'd
struggled with a perverse attraction that neither of them
honestly understood or particularly appreciated.

Ethan was an orthopedist at the Hospital for Joint Diseases, specializing in knee and hip replacements. Maggie,

as he saw it, specialized in wimps and whiners. Maggie didn't understand his love of human carpentry any more than he could comprehend her interest in emotional excavations. And that was only the tip of the difference.

She liked normal food: Italian and Chinese. His culinary tastes ranged from the exotic to the frankly bizarre. He hated ballet, which she loved. She loathed boxing, which was Ethan's life. She was a confirmed physical coward, he a devout daredevil. You name it, Ethan had risked it: helicopter skiing, rock climbing, visiting DisneyWorld during Christmas vacation. On those rare occasions when Maggie bothered to think about it, she found the only thing they really had in common was a short fuse. That, and they both had this thing about ear nibbling.

The East River Promenade was a meandering trail of footpaths and overpasses abutting the FDR Drive. Following her usual routine, Maggie took a brisk warm-up walk to the Seventy-first Street entrance and climbed the stairs.

Over the highway to the riverside path, she stopped to stretch out the kinks and commenced a listless northbound jog. It was too hot for serious exertion, she decided with a nod of satisfaction. She never felt entirely right about exercising until she'd established a compelling reason not to push herself too hard.

Sunbathers, newspaper perusers, and sleeping street people occupied the riverside benches. A dog walker strolling with a tangle of pedigreed pups was trailed by a uniformed nanny wheeling a set of identical infants. Maggie paused for a moment of cooing admiration. Normally she wasn't drawn to strangers' babies, but something about twins got to her every time.

"What are their names?" she asked.

"Jennifer and Jocelyn."

"They're adorable."

"Not so adorable at three A.M., honey. Believe me. Not so cute at four or five either."

Trudging up the steps to the next trestle, Maggie passed a line of serious runners. Marathoners, no doubt.

They had that unmistakable look about them, as if they'd been put through a juice press.

Maggie would never understand it. To her, exercise was a matter of health, definitely not a religion. She jogged to still her nagging conscience and to atone for the regular sins of her sweet tooth.

Put off by the trendy East Side gyms, she'd chosen jogging by default. Exploratory visits to neighborhood health clubs had confirmed her suspicions. Those places were infested by paper-thin women in thong leotards and men whose cut muscles appeared to be marinated in a light vinaigrette. Maggie had been appalled by the sight of bionic squads of them pumping and thumping in the weight rooms and exercise classes. No one perspired. No one had the decency to grunt or complain. Watching them, Maggie had vowed that if she ever found herself really enjoying a workout, she'd rethink the entire issue and give good old sedentary sloth another try.

She followed every straightaway and overpass to the northern terminus of the Promenade. An hour later, she returned to Seventy-first Street armed with a virtuous flush and a pleasant surge of energy. A germ of an idea had sprouted on one of her ponderous ascents over the highway. The more she considered it, the more promising it appeared. She couldn't wait to get home and start making the necessary calls.

She stopped on the way for battle provisions: bagels, barbecued chicken, rice pudding, microwave popcorn, Diet Coke, and iced tea. If this thing really got underway, it was going to be a very busy couple of days.

The thought energized her further. By the time she reached her building, she was running in overdrive.

"Help you with the packages, Dr. Lyons?"

"No, thanks, Pete. I'm fine. Couldn't be better in fact."

"Happy to hear that, because—"

Maggie was already at the elevator. Anxious to get started, she hurried inside and pressed nine. First, she'd have to check with the community outreach department, then public relations, then the facilities manager and the continuing education division. . . .

Her impatience grew with the list. The elevator was taking forever, stopping at every floor. The culprit had to be Mickey Glover, the building's resident delinquent. Little monster had started pressing all the elevator buttons as soon as he was big enough to reach them. He also bit people, threw things, screamed colorful obscenities, and teased the family's cocker spaniel so mercilessly the poor creature had developed a nervous tic. His mother, a round-shouldered wisp named Gretchen, never stopped or rebuked him. She was the type who figured everything her precious child did was simply darling. Someday, Maggie predicted, Gretchen Glover would be monitoring Mickey's adorable antics through the visitor's screen at Sing Sing.

Finally, the doors slid open at her floor. Juggling her groceries, Maggie worked the trio of locks on her door. The one controlling the dead bolt was highly temperamental. If not for the promise to her security-crazed mother, she would have removed the damned thing years ago. Maggie was fast on the verge of taking a sledge to it anyway when the lock clicked and the door swung open.

"There you are, Maggie. I was worried sick. Oh, my. Look at you. You're all flushed."

"Mom? What are you doing here? I thought you were at Aunt Hannah's." *Thought, wished, counted on it, said a prayer of thanks* . . .

Her mother sighed. "Hannah's impossible. You know."

Maggie did. Too well. Growing up, Aunt Hannah's family had lived two floors down in the same West Side apartment house. Maggie and her three cousins had played, fought, scuttled, and supported each other in typical sibling fashion, which had almost, but not quite, compensated for the sibling of her own that Maggie had always yearned to have. In the mothering department, Hannah and Maggie's mother, Francine, had served interchangeably, dispensing their bounty of neurotic cautions and concerns with equal fervor to all the cousins.

The two women even looked alike, though Maggie's mother was three years older or three years younger depending on which sister you asked. Both had terrific legs and dubious dispositions. Both, like three of their four offspring, had large green eyes, fair skin, and toy noses. Both Hannah and Fran shared the ability to disarm and dazzle when they smiled. Maggie suspected it had something to do with the rarity of the event.

"Why don't you change out of those sweaty clothes, Maggie? You'll catch something, all overheated like that."

"I'm fine, Mom. Listen. I don't mean to be inhospitable, but I have a ton of work to do this weekend. I really don't have time to visit."

"Of course. I understand, honey. Go about your business. You won't even know I'm here."

Maggie had hoped for a more literal disappearance, but she couldn't bring herself to show her mother the door. She loved the woman, no matter how impossible she tended to be.

The truth was Maggie would give anything to see her mother active and happy again, though she'd about run out of hope. After the divorce, Mom had dropped out of her normal existence. Ever since, she'd devoted herself full time to rage and recriminations, allowing only an occasional break for a psychosomatic illness or an anxiety attack.

"Want me to make you something, Maggie? You look a little washed out. Maybe you're working too hard."

"I'm fine. Excuse me, will you? I have some calls to make."

Sigh. "Of course. Do what you have to. Heaven knows I'm used to being alone." She sighed her way down the hall to the guest room. She sighed open the bureau drawers and deposited her things in the dresser. From the bulge of her suitcase and the number of drawer slams, Maggie calculated she was in for a long siege. Amazing how just when things seemed bleakest, something could happen to make them even worse.

But Maggie refused to let it get to her. Closing the study door, she placed the first crucial phone call. If she made a move without slogging through official channels, Poison Ivy would have her scalp.

An hour later, she left the study for a restorative dose of

Gail Weider's cookies and an iced tea. Her calls to the central office had been fruitless. Everyone on staff at East End worked Saturdays and Sundays on a rotating basis. But all the people she needed to reach were off this weekend. Using the staff directory, she'd tried home numbers next. Got nothing but phone machines, answering services, and apologetic relatives who promised to transmit her urgent message as soon as possible. Until she spoke to someone in proper authority and got the go-ahead, she'd have to put her possibly brilliant scheme on hold.

Her mother was out on the terrace, murmuring to the salvia. Favored by the sun, Francine's skin took on the soft glow of fine porcelain. Her hair shone, and her green eyes sparkled. She stooped to deadhead the bearded iris, moving with the grace and vigor of someone half her age. The woman was so bright, talented, and attractive, Maggie had an irresistible urge to go out there and give her a much needed boot in the rear.

She should have done it years ago, Maggie knew, before the depression had hardened to concrete. But she'd waited for her mother to take hold of her own life. Waited too damned long. Fortifying herself with a few more of Gail's sinful cookies, she virtuously stuffed the rest in the freezer and crossed the living room toward the sliding glass doors. It still wasn't too late.

On the way, she considered the best choice of words. This delicate task called for the precise mix of concern, support, confrontation, and quick reflexes to dodge any flying chunks of fury. Lady-and-tiger time. Not a pleasant prospect.

Approaching the door, Maggie was gripped by a sudden sick feeling. Her mouth parched, and her breaths went ragged. Clutching the arm of the sofa, she fought a wave of nausea and groped for a distraction to pull her out of the horrible moment.

Her seeking mind settled on the window dream. Two-year-old Maggie is kneeling at her bedside. Her tiny fingers are woven, eyes tight with concentration. The window glides open.

Now I lay me down to sleep . . .

Easy. Deep breath. There, better. Almost gone.

What the hell?

Maggie clung to the sofa a moment longer, willing the last of the awful sensation to pass. When it did, she straightened, took a deep, steadying breath, and headed for the hall. Had to be the stress. She hadn't had a spell like that in years, not since she'd been cured of her own paralyzing fear of heights. Before that, she'd known first-hand the hideous grip of a sudden panic, the terrifying sensation of being out of control, perched on the brink of unspeakable disaster. She'd known the irrational fear coupled with the seductive pull of the danger. It had taken months of steady work and treatment for her to put those paralyzing episodes behind her.

No backsliding, Maggie Lyons. That's the last thing you need right now.

Straightening the papers on her cluttered desk, she resolved to be fine. Maybe her brain was warning her not to take on anything else until she cleared up the money crisis at the clinic. Made sense to defer her mother's mountain of personal problems until she could devote her full attention to them anyway, Maggie thought. Knowing Mom, it was going to be a tricky climb.

With a little luck, she thought she could make a few more phone calls before her mother finished swabbing the mealybug off the coleus. But the porch door slid open an instant later.

"Maggie?"

She recognized the brittle voice and knew what would follow. Maggie didn't look up. Mom would surely read a problem on her face. The last thing she needed was more clucking concern.

"Sorry, Mom. I'm right in the middle. Have to run."

"Yes, dear. I was just wondering if you've heard from Prince Charming. Wondering what he was up to. Or should I say, *who*?"

"Honestly, Dad hasn't called in days. Guess he must be busy."

"I can imagine. Robert's always been a busy boy. Even when I had no idea. Amazing how blind a person can be."

Maggie continued making piles of her notes, not wanting to see the hurt look. If only her mother would let it go. If only she'd get on with her life already.

"Maggie, please. If he's seeing someone, I'd rather—"

The phone rang, giving Maggie a welcome excuse to scoop it up. She hoped it was one of the critical return calls. Something had to start working here. This day was not proceeding at all according to her careful design.

But the voice on the phone was not the relief she'd expected. He identified himself as Detective Frank Fazio of the Rhode Island State Police. It was about a suicide, he said. The victim had been one of her patients.

CHAPTER

10

Bannister's detective agency was headquartered on Federal Street in Boston's financial district. To cut expenses after the divorce separated him from his money, he'd relocated from a four-room office suite on nearby Milk Street. Now, he shared space and a secretary with a bail bondsman named Willy James and the personal injury law firm of Shatzkin, Shatzkin, Mulrooney & Glick.

His tiny, windowless office was sandwiched between the door that read "James's Bonds," and the one occupied by the senior Shatzkin, founding partner and first tenor in the firm's ubiquitous radio jingle:

> *Shatzkin, Shatzkin, Mulrooney & Glick.*
> *They're the names to call when you're injured or sick.*
> *Just dial Three-Two-One HELP, and we're there for you quick.*
> *That's Shatzkin, Shatzkin, Mulrooney & Glick.*

Hardly the most sumptuous surroundings. Noise ricocheted like stray bullets off the flecked linoleum floors and pressed tin ceilings. A haze of cheap cologne and cut-rate cigar fumes hung in the air. The decor was vintage Ho Jo's: orange sherbet plastic with aqua accents and faux-walnut trim. Most of the equipment, air-conditioning included, was dysfunctional or deceased.

Bannister barely noticed. Given the nature of his work, he reasoned he was rarely in the office anyway. As he saw it, there was no sense paying more than the bare minimum for what was basically a mail drop and a phone answering service. And Myra, the secretary who owed him one-seventh of her time, attentions, and loyalty, was exceptional at placating attention-starved clients and deflecting pesky creditors.

Bannister sat at the desk. Price occupied the not-so-easy chair and the second line on the extension phone across the room. Hanging up, he hugged himself and shivered.

"I'm freezing to death, Sammy. Can't you turn that thing off?"

"Sorry. The only two settings are 'steam bath' and 'meat locker.' Want me to ask Myra to bring you more tea?"

"No, thanks. The last cup froze to my lip."

"Hang in there, Lenny. We're going to hit the bull's-eye soon. I can feel it in my bones."

"That's good, Sam. 'Cause I'm too numb to feel anything."

Preoccupied with the task at hand, Bannister was oblivious to the chill. To him, there was nothing like the chase. Best part of the work next to the fee collecting. He loved tracking the stench, closing in on the trash pile, and hauling another heap of rotten waste to the dump. There was nothing like the moment when it all came together. Not even sex, from the little of that he could remember.

He especially enjoyed working a case with Price. Appearances aside, the guy was whip smart and able to milk a clue for every last drop of insight. Likable to a fault, there was someone he could call on for virtually anything they might happen to need. Best of all, though he was unfailingly agreeable, Price did not give up without a monumental, mule-worthy effort. Once he latched on to a line of investigation, you had to practically pry the guy loose with a crowbar. Bannister really admired that in a person. Reminded him of himself.

The two men had spent the entire afternoon in Bannister's deep freeze, trying to unearth Theodore Macklin's medical records and find out if the man had sought any psychiatric treatment in the year before his death. With

the aid of Price's crackerjack contacts, they'd managed to
procure copies of Macklin's canceled checks and tax re-
turns for the past two years. But there were no payments
to physicians and no medical deductions.

Macklin's business records were a little trickier to come
by, camouflaged as they were in a maze of interlocking
and dummy entities. But Price had finally gotten his
hands on the primary corporate filings through a sister of
a friend at the secretary of state's office. From there, he'd
been able to ferret out the name of the carrier for the
company's insurance plan.

Problem was, Macklin's health policy called for direct
payments to providers. Bannister had contacted Macklin's
former secretary and the firm's bookkeeper to see if either
remembered submitting any claims for the boss for visits
to a shrink, but the man's sudden death had left both
women mute and suffering from bad cases of selective
amnesia.

The claims adjustor Bannister questioned at Mass Mutual Insurance was no more helpful. Company policy pro-
hibited her from divulging information about individual
claims, she informed him in a grating nasal whine. Past
records were stored centrally and unavailable except
through special application. If Mr. Macklin wanted copies
of anything in his file, he'd have to go through channels.

Bannister was not pleased. He had no scruples about
impersonating Macklin to get the records, but channels
took time. Getting to the right person in the claims department had cost him three transfers and close to five
minutes on Muzak-ridden hold. Given that, he could
imagine how long it would take for a special application to
slog through the company's bureaucratic molasses. Meanwhile, someone would probably get around to informing
the computer that Theodore Macklin had been dropped
from the client rolls the hard way.

Out of ideas, Bannister saw no alternative but to throw
a tantrum.

"Damn it, Lenny! I hate corporations and records and
clerks and policies. I hate those phone systems where
you're bounced around like a goddamned Ping-Pong ball

until they finally figure out who's the right person to disconnect you or put you off."

Price nodded amiably. "Get it out, Sam. You'll feel better."

"And computers. I'd like to get my hands on the jackass who invented those goddamned machines. Last week alone, one ate my cash card and another told the kid at the Exxon station that I wasn't good for a lousy five bucks' worth of medium-grade oil. I ask you, Lenny, are my finances any of that kid's business?"

Price's head was still bobbling, but his expression had changed. Sporting a pensive frown, he raised a finger, requesting a moment's silence.

Bannister gave it to him, though it wasn't easy. Once his temper was on autopilot, it was no mean feat to unlock the landing gear and bring it down.

The moment was up. "So?"

"So your mentioning computers made something click, Sam. I remember reading a piece in one of the trade journals about a central data bank that insurance companies use to pool claim information. Not something they want the public to know about. And the feds have questioned whether it's an antitrust violation or restraint of trade. But it cuts fraud and helps insurers avoid bad-risk clients. So they've fought to keep it going."

Bannister reached for the phone. "Great. How do we reach them?"

"You can't call. It's a subscriber network. You have to be a member. Go directly to the mainframe. Takes an entry key and pass code to log on."

"So you're telling me you've got this great idea, only it's useless."

"No. I think I know who can break into the network for us."

Ten minutes later, Price managed to locate his source.

"His name's Harry Horgan, Sam. Golf buddy of mine. He's president and CEO of Compcom, a small but real successful computer hardware company. I caught him on his cellular, putting out the seventeenth green at

Fairview. He's willing to meet us back at the shop in an hour."

Bannister aimed the Camaro west and took the Mass Pike to Route 128, also known as America's Technology Highway. The road was bounded by sleek, modern buildings housing high-tech operations with cyberpunk staffers and technobabble names. Sun glinted off steel-and-glass facades and baked the great surrounding stretches of unused, unnoticed, unnecessary lawn. Several miles and billions of microchips later, they turned into the long ribbon of access road connecting the highway to Compcom Industries, Inc.

The chairman's suite occupied most of the second floor. An executive secretary with a brusque manner and pier-piling legs led them to Horgan's enormous corner office. A smoked-glass wall offered a muted view of the man-made duck pond in the rear and the emergency generators beyond. The black lacquer ultramodern furnishings could have been copped from a Spielberg movie.

Compcom's chief stood in the center of the space, clad in plaid knickers and a tam, practicing his tee shot. Guy had a walrus mustache and a sun-fried complexion. He acknowledged their arrival with a nod and kept swinging.

"That blasted slice came back, Lenny. Put me deep in the rough on fourteen. Cost me two strokes and a hundred bucks to Arnie Simpson, that arrogant son of a bitch from Paqsystems. Anyone but Arnie, it wouldn't have been so bad."

"Take it straight back the way I showed you, Harry," Price said. "You're breaking your wrist early."

Horgan swung again and cast an expectant look in Price's direction.

"Better. Focus on the arc and vector of the swing. Use the natural momentum to goose your velocity. Better. Easy does it now."

Another couple of swats and Horgan was ready to suspend the practice session. Peeling off his fingerless glove, he motioned them to choose one of the circle of plush chairs surrounding his gargantuan desk.

"Harry, this is Sam Bannister. He's the private eye I

work with once in a full moon. Sam, Harry here knows computers inside out and backward."

"And Lenny has been more help to my golf game than all the pros from here to eternity, Sam," Horgan said. "He's the only person I've ever met who's broken the game down to geometry and physics, language *real* people can understand. So what can I do for you boys? Like a drink?"

Price declined and told him what they were after. Horgan requested the necessary particulars, including Macklin's social security number, corporate name and carrier, and the company's group policy number. Then he pressed a button in a control panel on the desk, and the slick surface parted to expose a work station. He tapped the keys. Paused. Tapping again, he squinted at the screen.

"Damn. The network's got a Transprotect Cover."

"A what?" Bannister said.

"Security system. Electronic sentry. Guaranteed uncrackable. Sorry."

Price flipped up his palms. "So it goes. Guess it's back to the drawing board, Sam. Thanks for trying. Harry."

"God damn it. There has to be some way in," Bannister said.

"Easy, Sam. Harry's the best. If he can't do it, I'm afraid it can't be done."

Horgan frowned. "How important is this, Lenny?"

"Very."

"All right, then. But only this once and only for you." Compcom's chief pressed another button in the console and the intercom squawked on. "Call Levitt. Tell him I need him right away." He looked up. "Shouldn't take long."

"Who's Levitt?" Bannister demanded.

"First name's David, but he prefers plain Levitt, and we give him whatever he prefers. He's a computer genius. Best I've come across. We call him in to consult, but only on very special occasions. He's in huge demand, and his availability is strictly limited."

Horgan retrieved his driver and practiced his swing

under Price's direction. Ten minutes later, his secretary poked her head in.

"Levitt's here, Mr. Horgan."

"Great. Send him in."

A scrawny bespectacled kid in a scout uniform soon appeared. Bannister made him at nine or ten maximum, and small for that. The boy eyed his Mickey Mouse watch and cracked the giant gum wad orbiting in his jaw.

"What's the big emergency, Harry? I've got a troop meeting at five. We're making s'mores."

"This is Mr. Bannister and Mr. Price, Levitt. They need access to a national network with a Transprotect Cover. I know they bill it as uncrackable, but—"

The kid nodded impatiently and took Horgan's place at the terminal. "Okay, give me the specs."

As Horgan read off Macklin's personal and company data, the child's bony fingers worked the keyboard. He frowned at the screen and swiped a speck of debris from his glasses. Fiddling with his neckerchief, he watched and waited.

A minute later, the boy hefted his shoulders and puffed his lips.

"No luck?" Horgan said.

The kid pressed a final key causing a rush of unseen activity. Reaching under the edge of the desk, he extracted a sheet of paper.

"Here's your data. Okay if I leave now? I'm bringing the marshmallows."

Price brightened as he scanned the page. "A complete list of Macklin's medical claims for the last five years. That's terrific. Thanks, Levitt. So much for guaranteed uncrackable security, eh, Harry?"

Horgan ruffled the kid's hair. "True enough, Lenny. Those boys over at Mass Mutual really ought to demand their money back."

CHAPTER

11

On the phone, Detective Fazio had refused to part with any details. A suicide, he said, of one of her patients. He would not even offer Maggie the name of the victim or the reason for an inquiry into an apparently self-inflicted death. All he'd volunteered was that the police were investigating to clear up certain unspecified questions. According to a source, Dr. Margaret Lyons at East End Hospital had provided psychiatric treatment some months ago for the dead man. Fazio said he would greatly appreciate her cooperation. His tone said she would cooperate or else.

At his request, Maggie had agreed to see him at three. She'd have no problem keeping busy until then. If nothing else, she could spend the time worrying herself sick.

Suicide.

It was every psychiatrist's worst nightmare. The supreme failure. Maggie had considered herself fortunate. In ten years of practice, she'd never had to cope with a patient taking his own life.

Until now.

She reflected on the people she'd treated in the past months. No one had struck her as a potential suicide. Could she have missed a serious depressive? Worse, could something in her therapy have driven this particular patient, whoever he was, to commit such an act of desperation?

Conventional wisdom held that ridding someone of a phobia was liberating and life-affirming. But there was

nothing conventional about the uncertain course of individual human emotion. Maggie had never shared the
baseless confidence of some of her more dogmatic colleagues. Every treatment involved some measure of risk.
When you peeled away a defense or stripped off a habitu-
ated reaction, there was no guarantee you'd be left with a
healthy core of self-esteem and resilience. Usually it
worked that way, but what about the rule-proving exception? The so-called cure might conceivably expose a
screaming nerve. Leave nothing but raw, unendurable
pain.

She shivered. No use speculating. The suicide may
have had nothing at all to do with Maggie's treatment.
The pathogenic seeds could have been planted much earlier. Or the desperate death might have been precipitated
by a sudden shift of circumstance after the patient was out
of her care. Several plausible causes occurred to her immediately: a catastrophic illness, chemical imbalance, financial reverses, the sudden death or defection of a loved
one.

Still almost an hour until her meeting with Detective
Fazio. Maybe she could pry her mother out of the apartment before he showed up. The woman definitely did not
need an additional worry to add to her already extensive
collection.

Perusing the weekend section of yesterday's *Times,*
Maggie hit on the perfect diversion. Aware that her
mother would likely balk at any direct suggestion, she
opened the paper to the strategic page, dropped it on the
sofa, then made a soundless retreat to her office.

Perfect trap. In seconds, she heard the rush of the sliding terrace door and her mother's footsteps trailing into
the living room.

"Maggie, dear," Francine called. "You shouldn't leave
the paper on the couch like that. You'll get ink stains."

Maggie listened as the paper rustled, and footfalls
veered toward the kitchen. The nice thing about obses-
sive/compulsives was their absolute predictability. Her
mother always read the newspaper at the kitchen table
where any errant newsprint could be wiped clean. And

Mom always started by scanning for gardening-related articles and announcements. It took precisely the five minutes Maggie had anticipated before she heard the knock at her office door.

Her mother looked sheepish. "There's a show and sale through this evening at the Mid-Hudson Orchid Society, dear. Any chance you'd like to go with me?"

"Sorry, Mom. I told you I'm up to my ears. But you go ahead."

"You sure you wouldn't mind? I thought I'd stay around and make us a nice dinner. But they're featuring a new hybrid phalaenopsis. Hard to resist."

"Enjoy yourself."

Maggie stifled the smile until her mother was out the door. Finally, something had gone her way. Hoping it might signal a trend, she went to the kitchen for a couple of Gail Weider's chocolate chip cookies, which were even delicious frozen, and tried several of her calls again. She was on seemingly perpetual hold in the administration office when her other line started ringing.

She picked up, certain it was one of her crucial return calls, but that was far from the case.

"Maggie? Francis Kennedy. I was thinking what a nice day it is for a picnic supper. What do you say?"

She tried to keep the irritation out of her voice. Maggie reminded herself that the man was an old school chum of Alex Ivy's. And the last thing she wanted was to give Little Caesar yet another reason to climb on her case.

"I'm busy, F.X. And anyway, as I explained to you, I don't socialize with the aides in the program. It's against the rules."

"Rules are meant to be broken, Maggie. What could a picnic hurt? I'll cater. How's that?"

"Against the rules, as I told you. Please don't call me at home anymore, Francis. I'd appreciate that."

As she hung up, the lobby buzzer sounded.

"Two—uh—gentlemen to see you, Dr. Lyons."

"Thanks, Pete. Send them up."

The catch in the doorman's voice prepared her for an oddity, and she was not disappointed. The elevator soon disgorged a ruddy armed giant in uniform and a skeleton in a suit toting a briefcase. The cadaverous accountant type was in obvious command. Maggie accepted the hand he proffered and glanced at the laminated card identifying him as Detective Frank Fazio, Rhode Island State Police.

"That's Nelligan," Fazio said of his mammoth mute companion. "He's local out of the nineteenth."

Hiking his trousers by the crease, Fazio sat on the sofa, snapped open his briefcase, and extracted an accordion file crammed with documents.

"Theodore Macklin," he said, as if that explained everything. "According to his records, you saw him back in February. Remember?"

She did, though not fondly. Ted Macklin had been an overbearing, abrasive man who'd checked in for the course of intensive treatment the clinic offered for acute cases and out-of-towners. Maggie had suffered his crudeness and cynicism for a week or so and was frankly delighted when he'd elected to cut his program short and checked himself out.

"Theodore Macklin killed himself?"

"He did."

Maggie recalled the man's leering, his tactlessness and social ineptitude. Aside from his phobias, she'd thought him to be emotionally brain dead. "Any idea why? He certainly didn't seem the type."

"Frankly, Dr. Lyons, the state isn't all that interested in his motives. What we need is a firm and fast certification of the suicide, so we can proceed against Mr. Macklin's holdings."

Tersely, Fazio explained that Macklin had convinced several top state executives to entrust him with the management of a large pension fund. His performance there had been so impressive, he'd been placed in charge of several other sizeable state accounts.

Then, a week ago, an anonymous tipster had called the governor's office and claimed Macklin's operation was involved in shady dealings. The informant warned that the investment firm's illicit transactions would likely be uncovered as part of an ongoing federal probe.

Pending a full investigation, Rhode Island officials had moved immediately to freeze Macklin's assets. They knew that if the feds took after the man, any state funds in his control could be impounded indefinitely along with the rest of his holdings. Unfortunately, before they were able to complete the paperwork, Theodore Macklin was dead.

"As you can imagine, the governor is most anxious to protect the state's interests, Dr. Lyons. In these difficult times, the last thing he wants is to look like a losing player in a three-card monte game."

"I don't see how I can help you."

"Simple. Review your notes, listen to your tapes, whatever. There must have been some indication Macklin was depressed, possibly on the edge. You certify that, and I know we can get the coroner to sign off immediately, so we can expedite our claim. All we want is to secure our taxpayers' money."

"You're not going to find what you're looking for in my records. Mr. Macklin may have been many things, but there wasn't a hint of depression or suicidal tendencies."

Fazio shook his head. "I'm afraid you don't understand, Dr. Lyons. The man is dead. All you have to do is say you're not surprised he took his own life, and we can recover funds that rightly belong to the good citizens of the state of Rhode Island. I'm talking pensions, special accounts for emergency assistance to indigents and the elderly, programs for prenatal and infant nutrition and the disabled. Consider it a public service, why don't you?"

"Sorry, but I'd have to consider it a fraud. I won't lie for you, Detective. No matter how noble the cause."

Fazio frowned. "Get me a drink of water, will you, Nelligan?"

The big cop nodded and loped to the kitchen. Fazio leaned his ferret face closer to Maggie and spoke in a rasp. His breath was musty.

"I'd hoped we could do this without unpleasantness, Dr. Lyons. But I intend to get what I came for. Don't make me throw my weight around."

Maggie would have laughed, but outrage cooled the impulse. "I'm not going to be bullied into violating my

personal or professional ethics, Detective. I saw no indication that Ted Macklin was suicidal. If I'm asked to tes-
tify at an inquest, that's what I'll have to say."

Fazio attempted a minute of silent intimidation. He
gave up when Nelligan lumbered back in, his massive
mitt dwarfing a glassful of water that was dripping onto
the leg of his uniform pants and Maggie's carpet.

"Let's go, Nelligan. I'm through here."

The big man stalled. He stared at the drink in bewilder-
ment.

"Put that down, will you? You keep sloshing it around
like that, you'll drown yourself like Macklin did."

The words crept under Maggie's skin. "Macklin
drowned? I thought you said it was a suicide."

"He went off the Newport Bridge, Dr. Lyons," Fazio
hissed. "Either it was a suicide, or the guy had a mighty
strange idea about what made a decent diving board."

Fazio shoved the Macklin file back in his briefcase and
stood to leave. Watching him, Maggie's gaze drifted to the
terrace. Again, she was accosted by a terrible sensation.
The sky shuddered, and there was a rush of melting heat.
Her pulse raced, and the world slipped out of focus. She
imagined herself at the edge of the terrace floor, jumping
off. Plummeting.

The feeling soon passed. Caught in panic's grip, time
seemed suspended for an eternity, but the actual spells
never lasted more than a minute or two. Still, by the time
the terror released her, King Kong and Mr. Bones were at
the door. Fazio twisted the knob and stepped into the
corridor. Nelligan was about to lumber after him when
Maggie found her voice.

"Wait, Detective."

Fazio turned. His smile was a rictus. "Having second
thoughts?"

She told him she was. Now she was even more positive
that Theodore Macklin's death had not been a suicide.

CHAPTER

12

As Maggie spoke, Detective Fazio's mood decayed from scattered clouds to storm warnings.

She told him Theodore Macklin would never have gone on or off the Newport Bridge voluntarily. Macklin was intensely phobic about bridges. No matter how desperate he might have become, that would never have been his chosen mode of self-annihilation. Given that, she knew, the state could be in for a long and difficult murder investigation. Macklin's assets would be untouchable until it was over, giving the feds ample time to stake any claim they might have. Fazio kept pressing her for a more palatable conclusion.

"What kind of murderers would bother to take off the victim's shoes and socks and suit jacket before they tossed him over the side? And his jewelry. Divers found some of his things washed up on the bridge pilings."

Maggie shrugged. "I'm not the detective, Detective."

"And what about the way Macklin's Jaguar was left in the service lot? Parked nice and neat with the doors locked. Has suicide written all over it. Why the hell would a murderer worry about the car enough to lock the doors?"

"Maybe to make it look like a suicide," Maggie suggested. "Although, I really can't imagine why someone intent on suicide would worry about locking car doors."

Fazio smirked. "True, Doctor. But then, there's nothing rational about suicide. Which is exactly why Macklin might have forgotten about his phobia long enough to jump off that bridge."

"No way. He was more terrified of bridges than anything. Even death."

Fazio wasn't giving up. "So maybe he got treatment for that particular phobia after he left your program."

"Again, I'm not the detective."

"All right. I know. If he had, we probably would have turned up some record of it when we went through his papers. There are thousands of other shrinks. Maybe he went to one and wasn't billed yet. Or maybe he paid out of some account we haven't turned up. You're not the only game in town."

Maggie smiled sweetly. "You're absolutely right. There are many similar programs. Hundreds, in fact. I'll be happy to send you a list."

She was even happier to see him and his oversized escort to the door. Despite her relief at discovering that she probably hadn't pushed a patient over the edge, there was something in Fazio's accusatory manner that made her feel guilty.

Allowing the pair sufficient time to depart the neighborhood, she left the apartment and headed to the hospital. By now, Daisy Tyler should be over the worst effects of the tranquilizers.

Maggie went directly to the second floor, but the patient had not yet been transferred to her service. Taking the stairs to three, she found Daisy's room empty. Time for a shift change, so there were no nurses in the corridor to question about Ms. Tyler's whereabouts. Maggie decided to poke around until she found the woman on her own. She hoped poor Daisy wasn't cowering under a bed somewhere. Or locked in a supply closet. Or worse.

Trying to appear nonchalant, she strolled from room to room. No sign of Daisy. Not that she'd expected the woman to be out socializing with her fellow patients, but she had to be somewhere on the unit. Maggie seriously doubted that Daisy Tyler had the temerity to leave the floor, much less the hospital. No matter how intolerable the woman might be finding things here, she wasn't likely to prefer the milling crowd of imaginary horrors outside.

Maggie checked the lounge, smiling at the clusters of patients and visitors who turned at her entrance. No Daisy. Growing more concerned by the minute, she poked around in the supply closets and examining rooms. She even went back to Daisy's room to look in the shower stall and clothes closet.

Deciding that this qualified as a potential emergency, she knocked at the staff lounge and interrupted the change-of-shift conference to get whatever information she could from the nurses and residents. By all accounts, Daisy had not left her room since her admission. Anyone who'd looked in on her in the past eight or ten hours had found her asleep or resting in bed.

The shift supervisor left the meeting to help Maggie with the search. They agreed to make one more thorough sweep of the floor before calling security.

Maggie rechecked the patient rooms. She thought of Daisy's desperate state last night. Maybe she shouldn't have been left alone. Maggie could have posted a nurse in the room. She could have spent the night there herself.

She crossed in front of the elevator bank to check the rooms on the other side of the wing. A voice from behind stalled her before she came to the first door.

"Dr. Lyons? That you?"

Maggie turned. Mitch Goldberg was escorting Daisy Tyler off the elevator. Daisy's hand was looped through the young resident's cocked elbow. She had a bright smile and proud bearing. Except for the hospital-issue bathrobe, Daisy looked for all the world like the mother of the groom.

Maggie was incredulous. "Daisy, hi. I was searching all over for you. Where have you been?"

Daisy wrapped her blue robe tighter and smiled. "Dr. Goldberg took me down to the cafeteria."

"Ms. Tyler's been through enough," Goldberg said. "I didn't think she should have to put up with that slop they were trying to pass off as lunch."

"I owe you for the sandwich, Doctor. But my money—" Her lip quivered.

Goldberg dipped in a gallant bow. "Not at all. Not only were you charming company, but you got me out of a staff meeting."

He caught Maggie's eye and motioned for a private conference. She nodded and led Daisy into her room.

"I'll be back in a minute," Maggie told her.

"Sure, Dr. Lyons. I'm not going anywhere."

She found Goldberg waiting at the end of the hall. His arrogance had evaporated. An uncertain smile took its place. It was a definite improvement.

"I hope it was okay for me to take her," Goldberg began. "I stopped in earlier, and she was getting agitated again. I thought a little distraction might be in order. I tried calling you at home for permission, but I got your machine."

"It's fine. In fact, it's wonderful. You convinced her to do more than she has in the past twenty-two years. Maybe you'd like to give up the Ben Casey stuff and join us on the angst unit."

"Who's Ben Casey?"

For a second there, Maggie had forgotten the guy's age, or lack thereof. "TV character. Probably on after your bedtime. Or maybe before your conception."

"I'm not as young as I sometimes act, Dr. Lyons."

"It's Maggie. And I think you acted perfectly. Thanks, Doctor. Really. I owe you one."

"It's Mitch. And I'll remember. Profound indebtedness is one of my favorite things." He winked as he walked away. Forgetting herself, Maggie winked back. She covered it by pretending there was something in her eye. They're making little kids mighty precocious these days, she thought. Probably some additive in the milk.

Maggie spent the next hour explaining the clinic's intensive program to Daisy Tyler. They would meet privately for an hour a day to discuss progress, problems, and strategies. At least twice a day, Daisy would work on specific goals with her assigned aide.

Recovery hinged on planned, sequential exposure to

feared things or situations. Gradually, the patient became desensitized and was able to progress to more and more intimidating tasks.

"If you were phobic about snakes, we might start by having you think about them. Next step might be looking at pictures," Maggie said. "After you were comfortable with that, we'd probably ask you to touch the pictures or handle a rubber snake. Then, maybe you'd visit a pet store where they have live snakes in tanks. You'd get closer and closer until the experience stopped provoking any serious anxiety. Eventually, you'd learn to view or even hold a snake without particular fear."

Daisy shuddered. "Why would I want to do that?"

"It's just an example. Part of your treatment will be deciding exactly what you fear most. You'll be the one to set the goals. If you could wave a magic wand right now and get rid of one fear, what would it be?"

Daisy fingered her bathrobe. "Might be easier to tell you one thing I'm *not* afraid of."

"Can you remember a time when you weren't fearful?"

"I had general anesthetic once. For an appendectomy. Maybe when I was under."

She recounted a typical phobic history. Daisy had been reared by an overprotective mother and a salesman father who was rarely at home. She'd had the normal childhood fears: demons, the dark, separation, getting lost in crowds. But, unlike other children, she had failed to outgrow them.

Instead, the fears had outgrown her. Like a fire raging out of control, they had surrounded her, driven her back, confined her to a small, ever-shrinking safe zone. A living crypt.

"After my mother died, my dad used to practically drag me out of the apartment," Daisy said. "I couldn't hold a job, couldn't make myself get out and meet people. But every Sunday, even when it snowed, he'd force me to get all dressed up. We'd go to church together and then out for Sunday supper.

"The whole thing was torture for me. In church, I was sure I was going to scream or pass out and make a terrible spectacle of myself. I had to sit in the back row, right on the aisle. I spent the whole time watching the exit door. I had to be the first one out when the service was over. Otherwise, I was sure I'd get trapped. Maybe trampled to death.

"Afterward, at the restaurant, I'd get so nervous, I couldn't eat a bite. But I had to go through with that ritual every Sunday for as long as Daddy was alive. I'd beg him not to make me, but he insisted. Said I was just being a silly prima donna."

"And when he died?" Maggie said.

Daisy's eyes filled. "I couldn't even get myself out of the house for his funeral. He would have been so ashamed of me. I've been such a disappointment, Dr. Lyons. Especially to myself."

Listening, Maggie recognized the parallels between Daisy's experience and her own. Maggie, too, had a fearful mother who'd portrayed the world as hostile and unsafe. A mostly absent father. A childhood plagued by demons. Fortunately, Maggie's holdover anxiety had been restricted to a fear of heights, and she'd managed to work her way through that so it hadn't remained a serious impediment. All right, Ethan considered her severely restricted because she refused to consider hang gliding or sky-diving. But Ethan also deplored her refusal to eat pickled squid or roast yak.

"The important thing is the future, Daisy. You're going to get past the fears. You'll finally have the opportunity to live the life you want."

"It's hard to imagine."

Not so hard for Maggie. She'd seen it before with Henry and others as tortured and imprisoned.

Daisy's voice faded, and her lids drooped. As her breathing gentled, Maggie edged across the room and shut the door. The woman needed her rest. She'd taken the first step, but she had a long, hard hike ahead of her.

CHAPTER

13

The printout from the insurance network had confirmed Bannister's hunch. According to the claim records, Macklin had spent ten days in the psychiatric unit of a Manhattan hospital six months ago. The admitting diagnosis was nonspecific anxiety. From Horgan's office, Price phoned a psychology professor he knew who described the term as a catchall. Nonspecific anxiety could signify anything from insomnia to relationship problems to a total nervous collapse.

Things were no clearer after several exploratory calls to East End, the hospital where Macklin had been treated. No one on staff would surrender patient information on the phone.

So it was off to the Big Hassle.

Bannister had taken less than five minutes to toss his gear in a suitcase, collect the necessary files, and make it back to where he'd left Price and the Camaro idling at a bus stop.

His studio apartment was in Boston's North End, over an Italian deli on Hanover Street. In exchange for an occasional snooping job for his paranoid landlord, he lived rent-free, which was, as accountant types recommended, about a quarter of his monthly net income.

Next stop was Price's cozy Tudor on a quiet block in suburban Watertown. Ruthie, a solid, affable woman with paprika-toned hair and smiling eyes, bustled out to greet them in the driveway. She clucked over Price as if it had been months, not hours, since their parting. Then she led her husband upstairs to pack.

Knowing it could take quite a while for her to get the guy equipped and give him his marching orders, Bannister settled in the den with a Coke and his case notes.

All the circumstantial fingers had pointed straight at Theodore Macklin. From Martha Rafferty's friends, he and Price had discovered that the bad luck streak in their Harper School class had extended well beyond Martha and Ricky Bates.

Within a year of graduation, a star basketball player named Andy Gordon had drowned in the pool at a private midtown club. Several months later, Jerry Seiden, class salutatorian, had died of a rumored drug overdose. Very strange, given that no one could connect the studious young man to any former hint of substance abuse. Next, Robby Mercer, Harper's resident lady-killer, had taken a fall on the marble foyer floor in his apartment and lapsed into an irreversible coma.

At the time, no one had suspected a connection between the tragic events, but Price had spotted a clear one right away. All the victims had dated or at least shown an interest in Martha Rafferty. And all of the so-called accidents could have been engineered by Teddy Macklin.

Macklin's family belonged to the club where Andy Gordon drowned. Few people used the pool, so it would have been a simple matter for someone to sneak in while the Gordon boy was doing his regular early-morning laps and sneak out again once the kid was in a genuine dead man's float.

Jerry Seiden's alleged overdose might have been arranged by Macklin with the aid of supplies pilfered from one of the pharmacies in his father's citywide chain. As the owner's son, Teddy had easy access to the back rooms and supply closets where controlled substances were stored.

The Mercer apartment was one floor below the Macklins'. No one in the family was home at the time of the deadly fall. Teddy could have snuck down there, bashed in Robby's skull, and landed back on his family room couch in the time it took for a standard commercial break. Young Ted had fifty pounds and four inches on the Mercer kid. No contest.

Indications of Macklin's probable guilt had continued to pile up nicely. Several vintage Harper teachers confirmed that Teddy Macklin had been given to outbursts of serious temper. A couple remembered recommending that the boy have psychological counseling, but the Macklins had refused.

Bannister had even paid a visit to Macklin's parents, who'd relocated to a posh estate in Palm Beach. He'd passed himself off as an old friend of Ted's, and neither parent had questioned him or balked at his dogged curiosity. They seemed more than willing to unburden themselves.

As Macklin's father told it, Teddy had been the youngest of their five children and the one who'd failed to fit the family mold. The others had been exuberant, outgoing, and athletic. Ted was the eccentric, a demanding, troublesome boy.

Tearfully, Mrs. Macklin admitted that the child had been unplanned and unwanted. All of her earlier pregnancies had been difficult, straining her health. When, in her early forties, she became pregnant for the fifth time, her doctor had been dismayed but unwilling to perform a therapeutic abortion. Same result when they sought a second opinion. At that time, the procedure was only legal if the pregnancy posed a serious threat to the mother's life. Neither doctor was willing to go out on the necessary professional limb.

The Macklins had decided to seek the procedure on their own. Someone had recommended a clinic in Puerto Rico. But the attempt had been botched, and the pregnancy continued to term. There were no obvious ill effects on the child, but Macklin's parents blamed themselves thereafter for their son's every quirk and problem.

Yes, they'd recognized that the boy was withdrawn and temperamental. Yes, in retrospect, they wished they'd sought professional help when it was suggested by his school. But at the time, guilt had kept them from acknowledging their son's problems. Later, when it was clear that his emotional growth had been skewed and stunted, he was well beyond their influence. For the last several years, they'd had virtually no contact with Teddy.

Bannister had Macklin's parents in his pocket until he mentioned Martha Rafferty. The name triggered an automatic locking mechanism. Cold eyes, steely expressions. Fine with Bannister. Their silence spoke volumes. Even the guy's parents believed him guilty.

But he and Price were obligated to shore their suspicions with hard evidence. And dead or alive, the simplest, most effective proof of Macklin's involvement in Martha Rafferty's murder would still be the man's own confession. Bannister's gut told him that the shrink who'd treated Macklin's acute case of whatever was their best remaining hope.

His patience had run out. Checking the time, he bellowed up the stairs. "You almost ready, Lenny?"

"Almost. You think the place we're staying provides a blow dryer, Sam?"

"A who?"

"Guess I'll take mine in case. Did you bring a travel iron?"

"Come on. Enough already."

"Take it easy. I'll be down in a few minutes."

Bannister turned to the beginning and started flipping through the Macklin file again. His anger grew with the pile of pages. Rape, murder, a pack of young lives snuffed by an arrogant bastard who was able to wash off the blood again and again and walk away clean.

It was all the goddamned system. There were too many legalities and technicalities to trip over. Too many loopholes and exceptions to slip through. Damned system could be stretched and strained and distorted to cover any size heap of manure, even a pile as big as Theodore Macklin.

That's what had driven Bannister off the force five years ago. One Macklin case too many had coaxed him to shed the procedure-book straitjacket and try playing by a far more flexible set of rules. Five years, and he was still testing and resetting the boundaries.

Nice thing about solitaire was how you could change the game to suit you as you went along.

CHAPTER

14

The drive to New York took three hours and change. Felt like that much again before they were able to find a parking spot, and that one was tight as a tourniquet. Alternate side restrictions, the sign said. So tomorrow at half before the street sweeper, Bannister would have to get back in the saddle again.

Restless from the ride, he set off down the block as if his tail had caught fire. Price, burdened by his baggage and a lifetime of devout laziness, strained to keep up. Guy was huffing like a locomotive. Spewing garlic clouds from the salami sandwich Ruthie had packed for him to eat en route.

"Wait up, Sam. These bags are heavy."

"Must be the blow dryer."

Checking the address against the information he'd scrawled on the back of a past-due notice, Bannister turned into a dilapidated building near Second Avenue.

"What kind of hotel is this, Sam? Looks a little run-down."

"It's not a hotel. This guy I know rents apartments by the week. Much more comfortable. You'll see. More like home."

Price made a face. "Not my home."

"Trust me. Have I ever steered you wrong?"

"Actually, yeah. You steered me way wrong with the Schildhauer thing."

"You were the one who took the detours, Lenny."

"Maybe so, but you were the one who put us on the road."

"Besides Schildhauer then."

Price went silent a minute, thinking. "How about two Decembers ago, when you called me in to help you with those blond twins who were accused of servicing that old guy for his inheritance? What were their names again? Yummy and Tasty Divine? Something real subtle like that."

"That was charity."

"Oh, really? Then how come it wasn't deductible?"

"Some things you do for the good feeling, Lenny."

"Yeah, you and that old guy."

The lobby had all the charm of a holding cell. Everything was chained in place and scented with a fetching blend of cheap wine and weak bladders. Muttering, Price trailed Bannister up the slim staircase. Their apartment was on two. Bannister relocated the snoring vagrant at the threshold, worked the locks, and stepped inside.

"Hole, sweet hole. Hey, look, Lenny. It's not bad at all. Honest."

The place was doll-sized but clean and tidy. Every pillow was plumped, the chair arms snugged in crocheted condoms. Amazing how spiffy everything looked, given the probable vintage. The tiny Motorola in the casketlike case was about Price's age. The bookshelves were crammed with *Reader's Digest Condensed Books* circa the Year of the Flood.

Opening the narrow doors along the far wall, Bannister discovered a bathless bathroom and a chaste bedroom with a single bed shrouded in pink chenille. The final two doors revealed a broom closet crammed with Fuller Brushes and a cramped kitchen with ancient appliances. Peering inside the refrigerator, Bannister found a wall of ice streaked with green mold. The stove was home to a frolicking clan of cockroaches. He slammed the oven door and smiled. So much for budget home cooking.

"Seeing it's on Mrs. Rafferty, we might as well eat out. Right, Lenny?"

"Whatever you say."

"Flip you for the couch?"

Price clutched his lumbar region. "My back. You know."

Bannister nodded. Price had spasms. When one kicked in, the poor guy got all twisted with that sad puppy look on his hangdog face. Spent his days not complaining, which was enough to drive Bannister nuts. He had no patience for martyrs, not even that old-time French chick who got herself barbecued and became a saint. So no couch for Lenny.

Bannister flopped on the sofa. The cushions collapsed in a flatulent rush. Nothing under the fluff but springs and imagination. He forced another smile. Much more of this, and his lips were going to get charley horse. "Real comfy." You get what you goddamned pay for, he thought ruefully. Or less.

"Let's get to it, Price. Sooner we start, the sooner I get you back home to that sexy wife of yours."

"I'm for that."

Bannister led him out of the dump and down a block bristling with local color: methadone clinic, rat-infested warehouse, film studio that was definitely not connected to one of the majors. As they passed, Bannister peered through a crack in the door and caught a glimpse of a huge-breasted woman clad in nothing but a garter belt and matching mascara.

They walked past the Camaro. Someone had stuffed an ad for detailing under the wiper blade. Bannister took it out and read it. Two hundred a pop to get your car cleaned by some anal retentive armed with Q-Tips and toothbrushes. Who were they kidding? Whole goddamned car wasn't worth two hundred bucks.

The hospital was only a few blocks away. After hours or not, Bannister was anxious to start tracking down the shrink who'd treated Macklin. He was sure they were in the home stretch to the final answers.

Price stayed skeptical. "I don't know, Sammy. If Macklin was able to keep whatever he knew to himself all those years, why would he suddenly risk telling it to a psychiatrist?"

"Because, a thing like that can get heavier as you go along, that's why. Anyhow, with doctor-patient privilege, what was the big risk?"

"Even if you're right. That same privilege may make the doc unwilling to talk to us."

"We'll blow up that bridge when we come to it, Lenny."

They turned the corner, passed the hospital's emergency entrance, and filtered through a vestibule clogged with vending machines and visitors. Bannister eyed the place with something considerably less than affection. To him, the only decent part of any hospital was the way out.

An evening skeleton staff manned the main floor service stations. Two women with extremely high mileage guarded the patient files at reception. A young faux cop armed with a walkie-talkie staffed security. Admitting was deserted. Ditto billing. A single snail in an apron worked the coffee shop counter. The gift shop was still open. Bannister headed to it and found a cheap box of chocolates on the sale shelf. Looked a little rumpled, but then so did he.

He led Price to reception and requested a pair of visitor's passes for Mr. Brown.

"You want Nicholas Brown or Christopher?"

Bannister chose Christopher and headed for the stairs. They emerged on two and followed the trail of beige-walled corridors to the nurses' desk.

The psych unit was nothing like the movies. No raving lunatics or shuffling zombies. The open doors revealed reasonably normal-looking people watching the tube or chatting with visitors. All right, one or two were chatting with themselves, but from the little Bannister was able to pick up, the conversations sounded pretty rational.

He paused at the main office entrance. "Let me lead, Lenny. Deal?"

"Long as you stay off my feet, Sam."

Bannister spotted a promising pigeon at the nurses' station and got himself in the mood. He strode over and flashed his most beguiling smile.

"I can see why Uncle Ted still talks about this place. So many nice, attractive people," he boomed.

An inflated nurse with a blond bouffant hairdo answered his smile with a hefty one of her own. Woman was so well stuffed, her skin glistened. Bannister noticed she had great teeth. Pity she used them quite so often.

"Uncle Ted?"

"Ted Macklin. He was here a few months ago. Can't stop raving about the place." Raving. Bad choice of word, but she didn't seem to pick up on it.

"Macklin? Sorry. We get so many people through here. Most of them short term."

He deflected her remorse and whipped out the candy. "Doesn't matter. Uncle Ted asked me to drop this off as a token of his appreciation. Thought the staff might enjoy it. You can't imagine what you people did for him."

She cast a longing look at the box. "How nice. I'll put it out in the staff lounge."

"And he wanted me to say a special hello to his doctor. Oh, darn. What was that doctor's name again, Lenny?"

Bannister turned to Price, who shrugged on cue. "You know me and names, Sam. . . ."

"Uncle Ted will never forgive me," Bannister said. "You think you could look it up? I hate to bother you, but I promised."

"Oh, it's no bother." She bustled to the bank of files behind her and spent a few minutes poking through the *M*s. "Here it is. Mr. Macklin was admitted by Dr. Lyons. I should have guessed. Don't know what she does exactly, but it certainly seems to work. Lots of grateful ex-patients."

"You should hear Uncle Ted," Bannister said.

"Hope that helps," the receptionist said. She pulled out a calendar marked with staff schedules. "Dr. Lyons isn't on tonight, but she usually drops by to see her in-patients. Want to leave a note?"

"Actually, I'd rather give her a call. You have her number?"

"Sorry. I'm not permitted to give that out."

"Of course. I understand. Is that Lyons with a Y?"

"Exactly."

"Thanks. Where's the public phone? I'll try through her service."

The nurse directed them to a bank of phones near the elevators. Price dialed a realtor friend and got the doctor's address and home number from a reverse directory. What he couldn't get was Dr. Lyons's cooperation. The woman had sole control of her private patient files. This was one of the rare situations beyond the reach of his international network of contacts. As soon as Price explained that he needed to talk to her about a former patient, the lady shrink cut him off at the knees.

"I don't talk about my patients, former or otherwise."

"But you don't understand. This one is—"

"Doesn't matter. Patient information is privileged. Now, if you'll excuse me."

Price hung up. "Sorry, Sam. No dice. She sounded pretty miffed, too, like she resented my even asking."

Bannister scowled. "Follow me." He led Price back to the nurses' station. His portly pal with the terrific teeth was still around.

"You reach the doctor?" the nurse said.

"No problem. You think I could trouble you for one more favor?"

"Sure."

"Great. I'd like to make an appointment with Dr. Lyons. She said someone here could get hold of her schedule."

"No problem. You want an appointment for yourself?"

"Yeah. Guess these things run in families."

As she left to get the doctor's book, the nurse tossed him a peculiar look. Bannister hoped Macklin hadn't checked himself in for child molestation or lusting after sheep.

When she returned, he tried to smooth it over. "It's just for a consultation, to see if the doc thinks I need treatment. There wouldn't be any charge for that, would there?"

"For an introductory visit, no. I'd think not."

"Great. What's she got Monday?"

Dr. Lyons had an early opening. Bannister took it and left. He had two days to find out all he could to get himself into the right wrong frame of mind.

CHAPTER

15

She pulled her Honda into the drive. With her car still spewing plumes of exhaust, she leaned into the rearview mirror for a touch-up. Camouflaged by the drapes, Jason watched her plump her lacquered hair and slather on another coat of scarlet lipstick. Angling even closer to her reflection, she blotted her mouth on a tissue.

Jason had disliked her from the instant they were introduced after the first meeting of the phobia group. He'd hoped to stay with the aide who used to come to the house, but Dr. Lyons had paired him up with that creature. Woman reminded him of a beach ball. Round, flashy, nothing substantial inside. She had claw nails and raisin eyes rimmed in raccoon liner. Favored clothes in colors that hurt his eyes: scream pinks and purples. Her voice was like Yankee Stadium on a full count. And she smelled like chewing gum.

Her name was Binnie, for godsakes. What kind of a name was Binnie? What the hell were they trying to do to him? At least his other aide had been decent. In fact, Jason had hit it off pretty well with the guy. They'd even gotten sort of friendly. Same with the young doctor who'd come for the medical checkups the hospital required. Even the lady psychiatrist had been okay. Not too pushy, and definitely easy on the eyes.

But this one gave a whole new meaning to the word hopeless.

Jeez, no, now she was getting out. Coming up the walk toward the house. Dumb woman walked like one of Jessie's old pull toys. Wibble-wobble. She carried a bulging purse stamped with status initials. One of those designer fakes sold on street corners, he'd bet.

Jason backed away from the window and bolted up the stairs. Passing Jessie's room, he spotted his sister sitting cross-legged on her rug, back to him, playing with her Barbie beach set.

"Jess," he whispered. "You have to do me a favor."

Kid was lost in space, playing all the parts of one of her dippy fantasies. Normally, she was all over him, following him around, watching everything he did. He was forever catching her spying with those saucer eyes of hers. But now, when he needed her, she was off on Planet Nowhere.

The screen door creaked open, and the doorbell rang.

"Jessie, damn it! I'm talking to you," he rasped.

The kid didn't flinch. She acted as if he were mute and invisible. Jason stormed into the room and grabbed her hard by the arm. She yelped, startled, and tried to shake free.

"Jay-son," she whined. "You scared me."

"Get down there and answer that damned door. Say I'm sick."

The bell sounded again. Lucky thing his mother had gone shopping.

"Go on, now. Hurry up!"

She wrestled out of his grip and set her jaw. "You have to see that lady, Jay. Mommy said."

"I don't give a flying fish what Mommy said, Miss Prissy big mouth. Now get the hell down there and do what I told you."

Standing, she smoothed her T-shirt and stuck her hands on her hips. "You're being silly."

"You're asking for it, you little jerk. Move or you're gonna get it."

There was a firm knocking at the door followed by Binnie's strident: "Jason? Anybody home?"

"Get down there and get rid of her, Jessie. I mean it."

"I'm not scared of you, Jason. And I'm telling."

A molten rage filled him. Suddenly, he realized he

could kill her. He could just coil his fingers around that little pink neck of hers and squeeze until the bones were crushed to powder. He could rip her damned little arms off. Break her in two. Fury pounded in his temples. Grew so big he couldn't see around it.

"Jason?"

That broke through. Deflated his bloated bubble of rage as if someone had stuck it with a pin. It was his mother. What was she doing back already? Should have taken her hours at the mall.

"Get out of my room, you big stinker. I'm not talking to you ever again!"

Jessie's voice was brimming with tears. Her bottom lip curled and trembled. God almighty, had he really lost it and hurt the kid? Had it gone that far? Terrified, he looked her over. No marks on her neck. No welts or anything serious he could see. There was a band of color on her arm where he'd held on to her, but it was already dulled to an innocent pink.

Then, he spotted the parts gathered in her skirt. All he'd done was wreck her damned doll. Barbie had lost her head. And an arm.

"Hey, I didn't mean it, Jess. The thing just broke. It's put together like junk is all. See, there's nothing but these little wires and a couple of elastic bands. I'll get you a new one, okay?"

"Go away. I don't want you in here!"

"Damn it, Jessie, I said I was sorry. How about I get you that astronaut Barbie? You said you wanted that one, remember?"

"I *hate* you, Jason. I'm *never* talking to you ever again!"

His mother was on the steps now. Silently, she absorbed the scene. Jessie flushed and teary. The doll dismembered. And him. Lord knew what he looked like. Probably some wild creature from *Star Wars*. But Mom chose to stay out of it.

"Jason? Binnie's here to see you. Didn't you hear her at the door? Come on down now."

"Mommy, I need to talk to you. Real bad," Jess whimpered.

"A few minutes, Jessie. Let me just get things settled with Binnie and your brother."

"Okay. But come up soon. Please. It's really, really important."

Trapped, Jason trudged down the stairs. He kept his eyes downcast. Binnie was waiting in the foyer. He took in her shoes, pointy-toed things with pale puffs of fat rising in the middle like raw dough.

"Ready, Jason? I looked over the list of goals you and I wrote up after the meeting, and I thought we'd spend this first practice session taking a little walk around the neighborhood."

He'd been up all night, imagining this, expecting the horror to overwhelm him so badly he'd get sick. Maybe puke on the carpet. Maybe he'd even have a heart attack and drop dead. At least, that would be the end of it.

His old aide had never pushed him like this. They'd sat around and chewed the fat. Talked about Jason's experiments. Looked over the data. Guy had acted really impressed. Asked a million questions. So had that young doctor.

But this stupid bitch was bearing down on him like a steamroller. Jason wanted to tell her to get the hell away. He wanted to warn her off, to make her see the danger. But all he felt was a weird numbness as if his insides had been packed in ice.

"Beautiful day for a walk," his mom said. "Heat finally let up a little."

"Come on, Jason," Binnie said. "The hardest part is thinking about it, believe me."

Why the hell should he believe her? Binnie had given him a major line of crap. Claimed she'd been exactly like him only two years ago. Afraid to go out. Incapable of entering a store or a restaurant or church. Scared of tall buildings. Convinced a chunk of glass or concrete was going to break loose and fall on her. If it did, it'd probably bounce off, he thought. Woman looked like Miss Piggy. Even had the snout.

"All I'm asking is that you give it a try, Jason," Binnie said. "We can turn back whenever you say."

"Should I check first?" his mother asked.

Binnie waved her off. "Why don't we try without that? Okay, Jason? I'll be right with you every step of the way."

He felt his mother watching. Jason imagined her eyes filled with disgust and disappointment. Usually, his desire to win her approval was no match for the fear. But this time, there was nothing inside him. He was a blank.

He shrugged. "Okay. Let's go."

"Great."

Binnie breezed outside and Jason followed, letting the screen slam behind him. For a second, he was startled by the sun's glare, but the shock soon yielded to a rush of relief. Felt like plunging into a cold pool on a scorching day. How long since he'd done anything like that? How long since he'd done anything, period?

With Binnie waddling beside him, chattering like a fussy duck, he came to the end of the walk and stepped out on the pavement. Funny how he didn't feel anything. Maybe his damned demons had decided to take the morning off.

At this time of day, there were no cars. All the working people were long gone, the stay-at-home mothers already out for errands. Mail and deliveries wouldn't start for at least another hour, and all but the littlest kids were off to camps or jobs or summer school. So he was left with no distractions but Binnie's runaway tongue.

"Such a pretty street," she prattled. "Like the country with all the trees and everything. My place is in Lefrak City. Ever been there? Must be fifty billion people. Maybe more. They've got schools, churches, stores. You name it. Everything but room to move."

On and on. Like a bee buzzing in his ear. So irritating, Jason wanted to slap it out. Or her. He passed the last house on the block and kept going, quickening his pace. Anything to keep as far away as possible from that mouth.

The next street was deserted, too, but he paused at the corner to make sure. So much air out here. Felt as if he were swimming in a giant ocean of air, rushing and cool. Made him almost dizzy to breathe it, scented as it was with clipped grass, flowers, and motor fumes. Wasn't a

bad kind of dizzy either. The backs of his hands tingled.
He wafted them through the breeze and felt a charge of
satisfaction. He was actually doing this. Taking a walk.
Regular walk in the neighborhood like a normal person.
He was on the verge of a smile when the bitch started in
again.

"Well, here we are at a crossroads, aren't we? Hardest
thing for me is these small decisions. I've got no problem
at all with giant issues—war-and-peace stuff. But offer me
the choice of chicken salad or tuna, and I'm lost. What's
down that way?"

Motor Mouth was asking about the street to the left:
Hillandale. The right fork was Magruder, the way to
school and shopping and the few other places Jason had
dared to go in the past five years.

"Nothing special. A regular block," he said.

"Looks shadier. You care?"

He did vaguely. But not enough to admit. Suddenly, it
seemed ridiculous to prefer one direction over another.
He turned on to Hillandale. If he couldn't take it, they
could head back any time. He wasn't a prisoner. That
large-mouth ass couldn't make him do a damned thing
against his will.

"How's it going, Jason? Feeling all right?"

"Yeah. No problem." The truth surprised him, even as
he spoke it.

"No anxiety at all? It's okay to feel it, you know. The
practice sessions are meant to bring some out. That's the
only way you can learn to deal with it. We have exercises,
tools. Lots of things to help you."

"Well, I'm feeling okay. Sorry."

She laughed. A tinny giggle that reminded him of
cheap glass beads. The walk wasn't getting him, but she
sure was. He imagined holding her head under water until the bubbles stopped, and his smile came back.

"That's great, really. I didn't mean to make you think
you were doing anything wrong. Everyone reacts a different way. Whatever you feel is fine. It'll be up some days
and down others. That's the usual thing."

"Yeah. Right." The words kept pouring out of her, such

a hemorrhage of words you'd think the stupid woman would bleed herself dry and empty.

He quickened his pace. It felt good to stretch his legs out full. There wasn't much space in the house. The rooms were small and cramped with furniture. Most ended in a couple of strides.

Hillandale continued for a half-dozen houses. At the intersection of Somerset, he turned left again. That way, he could finish the loop in two more blocks and head home. He'd never imagined going so far this first time.

Not too shabby, Jason, my man. Not bad at all.

As he rounded the corner, the neighborhood changed abruptly. Unnerved, Jason slowed for a second. Forcing himself to keep going, he passed a rubble-strewn vacant lot and a body shop. Next came a seedy old Victorian that had been converted to apartments. After that was a tiny box of a house surrounded by chicken-wire fencing. He felt Binnie stall beside him, and then he heard it.

A low, throaty growl. Another. Then barks, sharp as gunshots. They pierced him. Left him bleeding rivers of fear.

Three enormous beasts lunged at the fence. Jason stood rooted as they leaped and flattened themselves against the wire, trying to get at him. Their eyes were ice black.

A scream rose in his throat. Stuck there deep and hard like a knife blade. Then the world shivered and went dim. Suddenly, everything was so far away he could barely touch or hear it. But he knew. They were out there. They would get him. Their snarls tore his flesh, crushed his bones.

"It's okay, Jason. They're all locked up. See? Can't come anywhere near you. Boy, they look fierce, don't they? Rottweilers, right? Anyone would be glad they're penned, not just you. That's why they *are* penned, in fact. Let's go, now. Come on. That's enough for today."

He was walled by blackness. Frozen. But the next thing he knew, they were back at his house. Binnie held the screen open for him and gave him a little nudge inside. His mother was waiting in the living room.

"He did beautifully," Binnie gushed. "We went all

around the long way. We even passed a yard with three big dogs, and he was all right. You had a little anxiety there, didn't you, Jason? But you managed. He was amazing, really."

Thinking of those snarling monsters, a hot rash scaled his spine and set fire to his face. She'd forced him out there with them. Dumb bitch had almost gotten him ripped to bloody shreds.

Binnie kept at it. "You okay now? Sometimes you feel so good, you take on too much too fast. We're going to do this step by step, young man. We're going to desensitize you and teach you ways to deal with the anxiety when it hits you. I've got a whole bunch of things in my little bag of tricks to help you out. There, you look better already. Feeling all right?"

He shook his head in dull compliance. No need to argue with her or anyone. He knew what he had to do.

Whatever it took, he was going to get through this.

CHAPTER

16

Bannister hung up, troubled. He'd had a long, hard talk with his daughter last night and another this morning, but she'd refused to reveal the source of her obvious unhappiness. Chloe wouldn't even admit she had a problem. But there was an unmistakable dull edge to her tone. Kid sounded like a box so jammed with troubles there was barely room for air.

He'd tested every imaginable angle: friends, school, boys. He'd even considered that the kid's funk might have his name on it.

"Is it because I had to postpone our visit this month, sweetheart?" he'd asked. "Because you know I wouldn't have if it wasn't absolutely necessary."

"It's not that."

"What then?"

"Nothing. I told you."

"Well, whatever it is, I'm here for you. Anything, any time. You know that."

"Sure, Daddy. Mind if I go now? I wanted to watch something."

Price tried to comfort him. "It's hormones, Sammy. Kids get hormones, there's no living with them for eight, nine years. Ruthie and I went through it with all three of ours. You're taking it much harder than she is. Believe me."

Bannister tried. But he couldn't shake the sense that this was something larger than normal adolescent turmoil. He knew his daughter. At least, he'd thought he did.

"I'm running late, Lenny. You'll call at exactly ten after?"

"I said I will, and I will. But I have to tell you the whole thing sounds pretty ridiculous to me. Not to mention a felony."

"Right. Don't mention it."

Price insisted on staying at the hovel to do some digging on the phone. He wanted to reconstruct what he could of Theodore Macklin's last few days. See what, if any, eleventh-hour contacts the creep had made.

The idea held no appeal for Bannister. Price's thoroughness had a way of complicating matters, contaminating a nice, straightforward case with lots of messy alternatives. All they needed to do was establish Macklin's guilt in the Rafferty murder. Why risk getting sidetracked by some silly quest for the whole, unvarnished truth?

Bannister headed out alone. Opening the apartment door, he found their wino curled up sleeping on the welcome mat. Hurdling him, Bannister hurried down and through the lobby where four more people slept in various states of undress and unconsciousness. The sight made him think of the toppling tower of unpaid bills on his nightstand, the maxed-out credit cards and eviscerated bank account. His fiscal house of cards had been verging on collapse for more months than he cared to consider. This Rafferty case could either plump the deck or strip him of the last of his dwindling store of trump cards.

Banishing the uneasy thought from his mind, he left the building. The call to Chloe had left him with only ten minutes to make his scheduled appointment at East End Hospital.

He worked the Camaro out of the spandex-tight space and eased down the block seeking a spot on the legal side of the street. Near the corner of Third Avenue, he spied a red sports number angling into traffic. With any luck, that precious scrap of real estate would be his. There were no cars ahead of him. But just as he was about to ease into the vacant slot, a black Porsche backed out of nowhere and blocked his way.

A patient, reasonable Bannister got out and ambled

toward the interloper. Guy at the wheel sported a road-kill toupee and a supercilious smirk.

"Excuse me, sir," Bannister said. "I guess you didn't see me. I was waiting for that spot."

"Fuck off."

Finishing school dropout, no doubt.

Bannister kept calm. "Believe me, I wouldn't argue over a parking space, but I'm in a hurry. So if you'd be so kind as to move."

"Kiss my ass."

"Certainly. Whatever you say, sir." He sauntered back to the Camaro. Turning, he raised his hands to frame the Porsche. Made a lovely picture in his mind. He imagined the bashed bumper, the busted taillights raining shards of million-dollar glass, the driver's apoplexy. Bannister's jalopy wasn't good for much, but he couldn't fathom a better battering ram.

Bannister backed up a fair distance and started gunning the engine, which sounded on its best days like a bad-tempered bull elephant. He gave Mr. Porsche plenty of time to decide between his macho crap and his dickmobile.

The car won.

Bannister claimed the spot triumphantly and headed for the hospital. He told himself he was prepared for this. At least, he'd done his homework.

Over the weekend, he and Price had spent hours doing research in the midtown library. First, they'd consulted the physicians' blue book, which listed Dr. Margaret Lyons as a board-certified psychiatrist specializing in anxiety disorders and phobia treatment. Woman was around thirty-five, thirty-six, judging from the year of her graduation. Had diplomas from Brown and Cornell Medical School. Did her residency at Johns Hopkins and worked there until coming to East End.

Bannister did some reading about her area of specialization. Therapists were split on the correct approach to patients with phobias. Traditional Freudians held that free-floating terrors were caused by an underlying trauma or conflict. The classic case was a child patient of Freud's named Little Hans whose abject terror of horses supposedly reflected an unresolved oedipal complex.

Shrinks who took Freud's view prescribed individual analysis, to cure the problem by digging for the roots. Without analysis, they believed patients would simply substitute a new symptom for the conquered phobia. And the new one might be worse.

Then, twenty or so years ago, a number of doctors in the field broke with Freud and decided it was more practical and productive to simply treat the phobic behavior directly. Pluck it like a weed and forget about the roots. They claimed symptom substitution was not a problem.

Phobia treatment centers sprang up across the country. Some programs used tranquilizers in combination with therapy. Some relied on acupuncture or relaxation techniques. Others worked to help the patient redefine his perceptions so feared situations could be seen in a new and less threatening light. A few held that phobias were sensory disturbances curable by medical means. More common were programs like the one at East End where patients were deliberately exposed to their anxiety triggers under controlled conditions and taught ways to overcome them.

There was a giant list of specific phobias. You name it, Bannister discovered, someone was terrified by it: birds, lightening, public speaking, dentists, swimming, balloons, in-laws, the sight of blood. Most severe phobics had a cluster of fears that ganged up to limit the scope of their lives, sometimes even keeping them housebound.

Many experienced panic attacks, episodes of intense physical reaction. Bannister memorized the symptoms: rapid heartbeat, sweating, shallow or labored breathing, tingling in the palms, dizziness or nausea, a sense of unreality.

Though the spells were brief and benign, panic victims believed they were seriously ill, even dying. They developed intense fears of losing control and making fools of themselves. In one of those ironic self-sustaining circles, the fear of the fear developed a life and power of its own.

Weird to think of Ted Macklin as phobic. Hard to imag-

ine that big gorilla cowering in the shadow of some imaginary menace. From what Bannister remembered, the guy
was all bulk and bluster. Jut-jawed, dare-me type. Then, it
could be he'd consulted Dr. Lyons on something outside
her specialty, say suicidal depression. Or it could be he'd
developed some kind of irrational fear as a smoke screen
for the guilt he harbored about the rape and murder of
Martha Rafferty.

Bannister paused at the hospital entrance and fortified
himself with a breath. Ready as he'd ever be, he strode to
reception and requested a pass to the phobia clinic. He
lowered his voice, suddenly self-conscious about his fresh,
unwelcome status as a psychiatric patient.

He went to the main office and gave the receptionist
his name. She directed Bannister to Dr. Lyons's office
down the hall and called ahead to announce his arrival.

His uneasy feeling intensified as he passed several
other offices where shrinks and their clients were locked
in earnest exchange. He could see the pairs through the
bubbled glass inserts in the doors. Each duo resembled a
plant tipped toward the sunlight. He imagined the air
thick with old hurts and musty questions. Therapy was
definitely not for him. Sure, he was as crazy as the next
guy, but he saw no reason to brag about it to a professional, especially when it cost over a dollar a minute for
the dubious privilege.

His knock brought a trim, green-eyed blonde with boy-
cut hair to the door. Tiny diamonds winked from her ears
and a miniature gold lion dangled from a chain around
her neck.

"Hello, I'm Maggie Lyons. Mr. Bannister?"

He pleaded guilty. Bannister was surprised and more
than a little unsettled by the doctor's appearance. He'd
expected someone stern and bookish, preferably with or-
thopedic shoes and a bun. Dr. Lyons had fire in her eyes
and a nice edge about her. If he hadn't sworn off women
forever, this one would be a definite maybe.

She motioned him toward the couch, and he sat pitched
forward like an expectant pinball. No way he was going to
lie down. She pulled up a chair and sat opposite him.

"So what brings you here, Mr. Bannister?"

Standard opening gambit. Bannister had picked up the usual session format from a book by Lucy Freeman, an author who wrote extensively on the psychoanalytic process. So he had his answer ready.

"It's really embarrassing, Doctor. I'm having this problem with heights. Came on me suddenly a couple of months ago. And I work in construction. Commercial stuff. Hard to be a job foreman when you can't bring yourself to go out on the rigging."

She was eyeing him strangely. "What happens to you when you try?"

"Rapid heartbeat, dizziness, sweaty palms. I feel as if I'm having a heart attack. And there's this sense of unreality."

Her curious look was curling at the edges. "And how long does this feeling last?"

"Oh, probably just a minute or two. But it seems much longer. And I have this sense everyone's watching me, as if I'm making a terrible fool of myself."

She bit back a smile. Here he was baring his invented agonies to the woman and she had the nerve to find them amusing. Real professional.

"And are you, Mr. Bannister?"

"Am I what?"

"Making a terrible fool of yourself?"

"What the hell is that supposed to mean?"

"You tell me. I was hoping to change the time of our appointment. I tried calling the number you left and found there was no such number. You aren't listed or unlisted with Manhattan Information. The address you gave turns out to be an armory. And the construction company you claim to work for doesn't happen to exist. My diagnosis is that you came here to pull some phony scam with my unwitting assistance. What's the game, Mr. Bannister, if that's your real name? Disability claim? Unemployment benefits? Insurance fraud? What?"

Bannister was dumbstruck. When he found his voice again, it had shrunk several sizes. "I'm a private investigator. I came because I need some information on one of your patients."

"Then why didn't you simply ask?"

"My partner tried that. You refused to talk to him."

"Then that should have been the end of it."

Maggie's beeper sounded. Training a wary eye on him, Dr. Lyons picked up the phone to answer the page.

"Who? Well, that makes absolutely no sense. Could you call down and get back to me? Right. Thanks." Her frown deepened. "You wouldn't be behind that bit of nonsense, too, would you?"

Bannister felt like a chastened child. "Not unless it was someone paging you to Emergency."

She puffed her lips. "Did you really think I was going to stroll out of my office and leave you behind to steal my patient records?"

"Not steal, borrow. Look, I'm sorry. I guess I was desperate."

"Good-bye, Mr. Bannister."

Bannister knew a futile situation when he saw one. But he'd never been one to let that stop him.

"Please, Dr. Lyons. This guy shouldn't be allowed to get away with what he did."

"I said, good-bye."

"We're talking human garbage. Lowest of the low. Macklin's not worth any goddamned privilege, and he's not worth protecting."

Her steely gaze faltered. "Macklin again?"

"What?"

"I had a visit from a Rhode Island detective over the weekend. He wanted information about Theodore Macklin also."

"How come?"

The doctor moved to speak but appeared to reconsider. "Why don't you tell me what your interest is first?"

He did, sketching the decades-old murder of Martha Rafferty and Macklin's probable but as yet unproven guilt in the case. Bannister left out the part about Mrs. Rafferty's posted fifty-thousand-dollar reward. The doctor's opinion of him was more than low enough already.

"Why was the Rhode Island cop asking about Macklin?"

Dr. Lyons hesitated. After a beat, she recounted what Detective Fazio had told her about the possibility of shady dealings by Macklin's investment firm and the state's interest in having the man's death certified as a suicide.

"So what did you tell him?"

"That's privileged."

"Why? Was this detective your patient, too?"

She bristled. "All right, Mr. Bannister. I told him I won't bend my professional ethics or opinions to suit anyone. That includes the state of Rhode Island. And it most certainly includes you."

Bannister frowned. "Are you saying you don't think Macklin went off that bridge on his own?"

"I'm saying I want you to leave."

"What makes you think it wasn't a suicide?"

"Good-bye, Mr. Bannister."

"But wait. I have to know."

"Will you go on your own, or do I have to call security?"

"Please, Dr. Lyons. Just tell me that much." He spotted a trace of softening in her eyes. Nice eyes, soft or no.

"All right. Theodore Macklin simply did not strike me as suicidal. And even if he were, given his intense bridge phobia, he would have chosen a different way out. Now, if you'll excuse me, I have work to do."

"Please, Doctor. All I need is to go through Macklin's file. I can do it under your supervision or anyway you say. The guy is dead. What can it hurt?"

"Good-bye, Mr. Bannister."

Bannister jotted his local address and phone number on the back of the detailing ad he'd found under his windshield wiper and tossed it on her desk.

"Here's where I'm staying in town. Please think it over. A young girl's life was stolen. Her mother's had to live all these years not knowing who did it. You might have the answers she's been looking for. She's an old woman, Dr. Lyons. All she wants is a little peace of mind."

She crumpled the number and tossed it in the trash.

Woman was very attractive when she was furious. Not so
bad the rest of the time either. Bannister found himself in
no particular hurry to adjourn the meeting.

"Look, Doc. I'm really sorry I wasn't straight with you
from the beginning. Isn't there some way I can make it up
to you?"

"Leaving would be a start."

"Come on. Macklin doesn't deserve to go out with a
clean slate."

"Good-*bye*, Mr. Bannister."

"Think about it. That could have been your kid. It
could have been you."

"Give it up, Detective. It's not going to work."

Bannister left her with a pleading look and a parting
shot to the conscience.

"You can keep that scum from getting away with murder, Dr. Lyons. You can make things right here."

Bannister had spent all his ammunition, but not a single
shot had hit the target. Dr. Margaret Lyons was a very
appealing, extremely well-constructed brick wall.

Leaving the office, Bannister knew he wasn't about to
let that or anything else stop him. When the stakes were
this high, you didn't fold over a little thing like a hopeless
hand.

CHAPTER

17

Maggie's schedule was packed. In the few spare minutes between patients, she finally managed to reach Richmond Steele, the hospital's vice president for community affairs. He listened without comment as she quickly outlined her idea for East End to host a national symposium on phobia treatment.

"I'm sure I can get several of the top names in the field to speak," she told him. "We can schedule it for a weekend and draw people from all over the country. It'd be good for East End and terrific for the clinic."

Steele raised the obvious issues. Maggie assured him that she would take care of getting all the necessary permits and insurance coverage. The clinic would assume full responsibility for all facility rentals, printing, publicity, and incidental costs. She was positive they could attract enough paying attendees to cover expenses and still realize a sizeable profit for the endangered phobia program.

While Steele made some notes, Maggie mused about the intriguing possibilities. If the symposium was the success she anticipated, she would make it an annual event. If that didn't generate sufficient revenue, she could hold regional or local meetings more often. She could even develop a training institute for area mental health professionals. All she needed was the necessary blessing from Steele, and Alex Ivy could have his precious twenty-percent increase in the clinic's bottom line. Maybe more.

"Sounds like an interesting idea," Steele conceded at last. "I'll run it by a few people and get back to you."

"Can't you just give me the okay? I thought you were in charge of all outreach activities."

He chuckled. "Outreach, yes, overreach, no. Let me just discuss it with President Ivy, and I'm sure I'll be able to give you the green light. Protocol. You understand."

Maggie's hopes plunged. "Yes. Unfortunately, I do."

"I'll have an answer for you as soon as possible."

No hurry, she wanted to tell him. Maggie knew what the answer would be. Poison Ivy wasn't about to make anything easy for her. He would find some reason to refuse her request. But there had to be some way around that little creep. Or through him.

All day, she kept turning the problem over and arguing it with herself from every conceivable angle. She had to force herself to pay attention during treatment sessions.

Her last scheduled patient was Daisy Tyler. Maggie noticed that the woman seemed much more relaxed. Daisy made surer eye contact, and her hands rested easily on her lap. A touch of optimism had even invaded her vocabulary. A couple of times, she said *when* I get better. Not *if*. Given enough time, work, and determination, Maggie was certain the woman could be cured. But there wouldn't be enough time if Alex Ivy had his way.

Maggie was in no financial position to open her own practice. If East End folded, she'd have to find another job. Start over, probably in a different city. Patients like Daisy would be forced to start again, too, a fresh, painful new beginning many of them would probably avoid.

There was a knock at Maggie's office door. This time it was Pam Richards's turn to suggest dinner.

"I heard about a new Italian place near Bloomingdale's, and it so happens Bloomie's is having a big sale," she said with a mischievous hitch of her brow. "We could do our patriotic bit to pump the economy."

"Tempting, but I think I'd better take a rain check."

Pam's eyes narrowed. "You all right?"

"I'll let you know in a day or two."

"Sure you don't want to talk about it?"

"I do, Pam. But right now, I'm talked out."

"Rain check it is, then." She hesitated at the door. "My shoulder's available any time, you know."

"Thanks. Consider it reserved."

Maggie was nowhere near ready to surrender, but the battle had left her energies a few quarts low. She craved a long, hot bath and a night of oblivion. She wanted to kick Alex Ivy and East End and suicides and irritating detectives as far out of her weary mind as possible. Fortunately, her mother was visiting Cousin Kathy in Roslyn for dinner and an overnight stay.

Cousin Kathy was one of Aunt Hannah's three children. She'd agreed immediately when Maggie called earlier seeking a little respite care for her mom. They had exchanged such favors before. Once, Maggie had taken her mother and Aunt Hannah to Miami Beach for a four-day stint, so Kathy could have her second caesarian in relative peace.

Kathy and her two sisters had always been close to Maggie, virtual siblings. But Maggie had always longed for a real sister, someone bound by blood and experience. Even at this age, she felt the lack as a small but real discomfort. It was like a vacant section in a jewel box, a visible reminder of a teasing, untenable wish.

Tony, the regular evening doorman, greeted her at the building's entrance. He was a gregarious fellow with a ponytail trailing from his uniform cap and a snake tattoo slithering forth from his cuff.

"Hey, Dr. Lyons. You watching the game tonight?"

"Only if it's playing inside my eyelids."

The elevator was taking forever. Mickey Glover had added to his mischief repertoire, stalling the cars between floors, pressing the emergency stop button. On the interminable ride to nine, Maggie reined her temper with positive thoughts. Someday, the little Glover brat would grow up and move out. Much sooner, she would be in sweet, warm, wet solitude. Even the thought was relaxing.

For a change, her apartment locks worked smoothly. Inside, she found several lights blazing. Surprising, given her mother's overblown opinion of the powers of electricity. As Francine saw it, a burning bulb could suddenly develop a temper and explode. A plugged-in appliance could engage in devilish acts of spontaneous mayhem. Usually, Mom left the place in a blitz-level blackout.

Maybe her mother was easing up a little, Maggie thought with a reckless shot of optimism. And maybe the moon was made of pickled herring.

She ran a tub and undressed. Slipping on a terry robe and plush slippers, she padded into the living room to check the mail. The usual stack of bills and circulars. Nothing that couldn't wait. Four messages had registered on the phone machine. There was her mother's tremulous voice announcing her safe arrival at Cousin Kathy's house. Ethan had called for the first time in weeks. He had two tickets to a grudge match at the Garden and was wondering if Maggie might want to go.

She could imagine the evening. First, they'd have dinner at a café specializing in Peruvian shashlik or candied root vegetables. After watching two brainless behemoths bash each other to pulp in the ring, Ethan would suggest something truly romantic to cap the night. Bungee-jumping off the World Trade Center, perhaps. Or spelunking in the New York City sewer system.

Next up was F.X. Kennedy. He was wondering about dinner. Wincing at his voice, Maggie found herself wondering about the persistent Mr. Kennedy. The man refused to be put off by polite refusals or firm reminders about hospital rules. A teensy obsession in progress? Last thing she needed at the moment was to play a home game of fatal attraction.

The final message was from that obnoxious detective, Sam Bannister. He hoped she was reconsidering his request to see Theodore Macklin's records, he said. They might contain crucial information about the murder case and more. Would she consider discussing the matter in person? Say, over lunch tomorrow?

Maggie shook her head and clicked off the machine. The man certainly suffered no shortage of unmitigated gall.

All day, she'd gotten reports that Bannister was snooping around the hospital, asking questions, trying to get his hands on Theodore Macklin's records. He'd attempted everything from blatant flattery to fibs to outright fraud.

He'd even barged into Pam's office while Maggie was with a patient and tried to pass himself off as a journalist doing an article on phobia programs.

Pam had found the whole thing amusing. "The reporter bit didn't fool me for a minute, Maggie, but he was very attractive, and sexy, and obviously very, very interested in you."

"Not in me, Pam. It's my patient files he's after."

"That's not all, Maggie. Believe me. There was definitely more on that man's agenda than files."

"Well, whatever it is, he can keep it."

Pam sighed. "If you're determined to throw this one back, toss him in my direction, will you?"

"With pleasure."

Maggie made a face at the phone machine. Having failed at every turn, the detective probably thought he could badger her into acquiescence. Fat chance. Maggie had been nagged by masters of her mother's caliber and managed to hold her ground.

She was not at all pleased that Sam Bannister had gotten her unlisted phone number. On the other hand, she was pretty sure she had his number as well. The man was good looking and knew it. Pam's assessment aside, he was probably a card-carrying narcissist with the sensitivity of a rock. The urban singles jungle was crawling with that species of predatory beast. Before she'd learned suitable vigilance, Maggie had been nipped a time or two herself.

Erasing the tape, she felt a surge of well-being. If only all her problems were that easy to eliminate.

The bath was perfect. Enveloping warmth, froth of bubbles. Maggie drifted on a soap-scented cloud. So soothing, it took a minute for the sound to penetrate.

Footsteps.

Fear gripped her. Someone was in the apartment. Pulse racing, she tried to rise soundlessly from the tub. As she lifted her leg, the water sloshed. Was it loud enough to give her away? Holding her breath, she tried to gauge the location of the footfalls. Living room or kitchen, she thought.

Slipping on her terry robe, she approached the bathroom door. Cracking it open, she peered into the dim hallway. She couldn't see anyone, but there was the distinct clack of leather soles on the kitchen tile.

With the building's security, she never bothered to use the apartment's burglar alarm system, another relic of her mother's galloping paranoia. But now, Maggie was grateful for the defensive overkill. There were several panic buttons scattered throughout the place. The nearest was in her study. All she had to do was slip into the next room and press it to sound a blaring siren and summon the police.

Her heart squirmed as she stole out of the bathroom.

Please let me make it.

Suddenly, a floorboard creaked under her weight. She stopped cold. No reaction from the intruder. After a few breathless seconds, she forced herself to continue.

Almost there, Maggie. A few more steps.

Her heart was racing, her throat was so parched she couldn't swallow. Forcing the terror aside, she focused on the panic button. One second of that screaming alarm and whoever it was would turn tail and run. All she had to do was reach it.

The study door was shut. Surely it was open when she passed earlier. What if someone were in there, waiting?

Hesitating, she heard sounds from the kitchen again. But there could be more than one of them.

Clutching the knob, she quickly assessed the risks. If she opened the door, she might be trapped immediately. The kitchen was occupied, but going in that direction, she'd have a better chance of reaching the panic button in the hall or fleeing the apartment before the intruder could get to her.

Maggie raced down the hall and into the foyer. She twisted hard at the door handle. It wouldn't open.

Damned locks. Which ones had she left open and which had she shut? Desperately, she wrenched and twisted at the trail of bolts and levers.

Open, damn it! Let me out of here!

"Maggie? Where did you come from? We thought you were out. I was just leaving a note."

Spinning around, she saw her father holding a pen and a note pad. He had a mischievous grin on his face and a nubile brunette dangling from his arm.

"Tina Brodsky, this is my daughter, Maggie Lyons."

"Maggie, hi. I'm so glad to meet you. Robbie talks about you all the time."

Robbie?

Maggie's incredulity grew as the last of her fear evaporated. Tina had a child's face. Shrink-wrapped skin. No wrinkles, not even a crow's-foot or two, for decency's sake. Her taut little body, untouched by gravity, was packaged in a black tank top and tight white jeans. The girl was brand-new, for godsakes. Probably still had the tags on her.

"Hope we're not interrupting anything, honey," her father said. "We wanted to surprise you."

"Well, you certainly did that. Give me a minute, will you? I'll get dressed."

She dripped her way back down the hall. With a wistful glance at the bubble-capped tub, she toweled off and slipped on a sweatsuit. Running a comb through her hair, she thanked the benevolent fates for her mother's timely trip to Cousin Kathy's. Mom had long viewed her father's affinity for younger women as a personal affront. And this one was practically fetal.

Maggie steeled herself and headed back down the hall. Cooing sounds emanated from the living room. There, she found her father and his little friend on the couch. Tina's trim feet were perched on Dad's lap. Wouldn't have surprised Maggie a bit if her father had commenced chanting, "This Little Piggy Goes to Market."

Her father was sixty-three. Tina was midtwenties, maximum. What could they possibly have in common? Country of origin?

"Where did you two meet?" Maggie asked. *Sesame Street?*

"One of those things." Tina giggled. "You know."

I definitely do not.

"I was out to lunch with a client," her father said. "Tina and a friend were at the next table. We got to talking."

About what? Toilet training? Kicking the pacifier habit?

"Can I get you anything?"

"No, sweetheart. We're all set. I made dinner reservations at Bella Vita. We were hoping you'd join us."

"Thanks, but tonight's really not good."

"Tomorrow then?"

Maggie gave him a hard look. "I have plans with Mom."

"Too bad. I really want you and Tina to get to know each other better. How's next Saturday?"

She couldn't put him off forever. "All right, I guess." *At least by then, Tina will be a few days older.*

"How about we have lunch in the meantime, Maggie? Just the two of us?" Tina asked.

Get real. "Sorry. Lunch is hit or miss depending on my schedule. I never make plans."

Tina's perkiness gave her the look of a wind-up toy. "No problem," she said eagerly. "I'll just stop by East End one of these days when I'm in the neighborhood. If you're free, great."

"Oh, I wouldn't want you to go out of your way." *Or get in mine.*

"Be my pleasure."

Maggie didn't debate that one. The pleasure would certainly not be hers.

Dad got to his feet. "See you Saturday, then. Bring someone if you like. Come on, Tina honey. We're running late."

He whisked his little friend out the door. Turning as he left, he fixed Maggie with a worried look. "Get some rest, will you? You look whipped."

She shut the door and locked it. Listening, she heard Tina's voice fade to a wordless trill. Trudging down the hall to the bedroom, Maggie wondered if her fatigue really showed. Maybe she only appeared worn by comparison to Lolita Brodsky.

Whipped, indeed. No matter how she looked, Maggie

was not ready to concede defeat by any means. In fact, she had an idea that might turn circumstances back in her favor. If she hurried, there was still time to take care of it tonight.

Changing into a more suitable outfit, she made the necessary call and shut the apartment door behind her.

CHAPTER

18

"You haven't eaten a thing, Jason. Aren't you feeling well?"

"Fine, Mom. Just not hungry."

"You sure? It's all your favorites."

"All right, for godsakes. Look, I'm eating. I'm stuffing my face. You happy now?"

He forced a bite. Felt like a mouthful of pebbles, choking dry. Usually, he loved steak off the barbecue. And the corn and roasted peppers and tossed salad with Ranch Dressing. But tonight, he was all jammed up inside.

Shying from his mother's fretful gaze, he glanced across the table at his father. Nothing to the guy but skin, bones, and glasses, Jason thought with a contemptuous sniff. Everything else about him was painfully nondescript. His clothes skimmed his narrow frame like flimsy curtains. He had hair almost the exact color of his face, so everything blended to near disappearance. Average features, eyes the color of rain. Guy hardly left footprints in the carpet, for chrissakes. Conscious of Jason's scrutiny, his old man looked over and blinked slowly, like a frog.

"So how's your summer going, son? Working on your experiments at all?"

"Some."

"Are *not*," Jessie taunted with a mean jut of her pointy chin. "You haven't been down there for weeks." She turned to her parents and spoke in a conspiratorial hush. "He's *afraid* of the basement. Thinks maybe there's a you-know-what hiding there."

There was a harsh silence. His father finally broke it. "Glad you're going to that group at the hospital for that problem, son. I was thinking, once you've got it licked, maybe you'll be ready to get a job, maybe come on board with the field force at Mutual Life."

Jason's stomach fisted. "Thanks anyway, Dad."

"Now, don't be hasty, son. Selling's not an easy profession, but there's always room for up-and-comers. You learn the ropes, who knows? Might find you've got the knack for it like your old man. Worth a try anyway. How about I put in a good word for you next time I see Mr. Pavia at the main office?"

Jason's cheeks went hot. Last thing he wanted was his father's stinking business or his useless good words or anything else. Guy was a big nerd of a failure. Always got the worst territory in the entire company. And he was forever scrambling to meet his quota. Worse, he only managed to sell his dumb policies to neighbors and family, people who felt too sorry or embarrassed to turn him down.

"The thing is, I'm getting college applications together, Dad. I've decided to go for that degree in chemistry after all. Maybe even a masters."

"Sure. That'd be nice." His father studied his plate, trying to mask his disbelief.

"And I *am* working on my experiments. Plenty of times I do it when you're off at your baby school or after your infant bedtime, Miss Bigmouth Know-it-all. So happens I'm going down right after dinner tonight. And you stay the hell away while I'm at it, or I'll wring your little neck. I'm sick and tired of you following me around all the time."

"Mommy," Jessie whined. "He doesn't *own* the basement, does he? Isn't it a *free* country?"

His mother's smile was wan. "Experiments take concentration, sweetheart. Anyway, I need your help in the kitchen after dinner. You're my chief plate dryer, aren't you?"

The child brightened. "Can we bake cupcakes after?"

"Good idea. We'll make our own concoction while Jay works on his down in the lab."

So Jason was trapped. After the dishes were cleared, they all sat waiting for him to get up and go downstairs. Daring him. The cellar door was directly across from the kitchen table; there was no way he could somehow escape and fake it.

"Have to go get a few things in my room first," he told them.

"I'm going up anyway," his father said. "What do you need?"

"Some papers and junk. They're scattered all over. Be easier if I get them myself."

"I know where your stuff is, Jay. Want me to get it?" Jessie chirped.

"Want me to get you, you nosy little creep?" Jason glowered.

"Stop teasing her, Jason," his mother said.

"She's a goddamned pain in the ass. I'm sick of her poking around in my business."

"Watch your language, son," his father said.

"When are all of you going to get off my goddamned case?"

Jason bolted and raced up to his room. Banging the door shut, he leaned against the wall until his breathing settled. The cellar was a place of eerie darkness and inexplicable dangers. He couldn't go back down there. Impossible.

He was startled by a knock. "Jason, honey. Are you all right?"

"Yeah. I told you. Just have to get some stuff together."

"Want Dad to go down there with you and check things out? He wouldn't mind."

"No, damn it. I said I'm going, and I am."

Anger pushed him out the door and down to the kitchen where Jessie was reading the instructions on the back of a cake mix box. Runt could read like she'd been born to it. Then, everything had always come easy to her. Little Miss Perfect.

"Two eggs well beaten. A half cup of water. Stir until barely moistened . . ."

Jason opened the basement door and started down. The risers crackled under his weight. His shadow spread over the dim stairs and spilled onto the cellar's stained concrete floor. His sister's voice faded to a drone in the distance.

"Pour in a well-greased pan . . ."

He passed quickly around the space, tugging the strings to activate the dangling scatter of bare bulbs. The light was glaring and uneven. There was the steady beat of dripping water in the crawl space under the den. A ripe moldy smell made his eyes water.

Two paint-freckled sawhorses marked the boundaries of the makeshift lab Jason had set up during his frenzied preparation for the Westinghouse Science Talent Search last year. His honors chemistry teacher, Otto Allen, had urged him to enter. Mr. Allen had lent him the latest texts and experimental journals and provided him with all the equipment and ingredients he requested. Guy was an oddball, true. But he'd warmed Jason to the competition with steady praise and encouragement. Mr. Allen kept telling Jason he had real talent for chemistry. Enough of that, and Jason had come to believe he had an actual chance at winning one of the prestigious awards.

For months, Jason had spent every spare second developing and refining his special formula. He'd tested his results on the dozen white mice Mr. Allen had ordered from a special lab animal breeding company known for their scrupulous genetic controls. Everything had been going along even better than Jason had dared to hope.

Then, one morning when he went to the basement to run his trials, he found one of the mice dead. The stiff remains were warped and bloodied, the skull crumpled like a paper bag.

What kind of a creature could have done that?

Jason had struggled to oust the incident from his mind and continue with his planned protocol. Completed contest entries were due in a week, and he needed to finish one final round of trials on his latest, most successful formulation: C2BU. If he could document its effectiveness with the remaining mice, he was sure he'd be named one of the Talent Search winners.

The next morning, he'd awakened early and gone down to his lab to check the mice. At first glance, things looked fine, but then he'd spotted another mutilated dead mouse in the rear corner of the cage.

Only one kind of beast could do this. It had to be one of them.

In a horrific flash, Jason could see the claws and smell the feral blood lust. He shriveled inside, became the tiny, tortured prey. Pitiful desperate thing, caught in the monster's grip. Wracked in every fiber of its being by a deathly terror. Phantom screams shrilled in his head, so sharp and fierce he thought his skull would split.

That was the end of it. No matter how he tried, Jason could not bring himself to go down there again. His doctor friend had urged him to continue with the experiment, and so had his aide. There were a number of comforting, alternative explanations for the violent deaths of the experimental mice, both had assured him. Maybe they'd overreacted to the courage drug and battered themselves in an attempt to escape the cage. Maybe the formula had induced some bizarre cannibalistic behavior in the animals. It was even possible that the deaths were unrelated to the drug altogether. The mice may have succumbed to an illness. Maybe some disorder that caused violent seizures.

Try though he did, Jason could not accept the rationalizations. Something evil was lurking in that cellar, a danger he could not risk.

He forged a doctor's note claiming that the experimental chemicals were making him sick. Adverse skin reaction from the fumes, he'd written in a decent imitation of their pediatrician's choppy hand. For good measure he'd played sick, faking a flu that kept him home from school until after the contest deadline had safely elapsed. Afterward, Jason paid Neil Ziegans from down the block to fetch the remaining mice and return them to Mr. Allen.

For months now, Jason's neat rows of prior formulas

had sat untouched in their corked beakers in the cellar. C2BU, his masterpiece, remained unproven, hidden in a corked bottle in the back of his closet. He couldn't bring himself to discard the sample and all the work it represented, so it remained where it was as a silent rebuke.

Jason tried not to think about it. Useless waste of time. Without experimental proof, no one would believe the formula worked. And what the hell did it matter at this point? The contest was way over. And he was the loser by miles.

He crossed to the racks of glass containers and ran a finger over the dusty corks. Killing time until he could beat a dignified retreat, he shuffled the beakers around, remembering how each variation had moved him a heady step closer to his goal. He'd been so hopeful then, carbonated with excitement. He remembered showing off the data to his aide and the young doctor. They were both so nice about it. Always acted interested and impressed. Jason had been only too glad to soak up the compliments about how smart and creative he was.

Creative like hell. Dumb hunk of human waste, that's what he was. No way he'd ever amount to anything but a futile, pathetic flop like his old man.

For an instant, he considered uncorking all the tubes and swallowing the contents. He imagined his family discovering him blue and cold on the cellar floor. Stiff and bloodied like one of those dead mice. He could almost hear them wailing and moaning over their tragic loss.

Oh, Jason. Our darling son. How will we live without him?

How? Very nicely, thank you. In fact, they'd probably celebrate. If he croaked, they'd be shed of a weirdo kid with no life and no future.

Then they'd be free to enjoy their precious, perfect baby daughter who was brave and brilliant and entirely sane. They'd sure as hell mourn their heads off if something happened to Jessie.

But who could blame them for not caring about him? What was he worth, after all? What had he ever done to make them proud? If only he'd won that Talent Search.

He'd have a bright future: school, career, everything. Even Rina Latham would have taken notice.

Eyeing the rows of formulas, he wished he could do it again, go back and have another chance. This time he wouldn't run away and foul it up. No copping out, no matter what happened.

And then it occurred to him that he didn't have to go back. There was more than one way to prove the success of his invention. He'd already taken the first step. He was ready to press ahead, no matter what the cost.

It still was not too late.

CHAPTER

19

They'd arranged to meet at six. Bannister slogged into the pocket park at five after and slumped on the bench where Price sat tossing the remains of a hot dog roll to a bobbling crowd of pigeons.

"Don't feed those things, Lenny. They're nothing but winged rats."

"They're God's creatures, Sam. Same as you and me."

"Oh, yeah? When was the last time you took a dump on somebody's head?"

Price's droopy eyes dripped empathy. "No luck?"

"I had plenty. All bad."

Careful to avoid Dr. Lyons, Bannister had spent the rest of the day at East End Hospital seeking an alternate way into Theodore Macklin's records. He'd hit all the departments: admitting, billing, research, records, accounting, even the lab. Flashing the tin special deputy's badge he'd gotten while under state contract on the Schildhauer case, he'd passed himself off as a cop from the Boston force assigned to investigate Theodore Macklin's suspicious death.

But every one of the desk jockeys had turned him down cold. Same with all the nurses and doctors and floor clerks and file clerks he'd approached with various stories, trying to get his hands on some scrap of useful information. Without exception, they'd referred him to the administration offices in the brownstone across the street. Hospital rules on releasing patient information were very strict, they'd echoed like a cageful of trained parrots. Official permission from the executive suite was the only key to the vault.

Bannister was shocked. Where were all the lax and lazy workers? Where was the screw-the-boss, ream-the-rules attitude? This was corporate America, for Chrissakes. Didn't these people have any patriotism?

Scraping bottom, he'd finally crossed to the administration building. The offices were housed in a converted mansion. Very fancy place. Had the original air and everything. A guard in the lobby eyed Bannister's phony badge with profound disinterest and pointed him toward the president's office. Fifth floor.

A pleasant fiftyish woman was at the extremely neat desk fronting the executive suite. She heard him out, called inside to the chief honcho, and advised Bannister to sit awhile. A while had stretched to more than an hour. The boss's secretary had endeavored to keep him comfortable. She'd offered him coffee, chitchat, magazines, sour balls, and pictures of her grandchildren. But Bannister was just as happy to spend the time pacing and cursing under his breath.

He'd worn tracks in the plush carpeting by the time he was summoned into the chief's sanctum. Predictably, the hospital's iron-fisted administrator was a tiny guy in designer doll clothes. He eyed Bannister, his little lips pursed in disdain. Funny how small men had such hostility for their taller counterparts. Bannister harbored no such biases, not even about pompous, overcompensating, puny runts like this jerk.

The president's name was Alexander Ivy. Ivy didn't flinch when Bannister handed him the line about being a detective on the Boston force. Figuring he was in the door, Bannister flashed the play badge. But when he went to slip it back in his pocket, the little prince waggled a finger, demanding a closer look. Bannister thought that would be the end of the act and him. Impersonating an officer was serious business. Getting caught at it was not only punishable by fine and imprisonment, it was downright embarrassing.

Fortunately, the guy was bat blind and too vain to put

on the glasses that were folded beside his blotter. Instead, he had squinted his beady brown eyes at the badge and shoved it back in Bannister's direction without comment.

"Lucky thing," Price said.

"Yeah, but staying out of jail wasn't all I'd hoped to accomplish."

Price looked surprised. "If he bought the cop act, why would he turn you down?"

"He didn't. He asked what East End could do to help," Bannister said. "I told him I needed to see the patient's records. I explained they might provide us with key evidence in our case. No problem, he says, so I figured I was home free.

"I give him the name. He gets on the horn and starts barking orders. A couple of minutes later, his secretary comes in with the info. The guy squints at the page and tells her to call extension eight-five-oh-two and tell them he's sending someone right over for the Macklin file."

Bannister went wistful. "Such a nice lady, that secretary. You ever notice how the worst pricks have the nicest secretaries?"

"That Myra who works for you is nice."

"Don't be a wiseass, Lenny. Myra's not that nice. Anyway, the secretary tells me to wait a second, and she'll write out directions to the person I need to see. I'm halfway across the hospital lobby when I realize she's sending me back to Dr. Lyons's office."

"Ouch." Price winced.

"Exactly. You sure you don't have someone you can call on this?"

"I told you, Sam. I know a lot of people, but getting into someone's private files is out of my range."

Bannister shrugged. "There's got to be some way I can get through to that woman."

"What's she like?"

"Two-legged mule. Stubborn. Hard-nosed. Unreasonable."

Price grinned. "Sounds like your type, Sammy."

"Could be. How'd it go with you?"

"Not bad."

Working from the checking account records, Price had
been able to contact Macklin's housekeeper and the head
of the service that cleaned the investment company offices. Both had last seen Macklin a week ago, five days
before his body washed up in Narragansett Bay.

That was the day he left Boston. Charges on his Mobil
card had him filling up with gas on the way to Newport.
There, according to his corporate American Express account, he'd checked into a suite at the Doubletree Inn.
He'd ordered all his meals from room service, portions for
one, and made a number of calls.

Price convinced another contact to run down the numbers itemized on the hotel bill. Some were in Boston. The
others were scattered around the New York area.

"I had Ed Simek, a cop friend of mine from the neighborhood, check out the Boston numbers," Price said. "All
squeaky clean. Legit clients of Macklin's investment firm.
We can start running down the list of calls to this area
after dinner."

"Only if you promise to give up anything that doesn't
relate directly to the Rafferty murder."

"You feel like a burger again tonight?"

"No wild goose chases, Lenny. I mean it."

"That's one thing about you, Sam. You're real sincere."

Bannister leaned back on the bench. So far, the entire
trip had been spent in useless wheel-spinning. They
hadn't even established as a certainty whether Macklin's
death had been take-out or deliverance.

Dr. Lyons's impressions aside, Macklin might have
taken that dive voluntarily. That certainly worked better
for Bannister. If someone had pushed the man off that
bridge, there loomed the huge open questions of who and
why. And chances were it had nothing at all to do with
Martha Rafferty's twenty-year-old murder.

Totally unacceptable.

Bannister ached for a quick, clean end to this endless
case. He wanted the open questions closed, for Leona
Rafferty's sake and his own.

"We're going after Macklin's scalp here, Lenny. Nothing else."

Price shook his head. "You think you can get things to go the way you want, Sam. That's your problem."

"Why is that a problem?"

"Because it's not reality. All you can find is what's there. And if you put on blinders, chances are you won't even find that much."

Price tossed the last of the bread balls to the birds. Brushing off his hands, he stood and started out of the park. Scattering pigeons, Bannister fell in beside him.

"Damn it, Lenny. Why do you have to be so logical all the time?"

CHAPTER

20

The cab deposited Maggie on the park side of the street. The sidewalk was crowded with summer strollers basking in the soft pink dusk. Horse-drawn carriages waited in a patient row at the curb. A hay-scented breeze ruffled her hair. Circling the line of hansom cabs, she crossed Central Park South and entered the opulent lobby of Lawrence Ivy's apartment building.

A wizened concierge announced her over the intercom and escorted her to a private elevator abutting the lavishly planted courtyard in the rear. Noting the terraced rock garden with its studied serenity and soothing flow of subtle colors, Maggie thought of her mother. That woman had the knack to make anything grow lush and lovely. Maggie had seen her work her magic on carrot ends and avocado pits and the tiniest bits of roots, leaves, or stems. So why was her own life all shriveled and brown at the edges and suffused with stubborn weeds?

The car arrived seconds after Maggie pressed the button. No delinquent little Mickey Glovers were allowed in a rarified joint like this, she presumed. They probably had an on-site exterminator to deal with the vaguest hint of such pestilence.

Entering the elevator, a sudden panic squeezed her throat tight. Her heart began to hammer and her focus shattered in a dizzying burst. Refusing to let the fear take hold, she trained her gaze on the ornate mirrored panels and fine wooden wainscoting in the elevator. *Distraction can work wonders. Even the worst fear will surrender given sufficient diversion.* Music seemed to swell through the walls. Her lips formed the words of the nightly rhyme. It was so important, Mommy said. So important, Maggie had to concentrate with all her tiny might. She had to shut her eyes, block out everything. *I pray the Lord my soul to take. . . .*

By the time the doors slid open at the penthouse, the hideous sensation had passed.

Stepping out, Maggie thought of her last visit to the senior Ivy's home. Over a year ago, Lawrence had requested a private meeting, so he could tell her of his retirement plans before he made his general announcement to the hospital staff.

Maggie's immediate reaction had been a selfish refusal to accept the necessary facts. She knew she was going to miss everything about the man: his courtly manners and kindness. His wisdom and infallible advice. His unfailing support.

But the truth was unavoidable. Physically, Lawrence could no longer manage the considerable responsibilities that came with the president's office. He was going to need all his remaining strength for his struggle against Lou Gehrig's disease. In the end, it would be a losing battle. But Lawrence was not the type to go gently.

Today, an attractive blond nurse greeted her in the apartment's foyer. She led Maggie to the sun room. The breathtaking view made the lovely green sprawl of Central Park appear to be Lawrence's personal front yard.

Maggie's friend sat in a paisley silk robe, propped in a wheelchair. A portable respirator, hooked by a plastic hose to the permanent tracheostomy in his neck, worked in jarring, percussive rhythm. Lawrence was painfully thin and pale. Even his hair had lost its vigor, the spare remaining strands lying limp and colorless across his mottled scalp.

Trying to mask her shock, Maggie crossed and kissed his cheek. The skin was unnaturally cool and draped his wasted frame like a rumpled sheet. He exuded the cloying scent of decay. Maggie had called several times since his retirement, hoping to see him, but until tonight's plea of urgent business, he'd put her off.

"Hi, Your Excellency. How's it going?" she said.

"It's going, as you can see. Sit, Maggie dear. It's been months since I looked at a lovely young woman who wasn't wielding a syringe or holding a bedpan." His words came in rushed clumps, punctuated by the harsh tides of the respirator.

"How are you feeling, Lawrence? Tell me what you've been up to."

"I'm a tiresome subject, Maggie. Nothing but numbers and doses these days, I'm afraid. Life reduced to fluid balance and the measure of my steady decline. I'd much rather talk about what brings you here. It's wonderful seeing you, really. I should have indulged myself sooner."

She hesitated. "I shouldn't be bothering you with my troubles, it's just—"

"Nonsense. I can't tell you how much it would mean to be useful again, if only for a moment. I suppose it's no secret that I've deliberately shut myself off these past months. Frankly, I couldn't see subjecting innocent souls to the repulsive sight of me when I could offer nothing in return but an object of pity."

"You're no such thing. Don't talk like that."

He chuckled. "Darling Maggie. Always the great defender of the faith and the fragile ego. I have missed you. I didn't allow myself to realize how much until you called earlier. Now, tell me, what can this old ruin possibly do for you?"

Trying to skirt the sticky personal issues, she described her idea for East End to host a national symposium on phobia treatment. Her enthusiasm grew as she spoke. The more she talked about it, the more convinced she was that the project would be a huge success. Beyond the profitability, there was the exciting prospect of gathering experts in the field for a valuable exchange of clinical experiences and strategies.

"Sounds like an excellent idea," Lawrence told her. "What's the problem?"

"I'm afraid there might be some—reluctance—on the part of the administration."

"Is my son still giving you the business, Maggie? What is the matter with that boy?"

"Apparently, he doesn't have your excellent taste in people."

He waved a frail hand in dismissal. "Nonsense. I know Alex lacks experience, but there's no excuse for allowing personal feelings to influence professional judgments. He doesn't have to like you, though Lord knows why he shouldn't, but he does have to treat you professionally and fairly. This symposium you're proposing would be a definite feather in East End's cap. Imagine the free publicity alone."

"I didn't come here to whine or tattle, Lawrence. And I'm not asking you to get in the middle of my relationship, or lack of one, with Alex. I'll work things out with him somehow. I'm just hoping to avoid his obstruction, so I can go ahead with the conference."

He flushed with the effort of his anger. "I'd like to take that boy over my knee."

Maggie laughed. "I'd definitely want front row center seats for that one. Meanwhile, all I was hoping you'd do is encourage him to expand the hospital's outreach programs in general. They're far from East End's strongest suit right now, so it'd be logical for you to bring it up. My proposal will just happen to be under consideration, and maybe he'll be less inclined to turn it down for arbitrary reasons."

He frowned deeply. "Allow me to handle Alex in my own way, will you, dear? My son has a few weak suits of his own to address. Before I die, I owe it to him and the hospital to point them out. Diplomatically, of course."

She nodded. "No one's more diplomatic than you."

A mischievous twinkle lightened his wan look. "And if diplomacy fails, there's always the direct double-barrel shot between the eyes. Lord knows I love my son. But he doesn't always respond well to subtlety. Alex is stopping by for lunch tomorrow. I'll speak with him then and get back to you first thing in the afternoon."

Maggie bit back her concerns. She'd have to trust Lawrence to handle this without deepening the animosity between her and Little Caesar. The truth was, she couldn't imagine how the situation could get much worse.

Anyway, if this last desperate scheme didn't work out, she had nothing much left to lose.

CHAPTER

21

Price and Bannister had a decidedly downscale dinner at Sergio's Café on First Avenue.

Sergio's, where the daily special was not, provided the fetching ambience of a prison mess and consistent service with a snarl. But it met Bannister's basic requirements: low prices and portions large enough to fill the considerable blanks. He and Price had eaten there at least once daily since their arrival. Lenny was already starting to smell like a cross between a Sergio burger, rancid fry grease, and the mosquito repellent the café tried to pass off as Diet Coke.

This evening, Price compounded the felony with a slice of Sergio's "world-famous" apple pie, and Bannister paid the check.

The first number on the list of calls Macklin had made from Newport to New York was in the Brighton Beach section of Brooklyn. Bannister dialed it from Sergio's pay phone. A woman with a dense accent answered. Hard to analyze its origin through the din. Crying baby, clatter of pots and dishes, running water, angry voices, the deafening blare of a television.

Claiming he had a package to deliver, Bannister confirmed that someone would be at home all evening. He and Price headed for the subway stop at Lexington Avenue and Seventy-seventh and caught a downtown local. At Lafayette they transferred to a Brooklyn-bound D train.

The littered cars were crammed with dead-eyed riders. Laughter erupted in jittery bursts. Troubled silence rode

the intermittent blackouts. An occasional pack of predatory toughs rippled through the crowd like a noxious
breeze. Tight fists. Taut nerves. Wariness crackled in their
wake like a live wire downed by a storm.

Bannister's cop's eye caught myriad other acts of casual
urban terrorism: a pickpocket working tote-bag patrol, a
man grinding himself into the rear end of a woman
mashed against a pole, a pimply kid snorting coke from a
Big Mac container. The transit cop posted at the end of
the car was oblivious. Too busy marking picks on a daily
racing form.

They exited at the Brighton Beach station and walked
to an address near the corner of Surf Avenue and Ocean
Parkway. The section was locally known as Little Odessa
for its large and burgeoning concentration of Russian im-
migrants. The building they sought was next to a market
whose name and sale items were spelled out in Cyrillic.
Bannister counted a dozen varieties of vodka in the window display.

They entered the apartment house through a vestibule
cluttered with overflow equipment: baby carriage, battered trike. Tracking the same pandemonium Bannister
had heard on the phone, they mounted the dim rear staircase to the third floor.

Their knock brought a doe-eyed young woman to the
door. Her face was a scrupulous blank, her posture
guarded. Blinking at them, she wiped her hands on a
food-spattered apron.

"Yeah?"

"Is this the Popov residence?" Price said.

"Popov, yeah," she intoned in choppy night-school English. A burst of noise from inside caught her like a dart.
She called over her shoulder: "Reuven, stop hitting your
sister. Bella, you change the baby now like I tell you."

"Is your husband home?" Bannister said.

"Husband? You wait." She shooed them outside with a
toss of her apron and shut the door. Soon, it was opened
by a somber man clad in a vested black mohair suit and a
hat.

Bannister flashed his Playskool badge. "Mr. Popov? I'm

Sam Bannister. This is Lenny Price. We're investigating the death of Theodore Macklin."

"I am Anatoly Popov. But this name you say, I do not know it."

Bannister had caught the second's flash before the guy's expression slammed shut. He was lying, and not well.

"Mind if we come in a minute?"

"I do not see for why, Mr. Bannister. I told you I do not—"

Bannister muscled his way into the apartment. Price hesitated in the hall, then followed. Lenny's good manners were like a tight girdle, hard to shed no matter what the circumstances.

Popov was agitated, but not in the manner of an upright private citizen beset by government bullies. His eyes darted around the cluttered living room as if he were checking for visible contraband. His wife had retreated to a rear bedroom, where the boisterous children, and anyone else on the premises, had been cowed into a macabre silence.

"Just a few questions," Bannister said. Without invitation, he sprawled on the plump green couch and pulled out a pad. "Where do you work?"

"Why do you want to know this?"

"I'm the curious type."

"I do not have to answer your questions."

"No, not if you have something to hide."

"You have warrant?"

Bannister sniffed. "Damn. I must have left it in my other purse."

"I ask you to leave now, Officer. This is my home. Home is castle."

"You telling me you refuse to cooperate?"

Popov was getting flushed and clammy. "What is to cooperate? I told you, I do not know this man you ask about, Mr.—"

"Macklin. Theodore Macklin. If you don't know him, I wonder why he'd be calling you."

"What calling?"

There was a burst of childish exuberance from the back room. It was quickly squelched.

Bannister nodded. "We have the phone company records."

Popov's eyes went steely. "You must be mistaken. There was no such call. I tell you I do not know this man Macklin."

Price had kept quiet, hanging near the door as Bannister questioned the Russian. He'd paced uneasily in the background as Bannister made his territorial claim on the couch. Now Price's grin was conciliatory.

"You heard him, Sam. He doesn't know anything. Excuse us, will you, Mr. Popov? You know how these things can get fouled up. Somebody probably reversed a number when they wrote it down."

Popov was all for that theory. "Of course." The Russian chuckled dryly, mopping his pale face with a hankie. "I understand. No problem, gentlemen. Sorry you come for nothing."

"Come on, Sam. Let's leave these nice people alone."

Bannister sat for a minute, seething for effect. "I don't know, Lenny—"

"But I do. 'Bye now, Mr. Popov. Sorry for the intrusion. Say good-bye to your wife for us, will you?"

"Of course. Good-bye, Officers."

Price left. Bannister followed a few grudging steps behind. They plodded noisily down to the second landing and ducked out of sight.

"Hand it over," Bannister demanded.

Price produced a wireless receiver. He'd planted the button-sized microphone on a pole lamp near the Popovs' couch.

Given the tension level they'd inspired, Bannister didn't think he'd have long to wait for an aftershock, and he wasn't disappointed. Everyone had gathered to talk in the Popovs' living room. Worried excited voices. No mistaking the tone.

"God damn it," Bannister said. "I knew this was going to be a waste of time."

"They didn't bite?" Price said.

"Oh, they bit. They're biting like crazy. Want to hear?"

Price pressed the receiver to his ear. Listening, he frowned. "Well, we wanted to get them talking, and we did."

"Yeah, right, Lenny. Only not in Russian."

Price produced a cassette recorder and taped the next fifteen minutes of conversation from the upstairs apartment.

"Problem isn't the Russian. That I expected," he whispered halfway through. "Trouble is how they all talk at once. I know a guy who'd be willing to translate, but he'd have a helluva time sorting out all the chatter."

"Want me to go up there and tell them to take turns?" Bannister said.

"I'd say yes. But knowing you, you'd probably do it."

The phone was ringing when they returned to their rental tenement. Price answered. All the calls since their arrival had been from salespeople, sales robots, wrong numbers, or Ruthie. But this time, Price extended the receiver in Bannister's direction.

"It's for you, Sam. Chloe."

Bannister took it with trepidation. "Hey, sweetheart. How's it going?"

A few words, and he relaxed. His daughter was bubbling over with news about a week-long babysitting job she'd just started and this cute kid Adam who almost certainly probably liked her. She was also pumped about an upcoming trip with her grandmother to the Berkshires.

"We're leaving Sunday. Gran says she can't wait to spoil me rotten."

"Sounds great, sweetheart. And it's great to hear you sounding like your old self again."

With that, the kid took a dizzying turn for the worse. She started bemoaning her fates, complaining about her friends, the weather, her mom treating her like an infant, how fat she was.

Fat? The kid weighed next to nothing, give or take.

"You're not fat. That's ridiculous."

"I'm huge, Daddy. You haven't seen me lately. My face looks like a balloon. And I'm getting thunder thighs. They make actual slapping noises when I walk. It's so gross, I could die."

"Come on. I saw you two weeks ago."

"I'm a horse."

"A very, very thin horse."

"Why won't anybody listen to me?" she wailed.

In record time she went from irritated to irate to unraveled. Bannister had no trouble making matters worse. Anything he said seemed to do the trick. Placating was useless. Ditto reassuring. Raw flattery sent the kid in a tailspin. Pleading for reason was even worse. Several frustrating minutes later, Bannister hung up. He felt as if he'd gone ten rounds with a dyspeptic alligator. And according to Price, that's exactly what he'd done.

"Hormones, Sam. I'm telling you. All kids go through it."

"Chloe's not like other kids."

"Thank goodness she is. You get an endocrine dysfunction, it's not pretty. Growth deficiencies are the least of it. You can be talking gross organic damage, intellectual sequelae. Just last month, I read in the *NEJM* about this kid who—"

Bannister stared him silent.

"Okay, Sam, okay. I just thought it might make you feel better."

The phone trilled again. Bannister didn't know whether to grab it or run. He decided to face the beast down. It was his beast after all.

Lifting the receiver gingerly, he spoke in a gentle lilt. "It's all right, sweetheart. I understand."

He confined himself to murmurs of agreement and occasional head nods. Kept his voice well below sea level.

Price eyed him warily as the conversation ended. "Better?"

"I don't know, Lenny. You should hear her. She tells me she has these moods. Kid doesn't know what to do with herself sometimes. Worries me sick."

"Normal, Sam. All normal."

"Oh, yeah? What about teen suicides? What about anorexia and drug abuse and babies having babies?"

Price narrowed his eyes. "Have you been watching Oprah again?"

"I don't like the way she sounds. I don't like having to walk around her like she's broken glass. I don't like the whole goddamned thing."

"Better get used to it, Sam. She's got a lot of teenage ahead of her."

But the child's voice echoed in Bannister's mind. Pained, troubled. No one and nothing could make him simply toss it off and forget about it. He knew how a single misstep could short-circuit a child's bright future. Take a wrong turn, trust the wrong person, and you could wind up like Martha Rafferty.

Bannister wasn't leaving anything to chance where Chloe was concerned. For his little girl, he was willing to go the limit.

CHAPTER

22

She floored the accelerator.

Mile marker six. Ten. Fifteen.

Flying phone poles. Black blur of passing trees. Raveling sprawl of power lines. Speed coursed through her in a white hot surge.

Incredible.

Mile marker twenty. Twenty-five. Hell on wheels. Racing the world. Winning.

Who'd believe it? She laughed aloud, straining her foot harder against the gas pedal. Milking the speed. Reveling in it.

Marker thirty. Forty.

She barely believed it herself. The whole thing had the grainy, distant feel of a dream. But it was true. True and real and wonderful beyond her wildest dreams.

It had started with the surprise visit from her sister Alice late this afternoon. After weeks of nagging and resistance, Alice had finally gone to the doctor. That worry was over. The lump had been nothing after all. No big C, no chemo. Only a scare, an innocent cyst.

They'd opened the split of champagne her sister had brought to celebrate. Paired the decadent indulgence with strawberries and a plate of cookies.

Crisp bubbles danced up her nose. One sip, and she'd felt the subtle shift inside. An odd pulse beat started, syncopated and insistent. Curious, but not at all unpleasant. Setting her glass aside, she'd decided not to mention it to Alice. She wouldn't have known what to say. Instead, she tried to counter the dizzy rush with food, but the tipsy feeling persisted.

By the time her sister left, the pulse had deepened to a restless throbbing. She'd splashed frigid water on her cheeks, pressed a cold cloth to the back of her neck. But instead of easing, the sensation spread and intensified.

Driven outside, she'd circled the block several times until a mindless urge prodded her down the ramp to the parking garage.

Oswaldo, the dark, toothy attendant, had fixed her with his standard look of raw contempt. But this time, she'd refused to let it shrink her. She held her ground and kept her expression neutral until he drove the Chevy up the ramp in a noisy haze of exhaust and flipped her the keys.

"Been weeks since you took her out, lady. Engine's real cold. Frozen almost," he'd said.

"Then I'll have to warm her up, won't I?" she'd replied with a mischievous smirk. "I'll have to give her a real good workout."

"Yeah, sure you will." His chuckle jiggled in his throat like loose change.

She'd roared up the exit ramp at peak speed, chuckling to herself at the thought of Oswaldo's astonishment.

Traffic parted magically as she raced through the weave of streets toward the Ninety-sixth Street entrance to the northbound FDR Drive.

A snap later, she was out of the city. Snap again, and the linked chain of Westchester suburbs yielded to long, twisting ribbons of deserted roadway. Nothing but her and the speed. Luscious, breathless speed. Speed that filled her with near-excruciating pleasure.

Marker fifty. Sixty-five.

Could this really be happening? For years, speed had been the enemy. She'd moved in deliberate slow motion, trapped in a cumbersome bubble of fear.

There had seemed no way out. She'd tried every imaginable remedy: numbing drugs, hypnosis, meditation, acupuncture. She'd plodded through every conceivable therapy. Individual analysis. Semantic restructuring. Self-help and support groups. Mountains of dollars. Thousands

of hours. She'd devoted her entire existence to a cure, but
nothing had worked to conquer the driving phobia. Her
other fears melted away, but that one refused to yield.

Lord knew she'd done everything, even put up with the
incessant insults as long as she could. When she couldn't
stand it any longer, she'd stopped going to the clinic. After
that, she'd figured she was lost for good. But she hadn't
seen a choice.

Now suddenly, the bubble had burst. Disappeared. She
was freed. Sprung like a pinball in a self-perpetuating
burst of momentum. Rubber rebounding off the corners
of the world. No end. No limits.

Go!

Marker one hundred.

She was through the roof. Erupting with joy. She didn't
need the damned hospital or anything else. She could
beat the fear on her own.

The road angled skyward. Dips and turns. Thrilling
bends and angles. She breezed past the string of yellow
signs bordering the narrow pavement. Snaking arrows.
Warnings to slow.

Never again. Slow was for lumbering mortals. She was
the wind. Free and indestructible.

Mile one twenty-one.

Twenty-one was her lucky number. She'd been born on
the twenty-first of June. Grew up on Twenty-first Street.
Had her first marriage proposal at twenty-one. First and
last as it had happened, but she'd had no way of knowing
that when she turned the young man down.

No way of knowing she was about to cross the threshold into perpetual darkness either. No boyfriend, no love,
no luck at work. One pink slip after another. Layoffs,
shutdowns, restructurings, personality clashes. Soon she'd
given up, stopped looking. Spent all her time cowering at
home, huddling with her family. Good little cook, she
was. Great baker. Her cookies and brownies were so
good, they'd pushed her to go into business. But she had
no talent for business. Her only talent was fear and worry.

Soon the worries had spawned reluctance and the re-

luctance had begat the fear and the fear had become her
and she had become the fear.

Girl in the bubble. Trapped. Immobile. Living the living death. Trying to fill the aching void with mountains of
food and great numbing gobs of sameness.

But now she was free of it. Another yellow sign her-
alded a convoluted trail of S-curves as the road began its
descent. Nothing but a flimsy guardrail to her right. No
sign of anyone ahead. A solid sheet of darkness filled the
rearview mirror.

The car was gathering speed on the downslope. She
clutched the wheel harder, trying to rehearse the perilous
curves ahead. Was it right first or left? Why couldn't she
remember? She struggled to picture the snaking arrow on
the yellow sign, but her mind was a quivering blank.

God, no!

The fear had snuck back. She was trapped in a terror
larger than herself. Consumed.

But she could get through it. All she had to do was slow
down. Bring herself back to the safe place, the place
where she was hardly moving.

Her fingers were cramped on the wheel. Muscles sear-
ing. Desperately, she worked her foot around, feeling for
the brake. The car was rushing like river rapids, carrying
her out of control. She found the brake pedal and pressed
with all her might. She had to stop it.

There, the speed was easing. She felt the dragging
weight of the brakes. Heard the reassuring squeal.
Slower, please. Please stop!

Sharp curve ahead. She could never make it at this
speed. Clenching her teeth so hard they ached, she
jammed harder on the brake. The speedometer was sinking, but not fast enough.

Tensing every fiber of her being, she braced for the
turn. Her heart was galloping, breath caught.

*You can make it. You can. Just ease into it. Concentrate.
Ignore the fear. Get your mind on something else.*

The curve began. She tugged at the wheel. Worked into
it. Halfway around.

You can do it. Almost there.

Turn the other way! The signal screamed in her mind. Fired like a thousand rockets. But the glare of a million flames couldn't penetrate the black bubble of fear that encased her. Held her stiff, stunned, and immobile.

There was a way out. There had to be.

But before she could find it, she was crashing through the barrier and hurtling off the edge of the world.

CHAPTER

23

Jason could hear them downstairs. Binnie's nasal shrill twined with his mother's low, patient tones. They were probably talking about him, he thought with a swat of annoyance. But he had far bigger things to occupy his mind.

He'd pretended to be asleep when his aide showed up for their nine o'clock practice session. The ruse was a necessary part of his experimental design. He'd calculated carefully. Given his weight and metabolism, the formula should reach peak effectiveness in fourteen minutes and remain near maximum for half an hour after that. Binnie was never on time, so he couldn't risk administering the dose until she was in the house. As soon as he heard her at the door, he entered the starting time in his log and made his soundless way to the bathroom.

He weighed one hundred sixty-five and a half pounds. Extrapolating from the gram weight of the experimental mice, he filled the bathroom glass with two precisely measured teaspoons of C2BU and swallowed it in a rush. He could not chance an overdose, and too small a measure would fail to overwhelm his inhibitions. With the others, he wasn't so cautious. But no matter how useless and desperate he sometimes felt, he had no desire to place himself in unnecessary jeopardy.

The liquid was dense and cloyingly sweet. Jason had made it that way on purpose, so it would be palatable to the rodents. Only a very rich confection would overpower the taste. He thought of the cupcakes on the kitchen counter, but he might lose the precision of measurement if he tried to bury the formula in food. Shuddering, he wished he could chase the putrid aftertaste with a swig of water, but he didn't want to risk diluting the impact.

"Ready yet, Jay?"

"Must've overslept. Be down in a minute."

Standing at the sink, he twisted the hot water tap and watched the mirror frost with steam. Tuning to his own visceral responses, he searched for a physical sign that his invention was taking effect. Pressing two fingers to his wrist, he measured his pulse rate against the second hand on his watch. It was dancing at the usual clip.

No changes yet.

Determined to waste ten full minutes, he returned to his room, opened and shut several drawers, and stepped into his closet.

His shirts and pants hung in an orderly row, all beiges or grays or other nameless neutrals. Same for the shoes and the shelf of winter sweaters shrouded in plastic bags. Jason had always taken pains to avoid attention. As a world-class nothing, he'd been in no real danger of drawing the spotlight. But he'd made doubly sure with his hunched posture, meek manner, downcast eyes, and drab wardrobe.

But all that was going to change. If this experiment worked, he'd take the bows he had coming and enjoy them. He imagined himself on a stage, facing a sea of admiring faces. Washed by applause. Jason the Brave, the Bold, the Magnificent. His cheeks blazed, and his lips spread in an irrepressible grin.

"Thank you, thank you," he mouthed with his hands lofted to still the imaginary tumult. "That's enough, really. You're too kind—"

"Jason. Come on, now. Binnie's waiting."

Checking his watch, he plodded down the stairs. From the foyer, he spotted his mother and his aide in the living room. He yawned broadly for effect.

"Sorry. Didn't hear my alarm go off."

Binnie cocked her head in sympathy. "Bad night, hon? Mine was terrible. Can't sleep for anything in this heat.

And the air-conditioning gives me such a sinus, I can hardly breathe. You ready to go?"

"I guess."

"Great. I was thinking maybe you'd like to take a little ride over to the boulevard. We can look at the stores while we walk. Be cooler, too."

Jason stifled a protest. Binnie couldn't know it, but the experiment called for precisely that sort of difficult trial. "Sounds okay."

His mother looked pleased. "You two want to stop for something at the luncheonette? My treat."

"A cold drink might be nice. Don't you think, Jason?" Binnie said.

Jason accepted the five-dollar bill his mother pulled from her wallet and followed the woman out the door.

The sky thrummed with haze and a melting heat. Sounds rent the morning stillness: a truck clattering over metal plates in the road, the chatter of a lawnmower, the hacking cough of a reluctant car engine. Jason sniffed and suppressed a tremor. Bad morning. Had a dangerous edge to it. If he could get through all this, the drug was an even bigger miracle than he'd dared to hope.

Distracted, Jason had lagged behind. By the time he tuned in again, Binnie was already at her car, fishing in her tote bag for the keys. He stalled at the edge of the flagstone walk. A raging sea of imagined hazards stretched between them. He was open, vulnerable.

"Come on, Jason hon. Sinus or no, you hop in, and I'll turn the air on full blast. It's hot as blazes out here."

He shied from her expectant gaze and tried to move. He needed to get back in the house for a minute; he needed to piece himself back together again. But terror had welded his feet to the walk. His heart was banging like a crazed prisoner.

"You okay, hon?"

He couldn't answer. Why the hell wasn't the formula working? Maybe he hadn't taken enough. But no, he'd checked his calculations fifty times. Two teaspoons was definitely right. Any more might push him to dangerous disinhibition.

He fiddled with the chain around his neck. The lion's head medallion had slipped to the back where it was poking him in the spine. With trembling fingers, he slid it back in place. He was filled with electric tension.

Come on, Jason. Get moving. What the hell's the matter with you?

"I'll start her up and get things cooling, okay?" Binnie said. "You take your time." She ducked into the car and closed the door. The engine caught, and stinking fumes spewed from the tailpipe. Waiting, Binnie tipped her dumb head toward the mirror and slathered a fresh hill of lipstick on her big mouth. Too bad it wasn't Krazy Glue. Maybe then she'd shut up for a blessed second.

The idea made Jason giggle. The fear was fading. Trying to speed it away, he tuned his thoughts to the experiment. He checked the time. Three more minutes until the drug reached optimum effectiveness. It had to work.

C2BU. The name was shorthand for "courage to be you." Jason's formula was designed to eradicate fear. No more phobias. No panic attacks or suffocating anxieties.

His work for the Talent Search had been inspired by studies he'd read on post-traumatic stress disorder: PTSD. Afflicted patients suffered from extreme irritability, troubled sleep, recurrent nightmares, and terrifying flashbacks of the precipitating trauma.

The problem had afflicted scores of Vietnam veterans, spurring an increase in research efforts. Recently, scientists had discovered physiological differences in PTSD patients. In one experiment, a mood-altering drug called yohimbine triggered an increase in panic attacks and flashbacks in PTSD patients but had no such effect in normal control subjects. Another study found that PTSD patients tended to oversecrete opioids, such as endorphin. That numbed the perception of pain, causing a sense of unreality and dislocation. Still another experiment established that PTSD patients released excessive amounts of the pituitary stress hormone, CRF, which caused the same symptoms as the original trauma: chills, trembling, panic.

Armed with those findings, Jason had searched for a

drug or drugs capable of blocking the actions of the body chemicals implicated in post-traumatic stress disorders. He reasoned that phobias were virtually identical to the recurrent panic attacks experienced by war veterans. For him and other severe phobics, mundane situations were as traumatic and fraught with perils as the front line in a raging battle.

His goal was to develop a pill that would blunt the terror, lower the volume on his hyperactive imagination, and allow him to live a normal life. And his efforts had been remarkably successful. Early versions of his formula had so emboldened his experimental mice that they were willing to risk pressing an electrified lever to retrieve a pellet of food.

With further refinements, he'd been able to spur increasingly dramatic risk behavior in the mice. He'd continued to modify the formula until he developed C2BU, which induced seemingly total fearlessness with no apparent side-effects.

In preliminary tests, mice given the drug displayed no startle response to loud noises. They lost their instinctive fear of normal predators. Placed in a clear container in the presence of a snarling cat, his experimental rodents evinced no physical or behavioral responses whatsoever. They appeared oblivious to the threat.

Jason was confident he'd discovered a cure for fear. All he needed was further work to confirm and document his findings. Then he could approach a pharmacological lab capable of conducting the extensive human studies required for FDA approval.

The potential was staggering. An approved courage drug could cure phobias and all disabling anxieties. It could eliminate combat stress and fortify soldiers for hazardous duty. Test pilots, stunt people, police, firefighters, and others in high-risk occupations could take the drug to reduce dangerous fear responses that might impair judgment or cripple performance. For creating a nation of heroes, Jason Childs would be the greatest hero of all. Respected. Adored.

Drawing a hard breath, he ventured off the sidewalk

and felt an immediate chill of elation. His stride was spring-loaded, his moves sure and fluid as a stalking cat. The drug was working.

As he approached the car, big-mouth Binnie ceased her primping and pushed open the passenger side door.

"There now, you look much better. Didn't want to push you, hon. Sometimes it takes a couple of minutes to get yourself together, isn't that so?"

"Yeah."

"Exactly how I used to be," she said smugly.

In fact he *was* worlds better. So improved he could barely relate to the simpering coward he'd been when he first stepped outside. A matter of minutes had made an incredible difference. Three minutes to be exact. Testing his pulse, he found it slow and regular. Kettle drum thumping with firm certainty in his veins. His brain was operating with startling clarity. Leaping blithely from thought to thought. Not a single dip into the dark chasms of self-doubt. Not a blip or hesitation.

Stifling an exultant shriek, Jason slipped into the car and slammed the door. He could do anything, go anywhere. And if it worked this way on him, it would surely have a similar effect on all phobics.

"Let's get going," he said. "I've had it with hanging around here."

Binnie laughed. "My, you're the changeable one, aren't you? Okay, then. Here we go."

Here I go, he wanted to shout. *Get ready, world, a new star is rising.* His brilliant formula was everything he'd dared to imagine.

And more.

CHAPTER

24

Maggie glared at the clock, trying to prod the lumbering seconds along. Lawrence Ivy had promised to call early this afternoon. As soon as she got the go-ahead, she could set the date for the symposium, book a suitable facility, and begin lining up key speakers. A conference of the magnitude she anticipated would be no small undertaking, and she was achingly anxious to get started. She needed the distraction.

"Now I lay me down to sleep . . ."

The window dream had continued to haunt her. Her mind kept skipping to it at odd moments during the day. Several times each night, she was transported to the room where she knelt to say her prayers on the flower-bordered rug.

"I pray the Lord my soul to keep."

Each time, the window slid up and she was cast out for the horrifying flight on the hawk's back. Circling, hurtling toward the ground.

"If I should die . . ."

Had to be the stress, she thought. Extreme psychic strain could churn up long dormant symptoms. The only way to deal with them was to apply the techniques she'd learned in treatment. The same ones she taught her patients.

Speaking of which, her morning schedule had been filled with two private patients and an intake evaluation for a woman with claustrophobia. Maggie had found her an amiable, attractive person who'd likely mesh well with

162

five others Maggie had already signed up for a group slated to start in two weeks. There were applications in progress from four other people, so the group was already at capacity. That left nothing for Maggie to do but choose a leader. She decided to see to it immediately and bump that issue from her overbooked brain.

Reviewing her roster of treatment aides, she eliminated those who had recently run groups. Eyeing the remaining candidates, she crossed off several who would be taking vacation time during the eight-week program. She further deleted those she judged too introverted or too shaky in their recovery to be effective. Another few had not proven themselves sufficiently reliable as aides to be trusted with the far more complex administration of a group program. She crossed off Francis Kennedy in self-defense. The last thing she needed was to give the man any encouragement, real or imagined.

She'd pared the list to five names. Scanning them, Maggie's immediate instinct was to ask Beverly Magida, a recovered claustrophobic with an ebullient personality and a delightful sense of humor. But her eye kept veering back to Gail Weider.

Gail had been a steady presence at the clinic since enrolling in a group for her multiple phobias nearly two years ago. In addition to her work as a treatment aide, she'd continued to attend self-help sessions and participated in the clinic's social and fund-raising projects. Gail had been one of a small core of dependable, readily available volunteers. But for the last couple of months, she'd been conspicuously absent.

At first, Gail's sudden defection had troubled Maggie, but she'd decided to leave it alone. It could be that distancing herself from East End was the woman's way of trying to further her recovery. Gail had come a considerable distance in treatment. She'd conquered her fear of crowds and open spaces, but she was plagued by a persistent fear of driving, especially on highways. Patients who hit that kind of frustrating wall were encouraged to test a variety of strategies. Hard to say what might work in a given case. The craziest things sometimes did.

Then, a couple of weeks ago, Maggie had run into Gail on First Avenue. The woman had been abrupt, verging on glacial. Maggie was at a loss. Clearly, her ex-patient was miffed at something. But no matter how she searched her memory for the culprit, she came up blank.

The mystery had been buried, however, under an avalanche of larger issues. And last week, after Gail had dropped off that batch of her delectable chocolate chip cookies, Maggie had concluded with relief that the difficulty, whatever it was, had been resolved.

But now it struck her, as she reviewed her roster, that she might be looking at the source of the woman's pique. Could it be that Gail was angry at not being selected as a leader?

Maggie chided herself for the oversight. Unfortunately, Gail Weider was the type that blended instantly and invisibly: human Covermark. She was assiduously average. Medium height and weight. Standard-issue brown hair and eyes. Personality unburdened by excesses of any sort. She was incredibly easy to overlook. But she was every bit as capable and dedicated as other aides who'd joined the program long after she had, and who'd already been chosen to run phobia groups.

Now, anxious to make things right, Maggie phoned Gail's apartment and left a detailed message on the answering machine.

"I'm looking forward to hearing from you," she concluded. "I know you'll do a terrific job as a leader."

That done, Maggie felt better, as if an invisible splinter had been removed. To feel better still, she decided to get something to eat. Tuning to the sandpaper growl from her stomach, she realized that Gail Weider was not the only one she'd been ignoring.

Lunchtime, and a long line of staff and visitors snaked out from the cafeteria entrance. Impatiently gauging a minimum fifteen-minute wait, Maggie was about to give up when she heard a beckoning voice.

"Maggie? Dr. Lyons? Come on. We've been holding your place."

She walked to the front of the queue where Mitch Goldberg was standing beside Daisy Tyler.

Eyeing the crush behind them, she shook her head. "I really shouldn't."

Daisy caught her eye. "Please, Doctor. I'd really love it if you'd join us."

A pair of nurses behind them pressed back to make room. "It's okay, Dr. Lyons. No big rush to eat in this place."

"Thanks, if you're sure." Maggie fell in beside Daisy and the resident and picked up a tray.

As they slipped into a sun-drenched booth near the window, Maggie noticed that Daisy had done her hair and even applied an artful trace of makeup. Soft gray shadow, peach blush, and a pale matching lipstick defined her features and replaced the prison pallor with a pleasant glow. Daisy wore the white blouse and black slacks one of the nurses had picked up for her at Macy's. The outfit was crisp and flattering, especially with the addition of a flowered neck scarf and red hoop earrings.

"You look great," Maggie said sincerely.

Daisy dipped her eyes. "You think so?"

"Absolutely. How's it going?"

"All right, I guess."

Goldberg grinned. "Come now, Ms. Tyler. We'll have none of that false modesty. This morning, Maggie, she walked all the way to the corner with her aide. Then they went down to the gift shop, and Daisy picked out a few things for herself."

Daisy touched the scarf. "You like it? The earrings were on sale."

"They're perfect. You have a real sense of style."

The woman flushed with pleasure. "I used to dream of working in a boutique someday. One of those small, elegant places on Madison Avenue. Pretty ridiculous, huh?"

"Not at all," Maggie assured her. "You can still do that, once you're feeling better."

Daisy tensed and studied at her salad plate.

"I meant after a lot of work and healing, Daisy. A goal

for the future. No one's going to make you do anything before you're ready."

But there was clearly no way to convince the woman that she'd ever be up to such an overwhelming challenge. Maggie caught Goldberg's eye and passed a cautionary look. *Don't push it.* Gradually, Daisy would come to the necessary new understandings on her own. The three fell silent and started on their food.

Goldberg broke the awkward hush with a string of hilarious stories. The young doctor was a natural comic. He had perfect timing and a real flair for impersonations. His George Bush was so perfect, the ex-president seemed a poor imitation.

Daisy's laugh was infectious. Maggie delighted in watching the woman enjoy herself, and she was very grateful to Goldberg. Resident schedules were notoriously impossible. The guy could be using this precious scrap of free time to catch up on sleep, friends, or family. Putting himself out to amuse a troubled patient was well beyond any reasonable call of duty.

When they finished their meals, Goldberg accompanied them to the second floor and saw Daisy to her room.

"I'm off tomorrow," he told her. "When I stop by to see you the day after, I expect you to have at least two adventures to report."

"I'll try, Doctor."

"So happens the best falafel in New York is just around the corner. You go once, you'll thank me."

Daisy dipped her eyes. "I'll do the best I can."

"That's a deal." Goldberg tagged beside Maggie as far as her office door. "Looks like she's coming along nicely," he said.

"Looks like you are, too."

His grin was mischievous. "So how come I'm still waiting for that special thanks you said you owe me?"

"Slipped my mind. Next time we dine at Chez Ivy, it's on me. I promise."

"Sorry, Dr. Lyons. If you want to express your appreciation for my selfless professionalism and astonishing wit, you'll have to do better than the hospital cafeteria."

Maggie couldn't help smiling. Guy was awfully cute. Probably appealed to the roving gang of mommy genes that bullied their way into her consciousness from time to time.

Which gave her a devilish notion.

"How's next Saturday? I'm having dinner with my father and a friend. You're welcome to join us."

He hesitated, then said: "I'd be delighted."

"Great. I'll let you know when we decide the time and place."

Closing the office door behind her, she enjoyed a moment of pure diabolical delight. Seeing Tina in the company of a juvenile peer like Mitch Goldberg was bound to bring her father closer to his misplaced senses. Maybe the two little ones would even hit it off and decide to form their own play group. True, that might bruise her Dad's ego. But Maggie was confident he'd soon forget this absurd relationship and move on to fresh unsuitable pursuits.

There was a knock. Knowing her next appointment wasn't expected for an hour, Maggie assumed it was someone on staff.

"Come in."

Too late, she found herself confronted by the relentless Bannister.

"What now, Detective?"

"Listen, I'm really sorry about yesterday. I should have told you straight out what I was looking for. I don't know what got into me."

Maggie knew exactly what he was full of, but she didn't bother to share her diagnosis. Instead, she decided to try the firm, reasoned approach. There had to be some way through the man's thick skull.

"I told you, I'm not giving you the Macklin file or anything else, Mr. Bannister. And I do not appreciate your snooping, trying to get information about him or me from other people on this staff. If you don't give it up, I'm going to ask hospital security to bar you from the building."

The threat didn't penetrate.

"I'd be glad to give it up if it wasn't so critical, Dr. Lyons. Believe me, the last thing I want to do is annoy you. But I need to see that file."

"Believe *me*, Detective. You are annoying the hell out of me, and it's not going to get you what you want."

Maggie expected further argument, but Bannister suddenly tacked and set the conversation on an entirely different course.

"Do you ever treat teenagers, Dr. Lyons?"

"Why do you ask?"

"I think my daughter's having a problem. She won't say what exactly, but she's not herself. I was hoping maybe we could have lunch or whatever and talk about it."

"If your daughter has a problem, she's the one who should be talking about it."

"I know, but she's in Boston. I just want to get your read on the situation. Figure out what I should do."

Maggie put it all through the processor and came out with a nice purée of horse manure. The man would use anything, even some invented crisis. Wouldn't surprise her if the daughter were invented as well. "Nice try, Mr. Bannister. But if I won't let you in the door, I'm not about to allow you to sneak in through a window."

"I'm not trying to do that, Dr. Lyons. At least, not now, I'm not. This honestly has nothing to do with the Macklin case. I'd really value your opinion about what's happening with my little girl. If lunch isn't good, how about meeting me for a drink after work?"

"I'm busy."

"Dinner? Breakfast? Coffee? You name it."

"I have named it, Detective. It's called 'no.'"

He hitched his head toward the door. "Afraid the boyfriend would object?"

She frowned. "I don't know what you're talking about, and frankly, I don't care."

He frowned harder. "I'll call you, Dr. Lyons."

"Threats will get you nowhere, Detective."

As soon as he was out the door, the phone trilled. Lifting the receiver, she heard the stertorous rush of Lawrence Ivy's respirator.

"I spoke with Alex, Maggie. Go ahead and plan your symposium. My son will not interfere."

"You mean it? That's wonderful. *You're* wonderful. Tell me what happened? I want the complete play-by-play."

He chuckled dryly. "No energy right now, my dear. Another time?"

"Of course. You get some rest. And thanks so much. I can't tell you what this means to me."

"My pleasure. Good-bye now."

Maggie's happiness was muted by her friend's obvious exhaustion. She was desperate to save the clinic, but she didn't want that or anything to be accomplished at the expense of Lawrence's frail health. Troubled, she dialed his apartment and spoke to his nurse. The woman assured Maggie that the old man always experienced a dip in energies after a visit, especially a visit from his son.

"He was thrilled to be able to help you with your conference, Dr. Lyons," the nurse said. "He's been talking about it nonstop since you left last night. Haven't seen him as up about anything in months. It was good medicine, honestly."

Relieved, Maggie hung up, then asked Henry to come in and help her make the preliminary conference arrangements. He arrived an instant later armed with a steno pad and a satisfied smile.

"Leave it to you. If there was any way to convince President Ivy to go along with your symposium, I knew you'd find it."

"Let's say I went around him."

Henry nodded. "That's you, Maggie. You want something, you don't quit until you get it."

"In this case, I guess you're right. This clinic is way too important to be scuttled by petty politics or personal grudges. I'm sure the symposium will solve our financial problem, but it's going to take a tremendous amount of work."

"We'd better get to it, then. Tell me exactly what needs doing."

Twenty minutes later, he left with a pile of assignments. He'd insisted on seeing to most of the arrangements himself, and Maggie didn't argue. Knowing Henry's unfailing efficiency and scrupulous attention to detail, she was confident that under his direction the conference planning would proceed without a glitch.

When her two o'clock patient arrived, she was able to set the symposium and the rest of her recent worries aside and focus completely on the man's intense fear of heights.

In his midforties, Phil Lustberg was a tall, rangy character with jug ears and large, limpid eyes. As he described his reaction to high places, Maggie tensed with her own remembered terrors.

"I feel as if I'm going to do something crazy, Dr. Lyons. Jump out the window or go off the theater balcony. It's an urge almost. I'm scared to death, but at the same time, I feel pulled toward the edge. I know it sounds nuts."

"Not at all. It's not uncommon."

Maggie knew the sensation only too well. Before her own treatment, she'd suffered precisely the same dread feelings. Fear drawing her like a seductive siren. Luring her to her own destruction.

"If I should die . . ."

Maggie suppressed a shudder. "The imagination can be extremely powerful, Mr. Lustberg. Sitting here, you know you're not going to jump out any windows, but when you're in the phobic situation, it's easy to get overwhelmed and lose your grip on reality.

"In this program, you'll learn how to work through those moments. Once you understand and accept the fear, there are ways to distract yourself until the worst of it passes and you're fully back in control. It takes time and practice, but you'll get to the point where the fear won't rule you anymore."

"I dearly hope you're right, Dr. Lyons. I can't do my job. My wife and friends are about out of patience. It's making me crazy."

"That's what we're here to help you with. You're going to learn to deal with your anxiety and get your life back on track."

"I'd give anything."

"All it takes is time and effort."

Maggie shook his hand. She set her face in a mask of confidence and held it until he was out the door.

Everything would work out, she thought. One way or the other.

CHAPTER

25

Bannister could not get his mind off his daughter. Waiting until he knew the child would have left for her babysitting job, he steeled himself and put in a call to his ex-wife.

When he expressed his concern about Chloe, Lila was her usual, compassionate self. The woman was full of helpful suggestions. If he had objections to the way she was raising the child, he could go to hell, she told him. And on the way there, he could mail off his support check. He was three days late, and she was sick of his crap. So sick, in fact, she was thinking of reporting the ailment to the domestic relations people.

As Lila saw it, there was nothing wrong with Chloe. But if the child had any problem, it was probably her irresponsible, insensitive father.

After all, her mother was perfect.

The perfect bitch.

Banging the receiver down, Bannister let Lila's accusation wash over him. Since he'd first felt the marriage crumbling several years back, he'd worried about the effects of a split on his daughter. He'd held on as long as inhumanly possible. He hadn't wanted Chloe to be subjected to the inevitable anger and hostility. The threats and retribution. The tug-of-war.

He knew it all too well. His own home had been broken, though not by divorce. Bannister's parents had stayed together to the bitter end, and a very bitter end it had been. Five years ago, after his father died of a heart attack, his mother had celebrated with the unbridled joy of a freed hostage. Bannister knew their love had predeceased his dad by thirty or more years, but it had still hurt to get slammed with the evidence.

Growing up, Bannister had fantasized that it would be different for his kids. He'd imagined having a noisy, boisterous pack of them. A real home and family full of love, light, and energy. He'd hoped that he and some hypothetical soulmate could give his kids solid walls of support and security. Two loving parents to shield them from life's hard knocks and rough edges. Neat trick. He just hadn't been able to figure out how to pull it off.

"Let's go to work, Sam," Lenny said, nudging him. "You can't spend all your time worrying."

"Says who?"

The next number on the call list Macklin had made from the Newport hotel was to Alter Ego, Inc. It turned out to be a theatrical costume company on lower Broadway.

The building's street level housed a luncheonette, a stationer's, and a shoe repair shop. Above were seven floors of dance studios and rehearsal halls. The costume company occupied the shabby building's ninth and tenth floors. The only access was a creaky commercial lift.

Price paled as the ancient mechanism stuttered its way to the top.

"You okay, Lenny?"

"Listen to that. Thing sounds like it's going to fall. You see an inspection sticker?"

"Since when are you afraid of elevators?"

"I'm not afraid of elevators. It's riding in them I don't like."

"Funny. I never noticed."

"Believe me, Sam. There's nothing funny about it."

"Hell. You should have been the one to go see Doc Lyons. You wouldn't have had to fake it."

Price nodded stiffly. "Aren't we there yet?"

The elevator disgorged them into a cavernous space crowded with racks of garish garments and bizarre accessories. Fake limbs, futuristic weapons, creature masks, a rainbow of wigs. Several people worked the inventory, boxing and tagging. Bannister and Price edged through the tight aisle between a pair of dress racks toward the line of offices in the rear.

Dusty, dirty, flying bits of frill and feathers. By the time they emerged at the far end of the racks, Bannister's nose itched and there was a fierce tickle at the back of his throat. Took three sneezes to neutralize the damage.

His knock at the first occupied office was answered by a plump, bald man with wide-set eyes and an odd hitch to his walk. Natural frog. No costume necessary.

Bannister explained the purpose of the visit. Froggy didn't blink when he mentioned Theodore Macklin.

"Name's not familiar to me. But I only handle the major theatrical accounts. What kind of business is this Macklin guy in?"

Bannister wished he knew. "Investments."

"Probably rented for a private party then. Sit. I should be able to look it right up for you."

The nameplate on the desk said Howard Storch. A photo on the wall showed Howard huddling with his wife and their three tadpoles on the lawn of a massive estate. Bannister watched as the man fingered through a giant Wheeldex.

"Funny. No Macklin on the customer list. Maybe Elva knows. She's our office manager. She knows everything."

Howard picked up his phone and dialed an extension. Seconds later, a round face capped by a blond beehive poked in.

"Elva darling. These detectives say someone named Theodore Macklin called here about a week ago. Sound familiar?"

"Nope. Who'd he talk to?"

"That's what we're trying to find out."

Elva batted a lethal set of false lashes. "Sorry. We don't log incomings."

"Do you keep message logs? Or records of calls out?" Price asked.

"Both, but I don't see—"

"Show them, Elva dear," said Howard. "Alter Ego is always glad to cooperate with the boys in blue."

Bannister and Price spent the next hour poring over a boxful of duplicate message slips. They found nothing from Theodore Macklin and no calls from anyone in Rhode Island. Next, helpful Elva produced a printed list of recent long-distance calls made from Alter Ego's phones. Each office was assigned a code number, she explained, so the bills could be charged to the right departments. Personal calls were strictly monitored and billed to employees. The aspiring actors they often hired for stock work on a temporary basis liked to reach out and touch an astounding number of people.

Price found the number for the Doubletree Inn on the second page of calls. "Got it, Sam. Whose code is twenty-eight?"

Elva looked it up and led them to the last office on the right. A thirtyish man with platinum hair and plastic features greeted them with a histrionic bow. His teeth were unnaturally white, and his voice was an octave or so deeper than God's.

"Clint Traynor," he said with a rakish heft of his sculpted brow. "If you gentlemen are seeking that *special* look for a memorable night on the town, you've come to the right place." He scanned Bannister's body with unabashed interest. "Anyone ever tell you you'd make a *fabulous* pirate?"

Elva snorted. "Can it, Clint. They're cops. They're interested in someone you called."

Clint frowned at the number. "Not me, Elva. I don't know a *soul* in area code four-oh-one."

"Business maybe? Think, dearie. It was made from your extension."

He eyed the list. "Oh, no. Not again. Last month Howard got me for almost ten dollars' worth of personals to numbers I didn't know. It was close to twelve the month before. I did not make that call, and I'm not paying."

Elva tamped the turbulent air. "All right, all right. Don't get excited. I'll check it out."

"You'd better. It's not the money. It's the principle," he sniffed.

Elva led them back to the antique elevator. "I have a

feeling who it might be," she told them, and asked for their number. "Either way, I'll call you later."

Price was eager to hit the next stop. Bannister was dragging. With the way things weren't going and his nagging worries about his daughter, he was about ready to cash his few remaining chips and head home. Maybe Chloe would perk up if he took a week off and spent some time with her. There were more important things in life than the damned Macklin case and solvency.

"I think you were right in the first place, Lenny. Why don't we just call it quits? I could surprise Chloe. Take her to my place for a couple of weeks."

"But you said she was really looking forward to going away with her grandmother next week."

"True."

"And didn't you tell me she loves the babysitting job she's got for the rest of this week?"

"Yes."

"So you think you should wait a couple of weeks or ask her to give up the things she's enjoying?"

"Where to next, Lenny?"

After their abortive visit to the Popov family the previous night, Price had contacted a friend at the Immigration and Naturalization Service. Price's INS connection had tracked the Popov clan to its origins in the town of Staritsa, north of Moscow.

From Staritsa, Anatoly, his wife, Luta, two of Anatoly's brothers, and the couple's two young children had applied for exit visas five years ago. Their entry to the states was approved after Luta's uncle agreed to sponsor the family's quest for U.S. citizenship.

The uncle, Mischa Nemichev, had provided the Popovs with interim housing and financial support. Once the adults qualified for work permits, Uncle Mischa had found jobs for them in his company: Nemichev and Sons, Jewelers.

IRS records confirmed that Luta and the brothers Popov—Anatoly, Arkady, and Danik—were all currently employed by the jewelry firm, which had thirty-eight workers on the weekly payroll. The retail end of the business was conducted out of booth twenty-seven of the Metallica Exchange in the midtown diamond district.

Passing the row of glassed storefronts, Bannister shaded his eyes against the glare of the display diamonds. There were doorknob rings, giant drop earrings, and icicle chains designed to choke only the most privileged throats. The priceless glitter stood in stark contrast to the somber proprietors, mostly Anatoly Popov clones with cheap, dark suits and dreary expressions.

The Metallica Exchange housed a labyrinth of cramped cubicles. Each was manned by a company elder and a couple of smiling underlings trained to hawk the wares. Many of the booths were deserted. At a few, customers scanned the crowded sample cases for bargains or indulgences or, better yet, both.

Bannister and Price circled booth twenty-seven and bowed their heads over the counter of a nearby vendor with similar merchandise and a fortunate view. A solicitous young woman approached them.

"Help you, gentlemen?"

"Thought maybe I'd pick up a little something for the wife," Price said. "Her birthday's coming up."

"Bracelet, pendant, necklace?"

"A ring maybe."

"Precious or semiprecious? Formal or informal? Fourteen- or eighteen-carat?"

Soon, they were surrounded by tottering trays of rings ranging from the mildly overstated to the frankly ostentatious. Ruthie, a sensible person whose home base was Earth, wouldn't be caught dead in any of them, Bannister knew. Fortunate, given that the cheapest cost about a two-bedroom condo in the Keys, even in a slack market.

Price was doing a commendable job of feigning interest. Borrowing the woman's jeweler's loupe, he spewed his standard overabundance of trivial information.

"I'd say this is G color, clarity near flawless. VVS grade, am I right?"

He handed back the loupe. The woman's eyes were stretched with astonishment. "Exactly."

Bannister was getting a headache. Probably the altitude

of the prices, he thought. While the saleswoman chirped on, he kept a surreptitious eye on booth twenty-seven.

Despite the general lull at most counters, business was brisk at Nemichev and Sons. A burly dark man presided over the operation. He was assisted by two slender women who sought his constant advice. "How much for this, Uncle Mischa? Can we do this in sapphire, Uncle Mischa?" A steady line of customers eyed the merchandise, made their choices, and slipped away. While Bannister watched, there were two tanned men with ponytails, a trim young couple in pastel jogging clothes, and a trio of jewel-encrusted women who'd obviously enjoyed a plentiful liquid lunch.

A couple of strange things caught Bannister's trained eye immediately. The packages the ponytailed pair took away were crude, paper-wrapped bundles in lieu of the neat velvet boxes and drawstring sacks the others received. And he caught no currency exchange between the bearish Uncle Mischa and the tanned guys. Not even the casual scrawl of signatures on notes of memoranda that were standard for the trade. No cash, no credit cards. Nothing but the satisfied look of the two departing men and the even deeper smile of contentment on the face of the proprietor.

Something was clearly not kosher. But Bannister strongly doubted that it had anything to do with the Martha Rafferty murder. He could feel another of Price's damned detours coming on.

"Ready to go, Lenny?"

"I don't know, Sam. The round cut, you think? Or the emerald? Round's a better investment, but I think Ruthie likes the classic less-faceted look."

"Your call."

"Yeah? So hard to decide. Guess I'd better think about it. You open tomorrow?"

"All day."

"Great. We'll be back."

She gave him a look that said she knew better and started packing away the samples.

Out on the street, Bannister sucked a breath to clear his

lungs of the extravagance. "My feeling is we're getting off the track here, Lenny. What do you think?"

"The truth? I think Ruthie would love a diamond solitaire and a wedding band to match. Nothing too fancy, mind you—"

"The way I see it, nothing here could possibly have anything to do with the Rafferty murder. You agree?"

Price's face was dreamy. "I bet she'd kill me if I showed up with the rings. But murder by Ruthie is not exactly what you'd call punishment. You know what I'm saying?"

"Stick with me here, Lenny. I'm suggesting we forget this other business Macklin might have been involved in, whatever it is, and concentrate on the Rafferty case."

"How can we forget what we don't know, Sammy? Have a little patience, will you? It's like I always tell you. You take your time, you'll get there much sooner."

CHAPTER

26

Closing the symposium file, Maggie rubbed her neck to ease the kinks. Henry was handling most of the conference plans, and Pam had agreed to do anything she could to help. But Maggie still had to line up the keynote speakers and the panel moderators. She'd spent the last hour and a half on the phone, and so far, things were going better than she'd dared to hope.

Initial enthusiasm for the project was high. Nearly everyone she'd contacted had agreed to participate. Several of her colleagues had offered help and useful suggestions. One director of a phobia program in Ohio had even volunteered to take charge of publicity.

Maggie was increasingly assured that the conference would be successful. By Henry's preliminary reckoning of costs and probable enrollment, they'd be able to raise more than enough to save the clinic.

Which definitely called for a celebration. Unfortunately, Pam was tied up with her niece's birthday party, and Henry had long-standing plans with a neighbor. Ethan took more energy than Maggie cared to expend at the moment, and the two other friends she tried were out.

Dialing her apartment, Maggie found herself hoping that her mother 'had decided to spend another night at Cousin Kathy's. A solitary celebration would be far more festive than dinner with the world champion wet blanket. But no such luck. Francine picked up, with her customary groan of greeting, after the third ring. Maggie managed to squelch her disappointment and muster a trace of enthusiasm.

"Mom? How about getting gussied up and meeting me at Grifone?"

The elegant Italian restaurant on East Forty-sixth was a favorite of Maggie's. Wonderful food, lovely atmosphere, fabulous service. Perfect place to mark an occasion.

"You mean where we went for Aunt Hannah's birthday? Isn't that awfully expensive?"

"It's my treat. I'm up for a special dinner."

Sigh. "You'd better count me out then, dear. I'm afraid I wouldn't be very good company."

Ask Mom to a picnic, she'll volunteer to bring the storm clouds. "What's wrong?"

Deeper sigh. "Oh, nothing. I called your father with a question a while ago, and some chippie answered. Acted like she owned the place."

Same old revolving door. At least once a week, her mother found an excuse to telephone her father's apartment. Then she sank into the doldrums over something she did or did not hear.

"Why do you keep doing this to yourself? You know it's always a problem for you when you call Dad."

"There was a financial matter I needed to discuss with him. After all those years together, you can't simply cut a person out of your life. You might have told me about his new flame, Maggie. I felt so foolish."

Maggie suppressed a sigh of her own. "Please come to dinner. We'll have fun."

"No, really. I'm exhausted, and I have no appetite. It'd be a waste of money. How old is this new one anyway? She sounds like a child."

So much for merrymaking. Her mother's blue funks required lavish doses of TLC. Take-out chicken and salad from Eddie's Deli with a side of sympathy it would be. Probably some humble pie à la crow for dessert.

Yes, I am a rotten daughter, Mom. I should certainly have told you about Dad's new lady love. After all, if you can't count on your children to torment you, who can you count on?

Talk about expensive.

Suddenly, Maggie was not all that anxious to leave her office. She dawdled, clearing up the mess on her desk. That done, she flipped through her book to see what pending matters she might be able to clear up before she headed home.

Her eye settled on the still-open question of a leader for the new group. Gail Weider hadn't returned her call. Maybe some further persuading was in order. Maggie decided to try again.

She dialed Gail's apartment and let the phone ring seven times. No answer. Funny. The machine had been on earlier. Gail had an admitted fetish about being reachable in case one of her multitudinous relatives tried to contact her. The Weiders were a very close and calamity-driven family. By Maggie's reckoning, they held the world record for near misses, medical scares, and harrowing escapes.

To remain firmly in the hysterical loop, Gail was forever investing in the latest model answering device. When she wasn't home, she called in at least hourly for messages. Maggie couldn't imagine Gail forgetting to turn on her machine.

Not unless there had been a *real* emergency for a change. What if Gail were sick or injured and unable to get to the phone? What if she'd been accosted by a burglar or rapist in her apartment?

Cut it out, Maggie. You're starting to think like your mother.

There had to be a simple explanation. Maybe Gail was in the shower. Or maybe she'd stepped out for a second to dump the garbage or do her wash. Maggie knew that Gail's building was only a few blocks from her own. She decided to stop by on her way home and discuss the group leadership in person.

Leaving the floor, she bumped into Francis Kennedy. The overgrown elf seemed to materialize out of thin air.

"Excuse me, F.X."

"No need." He flashed an insipid grin as he moved a

plant two centimeters to the left to conform to the others. "You can crash my wagon anytime, Doctor dear."

Maggie winced at his strong boozy smell and the higher-than-usual color staining his freckled cheeks. "You know better than to come here when you've been drinking. Please leave."

"With you? You bet."

"I mean, please leave by yourself. If you persist in breaking the rules, I'm not going to be able to keep you on as an aide." Alex Ivy's pal or not, Maggie was not putting up with this.

He raked his fingers through his carrot-curl hair, then straightened his tie. "Sure you're not up for dinner?"

"I'm positive." Maggie strode away, feeling an odd sense of menace. The man's harmless, she assured herself. Harmless.

Another muggy night. The sky was an ominous ash color and had the crackling feel of an impending storm. Quickening her pace, Maggie headed north on York Avenue. With a little luck, she could pay a fast visit, pick up dinner, and beat the rain home.

Gail's apartment house was an ivory brick box sandwiched between a firehouse and a vacant municipal building. The first drops of rain freckled the pavement as Maggie entered. In the tiny foyer, Maggie found two Weiders listed on the building directory. She pressed the button for G Weider in 4J.

After a pause, she buzzed again. No answer. So much for the shower and laundry theories. Gail would have been finished with either of those long before now. Maggie was sure there were other plausible innocent scenarios, but none came immediately to mind.

On impulse, she pressed the buzzer for the other Weider. Before she could question the wisdom of the move, a male voice squawked through the speaker.

"Yes?"

"Hello. I'm Maggie Lyons, a friend of Gail Weider's from East End. I'm—"

"I know. Eight B. Come on up."

The lock release droned. Maggie pressed open the inner door to the lobby. Inside, she hesitated. The voice over the intercom sounded as if she were expected. Either he'd mistaken her for someone else, or by fortunate coincidence Gail was in that apartment.

The other Weider could well be a relative, she decided. Lord knew Gail had plenty of those.

As the elevator opened on eight, Maggie was accosted by a crush of voices. She tracked the noise to the B apartment, last on the right. The door was open. From that and the decibel level, Maggie gathered that there was a party in progress. She was reluctant to intrude, but having come this far, she thought she might as well butt in long enough to confirm that Gail was all right.

She rapped on the door frame, drawing curious looks from a knot of people in the foyer beyond the open door. Given the physical resemblance, it had to be a Weider family gathering. Everyone shared the same amazingly unremarkable looks, size, and coloring. All fell silent.

Clearing her throat, she hastened to fill the awkward hush. "I'm Maggie Lyons. A friend of Gail's from East End. I hate to interrupt but—"

A man in his forties stepped forward. "Not at all. I'm Don Weider, Gail's cousin. I'll take you in. They're all in the den."

Grasping her elbow, he steered her forcefully down a hallway lined with family photographs and clusters of chatting relatives. No wonder Gail hadn't bothered to turn on her phone machine. Virtually everyone in her universe was gathered right here.

Maggie hesitated. "Maybe I should come back another time. . . ."

"Not at all. Go on in." Holding fast to her elbow, he paused at a closed door and knocked gently. "Estelle? Marion? It's a friend of Gail's from the hospital."

A line of Gail clones, men, women and children, sat on the L-shaped sofa inside. Another several stood talking near the window. At first, Maggie couldn't pluck her friend from the garden of look-alikes. But then, Maggie spotted her ex-patient.

Her knees buckled, and she felt the color drain from

her cheeks. A pair of faces, tight with concern, swam toward her through the thick, rippling air.

"Are you all right? Here, sit."

The throng on the couch parted to make room for her. Maggie slumped in the space, drew a tremulous breath, and waited for the walls to stop wavering.

"Feeling better? Can I get you a brandy? Something to eat?"

"No, I'm all right now. It was just such a shock."

"It was to everyone."

Maggie's eyes drifted back to the open coffin near the window. The group gathered in front of it had thinned, so she had a clearer view of Gail's ashen face.

"What happened?"

"Terrible accident upstate. Aunt Gail drove her car off a cliff rounding a turn. Went right through the guardrail. Troopers said she was going way over the speed limit. But that's the craziest thing I ever heard. If you're a friend from the hospital, you must know how scared Gail was of driving. Used to be she wouldn't get behind the wheel at all. Last few months, she was a little better about it. Even went to visit Aunt Grace in Merrick for her anniversary. But we all still teased about how slow and cautious she was. Gail the snail, we called her. Her brother always said if our Gail drove any slower she'd be moving in reverse."

Maggie's mind bristled with disbelief. Gail Weider would never have gone careening around some perilous curve. She'd never drive at excessive speed under any circumstances. No more than Theodore Macklin would have blithely hopped on a bridge railing and fallen to his death.

What was happening?

CHAPTER

27

True to her word, Elva from Alter Ego had cracked the mystery of the call to Newport in record time. Noting that the unauthorized charges from Clint Traynor's extension had been made in the evening, Elva had stayed at the costume company after hours to catch the culprit. First night out, and she'd bagged her bird.

"It was exactly who I suspected: the slut," Elva had informed Price triumphantly when she'd called earlier. Price had strained to hear her through the pelting rain that struck the flimsy windows of the hovel like buckshot. Howard the frog, Elva explained, had been fooling around with this woman for several months. Everyone knew about it except Howard's poor wife, May Ellen, who was a lovely woman and a saint and definitely did not deserve such shabby treatment.

"Men," Elva spat, summarizing her analysis of the gender.

As Elva told it, the slut was a cabaret singer named Fern Compton Harlow who traveled worldwide, performing in clubs. When Fern was in town, she often showed up at the costume company, but always after business hours. Employees working overtime had reported slut sightings. Elva suspected that Howard had one of the seamstresses stay late to run up new dresses for Ms. Harlow to wear in her no-talent act.

Elva described the songbird as a flamboyant harlot with hundreds of sequined gowns. Given that she was wearing one of them when Elva caught her on Clint Traynor's

186

phone, Ms. Harlow was probably off to one of her sleazy crooning jobs tonight. Price could find out where she was performing through her agent. Ever diligent, Elva provided the man's name and number.

"What's the point of chasing this, Lenny?" Bannister demanded. "What can Howard and his cabaret canary possibly have to do with Martha Rafferty's murder?"

"There's only one way to find out, Sam."

"Go yourself then. I'm really not interested."

"You don't have to be interested. All you have to do is drive and bring some of Mrs. Rafferty's advance money for expenses. The club is way downtown, so we'll never be able to find a cab back, especially in this weather."

"We won't need to if we don't bother to go."

"Coming here and continuing with this case was your idea, Sam. Remember?"

"I'm trying to forget."

After his fifth pass through the area, Bannister gave up trying to find a free space and pulled into a park-and-lock on West Broadway. The gap-toothed man in the booth demanded payment in advance. By the time the attendant counted out the change, giving each single a complete physical before handing it over, the rain had saturated Bannister's shirt and gotten a running start on his pants and shoes.

The Coco Loco Club was in TriBeCa, so named because the downtown Manhattan section formed a triangle below Canal Street.

The club claimed the ground floor of an office building and boasted a mock tropical motif. The lobby walls were done in a leopard print. Velvet monkeys and inflatable coconuts hung from a lush plastic bower of potted palms. From inside came the insistent pulse of synthesized jungle drums.

A large woman in cave-girl garb was posted at the door. She had three-mile legs and breasts so high-riding they resembled a flotation collar. She eyed Bannister and Price as if they were on a sale rack, then stepped aside to let them pass.

They picked through a curtain of fake vines fitted with

stuffed butterflies and found themselves at Alley Oops's bar mitzvah.

A tight crush of pumping, gyrating, undulating dancers crowded the dance floor. Outsized body parts jiggled behind tiny swatches of fake fur. The walls were draped in light-studded mosquito netting. The tables were tree trunks rendered in papier-mâché. Amorous couples cuddled on fake driftwood banquets. A waiter in a baboon suit slalomed through the throng wielding a tray of drinks in pineapple and coconut shells. As Price and Bannister stood absorbing the scene, another baboon in a loincloth and a shirtless collar caught Bannister by the wrist.

Bannister responded with his customary calm. "If you're fond of that hand, you'd better get it the hell off me—"

The guy's bravado melted like candle wax. Releasing Bannister, he set his hands on his hips.

"This happens to be a private club. I'll have to ask you two gentlemen to leave."

"We'll go after we speak to Fern Harlow."

"Sorry. Members only."

Bannister grabbed the guy by the collar and twisted hard. "But for us you'll make an exception, right?"

There was a gurgling.

"Was that a *yes*?"

Tight nod.

Bannister let go. The bouncer staggered and clutched his rumpled collar.

"Now where's Fern Harlow?"

"Right there."

The lights dimmed, and a striking woman appeared in a wavering cone of light. Her hair was an ebony satin spill. Eyes a haunting lilac. She was poured into a tube of floor-length red sequins slit to reveal a well-done thigh quarter. Gems glittered at her lobes, wrists, and neck. Bannister made her at six feet minimum and way too rich for his budget, even if he'd been in the market.

But there was no charge for window shopping.

She slunk to center stage, tossed her hair, and drew

enough breath to fill a parade float. Waiting out four bars
of sultry introduction, she started the set.

Her voice was warm syrup, her moves the sinuous coil
of a seeking vine. Everything she sang was slow and lan-
guid: "The Man I Love," "Just My Bill," "Stranger in
Paradise." And she made lazy love to herself as she oozed
out the notes.

Bannister knew better than to be seduced by slick visu-
als. He'd fallen into that trap with Lila. Bought the pretty
package blind. Owned it outright before he'd even
thought to fully examine the contents. At the time, the
rotten return policy hadn't even crossed his besotted
mind.

". . . *let's fa-a-a-all in love,*" Fern Compton trilled,
ending her final number. The lights came up. But before
Bannister and Price could reach center stage, a crush of
dancers had crowded the floor, masking the diva's departure. Bannister cornered the simian bouncer again.

"Where'd she go?"

The man planted a protective hand on his shirt collar.
"Dressing room. Right behind the grass shack."

Bannister and Price wove through the writhing dancers
and rounded the fake front of a jungle hut. Behind the
prop was a door marked by a frayed paper star.

Fern Compton Harlow responded to their knock with a
throaty invitation. At close range, she was far less attractive. Her skin was suffocated by beige pancake. The perfect features and flawless form had been given an obvious
surgical assist. Her eyes and expression were frosted over
and didn't look worth the effort to thaw.

The dressing room was cramped. There was a vanity, a
cot, a small settee, and a free-standing closet stuffed with
glittery dresses. Two suitcases and a steamer trunk occupied the remaining floor space.

Price asked the questions. Fern Harlow played it pleasant and cooperative. She admitted using Clint Traynor's
office on the occasional evenings she spent at Alter Ego.
Howard Storch was a fan and a good friend, she said, but
nothing more. He allowed her to use the company's facilities when she was in town. Living as she did in hotels, she

lacked access to fax, copiers, multiline phones, and other equipment she needed to conduct her business. She'd never had gowns or anything else made at the costume company, she said. She also denied any knowledge of Theodore Macklin. If she'd called the Doubletree Inn a week or so ago, it had to have been for some other reason.

"I travel all the time, Detective. If I phoned some hotel in Newport, I've probably got a gig coming up there. I like to book my own rooms. Make sure they don't stick me near the elevators or ice machines."

Price persisted. The woman was slick and convincing, but the coincidence of the Newport number was way too big a chunk to swallow. Macklin calls Alter Ego, Fern Harlow calls the Doubletree later the same day. You have two and two, four is a reasonable expectation.

Woman had a manufactured smile and lush lips that she kept moistening with her forked tongue. Her slow-crossing legs exposed a deliberate peek of lace. Bannister saw right through the diversionary tactics, but his hormones found them mildly amusing.

Still, she wouldn't budge from her story. "Guess that's it then," Price said, reaching for the doorknob. "Thank you, Miss Harlow."

"Sure you gentlemen don't want to catch the second show?"

"Thanks anyway," Bannister said. By his calculations, they'd already sat through two mediocre performances.

Back on the street, they dashed through the downpour to the car park. As they drove uptown, Price worked the pieces together.

"So there's Anatoly Popov and those oddball transactions at the Nemichev jewelry company. And there's Fern Harlow, traveling diva, and her friend Howard at Alter Ego. Interesting."

"Left field, Lenny. We're here about the Martha Rafferty murder. Nothing else."

"Did you notice the diva's wardrobe, Sam? And the airline tags on her luggage?"

Price went on about the odd ports of call Fern Harlow had visited. Third-world nations. Bucolic islands. Places where you wouldn't expect to find nightclubs or cabaret acts. And there was some complicated bit about the way her gown was sewn. Apparently Ruthie, an accomplished amateur seamstress, had made a sequined costume for their daughter, Rebecca, years back for a school play. Bannister tried, but he couldn't connect to the discussion. Price lost him somewhere between Bahrain and the notions counter.

His thoughts swerved back to Chloe. Given a hard enough shove in the wrong direction, any kid could get derailed, even one as smart, real, and together as his little girl had always seemed to be.

Daddy's girl.

He thought about their special mornings together. Before the divorce, they'd sneak out weekends while Lila was still asleep. Bannister would take Chloe for pancakes and laughs. Then they'd walk and talk until they'd exhausted a month's supply of words.

Bannister could still feel Chloe's little hand in his as she skipped to keep pace with his longer strides. Sweet hand, warm and boneless. Felt like a fragile bird, full of restless fluttering.

Chloe had always seemed so eager to grow up and away. Big-eyed, impatient, dressing up in Lila's heels and makeup. Bannister had often imagined the hard time he'd have dealing with her becoming a woman, a separate individual with other loves and a world and purpose of her own.

Until now, he'd never given much thought to the terrifying alternatives.

CHAPTER

28

"So I was in the company cafeteria, and I couldn't help but overhear these women talking at the next table. They were describing this girl in auditing who's having an affair with her periodontist. I kept picturing her in the chair, and the guy scraping her gums. Not my idea of a romantic interlude, that's for sure. Anyhow, before I knew it, I'd finished my whole sandwich."

Melissa, the blue-eyed beauty with the phobia about eating in public, was finishing her recitation to the young adult group. She was the third member of the Thursday Night Lyons Club to report her progress and the third who'd made remarkable gains since the group's initial meeting a week ago. There was a scatter of applause and congratulations, and the girl settled back in her seat, beaming.

"That's wonderful, Melissa. You should be really proud of yourself." Smiling, Henry turned to another group member.

"Stephen? You want to tell us about your week next?"

The musician shifted in his seat and cast a wary eye toward the window. Last night's thunderstorm must have been a torment for him, Maggie thought. On her walk home from the Weiders', she'd been accompanied by jarring thunderclaps and jagged spikes of lightning.

At the time, she'd been grateful for the tumultuous storm. It had provided a welcome distraction from the shock of Gail Weider's sudden death. At home, she was further distracted by her mother's hour-long diatribe against Maggie's duplicitous father. Mom saw her ex-husband as a well-oiled spite machine. She was convinced his every move was designed solely to hurt and humiliate her.

Maggie didn't make a futile attempt to reason with the woman. They'd had this discussion too many times. It always ended exactly where it began—no place. Instead, she listened and sought to fill the occasional pauses with attentive gestures and expressions of empathy. Anything was better than dwelling on Gail Weider's inexplicable death. Even this.

But the tragic accident returned to taunt Maggie as she lay in her bed hours later, well into the night but miles from sleep. She kept trying to envision Gail's Chevy wagon screaming around a perilous curve, splintering the guardrail, hurtling off a cliff. She struggled to make it real, to set the reported circumstances in a rational pocket of her mind. But the image kept exploding in a puff of incredulity.

What in the name of God was going on?

Tracy, the social phobic, was next to speak. When Henry asked about her progress, the young woman clutched her purse like a lifeline. Henry didn't press her, and the rest of the group waited patiently for a response. Everyone in the room understood only too well the wall Tracy was working to break through.

"My hardest thing is right here," she said finally. "I stood in the hall for twenty minutes before I could get myself to come inside." Her voice was tiny and rode on a tremor. "I felt like running away."

"But you didn't," Henry said. "That's what matters. And it's going to get easier. Now, can you tell us about your practice session with Rosalie?"

Tracy looked tense enough to snap. "We'd arranged to meet at the mall Saturday. I was on time, but no sign of Rosalie. I almost turned around and went home, but I figured maybe she'd gotten stuck in traffic or something. She showed up about fifteen minutes later. Said she'd been waiting for me the whole time in front of Macy's."

"What happened then?" Henry prompted.

Tracy allowed a meek smile. "I told her off, that's what

happened. She's supposed to be helping me, not leaving me stranded and scared half to death. She admitted it was her mistake. She apologized, too, but I didn't let it go at that. I'm afraid I really let her have it."

"Good for you," said Lauren with the big hair and matching mouth. "I have to tell you, Tracy, you don't exactly come across as the assertive type."

Tracy giggled. "I'm not. In fact, I couldn't believe what I was saying. But it felt great."

Henry was nodding enthusiastically. "Best thing is to get a feeling like that off your chest. Otherwise, it can eat you up inside."

Maggie covered her mouth to mask the grin. Henry was the least confrontational soul imaginable. If you parked your car on his foot, he'd probably apologize for denting your tire.

"Jason? Let's hear from you next. How did your session with Binnie go?" Henry looked expectantly at the lanky young man slouched in his chair.

"Two sessions," Jason amended with a shrug. "Went okay, I guess. We walked around the neighborhood the first time. Yesterday, we went to the boulevard and looked at the stores. Had a soda. No big deal."

"Sounds like an enormous deal to me," Henry said. "Could this be the same Jason Childs who had to be pried out of the house with a crowbar a week ago?"

"I sure didn't picture you strolling around the neighborhood, Jason," Lauren contributed. "Last week you said you were always thinking a dog could be around the corner. It's how I feel about bugs. Like one could be waiting for me any place, any time. That's why I always need to see what's ahead of me, to make sure I'm not going to run into a spider or something. Keeps me out of dark places, I'll tell you that much."

Jason shrugged again. "No big thing."

Maggie stiffened. How could he be so offhanded about such a monumental change? The young man even looked different. His eyes were brighter. No more webs of fear. An edge of authority had invaded his tone and bearing. And instead of the beige fade-in-the-wall outfit of last week, he was wearing a bright print shirt and sneakers with iridescent orange trim.

Eyeing the group, Maggie was struck by the enormous transformation in every one of them. They'd all come so far in one week. Was it too far? Too fast? Could there be something in this innocent-seeming process that moved patients to take deadly dangerous risks?

Like Gail?

She pushed the awful thought aside. Logic would not allow her to blame the clinic for what had happened to Gail Weider or Theodore Macklin. Hundreds of patients had gone through the group sessions. Thousands more had completed similar programs at other centers. There was no black magic here, nothing secret or sinister. Just proven techniques and hard work.

Maggie drank the rest of her iced tea. Her throat felt raw and fisted. *Get a grip, Maggie.* Gail's death and Macklin's were two separate cases. Cut through the terrible coincidence, and there had to be a rational, believable explanation for each shocking incident.

According to the Rhode Island police detective, Theodore Macklin's company had probably been involved in illegal dealings. Macklin might well have trampled some line and been marked for execution. If his murderers knew about his phobia, they could have arranged his killing on a bridge as a sadistic sweetener to their cup of revenge. Nothing illogical there.

There had been no witnesses to Gail's accident. The police were spouting pure supposition when they said she'd been speeding around a dangerous curve. The skid marks they'd found could have been made by another car altogether. Maybe Gail's brakes had failed at a critical moment. Or she might have spun out of control on an oil slick or wet patch. That kind of thing could happen at any speed.

Gail's reason for driving so far from home was a bit harder to fathom. But Maggie hadn't seen Gail in a while. It was possible the woman had managed to press past her former limits and decided not to tell anyone about it until she felt more confident. Stranger things had happened.

Comforted by those rational explanations, Maggie turned to Henry as he concluded the session.

"You're all off to a terrific start. From now on, I'd like you to keep personal journals. Write down any situations that give you trouble and instances where you deal well with your anxiety. It will be really nice to be able to look back and see how far you've come." He extracted a small spiral notebook from his jacket pocket and held it up. "I still refer to my own clinic journal from time to time. Helps me remember how things used to be."

"And next time, please bring in your charts. We'll collect and keep them until the final session," Maggie added. Each patient was asked to record anxiety reactions during outside practice sessions. The notes were another good way of tracking and documenting individual progress. Phobics tended to underrate their accomplishments. Building their creaky confidence was a crucial element of the program.

With the formal session over, the Thursday Night Lyons Club adjourned to the side of the conference room where Henry had arranged pitchers of iced tea and a platter of brownies. Maggie thought of the cookies from Gail Weider he'd served at last week's meeting. She'd been munching on the leftovers Henry had pressed on her all week. She still had a few on a plate on her kitchen counter. Strange to think of Gail's hands mixing and shaping the dough. Gail's fingers setting the finished confections on a doilied platter.

The group had split in fragments. Three of the girls stood near the back of the room. At the window, Lauren and Stephen were sipping iced tea and talking. Jason stood aside, watching warily. Very odd kid.

Henry was straightening up the refreshment table. He wore his special occasion suit, a shapeless banker blue. Maggie remembered that he'd planned to pay respects to Gail's family on his lunch hour.

She walked over and waited for him to finish brushing off the tabletop. "How did it go at the Weiders'?"

He blinked, then seemed to find his place. "They're

holding up as well as can be expected, I suppose. Such a blow for them."

"Yes. But I was asking about you."

Maggie knew the visit must have evoked painful memories of his mother's death. Henry and his mom had been unusually close. They'd enjoyed so many of the same things: gardening, cooking, watching old movies on cable. Henry refused to talk about it, but the old woman's passing had to have left an enormous hole in his life.

"I'm fine, Maggie. You needn't worry about me."

"Sure I do. I'm your friend. It's in the contract."

Henry was so intensely guarded and private. Reminded her of a long-locked room. Maggie wished she could find a way to open the man up and air him out.

She suspected that his visit to the Weiders' had been doubly difficult. Henry rarely socialized, but he had taken an observable interest in Gail Weider. Maggie had read the signs. Fluent body English. A sudden interest in slimming down. New clothes. The pair had taken to having an occasional lunch together while Gail was still a regular at the clinic.

"I said I'm fine."

She caught the annoyance. Rare defensive parry from Mr. Meek. Time to back off and respect his boundaries. Otherwise, the border patrol would be reinforced.

"See you tomorrow then, Henry. Great meeting."

Leaving the room, she was stalled by Tracy, who had a question about her medical insurance coverage. Next, Lauren cornered her to discuss whether it was reasonable for her to fear red grapes now that spiders had been discovered in several bunches in California supermarkets.

By the time Maggie finished that conversation, the others were straggling out. An attractive blond man in khaki slacks, a rep tie, and a navy blazer stood waiting in the corridor. Probably a friend or boyfriend of someone in the group, she thought. Curious, she hung back, waiting to see who approached him.

But there were no greetings or hints of recognition. The stranger held his place as the others peeled away and disappeared down the hall.

"Can I help you?" Maggie asked.

He eyed her badge. "You're Dr. Lyons?"

"Yes."

"Actually, I've come to see you."

"About what?"

He cast a meaningful eye into the conference room, where Henry was still restoring order. "It's best if we talk in private."

"Whatever it is, you can tell me here."

He nodded crisply. Flashing an ID, he met Maggie's eye. "My name is Dean Connell. I'm with the investigating unit of the State Board of Health. We've received serious allegations against you, Dr. Lyons. I've been assigned to check them out."

"Allegations? Is this some kind of a joke?"

A muscle twitched in his square jaw. Otherwise, he was stone, a statue of perfect bureaucratic control. "I can assure you, Doctor. It's no joke. Two patients in your care have died recently under highly questionable circumstances. If the charges against you are substantiated, professional censure may be the least of your worries."

Maggie was reeling. This could not be happening. Any second, someone would jump out from behind a corner and claim credit for the sick hoax.

So where was he?

Maggie peered into the diligent blue eyes, searched for a betraying trace of humor in the chiseled face. Nothing.

"This can't be happening."

"I'm afraid it is, Dr. Lyons. Now, can we go somewhere to talk privately?"

Dazed by the shock, she led him to her office. Looking around, she confirmed that everything was exactly as she'd left it: shelves, desk, files, pictures. Even the clutter was intact. But all that didn't change the terror that crept under her skin in a hideous electric rash.

CHAPTER

29

Jason's insides were dancing like crazed revelers, his brain a fast-bowed fiddle. Joy of such magnitude was an alien feeling, overwhelming. The world had been polished to a blinding sheen. Everything was so strikingly clear and resonant, the pleasure verged on excruciating. Even Jessie with her prissy nagging arrogance couldn't get to him today.

"I'm going out to play with Allison, Jay. I'll be back by lunch if you need me to check around for you outside or anything."

"I don't and I won't, sister dear," he said with a smile. "Stay away as long as you like. Do whatever pleases you. Have yourself the finest day in the recorded annals of mankind."

She narrowed her eyes. "Mommy, Jay's teasing," she whined toward the staircase.

"Jason?" came his mother's weary voice from downstairs.

"I just told her to enjoy herself, that's all. Isn't that what I said?"

"Jessie? Is that what happened?"

"He meant it teasing though. Make him stop."

He heard his mother sigh. "Allison's waiting outside for you, honey. You ready, or should I tell her to come back later?"

"I'm ready." The child backed down the hall, eyeing her brother warily. At the head of the staircase, she stalled and scowled at him.

"You better cut it out, Jay. I'm not fooling."

He waggled his fingers. "Have wonderful fun, little sister. Laugh and play and delight in this glorious day."

"I said stop. And you better not go in my room while I'm gone either. I know just exactly how many candies are in that box grandma sent me."

"That's because you're such a clever child. You should be grateful for that fine mind of yours. It will serve you well."

"That's it. I'm *telling*."

He watched her hasten down the stairs, her silken blond waves sinking out of view. Bless the little snippet. She was a major pain in his ass, true. But she was also a bobbling, bubbling mass of energy and adventure. Everything a kid ought to be.

Same thing he planned to become. A kid again. Full of life and devilment. Or had he ever really been one in the first place?

Well, no matter. That was history. The dark, dismal ages. The geek he'd been had nothing to do with the new improved model Jason Childs. Fearless and accomplished. Undaunted by life's trials and challenges. Pressing forward toward a brave, new act and outlook. Now that he'd passed into the light, he had no intention of looking back at the timorous troll he'd been in a bleak past incarnation.

The future view was far more enticing. From last night's group meeting, he'd learned that even small doses of the courage drug could work miracles. Every one of his fellow phobics had made startling progress. And he'd barely dabbed a trace of his special formula on the watchbands.

All he needed to do was run a few more preliminary trials on himself. Then, with his findings molded into a creditable report, he would consult with his old science teacher and mentor, Otto Allen.

Jason could imagine Mr. Allen's ebullient welcome, the pride in the science teacher's dull gray eyes as he recognized the renewed sheen on Jason's long-tarnished potential. Mr. Allen had selected him, nurtured him, believed in him. And now the old man would see that his faith had not been tragically misplaced.

Chemistry was Otto Allen's life. The man lived and breathed his molecules and catalysts and reagents. He constantly tracked the latest news and views in the field. He knew every player from minor lab drones to Nobel laureates. Mr. Allen would be able to direct Jason to a pharmaceutical lab where the testing on C2BU could be conducted for FDA approval.

More important, the man could help Jason to register and protect his invention. The necessity had occurred to him in the middle of a night marked by sleep-shattering excitement. Mr. Allen would know whether C2BU required a patent or a copyright or a whatever and how to go about getting one. Jason wasn't about to risk having some predatory corporate type steal his formula. If that happened, he'd never get a shred of the credit he deserved.

A finding of such magnitude had to be handled with utmost caution. Any scientist would be delighted to see his name on Jason's courage drug. The rights had to be worth a fat fortune. And there was the promise of international professional regard and recognition, the press, the possible prizes. Irresistible.

With a sickening jolt, Jason realized that a small-time nobody like Otto Allen would be every bit as vulnerable to such temptation as the next person. Maybe more. That guy would probably give his left test tube for a chance to be credited with Jason's discovery.

If the science teacher claimed C2BU as his own, who'd believe that Jason had been its real inventor? After all, old man Allen had been a known chemistry loon for decades. It was no secret that he was forever experimenting in the high school lab. Nights, weekends, holidays.

No, Jason could not risk sharing his discovery with his old science teacher or anyone else. At least, not yet. First, he'd have to figure out a way to document his findings and make an indisputable record of his authorship.

But how?

His brain was swimming in vain circles. He had to

move ahead, set a logical course. It still made sense to complete his planned series of personal trials first. While he was doing that, he could research the next essential moves to protect his discovery.

His Uncle Fred was a lawyer. Without surrendering any telling details, Jason was sure he could pick Uncle Fred's brain for the correct legal means to safeguard his invention.

By fortunate coincidence, Uncle Fred and Aunt Irene were scheduled to come to dinner Saturday night. By then, Jason would think of some way to slip the necessary questions into casual conversation. Once he found out how to register his formula, the rest would follow.

Fizzing over with anticipation, Jason went to the bathroom and measured a fresh dose of C2BU. Slugging it down, he checked the time. He'd be ready to commence the next experimental trial in fourteen minutes sharp. Ten forty-two and counting.

"Jason, honey? I'm going to the store. Need anything?"

Perfect. He could have worked around his mother, but now he wouldn't have to bother.

"No, Mom. I'm fine. See you later. Take your time."

"You'll keep an eye out for Jessie?"

"Of course."

"Bye then, dear."

He heard the door slam and the clack of her footsteps on the walk. A beat later, the car door smacked shut. The engine caught with a churning roar. As the sound faded, he checked his watch again. Nine minutes to maximum effectiveness. He'd use the time to set up.

All the clinic papers and pamphlets were in the manila folder on his desk. Extracting the list of long-term goals he and Binnie had devised together, Jason snickered. A week ago, a solo walk in the neighborhood had seemed as impossible as scaling Mount Everest. Now he could barely wait to breeze through the intermediate steps and venture out on his own.

He would have skipped all the silly preliminaries altogether, but he knew it was best to proceed through them sequentially. Valid experiments were painstaking and thorough. His ultimate goal was too precious to sacrifice to rashness or impatience.

Reviewing the list, he confirmed that he'd already completed the first three goals with his new aide. They had planned a neighborhood walk and completed the local outing together. Phase three was a walk in a familiar but more distant location. Their excursion to the boulevard covered that one.

Next, Jason was scheduled to view photos of dogs ranging from tiny lap pups to large, menacing breeds. Sequential desensitization, it was called. The theory held that fears could be dulled and finally deadened by systematic exposure to increasingly threatening situations. Binnie had provided him with the pictures. Now, Jason extracted the sealed envelope from his desk drawer, slashed open the top flap, and dumped the snapshots facedown on the scarred surface.

Four minutes to go.

After looking at the stills, the treatment plan called for Jason to watch a special videotape Binnie had prepared. Using her camcorder, she'd captured scenes of sleeping dogs, pooches at play, and finally, animals aroused to furious frenzy, straining at their leads.

Jason was reminded of the crazed curs leaping at him at the fenced horror house around the corner. Stupid Binnie had blithely led him there, set him squarely in the center of his blackest nightmare. But on his wondrous drug, even that horrific memory failed to arouse any serious anxieties.

As he checked the clock, the digital display advanced to ten fifty-six. Time to get started.

He turned the stack of photos over and began flipping through them. Without a twinge of apprehension, he progressed from the picture of a playful toy schnauzer to a somber-faced springer spaniel to the final entry, a mammoth rottweiler baring its mammoth teeth.

Finished with those, he went down to the family room and popped Binnie's tape in the VCR. Sprawled on the sofa, he watched the jerky parade of scenes. A small terrier napped in the shade of a towering oak. A mutt played a spirited game of Frisbee. A poodle, shorn in a show cut, strutted through a practiced routine of standard tricks: sit, speak, roll over, shake hands.

In Binnie's amateur grip, the camera twitched and wavered. Segments were wrenched out of focus and pulled back with a jolting choke-hold effect. Jason sniffed his contempt at the tape's clumsy quality. He was all but oblivious to the snarling Doberman that had lumbered into the center of the frame. The animal tensed and eyed the camera. An ominous threat rumbled deep in its chest.

Jason growled back. "Dumb dog, you're only a damned picture. And if you were real, I'd call your stupid bluff and scare you the hell away." He clapped his hands and the filmed animal turned tail as if in response. "Shoo, you dopey mutt. Get lost."

The reel ended. Jason turned off the set and bounded up the stairs for the next exercise. Binnie had packed a bunch of miniature dogs in a shoe box for him. Three-dimensional was supposed to be scarier, she'd claimed.

At the time, the absurd plan had seemed serious to him. But now, he felt the total fool, lifting the tiny creatures. Feeling their miniature muzzles and petite paws.

Next case.

He shoved the figures back in the box. From the paper bag under his bed, he retrieved the life-sized dog puppet Binnie had given him. Slipping his arm inside, he experienced a twinge of emotion. Not fear so much as repugnance, as if the puppet's insides were the slippery entrails of a living creature.

Shaking off his revulsion, he stroked the realistic fur, fingered the soft felt lining of the mouth. He couldn't make out the breed. It appeared to be a cross between a German shepherd, a collie, and an English sheepdog. Big, shaggy rag. He tried in vain to muster some anxiety or even a grudging touch of respect. Nothing.

"What do you have there, Jay?"

Jessie's flute voice startled him. "Don't you know how to knock, you little cretin?"

"The door was open. And you're not supposed to call me bad stuff." She edged closer and stroked between the puppet's pointed ears. "What's his name, Jay? He's so soft."

Curling his fingers inside the puppet's muzzle, he made a playful nip at his sister's dewy cheek and then nuzzled the side of her velvet neck. She chortled in delight as he spoke in a gruff canine voice.

"Boy, I'm hungry. What shall I have for lunch? Hmmm. Maybe a nice peanut-butter-and-little-girl sandwich on white."

She giggled. "That's funny. Do it some more."

He dipped the puppet to floor level, caught her bubble toes through her sandals, and made loud slurping noises. "Or maybe a foot-long little girl foot on a bun with mustard and relish. I'd *really* relish that."

Bright crystalline giggles trailed on the lustrous air. Crouching, she hugged the puppet in her boneless arms. Jessie's laugh was contagious. He felt her warmth through the mock fur, and he experienced a swell of satisfaction.

He was worthy, after all. Charming and lovable and accomplished. The black veil had lifted. A few more experiments, and he'd be ready to move ahead, to embrace the light.

Then no one and nothing would ever stand in his way again.

CHAPTER

30

Maggie's life had passed into total eclipse. It had started with the shocking visit from the State Health Department investigator. As soon as they stepped into her office and closed the door, young Mr. Connell had dropped the conciliatory act and let down his fangs.

Flashing a warrant, he'd demanded her complete treatment records for Theodore Macklin and Gail Weider. When she requested time to get the papers in order, he'd flatly refused, more than hinting that he suspected she might tamper with the files if he gave her the opportunity. She was welcome to consult her attorney, he said. But any lawyer would corroborate her obligation to provide the requested documents.

Maggie saw no point in arguing. She had nothing to hide and no reason to act as if she did. Once she collected the Macklin and Weider files and handed them over, Mr. Connell informed her that the investigation would not end with a review of the records. There would be a thorough examination of her professional conduct, he told her coldly, including interviews with staff and administration and, if necessary, patients.

In a month or two, when all that was completed and his preliminary report was ready, the department would hold a full, formal hearing. Connell advised Maggie several times of the serious nature of the charges against her and pointedly reminded her of her right to counsel. He dropped black hints about dire personal and legal consequences if the allegations against her were proven. The only thing the guy hadn't done was slap on the cuffs and leg irons. But then, he had promised to return again soon.

After the investigator left, Maggie had craved nothing but the peace and solitude she'd need to do some serious worrying. But she'd gone home to find her mother on the living room couch, weeping inconsolably. Seems Dad and Tina had dropped by earlier, hoping to lure Maggie out to a neighborhood movie. As if the moment hadn't been awkward and difficult enough, when Dad introduced his ex-wife to his exuberant little love bunny, Tina had gotten confused and taken Mom for Dad's mother.

"She called me *Grandma*, Maggie. And your son of a bitch father thought it was *funny*."

After nearly an hour of gentle reasoning and reassurance, Maggie had managed to douse that fire, but by then, another literal one was blazing in the building. Dear Mickey Glover had picked that unfortunate evening to add arson to his repertoire of creative amusements. Sweet child had shoved a garbage can stuffed with newspapers into the elevator, lit it, hopped out, and triggered the car to stop between floors. By the time the fire department managed to extract and extinguish the mess, the smoke was so thick that the entire building had to be evacuated.

Balmy, beautiful night, but Maggie's mother passed the entire time outside spewing dire predictions. Night air was virulent and hostile, she intoned with a sniff. So were night people. Out like this in their robes and slippers, they would surely catch something. Maggie didn't know about that, but the thought of throwing something had a definite and growing appeal.

When, after two A.M., they were finally allowed to reenter the building, Maggie was far too overcharged to sleep. Staring at the ceiling, she reviewed every tic and nuance of her brief treatment of Theodore Macklin.

She recalled their first session. Macklin had charged in, armored by defenses. Expensively dressed and oozing self-assurance, he'd informed her that he held her entire profession in extreme contempt and all but dared her to prove him wrong.

Maggie had been put off by everything from the man's

gruff demeanor to his pugnacious personality to the way he edged too close and invaded her personal space. Subsequent meetings had only reinforced her initial instinct. Theodore Macklin had all the charm and finesse of a B-52.

But Maggie had done her professional best. Replaying their sessions in her mind, she couldn't find a single moment when she'd permitted her temper to overwhelm her sense. Not a single instance where she'd revealed her enmity or distaste. She didn't have to like a patient to give him the care and treatment he deserved. All she had to do was objectively apply her training to the presenting problem. And that she had in Macklin's case. No question.

Examining her relationship with Gail Weider was much more complicated, however. She'd known the woman for years in a range of capacities: patient, aide, personal and professional acquaintance. But now she had to admit she had never known her all that well.

Gail was a lot like Henry: reserved, self-effacing, unobtrusive, locked in a terrible emotional vise. But nothing in her treatment at East End could have pushed her over an emotional precipice. The clinic had freed the woman from a number of difficult fears. Nothing more.

How could anyone think either of those deaths had been Maggie's fault?

In her own private theater of the absurd, Maggie tried to picture herself tossing Ted Macklin off that bridge, pressing Gail Weider's foot to the accelerator of that runaway car. But the scenes were too bizarre to play in even her wildest imagination. The whole thing was insane, a sick nightmare.

Sleep, when it came, brought no relief.

Maggie is kneeling on the flower-bordered rug. Listening to the distant music. Weaving her fingers together and shutting her eyes to concentrate.

"Now I lay me down to sleep."

"Lazy bit. Lazy!"

Maggie jerked awake, drenched in sweat. She found her mother still disconsolate over her unpleasant encounter with Dad and Tina. Several times over breakfast and the morning papers, Francine's stony resolve melted in a stream of mournful tears.

"Grandma," she wailed. "That little twit called me *Grandma*. Can you imagine? And all your father did was laugh."

Maggie finally managed to prod her mother toward her beloved plants. Gardening was the surest way to mute the volume on the woman's angst and leave Maggie free for a few minutes to wallow in her own.

But almost immediately after Francine stepped out on the terrace and Maggie shut the door to her office, the phone had started ringing. Every call was bad news, except for the one or two where the news was closer to terrible.

Daisy Tyler had relapsed during the night and required tranquilizers again. Two members of the upcoming group clinic had suffered second thoughts and canceled their applications. F.X. Kennedy would like to make amends for his bad behavior by taking her to dinner at 21.

Then came the killer call from Lawrence Ivy. Through the rasp of his ventilator, her former mentor informed Maggie of even larger troubles.

"Alex stopped by for breakfast, Maggie. He told me about the charges against you. It seems the state's health department investigator called him last evening, right after he left you. I'm afraid Alex is insistent that your symposium plans be postponed until all this nasty business is cleared up."

"But the allegations are pure nonsense!"

"I have no doubt of that, my dear. But I can see my son's point as well. The last thing you or East End needs right now is any extra attention. The publicity surrounding a major conference would be the worst thing possible. Baseless though they are, those charges could cause major problems for you and the hospital. Please try to understand."

Maggie took a long, hard breath. "Do I have a choice?"

"I'm sure they'll have this foolishness resolved in no time. Then you can go ahead with the symposium."

"Sure."

Fat chance is what she longed to say. Any significant delay, and it would be impossible to keep the date they'd chosen. If they put the conference off, the profits would come too late to save the clinic.

What more could go wrong?

As if in answer, there was a chilling scream. Maggie raced out of her room and tracked the din to the terrace. Flinging open the glass sliders, she spotted her mother at the distant edge. The woman was frozen in horror. Her mouth was distended in a strangled scream. Her face was sheet white.

"What happened, Mom? What was all that—"

Tracking her mother's gaze, Maggie too was shocked speechless. A section of the ornate wrought iron railing had fallen away. The supporting uprights dangled in space. Nothing stood between her mother and a deadly nine-story fall.

Inches away from the break in the rail, her mother began to whimper. Maggie fought back the dizzy waves crashing through her skull.

"Move back, Mom. Come inside." She held out a trembling hand.

"I can't." Her voice was a shiver. "Can't move."

"Yes, you can," Maggie said. "I'll help you." Proceeding with agonizing slowness, she forced herself onto the terrace. Her legs were wooden. A chill sweat drenched her, and her breaths came in shallow stabs.

Don't think about it. Don't let the fear take over!

"Oh, God, look. Hurry, Maggie. Please. Stop her. Don't let her fall."

Her?

The woman was disassociating, distancing herself from the horror by slipping out of her own skin. Inching forward, Maggie understood the feeling too well. She was splitting away herself. Unreality spread over her in a prickling rash. The city streets spilled beneath her. This was not happening.

Her gaze slid to the open edge of the terrace. Going over would be so easy. Tempting. She could see herself leaping in space, flying on the hawk's back. Circling in breathless arcs. *"If I should die . . ."* Terror tugged at her like a monstrous magnet. Why fight it? Much easier to let go. So much simpler.

Stop!

She made a desperate grab at reality, caught it by its disintegrating edges. The urge to surrender was a trap. She would not be caught. She *could* not. Distraction was the key. Grabbing the first trick that occurred to her, she started at a hundred and began counting backward by threes. The silent counting held her in place. Kept her in the awful moment.

"Hang on, Mom. I'm almost there."

Eighty-eight, eighty-five, eighty-two . . .

Maggie was halfway across the terrace now. With aching clarity, she saw how perilously close her mother stood to the unprotected brink. A breeze could push her over.

Careful, Maggie. Don't spook her, for godsakes. Watch it!

Her mother shrieked and pointed. "No, Maggie. Don't! Don't let her fall!"

Instinctively, Maggie dimmed her tone to a soothing lull. "I won't, Mom. Don't worry. Just stay right there. Don't move."

"She's falling. Oh, God, no!"

Her mother's hands flew to her throat. With an anguished wail, Francine wavered like a sapling in a storm. As Maggie watched in horror, her mother stumbled back, then tried to regain her balance with a forward step. In a desperate reflex, Maggie lunged. She grabbed Francine as she was about to pitch through the break in the railing.

Trembling, Maggie dragged her mother back across the terrace and into the living room. Once Francine was settled on the couch, Maggie made her shaky way across the room and locked the sliding terrace doors. With a satisfying rush of air, the menace was shut outside. Better.

But how had the railing broken like that? Peering out, Maggie saw the ragged ends. Probably rusted through from all the moisture from her mother's frequent watering of the precious plants.

Francine was in shock. Her pupils were dilated, skin

slicked with a chill sheen of perspiration. Maggie raised her mother's feet on a hill of throw pillows and loosened her clothing at the neck and waist.

"There, Mom. That's better. Now take a deep breath."

"Call someone. An ambulance," Francine cried. "They have to help her. She can't be dead. Can't be."

"Sssh. You're all right now. You're safe on the couch."

Her mother fixed her with a wide, uncomprehending stare. "Maggie?"

"It's over, Mom. You're fine now."

"I should have fallen. It's what I deserve. It's all my fault. Everything."

"Stop." Maggie dabbed the tears from her mother's ashen cheeks. "You've had a bad scare, that's all. Just try to relax."

There was a bristling stillness, aftermath of the horror. Maggie watched her mother slowly uncoil and surrender to a sleep of stone exhaustion. Staring at the bisque skin and fine features, Maggie felt a hard swell of affection.

Yes, the woman drove her crazy. But wasn't that par for the treacherous course? Mom had done her parenting job well enough, given it her best. Maggie had enjoyed the essentials: love, warmth, and protection. And her mother had provided an anchor. At times it dragged the bottom, true. But who was perfect?

The harrowing incident had dwarfed the rest of Maggie's problems. Daisy Tyler would get better in time. They'd find other applicants to fill the vacancies in the new group, or they'd run it below capacity. The recurrent window dream had to stop haunting her eventually. Maggie would find something that worked, even if it meant shooting the damned hawk. And if the symposium had to be shelved, she'd think of some other way to fulfill Alex Ivy's outlandish fiscal demands. There was more than one way to skin a rat.

As far as the state's investigation was concerned, Maggie knew she was innocent of professional misconduct, and she intended to prove it beyond a doubt, reasonable or otherwise.

Focusing on that, a crowd of fresh questions jammed

her mind. Who had lodged the absurd complaint against her? Could the whole thing be a further effort to undermine the clinic? Wouldn't surprise her in the least. Poison Ivy was not the type to be stalled by such frivolous issues as ethics, fairness, or truth.

As budding anger nosed out the last of her despair, the phone rang again. It was that obnoxious private investigator from Boston again, still trying to manipulate her into a meeting. More nonsense about his alleged daughter's alleged emotional problems.

As he spoke, the answer to all her impossible questions came into sharp, ugly focus. Alex Ivy was not the prime suspect at all. Detective Sam Bannister must have set up the whole phony state investigation bit to get his hands on the Macklin file. The so-called inspector from the health department was probably some actor Bannister had hired; the allegations were nothing but a vicious ruse. In the shock of the moment last night, Maggie hadn't thought to take a close look at Dean Connell's identification or the document he'd claimed to be a warrant authorizing him to take her files. Bannister. That man would stop at nothing, but Maggie was about to apply the brakes herself.

The black tide had turned. And the sludge was about to be carried out to sea.

CHAPTER

31

"I don't like it, Lenny."

"You don't have to like it, Sam. All you have to do is live with it."

Bannister choked down the last of an English muffin. Price savored the final bites of Sergio's special omelet, mushroom with extra shells, and corralled the remains with a scrap of buttered toast.

"No, I don't. I don't know what Lila's trying to pull, but I'm not going to stand for it."

Last night when Bannister called to speak to Chloe, his ex-wife had claimed the child was sleeping. It was only ten o'clock, and his daughter never turned in before midnight, minimum. You couldn't nail that kid's eyes closed by ten.

Early this morning, he'd phoned again, but Lila claimed Chloe wasn't up yet. When he called half an hour later, his ex-wife said the child had already left for her babysitting job. Bannister had dialed the number there, but the woman who answered informed him that Chloe wasn't expected for another hour.

"If Lila thinks she can keep me from talking to my own daughter, she's dead wrong."

"Get a grip, Sam. Why would Lila do a thing like that?"

"To twist the blade, that's why. To make me suffer. It's what she lives for."

"Maybe so, Sam. But I don't think this has anything to do with Lila. Kids Chloe's age are tough to reach, that's all."

"Are you saying Chloe doesn't want to speak to me? I don't buy that. No goddamned way!"

"Take it easy, will you? You're going to blow a fuse or something."

How was he supposed to take it easy? Bannister imagined a huge chasm yawning between him and his little girl. He pictured Chloe drifting beyond the breach, shrinking to a void in the swelling distance.

"What can I do, Lenny? All of a sudden I don't understand my own kid anymore."

"You're not supposed to, Sam. I told you. Teenagers speak a whole different language."

"Isn't there a Berlitz or something?"

Price patted his plumped belly. "Let's get going. I promised the guy we'd be on time."

Price had arranged an eight-thirty meeting with Kenneth Abby, an art dealer at the venerable Winslow-Gray Gallery at Madison Avenue and Fifty-seventh Street. Abby's home number was next on the list of numbers Theodore Macklin had dialed from the Doubletree Inn before his death. When Price called, the art dealer had not only admitted speaking to Macklin, he was willing to talk to them about it.

Small miracle.

When they arrived at the gallery, the iron security gate was locked. A camera lens scanned the street in rapid sweeps like a paranoid cyclops.

"He's not here, Lenny. Guy makes a big commotion about our being on time, and he's late. I say we take off."

"Be reasonable. It's only eight thirty-two."

"Late's late, Lenny. This whole business is a waste of time as it is."

Seconds later, a gray stretch Lincoln swept up to the curb. A liveried chauffeur emerged and held open the rear door for a dapper man in his forties. Abby was clad in a silver-gray Italian suit, a stiff white-on-white shirt, and gleaming wing tips. His salted hair was parted in the center and styled in dove's wings.

"Sorry to keep you, gentlemen. Traffic was simply

dreadful." Guy sounded as if his tongue had been done with extra starch.

"No problem. We just got here," Price said, ignoring Bannister's grunt of impatience.

"Come in, won't you? Welcome to the Winslow-Gray."

Abby unlatched the gate, unlocked the door, disarmed the security system, and bustled about the gallery flipping on lights and adjusting thermostats.

While he performed his opening exercises, Bannister and Price checked out the gallery collections. The walls in the main room were hung with modern masters. Price rhapsodized over early impressionist works by Berthe Morisot and Mary Cassatt and pieces by the American realists William Merritt Chase, Winslow Homer, and Thomas Eakins. Fizzing over like a kid on Christmas morning, he led Bannister through the small side rooms devoted to postimpressionists including Seurat, Pissarro, Cézanne, and Vuillard.

"You see that Derain, Sammy? Guy was the first to break with the fauvists. Created a huge flap."

"Sure, Lenny. I can imagine."

Having completed his morning ritual, Kenneth Abby joined them. "Now then. Would you gentlemen mind terribly if I catalog some new acquisitions while we chat?"

The walls and floors of the basement-level storeroom were neatly lined with the precious overflow: oils, watercolors, pastels, mixed media, constructions, stone and marble sculpture, graphics, sketches, and photographs. Many of the works were entombed in wooden crates, each scrupulously labeled.

Kenneth Abby spoke in derisive tones about Mary Boone and Leo Castelli and the other upstart art dealers who'd invaded SoHo in the seventies and eighties and promoted what he described as Hula Hoop modernists.

"Salle, Basquiat, Hockney, Motherwell." He sniffed. "All trash. Fads. Flashes in the pan."

He dismissed the entire roster of contemporary artists, including the most respected. Abby claimed their works were only purchased by dumb yuppies with bloated pockets and atrophied tastes.

Winslow-Gray represented over a century of dedicated contribution to the nation's creative consciousness, he said. They employed only the finest curators, catalogers, and restorers, and culled only the best of the best artists for their exclusive clients and exquisite shows.

"I will not allow my works to reside with just anyone," he said with a proprietary sweep of his arm. "These are my children, so to speak. I consider each sale an adoption. Every piece must be placed in a proper home, where it can be guaranteed the love, care, and attention it so richly deserves."

Bannister was tempted to duck the flying horseshit. Price was bobbing his head as if he actually agreed. But Lenny was about as argumentative as rice pudding.

"You said you had business dealings with Theodore Macklin?" Bannister said.

"Yes, many. Ted was quite the canny investor. Last month alone, I sold him a gorgeous bronze by Lipchitz and a fabulous oil by Juan Gris."

"Then the relationship was strictly business?"

"It began that way, though we developed a mutual regard and affection over time. I acted as his personal consultant," Abby answered. "When Ted came across a piece he liked or a new artist he admired, he'd solicit my advice. I also accompanied him to shows and auctions. Our tastes were most compatible."

"You consulted for a fee?" Bannister figured a guy who sold his children wasn't likely to give away his time.

The dealer stiffened. "An hourly rate and a percentage of any resultant purchases. Quite standard in the trade, I assure you."

Bannister didn't bother to say so, but the creep didn't assure him in the least.

"Do you remember what Ted Macklin phoned you about a week ago?" Price asked.

The dealer pressed a finger to his lips and hummed. "Honestly, I don't recall that specific conversation. We talked once or twice a week on average. Sometimes more. If I had to guess, we were probably discussing an upcoming auction at Christie's. Ted and I agreed that market conditions were ripe for some excellent bargain-hunting. And there's a scrumptious little Monet slated to go on the block in a couple of weeks."

While the dealer talked, Price studied the stored works and packing crates. "How many pieces would you say you sold Mr. Macklin over the years?"

"Oh, my. Hundreds. Maybe more."

"So he was a real good customer?"

"Absolutely," Abby said. "Ted will be sorely missed, personally and professionally. Terrible about his death. I can't imagine what prompted him to do such a thing."

"Can you imagine *anyone* who might have prompted him?" Price said.

"Murder, you mean? Heavens, no," Abby exclaimed. "Is that what you suspect?"

"Just covering all the bases," Price said.

Bannister was jangling with impatience. Chloe should be at her sitting job by now. He wanted to hear his daughter's voice. Start to repair the fractured connection between them. He tried to catch Price's attention, but the guy was absorbed in his offhanded snooping around the storeroom. Bannister knew he'd have to wait until his partner had satisfied his ravenous curiosity.

"Guess that about does it, Mr. Abby. Thanks for your time," Price said when Bannister was about to erupt.

"Yeah, it's been a real treat," Bannister said.

"Likewise, I'm sure."

Oven-hot day. The air thrummed with a blue haze, and the choking stench of exhaust fumes. Price shrugged off his plaid sports coat. Bannister shed his tie and rolled up his sleeves.

"That one was a curve ball," Price said. "Kenneth Abby didn't sell any art to Ted Macklin."

"How do you know that?"

"Remember the investment company offices? Macklin had bargain-bin prints on the walls. Starving artist stuff. If he was an art connoisseur, I'm the Easter bunny."

"Damn it, Lenny. I told you this was a waste of time—"

"I wouldn't say that. If anything, the lie makes Abby's connection to Macklin even more intriguing."

"Then how come I'm not the least goddamned bit intrigued?"

Price clacked his tongue. "You write things off too easily, Sammy. Use your imagination. It's even possible this will lead us to a final answer in the Rafferty case."

"How?"

Price gave it his creative best. Suppose Macklin had some unknown accomplice in Martha Rafferty's murder. The original task force had not been able to confirm or deny a possible conspiracy in the killing. But the existence of a confederate would tie up several loose ends in the case against Macklin.

According to Macklin's doorman, young Ted had arrived at the building no more than fifteen minutes after the Rafferty girl's other friends from the party departed, leaving Ted and Martha alone. An accomplice in the murder could have disposed of the girl's remains, freeing Macklin to make his rapid, squeaky-clean appearance at home.

All these years later, when the evidence was closing in on him, it would have been logical for Macklin to contact his former partner in crime for aid, advice, or reassurance. Whoever it was might then have murdered Macklin to ensure his continued silence.

Bannister snorted. "You really believe that?"

"It could be true."

"Yeah. And you *could* be the Easter bunny."

By the time they'd walked the mile and change back to their apartment, Bannister's shirt was glued to his back. Price was flushed and breathing in rasps.

In the dive, they turned the window fan up full, stirring a ponderous breeze. Price was anxious to get on the phone and find out what he could about Kenneth Abby and the Winslow-Gray Gallery, but he wasn't nearly as anxious as Bannister, who grabbed the line like the rip cord on a reserve chute.

Chloe answered on the second ring. Hearing her voice, Bannister's heart started knocking in his throat.

"Hey, sweetheart. How's it going?"

"What's wrong, Daddy? How come you're calling me here?"

"No reason. I just wanted to touch base, see how you're doing."

Her voice was sharp and impatient. "You know I'm working."

It was like a bad sitcom script. *I told you not to call me at the office, darling. What is it this time?*

"You sounded so down the last time we spoke. I just wanted to make sure you're okay."

"I'm not a baby."

"No one thinks you are."

"Then why do you keep checking up on me?"

"I'm not. I care about you, that's all."

"Well, I'm babysitting Timmy, Dad. Not having some wild party."

"I know that, sweetheart. You've just been sounding so down lately. Are you worried about going to high school next year? Is there a problem with Mom?"

Bannister was casting in the wind. Getting nowhere. She wouldn't even answer his questions.

"Can't you please tell me what's bothering you, Chloe? Whatever it is, I'd really like to help."

He'd tried to swallow Price's empty assurances. Hormones raging at flood stage. Temporary, seasonal storms that would recede without a trace of damage. But those pat explanations refused to go down.

"Nothing's bothering me, Daddy. I told you that. I told you and told you and told you. Now will you please get off my case!"

There was a jarring click.

Dial tone.

Bannister took a minute to shake the shock and accept that she'd hung up on him. His head had been lopped off and sent rolling. And his sweet baby girl had swung the ax. He stared at the receiver in disbelief, and then he started dialing again.

Price placed a restraining hand on his forearm. "Don't, Sam. At least give her a few minutes to get herself back together."

"I'm not calling Chloe."

This thing had gone too damned far. No matter how he had to twist her arm, he was going to pull a professional opinion from that mule-headed lady shrink from East End Hospital. If she said that Chloe needed counseling, he'd find some way around Lila and his lack of funds. His anemic insurance would cover only half the cost at best, but money or the lack of it was not going to stand in the way of Chloe's well-being.

A male secretary put him through to Dr. Lyons. Fearful that she'd hang up on him, too, Bannister blurted out the reason for his call. No hedging. His daughter had become moody and unapproachable. He needed to know whether this was normal teenage turbulence or something more. For some nameless reason, the lady shrink's read on the situation was important to him. Instinct told him he could trust her.

Listening to her response, his eyes widened in amazement. He'd expected any number of answers, but the one she offered was not on the list.

One thing he never suffered was a shortage of surprises.

CHAPTER

32

The building superintendent had positioned a makeshift barricade in front of the break in the terrace rail. He promised to replace the missing section as soon as possible.

"Only hang-up is getting the materials," he told Maggie. "Those ironwork places can take forever, and the piece I need isn't a stock size. Can't imagine how it rusted all the way through like that. The rest looks fine."

Maggie kept her eyes away from the jagged break. "It's really dangerous this way, Joe. Can't you tell them it's an emergency?"

"Oh, I'll tell them, Maggie. I'll tell them but good. I keep thinking how lucky it is you were here to help her back inside. Lucky those fallen pieces landed in the shrubbery, too. I thank the Lord no one was hurt, and you can bet I want it to stay that way."

Joe Gerard was a building fixture. He'd been around for the length of Maggie's memory and beyond. Time had dulled his jet hair to charcoal and tanned his ruddy skin to cordovan leather. At sixty-something, there was also a noticeable slackening of his gait and burly build. But Joe was still ready and able to remedy most any ill the building or its ninety residents might think to suffer.

When Maggie was a little girl, the kindly super had always been around to salve skinned knees or bruised feelings. Uncle Joe, as she'd called him then, had a seemingly inexhaustible supply of patience and understanding. Everyone liked and trusted the man, including Maggie's mother, whose very existence was based on the presumption of universal guilt.

"Is Mrs. Lyons all right?" He frowned at her sleeping mother on the couch. Francine hadn't budged in over an hour. Even Joe's hammering on the terrace had failed to rouse her.

"She's had a bad scare, that's all. The shock wiped her out. She'll be fine."

"Too bad it had to happen to her of all people. Fine woman, your mother. But not exactly what you'd call easygoing."

"Not exactly."

The landscape of Maggie's youth had been littered with her mother's incessant warnings and dire predictions. Mom was omnipresent, all-nervous, and a devout proponent of Lyons's Law of Perpetual Misfortune. Any rotten thing you could imagine happening would. Any horror you failed to fathom and fret about would occur that much sooner. No amount of worry or caution was nearly sufficient. The world was a malevolent place, pocked by obvious and invisible pitfalls. Small wonder Maggie had developed a few irrational fears of her own. The amazing thing was that she wasn't every bit as phobic as Daisy Tyler.

"Listen, Joe. I hate to ask, but I have to take care of something at work. I asked my aunt to come over, but it'll take her an hour or more to get here from Stamford."

"No problem. Be glad to keep an eye on your mom. My pleasure."

The bundle on Maggie's back lightened by several bricks. "You're a national treasure."

He flapped away the compliment. "Go on about your business now. With all the crazies running loose in this town, you can't afford to be taking time off."

Maggie hurried to the hospital. She was anxious to check on a couple of things before her scheduled meeting. Her first stop was the second-floor patient wing, where she found Daisy Tyler in bed, staring at a quiz show. Woman had the limp, sorry look of a picked-over buffet.

"Feeling better, Daisy? Heard you had a bad night."

Daisy issued a trembly sigh. "Can't imagine what got into me all of a sudden, Dr. Lyons. I was fine through dinner. Ate like a horse, in fact, especially the sweets. Afterward, I went to take a shower and wash my hair. I was having a grand old time, singing to myself and everything. But next thing I knew, I was Screaming Mimi again. Took three nurses to get me dried off, dressed, and back to bed."

"Try to forget it," Maggie said. "Everyone has times when they backslide. You'll have fewer and fewer bad moments as you go along."

Daisy shuddered. "I'm so embarrassed. Imagine me standing there dripping wet and buck naked. Screeching like a banshee. Can't imagine what they must think of me."

"They think you're a courageous woman who's dealing with a very difficult problem, that's what. Now get some rest. That's an order."

"I'm supposed to meet Dr. Goldberg for lunch at twelve-thirty. Thought I was even ready to try getting down there by myself. But I'm really not up to it today."

"I'll tell him. You just take it easy. Don't worry about a thing."

"That'll be the day," Daisy said. Her voice was winding down like a Victrola. "Guess I could use a little nap. . . ."

"Good idea. I'll check back with you later."

Still half an hour until her meeting. Restless, Maggie headed to her office. Henry greeted her with a worried look.

"I heard about the health department investigation. I'm so sorry, Maggie."

Maggie hadn't told her assistant or anyone about the charges against her. Henry had been gone by the time she'd finished talking to the so-called state investigator the previous night. Clearly, the news of her impending demise was already spreading like a bad flu.

He bristled. "Imagine them suggesting you hurt some of your patients. I'd like to tell them a thing or two."

"You're a pal, Henry."

"Are you all right? Anything I can do?"

"Don't worry. It's all going to work out. And soon."

"Of course it will. Coffee?"

"Thanks. That'd be nice."

Interrupted by the phony investigator's sudden appearance, she hadn't yet dictated her report on the latest meeting of the Thursday Night Lyons Club. Popping a fresh tape in her recorder, she worked to set the scene in her mind.

Reconstructing the session, she was struck again by the enthusiastic pitch of the group. She pictured the ring of shining eyes. The flushed faces. The flood of eager words. They'd been like kids playing chicken, pressing each other to edge past their usual limits.

But that was the whole point of the program. Group support was intended to inspire the phobic to take chances. Their brash risks were other people's baby steps. There was no danger in the clinic's approach. Nothing to move her to apology or regret.

So why was she still uneasy about the whole thing, even though she knew the investigation was a sham?

Finished taping her impressions, she headed out to her appointment. Drew Paulson, the department's chief creep, peered up as she passed his office. Thick lenses gave the doctor's eyes the look of snails bobbling in an aquarium. His smile bared teeth the color of old parchment.

"So sorry to hear of your dreadful troubles, Dr. Lyons."

"What troubles?"

She returned his phony grin. The man was dying to see her squirm. And Maggie had no intention of playing hooked worm to his starving sea bass.

Paulson stridently believed that phobics needed years of intensive analysis. He'd never hesitated to express his contempt for Maggie and the clinic's short-term approach. With regularity, his disdain erupted in a hot accusatory torrent.

Maggie vividly recalled his tirade at a recent staff meeting. "It's unconscionable, Dr. Lyons. Your so-called therapy puts your patients at risk for irreparable damage. *Physician, do no harm.* Remember?"

Refusing to be baited by his acidic challenge, Maggie had tried to view the issue from Paulson's unfortunate perspective. In Freudian terms, she could well understand what had triggered the man's idiotic outburst. Drew Paulson was fixated at the anal stage. He had his head firmly planted up his butt.

But that was his problem, and Maggie had an ample supply of her own.

"If the Health Department finds against you, I suppose it could mean your career. . . ."

"Sorry to disappoint you, Dr. Paulson. But that's not going to happen." She pushed through the outer doors, feeling his enraged eyes on her.

The day had heated to a boil. Maggie's skirt clung like plastic wrap, and her blouse was fusing to her skin. Many others consigned to the urban kiln had adapted by shedding their customary skins, opting instead for bare legs and midriffs, plunging necklines, and skeletal shoes. But Maggie's discomfort added welcome fuel to her raging ire.

Evenings, the Intensive Care Saloon on First Avenue was packed with East End staffers seeking to blunt the strain of the work with doses of anaesthetic on the rocks. At eleven on a weekday morning, however, only a few tables were occupied.

Maggie spotted the detective reading the *Times* and sipping coffee at a booth in the rear. She took in his smoky eyes, tousled hair, and chiseled features. Bannister had the sort of arrogant good looks that come packaged with a matching attitude.

She slid in opposite him, wove her fingers together, and held her tone at a strained neutral.

"I want you to know I have never harbored truly murderous urges before, Mr. Bannister. But you have managed to change that."

He looked startled. "Wait a minute. When I called this morning, you said you'd be delighted to meet with me. You said you were very anxious to hear what I had to say."

"And I am. But first, you will return my files. Next, you'll write a statement explaining your little scam in detail. Then I'll approach the proper authorities. After I have your license revoked and file the civil suit against you, I can't wait to hear exactly what you have to say."

"Try not to take this the wrong way, Doctor. But I think maybe you caught something from one of your patients."

"Get off it. The game's over, and you lost. I want the Weider and Macklin files back. Now. Today. You deliver them to me within the next thirty minutes, or I'll add criminal charges to the list. I'll be in my office."

She stood to leave. Bannister cuffed her wrist with firm fingers. "Look. I don't know what the hell you're talking about. The only reason I called was to get your advice about my little girl. Something's wrong with her, and she won't let me get close enough to find out what it is."

Maggie was incredulous. The man wouldn't even give up when he'd been hooked, reeled, and left flapping in the boat.

"*Enough*, Mr. Bannister. I told you, I'm not playing your stupid game. What can you possibly hope to accomplish by continuing with this line of nonsense?"

"All I'm trying to do is help my daughter, damn it. I wouldn't make up a thing like this." He tugged out his wallet and flipped it open. "Look what a beautiful kid she is. Always had a beautiful nature, too. But she's changed. She's upset, angry. Flies off at the slightest thing. I'm scared to death she's going to do something crazy, get herself into some kind of trouble."

Maggie searched for signs of insincerity, but found none. Eyeing the open wallet, she saw a photograph of Bannister with his arm around a pretty young girl. The resemblance was undeniable. Definitely daddy and daughter.

"You're serious," she stammered.

"Forget it. If you won't listen, I'll find someone who will." Catching the waiter's eye, he motioned angrily for the check.

The truth seeped under Maggie's skin. There was no perverse scheme or cruel practical joke. Bannister hadn't taken those files. Dean Connell and his terrifying investigation were for real. Maggie's work and future and the clinic she'd nurtured from its infancy were really on the line.

And maybe more.

Bannister tossed a bill on the check and pushed back his chair.

"Wait, Mr. Bannister. I'm sorry. I was wrong."

His anger flared. "No, I was. I thought you were smart and solid and really gave a damn about rescuing people in trouble. I thought maybe you could help me figure out what the hell to do about my little girl."

"Maybe I can."

"You expect me to believe you're anxious to help me all of a sudden? Forget it, lady. I'm not nearly as dumb as you obviously think."

"Not anxious, but I'm willing."

"And why is that?"

"Because I can see you really care about your daughter, and that scores a lot of points with me."

He stared at her. His eyes were coal hard and filled with challenge. "And?"

"And because I feel guilty for misjudging you."

"And?"

"That's not enough?"

"Even Mother Teresa has her own agenda," Bannister said. "What's in it for you?"

"I have a feeling you might be able to help me in exchange."

There was a bristling pause. Bannister stared at her as if she were mounted on a slide. "How?"

Maggie told him about the health department's inquiry into her professional conduct. She recounted the inexplicable circumstances of Theodore Macklin's and Gail Weider's deaths and the horrifying suspicions those deaths had spawned.

"The state investigator treated me like Jack the Ripper. Somehow, they've gotten it in their heads that those two deaths are connected and that I did something to cause them. I have to know exactly what's going on, and how to make it go away."

As she spoke, one disconcerting fact occurred to her for

the first time. Gail Weider had died only five days ago. The authorities in Albany could not have known anything about that incident or Maggie's brief, distant link to Theodore Macklin unless the information had been fed to them by someone at East End.

The entire dreadful business might be a further attempt by Poison Ivy to scuttle her and the clinic. Or it could be an attempt at professional subterfuge by someone else. Drew Paulson came immediately to mind. The doctor was unbalanced enough to attempt to destroy her. And Maggie knew there could be others. Any one of her more cordial colleagues might harbor secret resentments. There was always the possibility of a disgruntled ex-patient or someone on staff with a real or imagined gripe against her. She didn't have to be paranoid to acknowledge the grotesque possibilities. She'd learned long ago there was never a threatened shortage of the irrational or irate.

A glint of mischief lightened Bannister's grim expression. "If I agree, Doc, you'll have to give me full access to the information *I* need."

"You'll have it."

"Including Macklin's file."

"I'm afraid that's impossible. The state investigator took his records and Gail Weider's. I have no copies."

Before Bannister's face could fall the rest of the way, Maggie assured him that she could reconstruct much of Macklin's record from memory and whatever notes or tapes she might still have on hand.

"I've already spent hours reliving my sessions with him, Detective. But I have to be honest with you, I can't remember anything he said that was anything close to a murder confession."

"But you weren't looking for one. All I want is the best possible chance here, Dr. Lyons. And I'll do anything it takes to have that."

"My sentiments exactly."

Maggie was not about to sit back and play the helpless victim. Someone was out to get her, and she refused to do her fighting in the dark.

CHAPTER

33

From Maggie's office, Bannister phoned his daughter at her babysitting job. Waiting for an answer, he had the look of someone trapped with a ticking bomb.

As Maggie had suggested, he told Chloe a friend of his wanted to talk to her. He made sure the timing was acceptable. Fortunately, his daughter's small charge had just settled in for a nap. Bannister's eyes were dark with pleading as he handed the phone to Maggie.

At first, the girl sounded suitably tentative. Maggie explained who she was and why Bannister had suggested they speak. She was careful to couch it in terms even the testiest adolescent would find acceptable. No assignment of blame. No stifling parental concerns or suspicions. This was a simple fact-finding mission, hostile territory or no.

Maggie explained that it was her job to help people manage difficult feelings and troubling experiences. Everyone could benefit from an extra pair of ears once in a while. It had nothing to do with being weak or immature or abnormal in any way.

As the girl responded, Maggie probed gently, trying to part the child's defenses and peek inside. Checking for troubling undercurrents, she searched for chinks and cracks beneath the level surface, examining each stingy scrap of information, searching between the lines until she had enough to make a reasonable judgment. By the time she hung up, Bannister was on the brink of explosion.

"How was she? What did she say? What do you think? Did she tell you what's wrong?"

"No. And I'm not convinced there is anything wrong."

He looked stricken. "But you don't understand. I know Chloe better than anyone. She's not herself. You have to believe me. Anything happens to that kid, I don't know what I'll do. She's all that matters to me. Everything."

"I do understand. And I don't doubt she seems different to you. She probably *is* different. Kids her age go through major changes, physically and emotionally. It can be very disturbing for a parent, especially one who doesn't see the child every day."

"But it's more than that. There's something really wrong. I know it."

"She sounds all right to me, but I certainly can't make a firm assessment from one fifteen-minute call. Why don't I recommend someone in the Boston area? A session or two, and I'm sure any good therapist will be able to determine whether there's a significant problem or not."

She retrieved a professional directory from her bookshelf and started leafing through it.

"Why can't you do that?" Bannister demanded.

"Because I'm here and Chloe's there."

"But you were able to get through to her. Isn't it possible to do these sessions on the phone?"

"Yes, but it makes more sense for her to work with someone face-to-face."

He reached over and shut the directory. "I want you to do it. I liked the way you spoke to her. I liked that she didn't blow you off or get upset. Who says she'll click like that with somebody else?"

"I have no special magic, Mr. Bannister."

He caught her gaze and held it. "Please."

Maggie passed a beat in silent argument. "All right, but if she needs treatment, you'll have to find someone in her area."

"Deal. When's good for you to speak to her again? I'll set it up with Chloe."

Maggie suggested a time late that afternoon, and they agreed to meet again afterward. Meantime, Maggie would begin reconstructing Macklin's records. Bannister promised to use the time to start unraveling the inside story on the health department's investigation.

His smile was impish. "Looks like we're in this together, Doc."

"Only for as long as it takes, Detective."

In the hospital lobby, Maggie spotted Mitch Goldberg loitering outside the cafeteria. Aiming the detective toward the exit, she went over to talk to the resident. She didn't notice Bannister loitering at the door, watching her with the young doctor until envy forced him outside for a breath of stale air.

"You wouldn't happen to be waiting for Daisy Tyler?" Maggie asked Mitch.

He eyed his watch. "Actually, I am, but I think she's standing me up."

"Sorry, it's my fault. She asked me to tell you she wasn't feeling up to lunch today. Slipped my mind."

He grinned. "Then I'd say you have the moral obligation to take her place."

Maggie was tempted. Mitch was good company. And she could well imagine the scene at home with Aunt Hannah and her mother. Symphonic hysteria. The Doom Sisters performing in Be Major. But a guilt-edged chain was tugging her back to the apartment.

"Sorry. I'd honestly like to. But today's not good."

He registered a flattering trace of disappointment. "We still on for tomorrow night?"

"Tomorrow? Oh, right. My place at seven?"

"Sounds good."

The dinner had also slipped her mind. More to do. She'd have to call her father and make plans. Pick up snacks. Thinking of tiny Tina, she wondered what went with Shirley Temples. Her father most definitely did not.

Nor did her mother.

Before tomorrow night, Maggie would have to find some way to ease Mom out of the apartment. Even if they wound up meeting at the restaurant, her mother would not take well to Maggie's consorting with the enemy.

Entering her apartment, she found Hannah and her

mother huddled at the kitchen table. The sisters were sipping tea and sighing in practiced harmony.

"Feeling better, Mom?"

"How can I feel?"

"You can feel glad that you weren't hurt."

"What kind of a way is that to talk to your mother?" Hannah snapped.

"An honest way."

"Don't be fresh, Maggie," her mother chided.

Hannah clacked her tongue. "Such a terrible thing to happen. The worst."

"Come on, Aunt Hannah. Mom's fine. Thankfully, no damage was done. No one was hurt. That's hardly the worst."

Both sisters glowered at her. "I'd think you, of all people, would be more understanding," Hannah huffed.

"Then you'd be wrong." Normally, Maggie had the sense and forbearance to keep her unwelcome logic to herself, but the strain of the past few days and her dream-shattered sleep had frayed her patience.

Francine's eyes widened. "Margaret Lyons, what on earth's gotten into you? Apologize to your Aunt Hannah."

"For what?"

"I am shocked," her mother sputtered. "Shocked and disappointed."

"I know that, Mom. That is your response to everything: shock and disappointment. I just wish you could see that you have a choice. You could choose to be happy. You could choose to let the anger and frustration go. You could decide to enjoy your life for a change."

"That's easy for you to say. You haven't lived through the things I have."

"What things?" Maggie demanded. "What's been so goddamned awful?"

"You watch your tone, young lady."

"Damn it, Mom! When are you going to give it up?"

"The nerve of you, Maggie. Who do you think you are? I will not be spoken to that way. Let's go, Hannah."

Her mother stormed toward the guest room with Hannah trailing tightly in her wake. Drawers slammed, followed by the click of luggage latches. Maggie's reflex was to follow them and atone for some mystery sin. But she resisted the self-destructive urge.

For as long as she could remember, Maggie had caved under the weight of her mother's overwhelming demands and fragility. Even as a child, she'd felt the need to tiptoe around the woman's countless raw spots and sensitivities. Little girl or no, she'd viewed herself as stronger and therefore somehow responsible for preserving her mother's tenuous well-being.

During her training analysis, however, she'd learned to let much of it go. She could not be her mother's mother. Maggie had no power to repair her mother's wounds or unburden the woman of her corrosive secrets. Mom had to take responsibility for her own healing and happiness.

A door slammed down the hall. The sisters formed a wedge at the kitchen door. Hannah clutched a lace handkerchief. Francine led with a quivering lip. "I'm going now, Maggie. You can call me when you're ready to apologize."

"I'm sorry you're upset, Mom. But I will not apologize."

Hannah ticked her tongue. "You used to be such a sweet girl, Maggie. I don't know what's gotten into you."

"Maybe a little sense," Maggie muttered.

Tears welled in her mother's eyes. "You're getting to be just like your father. You know that, Maggie? You're getting to be as thoughtless and insensitive as that son of a bitch."

Faced with her mother's pain and anger, Maggie expected a penitent pull. But she felt none. Nothing pierced her numb weariness but a treacherous scrap of understanding for her father's defection. She had always viewed his leaving them as an inexcusable betrayal. But now she began to see it as a logical means to survive. Lash yourself to a sinking ship, you're asking to be pulled under.

"Bye, Mom," she said dully.

"Come, Fran." Aunt Hannah gripped her sister by the bent elbow like a broken bird. "You'll stay at my place. Take it easy for a few days." Turning from the room, Hannah stroked her sister's hair and soothed her with syrupy assurances.

"There, there. You know how selfish young people can be. She's a good girl. She'll come to her senses."

Maggie listened to the smack of the apartment door as it shut the women outside.

She had turned away wearily when she heard the knock. Mother must have forgotten something. A parting shot of some sort, no doubt, Maggie thought.

Opening the door, she was surprised and infuriated by the sight of F.X. Kennedy holding a paper sack. The aide's eyes were bloodshot, and there was a hard set to his mouth.

"You shouldn't have come here, F.X."

"I told the doorman I had groceries to deliver. Clever, huh?"

"What do you want?"

"I want to know what the hell I did to you, Maggie. Here I try to be nice and friendly, and all I get's the brush-off."

He was trying to bully his way through the door. Maggie refused to budge and give him an opening.

"Please leave, Francis. I don't appreciate your showing up at my door like this."

He glowered. "You don't appreciate anything, do you, you snobby bitch?"

"That's enough. Get out now, or I'll call the police. And don't bother coming back to the clinic. You'd be better off seeing some other doctor to get yourself back on track."

"What the hell do you know?"

He made a move toward her. With a firm push at his shoulders, Maggie maneuvered him back so she was able to slam the door. Then she went to the kitchen and sat at the table. Pressing her hands against the table's surface to keep them from trembling, she waited for his vicious hammering at the door to stop.

For a long time afterward, she sat alone in the gathering silence.

CHAPTER

34

Jessie carried a bag of beach toys to the car, her flip-flops slapping the walk. The ruffled rear of her swimsuit wobbled, ducklike, and her pigtails were a set of yellow swings.

Peering out from the living room, Jason could read his mother's impatience. She stood in the driveway beside the station wagon, tapping her sandaled foot. Mom took the toys from Jessie and stuffed them in the trunk alongside the picnic cooler, an old army blanket, the tote full of sunscreens and extra clothes, and the stack of candy-striped towels. Swiping the sweat from her forehead, she slammed the hatch.

"Hop in and buckle up, Jess. I'll be back in a minute."

Mom approached the house. Lit by hazy sunshine, her hair was a wreath of dried wheat. Jason sensed the hard press of heat around her. Her steps were plodding, her arms limp. She squinted in the glare.

With a squeeze of shame, Jason noticed how poor she looked. Ill-tended. He should be helping out, making money to ease the family burden. Mom was wearing one of Dad's old shirts over a shabby black tank suit. Beneath the slack elastic, her legs were milk-pale and mapped with bulging veins. A strap on her sandal was torn and flapping.

Stepping into the foyer, she breathed her relief. "Lord, it's hot out there. Nice and cool in the house, at least."

"Supposed to hit a hundred or more. Probably break the record," Jason said.

"Bound to be cooler at the beach, Jay. Sure you don't want to come along?"

"Nah. You go ahead. I'd as soon stay in the den with the air on."

"For once, I can't say I blame you. If I hadn't promised Jessie and her friends, that's where I'd be headed. Guess there are worse things than three little girls in hundred-degree weather. But I honestly can't think of any."

"Try a hundred little girls in three-degree weather."

Her laugh was a trill. "Now there's a thought to get me through the day."

"See you later then."

"We should be back around five or so, depending on traffic."

He shrugged. "Sure. Whenever."

"Bye now."

Once the car had slid out of sight, Jason felt a surge of triumph. Two down. One final interference to eliminate, and he could begin.

He dialed his aide's number. Binnie picked up on one of those godawful speakerphones. She was huffing like a steam train.

"Hullo?"

Her phone gave the connection a hollow timbre. Thing made Jason feel as if he were trapped in a bowling alley. Toss the voice. Catch the rumbling echo. Wait out the long, reverberating beat before the clash.

"Hi, Binnie. It's Jason. You sound out of breath."

"Working out on my stationary bike," she panted. "Very cardiovascular. Only two more miles to go, a quick shower, and I'm out of here. Should be your way right on schedule."

"Actually, I called to cancel for today. I'm not feeling well."

"Oh, that's too bad, hon. You running a fever?"

"No. Just a cold, I think."

"Maybe do you good to get out for a bit, then."

He raised his middle finger. "Not today. I'm really feeling lousy. And it's hot as a boiled bitch outside."

Her laugh was direct from the funhouse. "Never heard

that one before, but it's true enough. Guess we'll leave today alone. We can touch base first thing tomorrow morning and see how you're doing."

"Right."

"Bye, then. Keep cool. And feel better."

"Oh, I will."

Hanging up, he felt better already. In the kitchen, he bolted a chocolate doughnut and chased it back with a slug of orange juice from the plastic carton.

Bounding up the stairs, he headed for his closet. His remaining supply of C2BU was hidden behind the shoe box where he kept his skin magazines, his ossified condoms, and the pictures of Rina Latham he'd snapped sophomore year when she was cheerleading at a pep rally.

Jason could still see her bouncing boobs, the creamy turn of her thighs, the tiny skirt twirling up to reveal the white panties stretched over the V of her crotch.

Jason had been mesmerized by that V. He'd worked its endless possibilities in his fevered brain. V for Very Warm. V for the Village of his Vigorous, Voracious Longings. V for Victory over the choking chains of perpetual Virginity. Three years, and the titillating power of that V was undiminished. Even now, desire squeezed him so hard his eyes watered. But today he resisted the pressing urge to seek release. Proving himself and his formula had to come first. The rest would follow. Anything would be possible after that.

Retrieving his precious invention, he noticed that the beaker was more than half empty. Strange. He hadn't realized he'd used so much. Soon, he'd have to mix a fresh batch. That would mean a trip to the pharmacy for ingredients, a visit to Otto Allen at school for other necessary substances, and an hour or more down in the basement lab to do the actual measuring and mixing.

The thought sent his pulse racing and stole his breath. But he caught the panic before it could race away like a wild horse, dragging him helplessly behind. None of it would be difficult on the formula. On C2BU he could do anything.

Be anything.

Jason dosed himself and stepped into the shower. He turned the pressure up full. Raising his chin, he let the needle-hard spray pelt his face. Turning, he relished the tapping tingle on his shoulders.

He toweled off on the way to his room, dripping a trail on the hall carpet. Infused by the first jolts of power, he clipped the legs off a pair of jeans and sliced the neck and sleeves out of a T-shirt. Dressed, he slicked his wet hair straight back and slapped his cheeks with after-shave. Appraising his image in the mirror on the back of his door, he declared himself ready for the debut of his astonishing new role: *Jason Childs:* HUMAN.

Outside, he squinted to blunt the glare. The street was deserted. Straining hard, he caught the distant rush of traffic and the vague thunder of a passing plane. Overture and orchestra.

He started down the block, trampling the lanky sprawl of his own shadow. The heat was harsh and fiercely penetrating. His hair dried in a blink, and he started to perspire. Sweat stung his eyes and trailed south from his neck and armpits. Much more of this blasted heat, and he'd need another shower. But the show must go on.

"Curtain going up," he intoned. "At rise: Jason Childs, simpering nonperson, cowers into view from upstage right. Clutching the ewer with trembling hands, he imbibes the magic potion. There's a striking blast and a cloud of smoke. It clears, revealing the young man who's been recast as a sinewy giant. He moves with the skulking strides of a great cat. His eyes are hazard lights, flashing danger. He farts fire."

Jason laughed aloud. He had always been his own best audience. Best and only, for that matter. But this was a performance worthy of his standing ovation. He was out alone. Unafraid. Going somewhere.

But where?

Walking quickly, he came to the end of his block and continued straight to the intersection of Magruder and Hillandale. Hesitating at the corner, he remembered his last foray in the neighborhood with Binnie. He recalled the snarling dogs leaping at the fence. Lunging at him.

But there had been no real cause for concern. The fence was steel wire, eight feet high, chained, and locked. The trauma had been a simple product of his pretzel-twisted brain.

He veered left to the deeper shade and greater challenge of Hillandale. Passing a half-dozen somnolent houses, he came to the corner of Somerset. Stalled for a second at the corner, he inhaled deeply and prepared himself for the jolting change in the face of the neighborhood.

But he was not prepared for the red convertible that came barreling toward him as he was about to turn the corner. It spat a round of honks and a chorus of taunting voices.

"Hey, Jason!"

"Look, it's the Childs-monster!"

"Hey, Frankenstein old pal, how's it hanging?"

Mike Marchand was at the wheel. Brad Smith rode shotgun. Jason spotted Alyssa Hutt and Nancy Pearce seated like bookends at the rear windows. The last passenger remained obscured until the crimson car had come up idling beside him: Rina Latham.

A sledge pounded in Jason's chest, and he felt a rising flush.

"Hey, Rina, look. It's your number-one fan," Brad said.

"Come on over and give your dream girl a little smooch, Dr. Frankenstein," Alyssa taunted.

Blood thundered in Jason's head, and his heart started bucking like a mechanical bull. He couldn't do anything, couldn't say anything. The mocking voices pierced him like a rain of darts.

"Aw, look, he's embarrassed," Mike said.

Brad piped in. "Don't be embarrassed, Childs-man. Rina has that effect on lots of guys. In fact, she's just been named poster child for the National Wet Dream Association, haven't you, gorgeous?"

"Perfect match for Jason Childs, king of the nightmare dorks. Right, Rina baby?" Mike said.

"How can that be, Mike? I thought you were king of

the nightmare dorks." Jason heard Rina's voice and his cheeks burned with shame.

"Look at that. He's got a little lion hanging from his neck. Isn't that precious?" Nancy said.

"Very sweet," Brad said. "Come on, let's get out of here before all the sugar makes me puke."

His words evaporated in a trail of noisy exhaust as Mike gunned the engine and took off down the block.

Overwhelmed by rage and humiliation, Jason shivered in the heat. All the vicious moments from his past came flooding back. The taunts and insults. The loaded looks and whispered comments. The wire-capped wall of inclusion they'd built to keep his kind outside.

For as long as he could remember, the other kids had picked at him like a flock of predatory birds. Pecking away. Eroding every scrap of hope or confidence. His weaknesses were their seed and gravel. They honed their spiteful beaks on his inexcusable strengths. His clumsiness and shyness were fair targets. But so was his superior skill in science and math. Dr. Frankenstein, they called him. The mad scientist.

Well, now he was fuming mad. Sons of bitches had no right to mock or belittle him. Couldn't they see? He was tottering at the brink of greatness.

The hell with all of them. Rina Latham included. If she were worth a damn, she wouldn't have let them talk that way about her. Bitch probably enjoyed it. Probably got off on everyone wanting her, sniffing after her like animals in heat. She certainly asked for it with her clinging tops and her skimpy shorts and the skirts that barely covered her biggest question.

Probably got it, too. With a swell of revulsion, Jason imagined the ripe, provocative body crawling with sexually transmittable diseases.

The hell with her, too.

He'd show them. Sucking a ragged breath, Jason reaffirmed his sense of purpose. Those assholes weren't going to get him down or derail him. Jason Childs would show them all.

He rounded the corner onto Somerset. The vacant lot

was strewn with beer bottles, crack vials, crumpled food wrappers, paper scraps, and glinting shards of broken glass. Ripping the chain off his neck, he flung his stupid little silver lion at the sprawl of trash.

Jason continued on his way. Hammering and a spraying sound escaped the closed bays of the body shop. Passing the dilapidated Victorian, he thought of the fenced house beyond.

Nothing to fear.

They were only dumb animals.

As he approached the yard, the trio of growling beasts came lunging at the fence. Hatred rumbled deep in their chests, but Jason didn't feel a lick of anxiety.

He stopped to watch as they hurled themselves repeatedly against the wall of wire. Stupid mutts. Again and again, they heaved at the fence, smashed their dopey heads. Then they backed away dazed and whimpering only to recover and repeat the ridiculous exercise.

Jason snickered. "Hey, Bozo. Come on, come get me."

Gleefully, he egged them on. The dogs kept charging and stumbling backward until all three of them were limp and panting. Finally, they slunk away and settled under a leafy elm to sleep it off.

"Hey, you dopey jerks. Come back here. I'm not through with you yet."

One of the dogs shut his eyes and dropped his muzzle on his paws like a paperweight. The others were laid out like door mats, panting in the fierce heat.

"You hear me? I said, I'm not through."

No response.

"Don't you *dare* ignore me, you dumb bitches! Get back here!"

He waited, but although their eyes were on him, there wasn't a hint of movement.

"No? Fine, then. I'll come show you who's boss."

The lock was no problem. Prodding with his house key, Jason was able to free the loop of metal holding the chain. The line of links came away with a satisfying jingle; the gate squealed open.

Loping across the yard, Jason imagined Binnie's stupid camera on him.

"Lights . . . action. Our hero steps boldly toward the ring of sleeping giants. Unafraid, he walks into the lair and gives the stupid beasts their wake-up call."

He stopped beside the rottweiler. Rheumy-eyed beast's tongue was lolling like a fat pink scarf. Swallowing a swell of nausea, Jason nudged the heaving rib cage with the toe of his sneaker.

"Get up, you dumb jerk. You don't ignore me."

Jason assumed a boxing stance. He feinted and punched, working his feet around the somnolent beasts. Jabbing them playfully in turn.

"Right uppercut, left hook."

The nearest dog lifted its mammoth head off its muzzle and rose slowly to its feet. The others followed like swamp creatures rising from the muck. For the first time, Jason felt a tic of anxiety, and his feet stalled. He searched for a joke to chase away the rising terror. But he couldn't think of one. Nothing penetrated the tidal wave of fear.

The dogs began circling like vultures over dead flesh. Jason struggled against the dark waves of dizzy terror that threatened to drag him under.

Think, Jason. Get a hold of yourself.

Scraps of sense invaded the blackness. All he had to do was run. He could race through the gate and shut the beasts inside. All he had to do was find a way to get the signals from his mind to his frozen muscles.

You can do it, Jason. You have to do it!

The thoughts were beginning to penetrate as the first vice of teeth clamped his leg. As he struggled to get away, a massive weight was hurled at him, knocking him defenseless to the ground.

CHAPTER

35

Bannister left the hospital humming. Things were definitely on the upswing. One of Price's countless contacts would get the scoop on the State Health Department's probe of Dr. Lyons. In exchange, the lady shrink would help him get a handle on what was going on with his daughter. In the bargain, he'd finally have his look at the rotten lining of Theodore Macklin's psyche.

Bannister remained confident that Macklin's couch confessionals would contain some sort of damning evidence of his guilt in the murder of Martha Rafferty. Mrs. Rafferty's reward check was so close, Bannister barely had to stretch to get the feel of it. And there would be the satisfying bonus of nailing that scumbag Macklin, even in death. Bannister had always believed in judicial symmetry. What goes around should definitely come around.

But sometimes what goes around, goes flat. Passing the Camaro, he spied a ticket drooping from the windshield wiper. Reading the citation, he discovered that the parking spot he'd found yesterday after a nationwide search was for vehicles with diplomatic permits only. Half a block away, a sign the size of a flea bite confirmed the bad news. And to add injury to the forty-five-buck insult, now he had to find another space.

Twice during the scouting expedition, the heat warning light flashed on his dashboard, and a steam genie levitated from the hood. By the time he finally landed a legal spot ten blocks up and two over, his radiator wasn't the only thing boiling over.

On the way back to the dump, he dined on a street vendor hot dog with a frozen center and a rock-solid roll. Half a block from home base, he stepped in a flagrant violation of the pooper scooper laws. Some years, it honestly didn't pay to get out of bed in the morning.

Parking his soiled shoes and simmering temper on the doormat, he let himself into the dump. Price was sprawled on the couch in his skivvies, reading the paper.

"Hi, honey, I'm home," Bannister said.

"Hey, Sam. Hot enough for you?"

As usual, Price was in fine humor and had a productive morning to report. A contact at Customs was tracing import-export invoices from the Winslow-Gray Gallery. A friend-of-a-friend from an international news clipping service was running down the peripatetic career of songbird Fern Compton Harlow. Nemichev and Sons, Anatoly Popov, Howard the Frog, and Alter Ego, Inc., were being dissected by a team including a friend of Price's at Internal Revenue, a mole in the Attorney General's office, and a pal from Rackets and Frauds. Price also had phone company and banking buddies working on any hidden links between the diverse characters and companies on Macklin's final call list from the Newport hotel.

"Looks like you've been a busy bee," Bannister said. "All I managed to do was get a full promise of cooperation from Macklin's lady shrink."

Price was suitably impressed. Bannister could tell by the way he flipped from the sports section to Op Ed and scratched behind an ear.

"I mean it, Lenny. Dr. Lyons is going to give us everything she's got on Macklin."

This time, Price was so moved, he shut the paper and yawned. "In exchange for what, Sammy?"

"Nothing. A few phone calls, a half hour's work, tops."

"What work? Which calls? Come on, Sam. This thing has gotten way bigger than we bargained for already. It's starting to get that Schildhauer smell about it."

"Don't get yourself in an uproar. I'm willing to take on all the tough stuff. All you have to do is run down the source of a complaint for me, and we get the Macklin file."

Price frowned. "I still think you're barking up an empty tree, Sam. I bet Macklin didn't confess the Rafferty murder to that lady shrink or anybody else."

"Thanks, Lenny. I knew you'd go along."

"When did I agree to do that?"

Bannister waggled a finger. "You see? That's what happens when you don't pay attention."

He briefed Price about the allegations against Dr. Lyons and her visit last night from Dean Connell of the State Health Department's investigation unit.

Price's frown deepened. "Pretty strange that two of her patients died one right after the other like that."

"It's a coincidence, Lenny. There's no way in hell Maggie Lyons is responsible. Don't even suggest it. Not for a damned second."

Price held up a hand. "Down, boy. Easy. I'm not suggesting anything." His face went coy. "Except maybe that someone I know seems to have fallen like a brick for a lady shrink."

"My ass, Lenny. This is strictly business."

Price smirked. "Sure, Sam. Sure."

"I mean it, Price. I told you, I'm off women. Besides, this one's got a boyfriend. Some jerky, smooth-cheeked doctor-in-training. Looks like a dark Dennis the Menace. Can't imagine what she sees in him. Not that I care."

Price's look was impish. "Of course you don't. After all, it's strictly business."

"Right. So what do you think about this Health Department thing?"

"Odd that the investigator would demand those patient files right off like that," Price mused.

"That occurred to me, too. I figure this Connell character must have storm trooper tendencies."

Price mulled it over for a minute. "Or it could be this case has been placed on the center front burner for some reason. Sounds as if that investigator was real eager not to let anything slip. So eager, he was willing to risk being accused of trampling Dr. Lyons's legal rights."

"Why would that be? You're not talking serial murder or the death of a Vanderbilt here."

"Can't tell you why, Sammy. But I am curious."

"Don't be, Lenny. Okay? We've got enough troubles without your damned curiosity."

Price got busy on the phone. He had no contacts at the New York State Health Department, but that was a minor obstacle. A call or two, and he'd unearth a friend twice removed or the grateful sister-in-law of an ex-victim he'd vindicated, and the wheels would start spinning in their direction.

Price's popularity was miles beyond Bannister's comprehension. The more people he knew, the more people he knew disliked him. Price had managed to web his world with spun sugar. Everyone the man had ever touched was willing and eager to return the favor.

This assignment proved more challenging than most. According to Bannister's Timex, it took almost seventeen minutes and four calls for Price to get the confidential dope on the Health Department's complaint against Dr. Margaret Lyons.

The alleged professional misconduct had been reported by phone by William Weider, father of one of the deceased patients. According to Mr. Weider's complaint, Dr. Lyons had brainwashed and manipulated his only daughter, causing the woman to engage in highly uncharacteristic reckless behavior that had resulted in her tragic death.

Hanging up, Price went wistful.

"That was really nice, Sam. Haven't touched base with Carl Blake from the A.G.'s office in an age."

"The Attorney General's office? Who's Carl Blake?"

"Old friend. Ruthie and I had a ballet subscription with the Blakes for years before we moved to Boston. Played bridge together, too."

"You've got more damned friends, Lenny."

Price shrugged. "Guess I'm just a people person."

"Good guess."

To each his own. Bannister had no desire to vie for the Miss Congeniality award. But there were certain clear advantages to being well loved and even better connected. While Price got to let his fingers do the stalking, Bannister had to brave the heat and make a very cold condolence call.

On the way to Gail Weider's former apartment, he toyed with a few alternative approaches. Given how little he knew of the dead woman, claiming to be her friend was too risky. From Dr. Lyons, he'd learned that Ms. Weider was a former patient and sometimes aide in the phobia program. Maggie had shown him an obituary from the *Times* that listed a staggering number of family ties and the dates and site of the planned mourning period. Beyond those meager bits, Bannister was flying on instruments.

Pressing the buzzer in the front vestibule, he announced himself as an acquaintance of Gail's from East End. In the elevator, he decided to go the conservative route and claim to be a fellow program aide. "Dr. Sam Bannister" had a certain ring to it, but it was nowhere near the ring of truth.

Turned out he'd been worried for nothing. Bannister was not asked to field any sticky questions or quell any skepticism. He was greeted with open arms and a parade of food platters. Hating to be rude, he allowed Cousin Whoever to force a pile of chocolate chip cookies on him. Best he'd ever tasted, and he considered himself something of a junk food gourmet. Eating the sweets, he held a studied frown. But it was tough to act properly morose while your taste buds were singing the Hallelujah chorus.

Aunt Whatsis took him in hand and made the introductions. He was presented to a roomful of rubber-stamp relatives, uniformly pleasant and unassuming. Bannister expressed his desire to pay respects to Gail's parents, and the aunt propelled him toward a weeping woman on the couch.

"Evelyn, dear. This is Sam Bannister. He knew Gail from the clinic."

"So sorry for your loss, Mrs. Weider," Bannister said.

Gail's mother snuffled and wiped her eyes. The moon-faced man to her right draped a comforting arm around her shoulders.

Bannister nodded gravely. "Mr. Weider? I knew your daughter from East End. So sorry."

The man shook his head. "Gail was my niece. Her father passed on several years ago."

Bannister was taken aback. Dead men rarely lodge official complaints. Talk about long distance. "Sorry. I didn't know."

Gail's mother spoke in a tear-filled voice. "That's all right. We all feel as if Thomas is still here with us. Gail, too."

Beating a clumsy retreat, Bannister settled next to a woman named Alice, who turned out to be Gail's younger sister. So much for a father named William whose only daughter had been brainwashed and imperiled by Dr. Lyons.

"Gail will be sorely missed at East End," Bannister said.

Alice swiped her fevered nose with a napkin. "She missed the place herself. In fact, she was finally thinking of going back when this happened."

"Back?"

"I kept telling her she was spiting herself staying away. Gail enjoyed the hospital so. Gave her something to do. A sense of purpose. But that girl always was one to hold a grudge until it yelled for mercy."

"Who did she have a grudge against at East End?"

Alice eyed Bannister. "You didn't know? Mad as she was, I figured it must have been common knowledge."

Having opted not to play doctor, Bannister was certainly not up for pulling teeth.

"Not to me. Who was she mad at?"

Alice shrugged. "Gail didn't mention the name. Said it wouldn't mean anything to me. All she told me was she wasn't putting up with any more insults."

"Could it have been Dr. Lyons?"

"Are you kidding? Gail worshiped the ground that woman walked on. Dr. Lyons saved my sister's life. No question. Before the clinic, all Gail ever did was stay home, watch the soaps, and bake cookies."

At the mention, Bannister searched the room for seconds. "If they were anything like the ones I just had, that was a job worth doing."

"They're from Gail's recipe. Used to be top secret. Gail wouldn't even give it to any of us in the family. Had the notion she might go into the cookie business someday. Sell to fancy delis and the like. But first, she had to get over her driving phobia." Alice whimpered. "Gail thought all her problems would be solved if only she could get herself over that fear."

Bannister steered the conversation back on course. "You have no idea who she was fighting with at the hospital?"

"Only that it was a man. I remember her saying, 'The nerve of him treating me that way. Saying those things, and he's not even a real doctor.'" The memory spurred a fresh flood of tears.

"It's hard, I know," Bannister said.

"You know what gets me the most? All her life, Gail battled a weight problem. Three months ago, she finally hit on a diet that worked for her. She started exercising, stopped baking. Even gave out her precious cookie recipe to a few people, so no one would be nagging her to start making them again. I saw my sister the day she died. When I left her, I remember thinking she'd never looked better in her whole life."

Alice was consumed by wracking sobs. Uncle Whochamacallit swooped down to comfort her.

For the next hour, Bannister worked the gloomy room. Everyone expressed wholly positive feelings about Dr. Lyons and Gail's experience at East End. There wasn't a spoken hint of suspicion that Gail's death might have been connected in any way to her work or phobia therapy at the clinic. Without exception, her relatives believed the woman's death had been a bizarre accident.

Bannister tried to get more information about the mysterious blowup Gail's sister had mentioned, but no luck. Must have been a doozy to keep the woman away from her sole work and purpose outside the tight family circle.

On his way back to the dump, a nasty thought burrowed under Bannister's skin. Had the so-called accident been arranged by Gail Weider's unnamed adversary at East End? Murder would account for the incomprehensible circumstances of the woman's death. Given Gail's terror of the road, it was completely illogical that she'd taken that final killing spin voluntarily. But feuding parties rarely resolve their differences by burying the hatchet in the other guy's head.

That thought stalled him for an instant, but Bannister was able to cast it quickly aside. Reduced to their lowest common denominator, people were just animals after all. And it didn't take all that much to strip some human beasts of their sheep suits.

Lucky thing for him, Bannister thought with a sardonic smirk. If everyone started behaving by the rules of sane civility, he'd have to go find himself a brand-new line of work.

CHAPTER

36

Maggie often reused or discarded old dictation tapes after having them transcribed for inclusion in a patient's record, but she managed to locate a couple containing session summaries from her work with Theodore Macklin.

Playing them back, she was struck by the sharp edge in her own voice. Even after the man had left her office, she'd remained tense and unsettled.

That was the way Macklin had always made her feel. And he'd done it with obvious relish. Most patients played by the unstated rules, instinctively allowing her to claim the necessary position of trust and authority. Even when they passed through the normal phase of transference, temporarily substituting doctor love for their obstructive defenses, most clients kept their appropriate distance. But Theodore Macklin had been a memorable exception.

From the first, he'd taken small liberties designed to upset the equilibrium. Entering the office, he'd moved to shake Maggie's hand. But he'd held it well past the point of comfort or necessity.

The first time he pulled that stunt, Maggie had been flustered and at a loss for an instant, effective response. Refusing the gesture would be admitting her uneasiness, giving him the edge he sought. If she accepted, she invited or, at least, appeared to condone his boorish behavior.

Having relived the awkward moment several times by the following session, Maggie had thought she was ready for him. But Macklin, too, had prepared. Instead of extending a hand, he'd pretended to stumble on his way to the couch. Maggie had grabbed him reflexively by his thick upper arms. Macklin had languished there, leaning heavily into her with parted lips and a lascivious glint in his eyes.

Maggie had itched to drop him on his head, but she knew any such passionate response was exactly what he wanted. Instead, she sat the jerk down and set out the ground rules in terms even he could understand.

Macklin had suffered from a classic case of sexual insecurity. Beneath the blowhard macho posturing, beat the heart of a little boy with severe libidinous stage fright. He deeply doubted his power to attract, connect, and perform with a woman. He was as phobic about carnal encounters as he was about bridges or tunnels. Freudian or not, it was hard to overlook the obvious symbolic connections.

Any female, regardless of age, role, or eligibility, had the power to stir Macklin's terror. But his response to the fear of sex was not typical phobic avoidance. Like a timorous kid in a schoolyard, Macklin reacted by becoming a sexual bully.

Maggie tried to imagine that bullying response pushed to its grisliest extreme. Could a teenage Ted Macklin have brutally raped and murdered Martha Rafferty? Bannister had described the victim as the one person in Macklin's class who'd gone out of her way to be kind to Ted. Martha Rafferty had encouraged Macklin to get out more. She'd pushed the others to accept the boy.

Given his terror of females, Macklin might have been threatened by the girl's attentions. But was he capable of responding with murderous violence? And after committing such a heinous act, would he have been capable of making all the bloodless calculations necessary to bury the crime in fact and eradicate it from his own conscience?

Or did the man lack a conscience altogether?

The question haunted Maggie. Had Theodore Macklin been a true psychopath, completely devoid of human caring or remorse?

Every potential clinic patient was given a thorough intake evaluation, including medical and psychological testing. Maggie had spotted no red flags in Ted Macklin's profile, but the program's questionnaire was not designed to smoke out clandestine criminal types. Most of Maggie's patients lacked the nerve to jaywalk, much less commit and conceal a rape and homicide.

She searched her memory for signs of psychopathic development in Macklin's history. By his own description, Theodore Macklin had been a loner with poor and sometimes stormy family relationships. As a young boy, he'd had trouble getting along with other children and was often punished for his poor conduct in school. All were typical of a psychopath-in-training.

It wasn't standard practice to question phobic patients about a record of animal abuse or fire setting, both common in the early lives of psychopaths. But if Macklin had been capable of normal caring, kindness, or empathy, he'd hidden the ability well. When, on rare occasions, he'd referred to other people in his life, it was in terms of their use or value to Theodore Macklin. New acquaintances were opportunities. Clients were portfolios. Employees were gofers or go-getters. Socializing was business with food.

Maggie spent the next several hours carefully reconstructing Macklin's file from her notes, tapes, and memory. Certainly the man had been among the more spectacular failures in the history of the phobia clinic. Ten days of daily individual sessions, group meetings, and supervised practice hadn't even gotten him to the point of true acceptance of his phobic condition, the first essential step toward recovery.

Macklin contended to the end that every bridge was a very real danger. Ditto tunnels. He'd come to East End armed with harrowing statistics about the country's tottering infrastructure. And the superstructure wasn't much better. The man had memorized a grim litany of building, bridge, and tunnel collapses. He knew the site and circumstance of every major construction debacle in the last twenty years. He could reel off the bruise and body counts and offer a description of each victim's wounds in macabre detail.

Macklin had been a source of tremendous frustration to Henry, who had acted as his aide. Maggie had asked her star assistant to assume the odious assignment as a special favor. But this patient had proved even more impossible than Maggie had dared to anticipate. Animals could smell fear, and Macklin was no exception. He'd sniffed out Henry's residual anxieties. With vicious deliberation, Macklin had preyed on poor Henry's fears.

One instance stuck in Maggie's mind. Henry had planned to take Macklin for a ride on the FDR drive, which would involve close-range sightings of several formidable bridges. Henry was a cautious driver who always kept to the right lane and the speed limit. Sensing his aide's uneasiness, Macklin had spent the entire practice session harping on the snail's pace. Henry hadn't been able to get Macklin to focus on the real purpose of the exercise.

Maggie remembered Henry's report of the irritating session. "He was so busy teasing me about life in the slow lane, he wouldn't even look at the bridges," Henry had complained. "I don't get it, Maggie. Why did he come to East End in the first place? What can he possibly hope to accomplish if he refuses to cooperate?"

"I guess he hopes to drive us all crazy."

"But how can we help the man if he won't even try?"

"We can't. Don't let him get to you, Henry. Try to look on the bright side. He'll be gone in a couple of weeks."

Turned out to be a very long brief stay. Macklin had been a pariah to his phobia group, where no one appreciated his superior attitude or steady portents of doom. He'd aroused even gentle Henry to something akin to actual anger. The floor staff and other patients had avoided Macklin. Maggie, who could not avoid him, had anticipated their daily sessions with the same eagerness she brought to root canal.

After a week and a half, Macklin had simply packed his bags and left. No official checkout. No farewells. The man hadn't even paused to fire a parting shot before riding off into the sunset.

Shaking out her cramped fingers, Maggie wished she'd never heard of Theodore Macklin. Six months later and dead, he was still leaving muddy footprints all over her life. When was it going to end?

Was it going to end?

She was damned well going to do her part to hurry this mess to its best possible conclusion. Four o'clock. Time to call the detective's daughter and do a little detecting of her own.

CHAPTER

37

Sick headache. Jangling nerves. Too little sleep; too much coffee. A crowd of shrill worries jockeyed noisily for the conscious center stage.

The first two had gone perfectly. The next was in process. The plan had to proceed in perfect order.

The cab ride intensified the sense of uneasiness. The taxi had brick seats, liquid shock absorbers, and a lead-footed driver. At intervals, garbled squawking spat from the two-way radio. In response, the cabbie pressed the mike to his cracked lips and rasped in a nasty, alien tongue.

Rotten city was bad enough in the winter. Summer heated the ozone-tainted air and brought the simmering populace to a boil. The cab passed masses of plodding bodies. The faces were squint-eyed and grim. Even the smallest kids had a grave, edgy look about them. How awful being out among them, open and vulnerable. How wonderful to have the peace and solitude of the special place. But there would be no retreating to that until the work was done, the retribution ensured.

The cab stopped in front of the store. The door opened with a whine. The necessary moves were a silent mental echo. Step out. Breathe. Exhale the stalking demons.

Nothing could get in the way. Everything had been planned to the most minute contingency. Everything must be perfect, beginning to end.

The next hour was focused on the final details. Armed with the essential purchases, the voice urged another foray outside. Wait for a cab. Raise a seeking arm. Flash a fetching smile.

The moment was coming. A few more days of this hideous charade, and it would be time to attend the bitch's funeral.

CHAPTER

38

Maggie could read his aching uncertainty. The detective's eyes were pained; his jaw worked as if he were chewing on stones.

Nothing she'd told him had done a bit of good. No amount of reassurance from her or anyone was going to convince the man that his daughter was doing all right. He had to come to that risky understanding on his own. And to get there, he'd have to traverse some very rocky personal terrain.

Two hours ago, when he'd shown up at her apartment uninvited and unannounced, Maggie had been miffed, to say the least. But recognizing the depth of his pain and worry, she'd quickly forgiven the intrusion.

Now he sat on the couch in her living room, his hands knotted.

"You don't understand. Chloe's very smart. Smart enough to tell you what she knows you want to hear."

"That's not what happened, Detective."

"How can you be so damned sure?"

"We've been riding this merry-go-round for over an hour now. I'm satisfied that Chloe isn't in any serious psychic distress. If she were, there would be some obvious impact on her behavior or her ability to function. She'd be having sleep problems or a loss of appetite or psychosomatic symptoms. She'd be sullen or withdrawn or distracted or running with a new crowd or all of the above. You said yourself that none of those things are true.

And you told me Chloe's mother doesn't see a problem either."

"Chloe's mother *is* a problem."

"Maybe so. But you yourself described her as a loving, caring parent who has your daughter's welfare and best interests at heart. Do you think she'd deny signs of serious problems in your daughter just to spite you?"

"No." Bannister shook his head wearily. "But Lila doesn't hear what I hear when I speak to Chloe. And neither do you."

"I'm sure that's true."

Patiently, Maggie tried to explain why his perception was separate and unique. He was listening to his child through a stack of distorting filters: distance, the marital breakup, guilt, uncertainty, fear.

"It's natural for you to worry about what effects the divorce might have on Chloe and your relationship with her. The parent-child tie is very close and extremely complicated. A stressful change like a divorce can work that tight bond in tangles. It's going to take a lot of effort on your part to learn how to separate your own fears and worries from what your daughter is feeling, Mr. Bannister."

"Call me Sam, will you? Seems ridiculous being so formal while you're digging around in my underwear drawer."

"Interesting way to put it."

"Look. I appreciate your talking to Chloe. And, whether I buy it or not, I'm glad to hear you don't think she has a serious problem. But if you're trying to shrink me, don't waste your time. I'm way too big a piece of work."

Maggie repressed a smile. "I don't treat people against their will, Sam. All I'm suggesting is that you might have a few things to work through yourself. Most of us do."

"Only a few?"

"I'm not a mathematician. And I'm not your doctor. But if you get your stuff worked out, I can guarantee you'll be more comfortable about the job you're doing as Chloe's father."

"Is that the whole commercial?"

Maggie spotted his stubborn expression and shrugged. "So it seems."

"Time to return to our regular programming then."

Bannister explained the oddities he'd discovered in the health department complaint against her. The complainant's name and several surrounding facts had been falsified. From Bannister's visit to the grieving Weider family, he seriously doubted that the gripe against Maggie had been lodged by anyone on the dead woman's side of the fence.

"Those people think you walk on water," Bannister concluded.

"Only when it's absolutely necessary." Maggie's grin evaporated. "So I was right. The charges came from someone at the hospital."

"Looks that way. Question is who?"

"And why."

"Yes," Bannister said. "But you're forgetting your Abbott and Costello. Who's always on first."

He told Maggie that his partner was trying to get his hands on a copy of the complaint. The exact wording of the allegation might tell them something. Beyond that, there wasn't much to go on.

Maggie seethed awhile in silence. "There has to be a way to find out who did this," she said at last.

"We can't interview the entire East End population. And even if we did, I don't think anyone would run to take credit for the charges. If whoever it was hadn't wanted anonymity, he wouldn't have made up the phony name and pedigree in the first place."

"I feel like I'm shadow boxing, only the shadow has all the advantages. There has to be something I can do."

"Why don't you make up a list of four or five key suspects? I can turn the screws that many times and see if anyone yells 'Uncle.' "

"No problem." Maggie's expression was grim as she listed the obvious front runners: Francis Kennedy, Drew Paulson, Alex Ivy, and two other psychiatrists in the de-

partment who'd competed for the job as head of the phobia clinic. She handed over the list.

"You sure you don't want time to think about this?"
Bannister said.

"Believe me. It's all I've been thinking about."

The discussion shifted to Theodore Macklin's recon-
structed record. Maggie led Bannister on a guided
session-by-session tour of the man's brief stay at East
End. She described Macklin's social ineptitude and the
disturbing facets of his past and personality.

"Viewing the case with the benefit of my perfect
twenty-twenty hindsight, Theodore Macklin had several
attributes of the classic psychopath," Maggie said.
"Wouldn't surprise me to learn that someone with his profile had committed violent criminal acts."

"Unfortunately, that's not good enough." Bannister
scowled. He needed hard facts. Evidence. He needed to
hear that Macklin had made some sort of an admission in
therapy about the Martha Rafferty murder.

Maggie searched her memory again. "There was nothing like that."

"There *had* to be."

"Believe me. I'd remember."

"I know you'd remember an outright confession. But it
might have been more subtle than that. Maybe he used a
kind of code. Maybe it was in a dream he described.
Think, Doctor. Please."

All the word "dream" did was remind Maggie of her
recurrent nightmare. Circling on the hawk's back.
Screaming the nonsense words: *Lazy bit.* Lazy bit?

Forcing herself back to the moment, she couldn't come
up with anything to fill in the blanks for Sam. "Sorry."

"Damn it. Why isn't anything ever easy?"

Maggie smiled. "My mother would say it's because the
world is full of evil and darkness."

Bannister couldn't help but smile back at her. "Your
mother sounds as impossible as my mother."

"No way, Sam. I'm not usually competitive about things
like this, but I can guarantee you my mother wins the
impossible award hands down."

Their eyes met. What Maggie saw there made her glance away and change the subject quickly. Under other circumstances, the guy's visible interest might have been flattering. But under other circumstances, she might be able to breathe and swallow.

"So, I guess that's it for now," she said.

Bannister eyed his watch. "I'm starved. You up for some dinner?"

"Sorry. Tonight's not good."

"How about tomorrow then?"

"I'm busy then, too. Thanks anyway."

Bannister frowned. "The resident?"

"Actually, yes. How did you know?"

"Not important." He stood to leave, pausing at the kitchen door. "There was one more thing."

Bannister recounted what he'd heard about a feud between Gail Weider and some nameless foe at East End. The argument had been enough to keep the woman away from the clinic for the last few months. Gail's sister had mentioned an insult by a mystery male whom she'd described as not even a real doctor.

"You know about that?"

Maggie shook her head. "I had no idea why Gail stopped coming to the clinic. I figured I must have done something to upset her."

"Not according to her family."

Bannister's gnawing hunger drew his eye to the plate of cookies on the counter. At Maggie's nod, he helped himself to a handful.

"That's strange," Maggie mused. "I can't picture a submissive soul like Gail Weider having a big blowup with anybody. And if she did, I can't imagine not hearing about it. East End has a remarkable rumor mill. Sneeze on two west, they'll bless you on fourteen."

"Wonder why it didn't work this time?"

Maggie didn't answer. She was caught by the sick paradox of her own remark. These days it seemed every time she sneezed on two west, some distant soul wound up wearing a toe tag.

CHAPTER

39

Bannister spent the next hour trying to walk off a jittery sense of confusion.

Someone had reshuffled his deck, fixed it so he couldn't tell the trump cards from the jokers anymore. Correct or mistaken, he'd always known exactly how to play the hand he'd been dealt. But suddenly the world was operating by an unfamiliar set of rules. And they were written in hieroglyphics.

He struggled to decipher the dips and squiggles. Dirty was clean. Guilty was not. Down was up. Chloe's problems were in his mind, not hers. Lila was the sensible one.

Other unthinkable thoughts kept bubbling up through the muck. An emerald-eyed shrink had captured his muddled fancy. Woman was smart, swift, and equipped with a state-of-the-art bullshit detector. Bannister appreciated all of the above. Good solid contents. And the package wasn't bad either.

He tried to push away the treacherous idea. Maggie Lyons was obviously not interested in him. And she was unavailable. For some inconceivable reason, she'd hooked up with that damned resident. Bannister had disliked and distrusted that dippy kid doctor on sight.

But the resident wasn't his problem, and neither was Maggie. He sternly reminded himself he'd sworn off women. Permanently on the wagon. Start something with the wrong one, and you were guaranteed a nasty finish. Given his unblemished record of disastrous choices, he wasn't about to trust his instincts in the romance department. His excellent nose simply went blank in that direction. Total abstinence was the only certain defense.

He remembered how it had been with Lila. Woman had intoxicated him instantly and completely. By the time he'd sobered up, he was paying alimony, making appointments to see his kid and visit his money, and living in a single room over a pepperoni palace. Most people dreamed in black and white. His dreams were in provolone and garlic.

Bannister had drifted north to Spanish Harlem, not the greatest place for a solitary stroll after dark. He tried to muster a sensible measure of self-protective fear and turn back, but he found he didn't give a damn. No one was going to get in his face tonight. He simply wasn't in the mood.

Night had fallen, but the temperature had failed to sink along. Mopping his brow, he turned into a small, decayed park slipped between an abandoned tenement and a caged bodega.

Patchy darkness shrouded the parched grass and blistered benches. The few streetlamps that hadn't been shot out dripped stingy puddles of tepid light. Flies ambled over a man sleeping fitfully in the failed shade of a scrawny pin oak. A kid swaggered by, carting a house-sized ghetto blaster that screamed songs of rage and promises of retribution.

Long after the kid disappeared, the alleged music rang in Bannister's ears. When the echo finally faded, an unwelcome vision slipped in to claim its place. Bannister saw Theodore Macklin's ugly face in the morgue and the timid guise of Gail Weider from the brief *Times* obituary. Try as he did to keep them separate, the images bled together like paint swirls on wet paper.

There had to be a connection.

What was it Price was always saying? *You take your time, you'll get there sooner.* And there was Lenny's other favorite. *You can only find what's there.* The truth is too big to ignore or step around. You try, you're only going to go miles out of your way to get to the place you can't avoid.

Why hadn't he seen it before?

Bannister's mind was working a fast shuffle. His heart was racing, mouth dry as chalk. He had to get back to the dump and talk to Price.

Turning fast, Bannister bumped head-on into a nasty-looking Hispanic kid. Guy had bad teeth, worse hair, and a silver hoop earring. He wore a studded leather vest over skin that was mottled with ruts and bruises.

"Watch yourself, asshole," he snarled.

Kid had a raw, mean look in his eyes. Normally, Bannister would read it as a caution sign, but it didn't seem worth the bother.

"Who do you think you're calling asshole, asshole?" Bannister snapped back.

"That's it, man. You're out."

Bannister looked the kid over and laughed. Real fashion statement. The dead black leather matched his eyes. The studs and earring matched the knife blade.

He came at Bannister with a feral growl. The slash was at warp speed. The move reminded Bannister of a teasing wink. It was almost flirtatious. And the punk was definitely not his type.

Bannister caught the wrist of the hand holding the blade. Flipping the guy around so he was facing away, Bannister compressed the creep's bulging windpipe with a forearm.

Big shot made a sound like a stuffed sink. Bannister caught his breath, dismissed the throbbing pain in his gut, and concentrated on the plumbing problem. His assailant was taller by several inches. Had a hard, lanky body. Long drink of *agua*. But water wasn't the only thing this one ran through his pipes. He had the nervous feel of a needy junkie and that cloying junkie stench. Wormlike tracks crawled the length of his inner arm. Walking waste dump.

"You got a name?"

"Lemme go, man. I can't fucking breathe."

"That's a step in the right direction."

"Hey! You're choking me. You fucking nuts or something?"

His sanity might be questionable. But Bannister was not up for a debate. Creep needed a lesson, and it had been way too long since Bannister had played a nice game of school.

Still clutching the guy in a choke hold, Bannister used the knife to slice open the pocket bulging with the kid's wallet. Rifling through it, he found what he was after.

Moving in a muggers' tango, Bannister maneuvered the jerk to the pay phone on the corner. Incredibly, the thing was in working order. His first call was to the local precinct, requesting immediate trash collection. But it was his next contact that put a nice gleam of fear into the punk's dead eyes.

"Hey. Don't do that, man. You don't know—"

Bannister smiled. "Oh, yes, I do, Ernesto. I know exactly. It's ringing, Ernesto. Someone's picking up now."

"No, man. Really."

The punk struggled in his grip. But Bannister held fast. He was grateful for the moment. He was grateful to Señor Feldman, his high school Spanish teacher, who'd been a stickler for oral practice. Even all these years later, he had no trouble finding the necessary words.

"Hola. Señora Nuñez? Policía aquí. Tengo su hijo."

As the storm gathered on the other end of the line, Bannister felt the kid go limp.

"Fuck, man. What'd you have to go call my old lady for?"

"Because I'm sure she's very concerned about you, Ernesto. She sounded extremely concerned, in fact."

"Woman's got a temper on her like you never seen. She'll rip my fucking head off."

He caught the approaching headlights. "Maybe so, but she's going to have to wait her turn, *hijo*."

Waiting for the strategic moment, Bannister released the kid so he was catapulted toward the squad car barreling up the block. Even if the cops released him, *mamacita* would see to Ernesto's proper punishment. Bannister had neither the time nor patience to go with them and make a formal complaint. His insides were hosting a grasshopper's convention.

Ducked out of sight, he watched the cops nab the punk, cuff him, and roar off with their sirens wailing. They were out of sight before a pain again drew Bannister's attention toward his abdomen.

Glancing down, he saw the slash across his shirt and the spreading fingers of blood. Wincing, he peeled back the matted fabric and appraised the seeping wound.

All he'd bargained for was a little satisfaction. Looked like sweet Ernesto had given him a nice big tip.

CHAPTER

40

She couldn't sleep. The air danced with sparks and currents. Daisy didn't know what to make of the odd feeling. It bore no resemblance to her usual anxieties: ponderous, and suffocating. This was a live wire. Hissing and seductive. Exotic vixen. Danger dancing under a teasing stack of veils.

Intriguing.

Daisy stared at the ceiling. Maybe it was something she ate. Or maybe it was the result of eating everything. These past few days, her appetite had been overwhelming. A gaping chasm. She'd always downed her food out of dull, mechanical need, but now she was ravenous all the time. Between meals, she was forever rooting in the refrigerator near the nurses' station. She ordered nearly all the items on the menu. Double portions of starches and sweets. And with all that, she eagerly awaited the plate of cookies she knew she'd find on her nightstand late each afternoon with a note signed by her "not-so-secret admirer."

At first, his attentions had flustered her, left her at a breathless loss. She'd never considered herself worthy of such special regard. But now she'd come to expect and rely on the pleasant extra touches he provided. Such a sweet person, he was. Exactly the sort you'd hope to find working with sick people. The compliments and gifts didn't even seem strange anymore. They felt lovely.

The odd thing was that she hadn't gained any weight. Maybe she'd even lost a few pounds. She didn't have to step on a scale for confirmation. Her body was leaner than usual, the muscles better toned.

Not that she'd ever paid her figure all that much attention. Appearance doesn't count for much when terror is your sole and constant companion.

Reading herself in Braille, Daisy traced the proud jut of her cheekbones and the startling hollows beneath. The puff of gelid flesh beneath her jaw had disappeared. Her breasts were firmer than she remembered, spongy hillocks mounted on a curved ladder of protruding ribs. Her belly lay like a vacant hammock between the bony ridges of her hips.

Where were the doughy masses surrounding her thighs? Where was the excess rump tissue oozing out from beneath her like melted marshmallows? What had become of the *real* Daisy Tyler, the one long since gone to middle-aged seed?

Maybe the fountain of youth was hooked to the hospital water supply or lurking in the laundry detergent. Or maybe she was crazier than she or anyone suspected.

Weird how the idea failed to disturb her. What was crazy after all, and what was so terrible about it? During the past few days, whenever she'd mustered the nerve to leave her room or even peer out the door, she'd observed the other patients on the psych ward. Nothing in particular distinguished them from so-called normal people. As her mother used to say, it was all mind over matter. If you don't mind, it doesn't matter.

Slipping out of bed, Daisy went to the bathroom. Shutting the door, she flipped on the harsh fluorescent lights. Leaning over the sink, she viewed herself critically in the mirror.

Definite improvement. Her skin had a pleasing flush, her eyes the clear sparkle of a rushing stream. Was it her imagination, or had the wrinkles faded? She recalled the map of age on her former face. Where were the tire ruts running from her nose to the edges of her mouth? And who'd stolen the splash of lines circling her eyes like cracked ice?

"What's gotten into you, Daisy Erin Tyler? Have you gone totally daft?"

The words and the startled sound of her own voice set her laughing. Unconsciously, she'd slipped into a fine approximation of her father's stern Irish brogue.

"Dress yourself this instant, girl. Put on your Sunday finest, and let's be going before we miss the opening hymn altogether."

"Nearer my God to thee . . ." she sang to her shining reflection in a thready voice.

"That's better, girl. Don't you be cowering in the corner like that. Afraid of your own shadow, aren't you? A shame on your own house. That's what you are."

Yes, Poppa. No, Poppa. Whatever you say, Poppa.

Daisy made a face, sassing the miserable memory. She could barely connect with the cringing creature she had been. If this was crazy, crazy suited her just fine.

Slipping back into the room, she dressed in the dark, tugging on her navy skirt and white blouse. It felt sinful and delicious to have the fabrics draped over her bare breasts and buttocks. They slid in a delicate caress as she moved. Lover's fingers.

"Crazy as a bedbug you are, Daisy Erin."

You bet your sweet ass I am, Poppa.

Wiggling her toes, she decided not to bother with shoes and stockings. The floor felt wonderful. Cool and daring.

Peering into the hall, she waited for the patrolling charge nurse to round the distant corner. As soon as the woman was out of sight, Daisy hastened from her room, raced down the hall, and ducked through the emergency exit to the stairs.

The metal risers nipped her bare soles as she scrambled down the double flight to the lobby level. There was an echo in the stairwell, the clamorous clang reminiscent of church bells heralding a blessed event.

Hear ye, hear ye. Daisy Tyler is alive and well. Daisy Erin Tyler has risen this day from the living dead.

Hallelujah and a rousing amen!

Waiting impatiently for the security guard to abandon

his post at the door, she tried to form a plan. Unfettered by the fear, she could go anyplace. Do anything.

A lifetime of denied dreams looped through her humming brain. She could go dancing at the Rainbow Room. Have drinks at the Helmsley Palace and dinner at Lutèce. She could take a carriage ride through Central Park and stop for a rich dessert at Tavern on the Green. She could do some or all of the above, or none of it, with no better reason than whim or fancy. Maybe she'd go dunk her head in the spouting fountain at Rockefeller Center. Or was that fountain only operative at Christmastime? No matter. If she wanted to soak her skull, soak it she would.

Finally, the portly guard stood, yawned extravagantly, and strolled toward the men's room. Daisy barely felt the tile beneath her feet as she half ran, half flew through the lobby and out the revolving door. Joy overwhelmed her as she stood outside, absorbing the summer night's bounty. Twinkling bridge lights. Aura of the skyline. Crackling whisper of the tepid breeze.

At the curb, she closed her eyes and let the swell of city sounds saturate her hearing. Crying babies, people talking, lines of cars passing, the squealing brakes of a bus.

A villainous idea edged out all the others. Dropping her arms to her sides, Daisy tuned to her inner rhythms. Her pulse was a kettle drum, deep and insistent. The blood surged through her like rush hour traffic on a fortunate day.

Nothing can stop you. Nothing will harm you. You are beyond caution or peril.

Imagining the gasp of a gathered throng of admirers, she nodded decisively and stepped off the curb. She would cross to the other side with her eyes closed.

Fearless Daisy Tyler. Daisy the daring. Watch out, World. Here she comes!

She was too filled with wonder to sense the gathering risk. The truck bearing down on her. The driver unaware.

"Wait up, girl. Who can keep up with you, Daisy Erin? You're going to get yourself killed, running reckless like that."

Go to hell, Poppa. And don't hurry back.

Step by solid step, she stepped closer to the traffic lane. She was the tide, a giant, unstoppable force.

But she was about to be stopped. The truck was closer. Aimed for disaster. Twenty yards away. Ten.

Suddenly rough hands reached out and wrenched her backward to safety.

The truck sped past, slapping her with a hard rush of air.

Flustered, Daisy turned and found herself in Dr. Goldberg's powerful grip. His face was taut. "My God, Daisy. Are you all right?"

"What? Yes, I'm fine. Just stepped out for some air. So stuffy inside."

Her heart was pounding wildly. What in hell had she been thinking? What was she doing out like this, half naked? Barefoot? She must be completely insane. She could have gotten herself killed.

The thought made her tremble. For the first time, she felt a rush of fear. Circling his arm around her, the young doctor led her back through the lobby and summoned a nurse to plant her safely back in bed. Out of Daisy's hearing, he ordered a sedative guaranteed to deliver a sound night's sleep.

The nurse soon reappeared in the hall, nodding to let him know that Ms. Tyler was down and decent. Goldberg entered the room sporting a studied smile.

"There. That's better."

Daisy's eyes filled. Angry with herself, she swiped the tears away. "Can't imagine what got into me, Dr. Goldberg. I must have taken leave of my senses altogether."

"No such thing," he said, pulling the blanket to her chin. "Just feeling your oats."

"Honestly? You don't think I'm certifiable?"

"Not at all. In fact, I'd bet you'll be ready for midnight strolls and plenty more before you know it."

She drew a deep breath. Such a dear young man. So reassuring. And look at how he'd gone out of his way for her at every turn. If Dr. Goldberg said things were fine, Daisy would make it her business to believe him.

"I dearly hope you're right, Dr. Goldberg."

"Trust me, Daisy. Very soon, you'll be doing things you never imagined possible. Tonight just wasn't the time."

CHAPTER

41

Price blew an exasperated breath. "You should have known better, Sam. You're not carrying, and a junkie jerk comes at you with a blade that way, you give him whatever the hell he wants."

"I did, Lenny. What he wanted was to cut me."

"What the hell were you doing up there anyway? You know better than to go walking around alone at night in a neighborhood like that."

Bannister shrugged, and instantly regretted the movement. "Apparently, I don't."

"And you should have called. I was worried sick about you."

"Please forgive me, sweetheart. You know how hard it can be to break away in the middle of a hemorrhage."

"No kidding, Sam. You really okay?"

Bannister flapped a hand. "It was nothing. Doc in emergency shoved my guts back in place. Gave me a couple of hundred stitches, and I'm good as used."

Price's forehead was still pleated in worry lines. "Get some rest. Go on. You take the bed."

"What about your back?"

"My back, your front. We're a regular pair of bargains. But right now, you're the bigger one. So go. Sleep tight."

Very tempting. Bannister was drained. The mugging in the park was bad enough. But then he'd suffered the second, longer assault in the emergency room at East End. The place had all the amenities you'd expect from a fine, modern house of healing. Nasty receptionist. Endless

275

waiting. Giant stack of forms. Bannister had sat trying to stanch his bleeding in the pleasant company of a gunshot victim, a projectile vomiter, a screaming woman with a pretzel-twisted arm, and a kid who'd left most of two fingers in a garbage disposal.

When his turn came at last, he was ushered in to see a doctor with an impenetrable accent and a tic. From what Bannister had forced himself to watch, the guy had no knack at all for embroidery. So there went the swimsuit modeling career. And to top it off, he'd been subjected to a lecture on his runaway blood pressure, a problem he'd never had before and definitely didn't need now.

"All right, Lenny. I'll take the bed. But first there's something serious we have to discuss."

"Your near-death experience isn't enough for one night?"

Bannister recapped the conclusion he'd come to just before colliding with Ernesto Nuñez's runaway temper in the park. He and Price had been interested in the life and crimes of Theodore Macklin only. Even after they'd tripped over Gail Weider's surprise ending, they'd never stopped to wonder whether the two corpses might be connected by something more than coincidence. But what Bannister had heard about the dead woman's feud with someone at the hospital had put a fresh spin on things.

"Suppose some nut got mad enough at Gail Weider to whack her, Lenny. Macklin, charmer that he was, might have ticked off the same time bomb while he was at that hospital."

"And?"

"And nothing. Isn't that enough? Didn't you hear me? We might be looking at a double homicide here. And if someone at East End likes to solve his little disagreements by tossing people off roads and bridges, we damned well better find out who it is and put a stop to him."

Price shook his head. "Don't you think I know that, Sam? What do you think I've spent the last eight hours on?"

"You've already started checking out the double homicide angle?"

"I figured you knew that. Soon as you mentioned the other patient's death and the Health Department investigation, I told you I was curious."

Bannister's own curiosity overwhelmed his urge to argue. "So what the hell did you find?"

Price had run the double-murder possibility by Joey McKenna, a friend and homicide detective on the District Attorney's squad. McKenna had found the theory interesting. But as Price had suspected, given the current budget crunch, no official agency was about to get involved on the strength of supposition.

"As Joey said, Sam. At this point, we don't even know for sure whether the Macklin and Weider deaths were homicides, accidents, or suicides. Of course, they'll be glad to hop on once we build them a firm enough platform."

"Exactly how many stiffs does it take to make a platform?"

"No more, I hope."

Price's work on the case hadn't ended with McKenna. He'd pulled the necessary strings to get copies of the Macklin and Weider autopsy reports faxed to a toxicologist friend at the Manhattan coroner's office. The doctor had agreed to review the records first thing in the morning.

"I figured Doc Lepczek might find something in the postmortems that would show a link between the deaths, if one exists."

"Good thinking."

"And I got a list of Dr. Lyons's other patients. I figure we'd better start checking them all out, see if any of the others look to have targets painted on their backs."

Bannister went grim. "I told you, Lenny. Maggie Lyons had nothing to do with those deaths. You don't know her, but she's definitely no murderer. I'd stake my life on it."

"All I'm saying is that if the trees start falling in the forest, you check the others to keep the blight from spreading. Maggie Lyons is far from the only one at East End who deals with her patients."

Bannister pressed his lips in a seam. "Fair enough. Guess we better catch some sleep. Looks like we've got a busy day ahead of us."

Price settled on the couch. Bannister dropped his brick head and aching body on the narrow bed. Only a couple of hours until the world opened for business again, and they could start trying to figure out what the hell they were really up against.

Suicides? Serial murder? Bizarre coincidence? One from column A and one from B?

Stow it, Bannister. You don't get your beauty sleep, you're going to look like hell in the morning.

He tried to empty his mind. When that didn't work, he rummaged around for a relaxing thought. But every channel was playing a horror flick. He saw Ernesto with the gleaming blade. Macklin with pretty young Martha Rafferty. A crazed killer on every corner, hawking his unlicensed wares.

Counting sheep was for farm boys. Bannister finally drifted off tallying up the corpse count.

CHAPTER

42

Double feature.

Twice during the night, Maggie was startled awake by the terrifying end of the window dream. She slips out the window. The hawk flies her in dizzy circles. She's falling away. Plummeting toward the ground in a helpless, endless spiral.

"Lazy Bit. Lazy!"

No!

After the second time, she gave up and declared the night a forfeit. One of these days, when all the real horror was behind her, she'd have to make an appointment with Dr. Grayboys and try to get at the elusive root of that dumb dream once and for all. They had worked to dredge up the subterranean significance many times during her training analysis. But Maggie's memory drill kept hitting ledge.

Meanwhile, she had her hands more than full with the weighty present. And at the moment, there was nothing she could think to do to hurry a lighter, brighter future along. Sam Bannister had promised to find out who'd lodged the complaint against her. The state department investigators would take care of mixing the tar and feathers. Maggie's impossible role was to await the outcome, whatever it might be.

Patient waiting was far from her favorite activity. In truth, she'd never been able to get the hang of it. Maggie decided she'd better figure out some way to fill the sprawl of empty hours that threatened to suck her up like a pool of quicksand.

Dressed in shorts and a T-shirt, she went for an early jog. Six A.M., and the sky was tarnished silver. A vague shimmer capped the horizon. Pilot light. From the edgy aura of the atmosphere, it felt as if the blaze would catch again in earnest at any second.

She took a brisk walk to Seventy-first Street and crossed the connecting overpass to the East River Promenade. Only a scatter of restless souls were out this early on a Saturday dawn. The eyes she passed were locked and bolted. Take the standard city distrust, add heaping helpings of sweltering heat and sore tempers, shake it up and dish it out before the sun shines, and you've got yourself a fat slice of paranoia pie.

Maggie didn't want any. In active defiance, she started greeting the wary strangers she passed with a wave and a smile. A couple backed away as if they'd been slapped. Most countered with reflexive courtesies: cautious grin, guarded wave. A few muttered "hello" or "good morning." One young man in sweats and a headband paused long enough to trade friendly complaints about the weather.

Better. Living in a jungle didn't mean she had to walk on all fours.

The run and the satisfying exercise in civility gave Maggie a critical boost. Eddie's Deli had opened by the time she was headed home, and she felt up to the task of buying snacks for the planned cocktail hour visit by Mitch Goldberg, Dad, and Babycakes.

Fifteen minutes later, she left the market toting a bagful of cheeses, crackers, crudités fixings, and mixers. On the two-block walk to her building, she tried to decide between the black dress and the red, the sum of her summer evening wardrobe. Both were comfortable and appropriate. Pity she couldn't say the same about her father's date.

Half a block from her apartment house, Maggie spotted the doorman and the super at the curb. She couldn't catch the words, but Pete and Joe were talking in grim, rough voices. Joe worked his hands in the extravagant angry gestures of a revival tent preacher.

As she neared the building, she overheard the magic words. Mickey Glover strikes again.

"What was it this time, Joe?" she said.

Spotting her, the super shook his head in disgust. "Because of the fire that little monster set the other night, I had a surprise visit this morning from the city inspector. Guy really busted my chops. Went looking for infractions and wouldn't quit until he found some trumped-up nonsense to cite us for. Bottom line is we have to empty out the entire storage room."

"Sorry, Joe. Sounds like a major pain."

He nodded. "I'm asking all the tenants to come and claim the stuff they want. I'd bring it around myself, but it'd take a while. If that inspector shows up before we get it emptied, it's another citation."

"I don't have anything in storage," Maggie said.

"No?" Joe pulled a folded page from his pocket. "I made a quick list. Thought I saw something of yours. Yes. Here it is. There's a carton with your name on it. Maybe stuff from your folks."

Maggie followed Joe down the back stairs to the basement. They passed the utility room and the laundry. The storage room was in the rear, a concrete bunker crammed with castoff baby equipment, out-of-season sports gear, and layers of boxed memorabilia.

"Wait here. I think I can put my hands on it quickly," Joe told her.

He entered the cluttered chamber. Moments later, he emerged carrying a battered box marked "Lyons."

Maggie took it, balancing the grocery bag on top.

"Sure you can manage?" Joe asked.

"I'm fine."

Another tenant appeared to collect his stored belongings, and Joe got busy with him. Leaving the basement, Maggie's curiosity was piqued. After the divorce, her mother had gone on a discard binge, ridding the apartment of all conceivable evidence of her husband's duplicitous existence. Mom had sold or donated all the furniture

Dad had left behind. She'd packed up the books, souvenirs, and knickknacks for collection by charity thrift shops. But stripping the place bare had not been enough to evict the demons. Eventually, her mother had felt the need to abandon the apartment altogether, leaving Maggie to rattle around in the glut of sanitized space.

Maggie had envied friends whose homes overflowed with nostalgic paraphernalia: photo albums, bronzed baby shoes, dusty cartons crammed with priceless, worthless treasures. At times, she felt like a player on a bare stage, acting out her life without benefit of props or backdrop. Neither her mother nor her father liked to muse about the past. And there was no physical evidence to flesh out Maggie's sketchy recollections.

Until now.

Riding the elevator, she studied the carton. She estimated it at two feet across and three deep. Had a solid feel, but there was enough play to allow the contents to slip and jiggle when she gave it a hard shake.

Balancing the awkward burden on her hip and forearm, Maggie opened the trail of locks. Entering the apartment, she went directly to the phone and dialed. Her aunt answered before Maggie heard a ring. Learning who it was, Hannah's voice went brittle.

"I hope you're calling to apologize, Maggie. Your mother has been beside herself."

"Is she there? I have to ask her something."

"She won't talk unless it's to hear you say you're sorry."

Maggie held her tone level. "Will you please tell her I'm on the phone?"

Hannah's palm smothered the receiver. Maggie caught the muffled play of voices. Drone meets groan. A discussion between those two was never what one would call uplifting.

"Fran told me to tell you she's simply too upset to speak to you, Maggie. What is it you wanted to ask her?"

Anxious to break the odious connection, Maggie told her aunt about the box from the basement storeroom. Hannah was only half listening. Her attention was diverted by her sister's plaintive wailing in the background.

"Ssh, Fran. Please. Take it easy." Hannah came back on the line. "Now's not the time, Maggie. You can hear how aggravated she is."

"But what about the box?"

"Can't be too important. Let it wait, or look through it yourself. Up to you."

"Okay."

Hannah's voice dipped to a harsh whisper. "Would it kill you to apologize?"

"No, but my phony apology isn't going to give her what she needs."

"What's that supposed to mean? For the life of me, I can't understand what's gotten into you, Maggie."

"Forget it. Just tell Mom to give me a call when she feels up to it, will you?"

"All right. I'll speak to her as soon as she calms down a little."

Maggie hung up thinking she could be in for a very, very long wait.

She'd settled the box on the floor. Eyeing it gave her an uneasy feeling. Silly. If the carton had contained anything private or critical, her parents wouldn't have left it in the communal storeroom.

She used a paring knife to slice the cords. The box flaps had been stuffed together. They came apart with a sucking sound and a puff of dust.

Inside was a layer of yellowed newspaper. It was a thirty-year-old copy of the *New York Times* from November 15, less than a month after Maggie's second birthday.

Underneath were baby things: a pair of worn receiving blankets, two knitted cap and sweater sets, tiny kimonos, and Dr. Denton pajamas with flap bottoms. Holding them, Maggie marveled at the tiny sizes. Hard to believe her feet had ever fit into the booties that now barely stretched to accommodate her thumb. She smiled at the absurdity of how small a person starts. But everyone remains small and vulnerable in certain pieces of the uncertain self. Scraps of the tiny infant she'd been remained buried deep within her. For a second, her nightmare pressed to the surface. But she was also the sound, inde-

pendent woman whose pragmatic voice urged her to get
to the bottom of the carton.

Under the clothes were a scatter of infant toys: rattles,
pop-beads, wooden blocks with alphabet markings, music
boxes. So many toys. So much alike. Then, her mother
had always been the type to have extras of everything: in
case.

At the bottom of the box was another section of the
ancient newspaper. Maggie lifted it out. Nothing underneath. Scanning the piles of things, she tried to make
some meaningful connection. But a mountain of dark
space loomed between her and the infant girl she'd once
been.

So much for Memory Lane. Maggie started replacing
the stacks of toys and clothes and equipment. Ten minutes
later, she added the top paper layer, sealed the carton,
and stuffed it in the back of the guest room closet.

Washing her filthy hands, she felt a tug of disappointment. Would be nice to find a boxful of easy answers, she
supposed. But knowing human nature, she'd be forced to
concoct a fresh batch of personal enigmas if that ever
happened.

Heading for the living room, she decided to get the
place presentable for her expected guests. She straightened the cushions, made neat piles of the scattered papers
and magazines she was forever meaning to get to, and
picked up the obvious debris.

Maggie was about to deposit the messy heap in the
trash can when she realized that the paper slip she'd
picked off the foyer floor was the back of a faded photograph. There was a date penciled in her mother's graceful
hand. Turning it over, she found a snapshot that had fallen
out of the box of baby things.

As the image pierced her shock, Maggie understood
that she had discovered a boxful of answers after all. Here
was the explanation for all the blanks and inconsistencies
that had plagued her for a lifetime.

And now she would have to face them.

CHAPTER

43

The toxicologist slipped her reading glasses in the pocket of her lab coat and folded her hands.

"Sorry, Mr. Price. I'd be glad to help, but I can't give you what I don't have."

Price nodded. Bannister was not inclined to be so agreeable. "But you said you spotted the same peculiarity in both autopsy reports."

Imke Lepczek nodded. She was a rangy woman with silken blond hair and a dense accent. According to Price, Dr. Lepczek knew her way around lab values better than anyone else in the bagged-body business. For her old friend Lenny, she'd agreed to give up part of her day off to meet the two detectives in her lab at the coroner's office on Thirtieth Street and First Avenue. She'd spent the last hour there, reviewing and comparing the results of the postmortems from Gail Weider and Theodore Macklin.

"That's true, Mr. Bannister," she said. "Both blood scans showed an excess of a stress hormone called CRF and a slight depression of normal endorphin levels. Strange combination."

"Strange how?" Bannister said.

"Normally, you'd expect to see an elevation of both factors. It's a common pattern in patients with post-traumatic stress disorders."

Price scratched behind an ear. "Macklin and Weider were both severe phobics. Wouldn't it make sense for them to react like PTSD patients?"

285

"Absolutely," the toxicologist said. "That's why I find this unusual combination of factors so surprising. But the problem, as I told you, is that I can't assess them in a vacuum. I'd have to have longitudinal data to tell whether this was a transitory anomaly or indicative of external contaminants."

Price read Bannister's confusion. "She's saying that she'd have to see blood samples from a living patient for a couple of days to tell anything, Sammy. Without that, Dr. Lepczek doesn't know what to make of results like this. Those weird numbers could have come from somebody giving Weider and Macklin a drug of some sort. Or it could have been a fluke."

"You mean two flukes," Bannister said. "That's pretty hard to swallow."

"Maybe not. What if Dr. Lyons prescribed some medicine that caused those changes in both victims?" Price said.

"No way. Maggie wouldn't mess with any drug that would hurt a patient."

"Easy, Sam. I'm not accusing her of anything, I'm just suggesting a possible reason for those strange lab results. What do you think, Dr. Lepczek?"

The toxicologist frowned. "It's possible, I suppose. But only if she were involved in experimental trials of a new drug. I know of nothing on the market that would cause this odd pattern."

"Can't hurt to ask Dr. Lyons," Price said.

"I'll do it, Lenny. Use your phone?" Bannister strode to the one on Dr. Lepczek's desk in a tiny rear office.

"Be there, damn it. Please be there." Bannister needed to hear that Maggie hadn't been dosing her patients with some unproven concoction. He couldn't bear the thought that she might have been responsible for those deaths, even inadvertently.

Watch it, Sammy boy. You fall for a woman, you're liable to keep right on falling.

There was no answer at Maggie's apartment. He left a message on her machine and tried her office at the hospital. According to her assistant, Maggie hadn't been in and wasn't expected. When Bannister said it was an emergency, the guy clacked his tongue.

"Ordinarily, she can be reached by pager, but I've been trying her since early this morning and no luck. Isn't it just the way to have her unavailable with all these emergencies."

"Why? What's going on?"

Bannister heard the assistant out. Hanging up, he returned to Price and the toxicologist.

"What's wrong, Sammy? You feel okay?" Price said.

Bannister told them, his wound throbbing in sympathy for the latest victims. Last night, a female patient of Maggie's in the hospital had wandered outside in her bare feet. The woman had ventured into traffic and narrowly missed being run down by a truck.

Another patient, a member of Maggie's young adult group, had let himself into a fenced yard where three killer dogs were lurking. In a vivid rush, Bannister felt the catch of teeth, the sickening rip of flesh. His throat filled with the sour taste of fear. Looked like Ernesto Nuñez had left him with more than the scar across his middle. The work had its moments. But this wasn't one of them.

"You okay, Sammy? Christ, you're green. Sit down. Let your head hang between your knees."

Bannister tried to shake the queasiness. "I'm all right. Something just got to me there for a second."

This was no time to fall apart. They had to pay a visit to the newest clinic casualty. Maybe this one could provide the necessary answers. They had to find the magic words to make the nightmare disappear.

CHAPTER

44

The cab ride from her building to Grand Central Station was a blur. So was the moment outside the Pan Am Building when she changed her mind and asked the driver to take her to Stamford, Connecticut. He'd turned to Maggie, the insanity verdict printed on his face.

"Cost you hundred fifty dollars."

"That's all right."

"Tolls extra. Waiting time, too."

"I understand."

The cost had no meaning for her. All she cared about was reaching her destination as quickly as possible with the fewest possible turns and detours. She could not tolerate further complications or delays. She'd waited far too long already. Nearly her entire life.

The cab's radio was too loud, the music nail-sharp and grating, but Maggie experienced it from a benign distance. Everything seemed blunted and flat, including time, which passed in jarring bursts. With jolting suddenness, they'd completed the bulk of the trip and turned off the Merritt Parkway at the second Stamford exit. At Maggie's direction, the cabbie headed north through the confusing weave of streets that led to Aunt Hannah's house.

"Turn here?" the driver said.

"At the church sign. Then make the second left."

The cabbie clutched the wheel and negotiated the meandering back roads at a timorous crawl. He was suffering from a fear of the unfamiliar, she suspected. Definitely a feeling Maggie could understand.

Or could she really understand anything?

Pulling the faded photo from her purse, she stared at it again. The meaning was undeniable, but she couldn't find a place for it. Her mind was a wall. The incredible truth could only bump and bounce away.

Aunt Hannah's house was a prim Dutch colonial screened by a dense privet hedge. Maggie knocked at the door frame and watched as her aunt appeared in silhouette behind the dark screen door. Peering out, Hannah shaded her eyes with cupped fingers.

"Maggie? Is that you?"

"I have to see my mother."

Hannah unlatched the screen and pulled it open. Spotting the waiting city cab at the curb, her hand flew to her mouth. "My God. What happened? Did somebody die?"

Maggie's mother had moved from the kitchen into the hall.

"That's what I'd like to know. Who was Elizabeth? And what happened to her?" Maggie stepped inside and squinted as her eyes adjusted to the gloom.

Hannah moved quickly, circling her sister in a protective embrace. "It's all right, Fran. Let me handle this."

"Tell me, Mom," Maggie said.

"Ssh," Hannah crooned, stroking her sister's hair. "Don't let her upset you."

Maggie gripped her mother by an elbow and drew her out of Hannah's grasp. "I have to hear it, Mom. I have to hear it from you."

Her mother nodded dully. "How did you find out?"

"This was in the carton you had in storage."

Maggie pulled the old photo out of her purse and set it in her mother's palm. For a long time, her mother stared at the snapshot. She looked like a photograph herself, captured and still.

By now, the image on the old picture was etched in Maggie's mind. It was the room from her window dream. Same twin beds with the matching flowered spreads and curtains; same flower-bordered rug. The two objects that hadn't survived in her nightmare explained everything.

On each bed was a large embroidered pillow. One said, *Margaret*, the other, *Elizabeth*.

"Elizabeth was my sister?"

"Your twin."

"Twin?"

Her mother's eyes were fogged with pain and memory. "You were identical, almost impossible to tell apart. I always kept name bracelets on you to make sure there wasn't a mix-up.

"But there was really no chance of that from the way you acted. Your personalities were entirely different. You were the brave one, Maggie. Always the first to try something new. Always the one we had to keep an eye on. Lizzie was shy and quiet. Much less active. Lazy Elizabeth, we used to call her."

Lazy Elizabeth. Lazy Bit.

"What happened to her?" Maggie said.

Aunt Hannah had slipped back in her regular role: human shield. For once, Maggie's mother raised a protesting hand and edged clear of the cover.

"It's no good, Hannah. It has to come out. I always knew it would, sooner or later."

Her mother's voice wavered. "Your father and I had a dinner party to go to. Business thing. Usually, we left you girls with Hannah and Bill when we went out, but they were away that weekend."

"Bill's niece's wedding in Philadelphia," Hannah said.

"So we hired a sitter from an agency," Maggie's mother went on. "She seemed like such a nice young woman. Smart, responsible. Good references.

"I gave her all the instructions. Told her your exact routine. And of course, I left the number where we'd be. It was a midtown hotel, no more than a mile or two from home. Still, I felt nervous for some reason. As if I had a premonition. Your father kept telling me I was being neurotic. That I had to learn to ease up, let you two go."

Tears consumed her. She yielded for a moment, then patched herself back in control.

"We got the call in the middle of dinner. The sitter was hysterical, barely able to speak. She'd put you girls to bed.

There wasn't a peep out of you, so she thought everything was fine. She was listening to the radio when she heard the sirens in the street. From the window, she saw something that looked like a broken doll lying on the sidewalk. How terrible, she thought. Some child must have fallen. Until the police came knocking at our door, she'd had no idea it was Elizabeth."

"Why didn't you tell me?"

Tears spilled over in Francine's eyes. "You were just a baby. Close as you were to Lizzie, you stopped asking about her after a few days. The pediatrician thought it was best to leave it alone for the time being. We always intended to tell you later on, but it never seemed like the right moment."

"I told you dozens of times about that recurrent nightmare. You knew it was about Elizabeth falling. Why didn't you say so?"

"I couldn't, Maggie. Don't you see?"

The dream played against the coating of ice over Maggie's consciousness. She was pushing up the window with a smooth easy glide. Soaring out. Landing on the hawk's back. Starting the dizzy descent.

But it was not her.

Lazy bit.

"How did she fall? Tell me what happened." Maggie caught the silent warning look that passed between the two sisters. "Tell me."

Her mother was crying again. "It was an accident. Somehow, the window got opened wide enough so Elizabeth was able to slip out."

Somehow.

Maggie was numb, her head reeling with the impossible new twists.

"All she wanted was to protect you, to keep you safe and happy. What more can a mother do?" Hannah said.

"Nothing," Maggie said dully. "I have to go now. The taxi's waiting."

Hannah followed her out the door and down the walk. "It wasn't her fault, Maggie. Don't you understand? Don't you see?"

Pulling the taxi door shut, Maggie asked the driver to turn up the radio. They drove off in a burst of enveloping noise. But nothing was sufficient to mute the strident facts.

For the first time in her life, Maggie understood and saw perfectly. She'd been born with a twin sister, an identical other half. And once upon a tragic time, Maggie's mischief had sent that innocent angel to her death.

CHAPTER

45

Order was the essence. Good fortune followed meticulous planning and attention to the basest detail. Tragedy trod the heels of sloppiness and neglect, no matter how brief or transitory. A blink, a moment's breach of the guard, and events could spin eternally out of control.

It had happened once. It would never happen again.

In school, there had been endless lessons in the value of redundancy. Check and double-check. Test and retest. Backup and contingency systems were the best insurance against accidental failure.

All was in readiness. And that readiness would pay suitable dividends.

Needing to get the bitch doctor out of her apartment during the final preparations, several alternative strategies had been devised. It would only take a few minutes alone in the place.

Tonight was the finest imaginable night: her final one.

Any number of ways to lure her out had seemed foolproof. But such intervention had proven unnecessary. Before dawn, the bitch had left the building on her own. Her departure had been so precipitous, she'd even forgotten her beeper. There it was, on the foyer table. Opening the door with the duplicate keys made from the ones lifted temporarily from Maggie's purse in her office, the beeper was sitting there in plain sight, a pleasurable bonus. The very best of good fortune. Out of touch, Dr. Maggie Lyons was even more vulnerable to the plan.

This was the finest imaginable chess match. The queen was the pawn. The pawn was the king. And the end game would be a real one.

CHAPTER

46

After twenty years in the business, Bannister thought he'd developed professional immunity to the effects of violence. But nothing had prepared him for the sickening spectacle of Jason Childs.

Kid was mummified, his bandages oozing a rainbow of revolting fluids. A staggering array of lines linked the teenager to medications and machines. The monitors shrilled and beeped in dissonant chorus, filling the room like swarms of warring bugs.

According to Mrs. Childs, the dogs had separated Jason from part of his lower lip, a piece of his left ear, and the tips of three fingers. The rest of him was marred by ruts and bruises. His recovery would take numerous grafts and several rounds of plastic surgery. But the largest damage was to his mind. The kid was in a near catatonic state, totally unresponsive to all stimuli, including deep pain.

Price shook his head. "It's a defensive thing, Sammy. He'll come back eventually. Might be soon, but it could take days or weeks."

"Damn it, Lenny. Why can't we get a break?"

"You're looking at him and wondering why *we* can't get a break?"

Bannister fell silent. There but for the gracelessness of Ernesto Nuñez he knew he might be as well. Going mouth to mouth with that punk had been just as risky as Jason's foolhardy attempt to get up close and personal with the rottweiler sisters. And Bannister's dumb stunt could have had a similarly unfortunate outcome. Funny to be grateful for a throbbing gut and twenty-seven stitches. But all things were relative.

"I just mean I wish he could tell us what happened," Bannister said for the fifteenth time.

"Maybe he still can. Follow me."

Mrs. Childs was waiting in the hall, cuddling a little blond girl on her lap. Cute kid, Bannister thought. Reminded him of Chloe. But then most things did.

"Are you policemen?" the child chirped.

"Detectives," Price said.

"You going to punish those nasty dogs that hurt my brother?"

"That's the dog warden's job. Ours is to try to figure out what happened," Price told her.

"Jason would never tease a dog," the little girl said gravely. "Never."

Price sat beside the mother and questioned her gently. No, she said. Jason hadn't been on any medication. No. She couldn't imagine him going into that fenced yard voluntarily. To her knowledge, the boy had no enemies. In fact, he was pretty much a loner. He hadn't complained about anyone at the hospital in particular.

"He *hated* Binnie," the little girl said.

"No, he didn't, Jess. Binnie was Jason's new therapy aide," Mrs. Childs explained. "He didn't hate her; he just hated having to go to the hospital for that group. He didn't mind when his old aide and the doctors came to treat him at the house, but it's a torment for Jason to go out."

"He stays home all the time?" Bannister asked.

"Mostly. For the last six years, I've had to drag him out for essentials like school. And even then, I had to deliver him to the door and pick him up."

"But he did make it to the group sessions," Price said.

A ghost of a nod. "Only after months and months of nagging from his father and me. I feel so guilty. None of this would have happened if we hadn't pushed him."

"What makes you say that?" Price asked.

She gnawed her lower lip. "Jason's changed since he started that program. Gotten nervier. I was hoping it was a sign of some improvement. But now this." Her eyes filled. "He would never have gone into that fenced yard if we hadn't made him desperate. I'd bet he did it to get us and everyone off his back."

"It might have had nothing to do with you or the clinic, Mrs. Childs. That's what we're trying to find out," Price said.

"I should have left him alone," his mother sobbed. "This is all my fault. I know it."

The little girl stroked her mother's cheek. "It's not, Mommy. It's Jason's own fault." She faced Bannister and Price, her jaw set. "He did take medicine. I saw him swallow some of his experiment stuff."

"Experiment?" Bannister felt his heart quicken.

Mrs. Childs mopped her eyes and drew a shuddering breath. "That's silly, Jessie. Jason wouldn't do a thing like that. He must've been fooling you."

The child's head swung in an adamant arc. "He wasn't, Mommy. He didn't even know I was watching. He took that stuff, and then he started acting real funny."

"What kind of experiment was he doing, Mrs. Childs?" Bannister asked.

"It was some project he was working on last year for the Westinghouse Talent Search," she said. "Never came to anything, but he still tinkers with it from time to time. I'm honestly not even sure what he was trying to develop. Jason was very secretive about his experiments."

"I know," the child said. "It was this magic medicine that could make you very, very brave."

Bannister tensed. Price caught his eye. *Go easy,* his stern look said.

"That's silly, Jess. There's no such thing." Mrs. Childs turned to the men. "I'm afraid she has an active imagination."

"What makes you think it was a bravery drug, sweetheart?" Price asked.

"It said so in Jay's experiment book." Her eyes widened. "Please don't tell him I looked in there. He'll get furious."

The woman shook her head. "Jason was only teasing, Jessie."

"He never teases in his experiment book, Mommy. You know that."

"We need a sample of that formula, Mrs. Childs," Bannister said.

"But why? Jason would never make anything harmful. He's the gentlest soul imaginable."

Bannister held his calm. "I'm sure he is. But we have a friend who can analyze the compound and make sure there's nothing about it that could affect Jason's care. You know, sometimes drugs can interact and cause troubles."

"Right. It's for Jason's sake, Mrs. Childs," Price said.

She worked it over. "All right, if you think it's important . . ."

"I do. And we should have a copy of Jason's hospital record, in case my friend in the lab needs to check his medications or whatever," Price said.

"Okay, Detective. I'll go ask the nurse."

The little girl watched until her mother was safely out of earshot. "Is Jay in trouble?" she demanded.

"We just want to find out what happened, sweetheart," Price said.

Mrs. Childs was returning, her steps crisp against the tile. The child lowered her voice to a fretful breath.

"Please don't say I told on him," she rasped. "Jay will *kill* me. I know he will."

CHAPTER

47

Maggie couldn't bring herself to return to the apartment. Suddenly, she didn't seem to belong there. Or anywhere else, for that matter. She'd been evicted from her normal slot in the universe. Set out for random collection like a castoff piece of furniture.

She'd had the cabbie drop her at the north terminus of the East River Promenade. For hours, she wandered aimlessly, trying to weave her unruly thoughts into something approaching bearable order.

She'd been redefined, rewritten. Her entire conscious existence before today had been a tentative first draft.

New main character: Margaret Lyons, identical twin. Maggie struggled to dredge up some memory of the lost Elizabeth. Images teased at her, vague as moth wings. She was clutching at chubby, dancing fingers. Tumbling over a small hill of giggling flesh. Making silly faces at a living mirror.

Voices trilled the birthday song, and she pictured a cake capped with sugar roses. "Happy birthday to—"

"*You.*"

The "you" part must have been Elizabeth's.

Lizzie, the lazy one.

Lazy Bit.

Lizzie the lost.

Having a twin sister cleared up so many lifelong riddles. Maggie had always had an inexplicably strong reaction to twins. Once, after reading an article about a meeting of a national twins organization, she'd been

moved nearly to tears. The response had seemed sense-
less at the time. The story had been entirely upbeat and
whimsical. But it had haunted Maggie for days. She'd
even joked with Henry that she must have been a twin in
a former incarnation.

And so she had.

"Ring around the rosies.

Pocket full of posies.

Ashes, *ashes.*

We all fall down!"

Now her mind could split the ancient rhymes into her
part and Lizzie's. Chilling echo from a distant other side.
Her mother must have taught them all the baby songs and
chants that way, playing the pair of them like two slats on
a xylophone.

The photograph had shown identical bedspreads and
pillows, the two of them dressed in the same dotted
dresses, frilled socks, and patent leather Mary Janes.
Maggie's mother had mentioned name bracelets and distinct personalities. Otherwise, they'd been given doubles
of everything. The carton from the storeroom had contained duplicate toys, outfits, blankets.

The current wisdom on raising twins was to encourage
them to be separate and distinct. But there had been no
reason for Maggie's mother to worry about helping her
and Lizzie establish individual identities. Only one of
them had been destined to survive.

Lazy Lizzie. Flying on the hawk's back. *If I should
die . . .*

The bird that haunted Maggie's dreams must have been
a passing cloud or plane, some visual quirk printed indeli-
bly on her infant imagination.

New plot: Maggie Lyons murders her second self and
spends the rest of her unnatural life struggling with the
unthinkable consequences.

Infant or no, she had been responsible for her sister's
death. From the look that had passed between her mother
and her aunt, Maggie knew she'd always been held to
blame for that tragic event and the avalanche of troubles it
unleashed. Maggie was seen as the source of her mother's

suffocating overprotection and irrational fears. Maggie was the fuel that had fed her mother's blazing need for self-denial. Maggie had stolen her mother's youth and courage and strength. She was deemed responsible for killing her parents' marriage, dooming her mother to a dark life of loneliness and regret.

Lazy Lizzie and Murdering Maggie. Maggie, the destroyer of her home and family.

Maggie knew it was unfair and untrue. She'd been a baby at the time of Lizzie's death. Anyway, her mother was responsible for her own happiness. Everyone was. But Maggie couldn't shake the illogical burden of guilt and shame. She kept viewing the act from her adult perspective. In horrific detail, she saw her tiny hands raising the window. She felt her willful fingers urging the infant Elizabeth to her death.

In a daze, she left the promenade. Heading west, she walked through Central Park and followed Central Park West to Eighty-second Street. All those years ago, her family had lived in a majestic old apartment building called the Beresford. Maggie remembered that they'd occupied a north-facing apartment on the tenth floor. Standing across the street, she counted until she was staring at the windows to her parents' old apartment.

She tried to envision herself and Lizzie inside, playing in their room with the flowered spreads and curtains and the flower-bordered rug. She struggled to conjure the smell and feel and sound of that brief safe time before the world was shattered in irrevocable fragments.

Shivering in the heat, she was overwhelmed by the sudden loss of what she hadn't known she'd had. And her mind filled with the child's prayer her mother had taught and urged the tiny pair of them to say each night without fail:

"Now I lay me down to sleep.
I pray the lord my soul to keep.
If I should die before I wake.
I pray the lord my soul to take."

CHAPTER

48

While Bannister circled the block searching for a parking space, Price dashed into the coroner's office to deliver the sample of Jason Childs's experimental formula and a copy of the young man's hospital record to Dr. Lepczek.

From the Childs's house, Price had reached the toxicologist at her home in Riverdale. Dr. Lepczek had agreed to return to the lab immediately to analyze the experimental compound and compare Jason's blood values to the odd ones she'd discovered in the Macklin and Weider autopsy reports.

Near the corner of Thirty-third Street, Bannister spotted a boisterous family piling into a minivan. He pulled the Camaro alongside and waited out the laborious loading process. There were two parents, three kids, two dogs, one grandma, and an accompanying jumble of purchases and paraphernalia. Bannister thought of his own world, the entire inventory small enough to stuff in a lunch bag. Not much to show for nearly forty years on the planet.

At least there was Chloe, he reminded himself. That kid was his ticket to immortality. And the ticket was definitely first class. His little girl had way more to offer than most people, Bannister thought with a swell of pride, even with her occasional bouts of distemper.

Bannister had spotted the same proud parental gleam in Mrs. Childs. The woman was visibly moved by her young daughter's poise and self-possession. Jessie had taken things in hand, especially after they all arrived at the family home in Bayside. The little girl had led them directly to the spot where Jason stashed his formula at the back of his closet. She reported how Jason had dropped out of the Talent Search competition, too fearful to continue with the experiment after finding one of his test animals dead.

"I saw Jay carry this mouse up from the cellar in one of those flower shovel things. It was all smashed and yucky, and he flushed it down the toilet. That was the day he called his chemistry teacher and said he had the flu. Remember, Mommy?"

Bannister thought about how kids are taught not to snoop or tattle. Lucky thing Jason's little sister had chosen to ignore that particular lesson.

The minivan finally vacated the spot. Bannister angled in and headed to the Medical Examiner's office, a blue-and-white tile building on First Avenue near Bellevue Hospital.

He found Price and Dr. Lepczek huddled over a spiky readout in the toxicology lab.

"You see the skewing in the pattern from the baseline to the pretrauma sample, Lenny? And then the severe dip?" Dr. Lepczek said.

"Very interesting. See that, Sam? You notice the steady phase overload followed by a major spike in the opioid levels? Ever see a more obvious rebound?"

Bannister stared at the paper. "Once or twice at a Knick's game."

Explaining, Imke Lepczek ran her square finger along the sharp trail of lines. "We found the same odd pattern in the Childs blood samples that we saw in the Weider and Macklin autopsy reports. Fortunately, we also have a copy of blood work done on Jason at intervals since his admission to the hospital. And we have reports from his last several regular checkups. Jason's doctor is on staff at Elmhurst General, so the chart goes back a few years."

"What does it mean?"

Dr. Lepczek made a tent with her fingers. "It means Jason was taking a maintenance dose of some drug that elevated his CRF stress hormone level and depressed his normal production of endorphins. Shortly before his admission, he ingested a much larger quantity of the drug. That would account for the major and continuing change in his levels of both substances."

"You're saying the Childs kid really did develop a courage drug?" Bannister said.

Price's nod was grim. "Suicide drug's more like it. Apparently, whatever this substance is, it strips normal inhibitions altogether. Makes it so a person takes risks he never would in his right mind."

"From what I see here, I'd bet on a time-release preliminary exposure for several days before the booster dose," Dr. Lepczek said.

"Time-release like one of those cold capsules, you mean?" Bannister asked.

Price shrugged. "Doubtful, Sammy. No matter how clever this kid was in chemistry, it's unlikely he'd figure out how to fabricate something like that. Imke agrees it was probably a topical thing, something taken in through the skin."

Bannister called Elmhurst General and tracked Mrs. Childs to Jason's room. Again, the little sister was the one with ready information. Jessie had seen Jason apply some of his magic bravery drug inside the plastic watchbands he'd distributed to his phobia group.

Cupping his hand over the receiver, Bannister reported the finding to Dr. Lepczek.

"That could work. He might have inserted some absorbent substance between the plastic layers," she said.

Bannister picked up his hand for a high five. "So, partner, looks like we've deduced the hell out of this one. Jason Childs is our man, and he's certainly in no condition to hurt anyone else. We take back the watches from the other group members, and the party's over."

Price didn't return the gesture. His face had fallen like a failed soufflé.

"Only one major fly in that ointment, Sammy. According to Mrs. Childs, Jason never left the house without her, remember?"

Reality crept over Bannister like a rash. "Which means he couldn't have gotten to Macklin and Gail Weider."

"Exactly."

"So maybe the mother is wrong. He could have snuck out when she was out shopping or whatever."

"Not likely, Sammy. Everyone swears that Jason Childs was a shut-in, even his little sister who knows all and sees all. Besides, what connection would Jason have had to Macklin and Gail Weider, much less that woman patient at the hospital who tried to play chicken with a truck last night?"

Bannister couldn't pull a single rabbit out of the hat. "None I can think of. But that doesn't mean there wasn't any. Don't you always tell me to take it where it leads you, Lenny? Aren't you the one who's always saying I shouldn't overlook anything?"

"Yeah, Sam. And of course, we'll check all the angles. But you also can't overlook the very large possibility that the snake we're after is still hiding out there in the grass."

CHAPTER

49

All day, Bannister had been running on nothing but pain-killers and frustration. At Price's insistence, he agreed to a pit stop at Sergio's for refueling. Now he sat prodding his food around the plate. Nothing could come between Lenny and his appetite, but Bannister's only hunger was for an end to this mess.

"Eat, Sammy. You're pale as a ghost. Last thing anyone needs is for you to get yourself sick."

Bannister couldn't see the point. "Maybe food would help. But this stuff?"

"Come on. We need you big and strong."

They certainly needed something. Three victims already, one harrowing near miss, and, if Price was correct as usual, an untold number of people could be waiting in the on-deck circle.

Between hearty bites of his turkey club, Price outlined his plan and scribbled a wish list on the paper place mat.

"First, we need the names of all hospital personnel that dealt with the Childs kid. Then, we find out which of those also had dealings with Weider, Macklin, and that woman who almost had the head-on collision with the truck last night. What's her name again, Sam?"

"Tyler. Daisy Tyler."

"Right. I say, first we call the Childs woman to find out who worked with Jason. Would have been someone who spent a fair amount of time with the kid, I figure. No one would believe Jason had actually developed a courage drug without a decent amount of talk and demonstration.

Also, the mother said Jason was secretive about his experiments. So it's not likely he opened up to a casual acquaintance."

"I'll call."

Bannister went to the pay phone in the rear and dialed Maggie's number first. He'd been trying to reach her all day. One conversation would clear so many open questions, he thought as he listened to her taped voice on the answering machine.

Maggie would know who'd worked with the Childs boy and the other victims. Maggie could tell him and Price about the suspects, help them get a handle on who might be capable of stealing the kid's formula and using it to murder and maim.

So where the hell was she? Bannister's gut fisted. What if something had happened to her? But no, that wasn't a possibility he was willing to entertain.

Mrs. Childs had gone home for dinner. Bannister caught her there and got the list of East End personnel who'd worked with Jason during his first round of therapy. Several of the names were familiar from the grand rounds he'd made when he was trying to get his hands on Macklin's records.

Next, he phoned the psych ward at East End, hoping to reach his portly nurse friend. Unfortunately, she was at some unknown out-of-town location for the rest of the weekend. Not surprisingly, the woman on the line wouldn't budge when he tried to pass himself off as Ted Macklin's new doctor and requested the names of the people who'd treated Macklin during his stay at the hospital. Bannister knew only too well that East End wrapped barbed wire around patient information. As usual, they were going to have to go around the long way.

Returning to the table, he found Price seated with a chunk of cherry pie and an expectant look. Bannister read from the notes he'd scrawled during his conversation with Mrs. Childs.

"Starting about eight months ago, Jason had weekly sessions with a psychiatrist named Pam Richards, a good friend of Maggie's. A young resident came by several times to check him medically, but Mrs. Childs doesn't remember the guy's name. His aide was Francis Kennedy, better known as F.X., pleasant enough according to the mother. Got along fine with Jason. When F.X. couldn't make it to Jason's for practice sessions, another aide filled in. Mrs. Childs couldn't remember that name either."

Price wiped a slick of cherry filling off his chin. "You still couldn't reach Dr. Lyons to find out who worked with Macklin and Weider?"

"No, and I have to tell you, I'm worried about her."

"You don't have to tell me, Sammy. It's obvious." He motioned for the check. "Let's go see that Daisy Tyler woman at the hospital. Maybe she can hand us the missing link."

CHAPTER

50

They found Daisy Tyler in bed, watching a Fred Astaire–Ginger Rogers movie. At Price's knock, she cast an expectant look toward the door. Spotting them, her face registered disappointment.

"Daisy Tyler? I'm Sam Bannister, and this is my partner, Lenny Price. We're consultants to the hospital. If you're not busy, we'd appreciate it if you'd help us with a survey we're conducting. It'll only take a few minutes."

The woman's face went wary. "What kind of survey?"

Price picked up the ball and ran with it. "It's a staff evaluation poll. Just routine. Dr. Lyons recommended you as one of the people we should talk to."

Her face softened. "Sure. I'll be glad to help if Dr. Lyons wants me to."

"We appreciate your cooperation, Ms. Tyler. Can you tell us which doctors and aides you've worked with here at the hospital?"

Daisy's eyes narrowed. "Dr. Lyons could have told you that."

"Just procedure. We have to get the answers directly from the patients."

She nodded. "Okay. My aide is a woman named Beverly Magida. She's a great person, with a wonderful sense of humor. As you probably know, I see Dr. Lyons for therapy. And there are tons of nurses. Three shifts. At least eight or more a shift. Plus the weekend people. They've all been so nice."

Price kept pressing. "How about other aides? What happens when this Beverly Magida can't make it?"

"Bev hasn't missed a session so far. I suppose they'd substitute someone else if she got sick or something."

"Have you had any dealings with F.X. Kennedy?"

"That redheaded aide? He works with another patient here. Woman named Liza something. She introduced me to him in the lounge. Friendly man. Drops in from time to time to see how I'm doing."

"Have you seen any psychiatrists other than Dr. Lyons?" Bannister asked.

"Once or twice, Dr. Lyons had another doctor stop by. A woman named Dr. Richards. Very nice. Everyone here has been just wonderful to me. You can put that down in your evaluation report in big letters."

Her eye drifted toward a doilied plate covered with hand-dipped chocolates. Bannister spotted the accompanying note. It read: *From your not-so-secret admirer.*

Daisy giggled. "I know it's silly. But it does give me a lift. Every day, someone manages to sneak in and leave me a treat." She fingered her watch. "This was the first gift. Most nights it's cookies or candy."

"Who do you think sends them?" Bannister demanded.

"I'm almost ashamed to say," she said. "The man's half my age, and I know it isn't real interest."

"A young resident?" Bannister pressed.

"How did you know?"

"What's his name?"

Bannister held his breath, waiting for what he knew he was about to hear. A young resident had made several visits to Jason Childs. A resident had free run of the hospital and free access to patients.

Son of a bitch must have had some hidden agenda, maybe a murderous obsession. Bannister's suspicions had been aroused the first time he saw the guy sniffing around Maggie. A vicious pulse was thundering in his ears. He should have listened to his instincts. Why hadn't he warned Maggie to stay away?

Daisy's smile was wistful. "He's the sweetest young man you ever want to meet, Mr. Bannister. His name's Mitch. Dr. Mitchell Goldberg."

CHAPTER

51

A wrapped package and a banded stack of mail awaited Maggie at the door to her apartment. Carrying them in, she found the place awash in eerie stillness. She passed from room to room, flipping on lights, televisions, radios. Anything to fill the lethal hush.

In her office, she noticed that it was nearing six-thirty. The day had been swallowed whole. Back in the foyer, she leafed through the mail and opened the package. It was a box of hand-dipped chocolates from a posh Madison Avenue shop. The note was from a "not-so-secret admirer." Fishing for a list of possible suspects, she suddenly remembered that she had a dinner appointment with Mitch Goldberg for *this* evening. If she didn't hurry, her unwelcome company would soon be on the way.

She called her father first and was delighted for once to hear Tina's voice on the line. Maggie begged out of the evening, claiming a work emergency. Without pause or question, Tina was willing to trade Maggie's lame excuse for a polite expression of disappointment and a promise to reschedule soon. No doubt her father would have been a tougher sell.

Mitch Goldberg didn't answer his home phone, and he didn't respond to his page at the hospital. Maggie was not up to seeing him or anyone tonight. She called down to Tony, the night doorman, and asked him to head off her guest at the pass.

"Tell him I'm not feeling well, will you, Tony? I haven't been able to reach him, so he might be on the way."

"Sure thing, Dr. Lyons. Need anything?"

"No, thanks."

What she needed couldn't be sent up from the pharmacy or the corner market. She ached for peace. Maggie wanted her life back in reasonable order. She was like a drawer rifled by a thief, her contents violated and thrown in chaos.

Maggie plodded to her bedroom and sprawled atop the covers. She tried to sort through the disconcerting mess, to impose some hint of harmony on the jumble of thoughts and thorny feelings. But it was all too new and overwhelming.

Weighted by the day, she pressed her cheek against her pillow and succumbed to a dreamless sleep. She could have used a week of numb unconsciousness, but she was yanked awake moments later by the drone of the doorbell.

Who the hell?

Maggie lay still, willing whoever it was to give up and go away. But the buzzer kept sounding.

"All right, I'm coming."

She padded down the hall and peered through the peephole. The young resident was at the door. Why hadn't Tony turned him away as she'd asked? And why, in any event, had Goldberg been allowed upstairs without the customary announcement? It wasn't like Tony to slip like this.

Maggie spoke through the door. "Mitch? Sorry. I tried to reach you. Didn't the doorman tell you I'm not feeling well?"

"No one was down there, but if you're sick, there's all the more reason for you to accept the company of a fine physician such as myself."

Angling her eyes down, she saw that he was cradling a bottle of champagne.

"Thanks, but really, I'm not up to it tonight."

"Can't I just come in for a second to give you a little gift of good cheer?"

Maggie felt a guilty twinge. "All right, I guess. But you really shouldn't have gone to so much trouble."

She worked the locks. Opening the door, she saw that

Goldberg had gone all out. New clothes, fresh haircut, the heady scent of an extravagant cologne. The champagne was vintage Dom Perignon.

"This is too much, Mitch. Honestly."

"It's my pleasure. Sorry you're under the weather."

Under the weather didn't begin to cover it. Maggie was a mess. She was still wearing the running shorts and sneakers from her morning jog. Her T-shirt was soiled from the dirty carton she'd carried up from the storeroom. Her eyes were grainy with sleep, and a jackhammer was working at her temples.

"As you can see, I'm in no condition for a night on the town. How about a rain check?"

He breezed past her and set the champagne on the kitchen counter. With deft moves, he uncorked the bottle.

"You shouldn't have gone to such expense."

He flapped away her concern. "Sit down and put your feet up. Doctor's orders."

Plumping a pair of throw pillows, he slipped them behind her neck. "First, I prescribe a spot of bubbly."

"I don't know—"

"But I do," he said firmly. Rummaging through the kitchen cabinets, he found two stemmed wine glasses. Filling them with measures of the crackling liquid, he offered one to Maggie.

She took a sip. The champagne tasted wonderful. The bubbles tickled her nose and fizzed at the dull rubber swaddling her brain. Nice.

Goldberg plied her with more champagne. After seeking her permission, he opened the box of chocolates and offered her several luscious selections. Two glasses of bubbly and many sinful calories later, she had to admit the therapy was having a positive effect.

"Better?" he said.

"Much."

"Good. Why don't you go slip into something more uncomfortable? I'll call the restaurant and tell them we'll be a little late."

Maggie shook her head. "I'm honestly not up for that, Mitch."

"Woman can't live by chocolates and champagne alone."

"Yes, she can. And very happily so, I might add."

He waggled a finger. "I'm the doctor here, Doctor. And I say you need some real nourishment."

"How about we compromise, and I order up a pizza?"

"Mushroom and pepperoni?"

"You've got yourself a deal."

Maggie called Ray's Original. Leaving Goldberg to await the delivery, she took a quick shower and dressed in fresh jeans and a clean T-shirt.

The young resident turned out to be a pleasant distraction. His company kept her from dwelling on the horrific turn her life had abruptly taken. The champagne helped dull the shock of the day's revelations. Maggie wasn't aware of how well until the walls wavered and her pulse started to race.

"Whoa. I'm afraid my brain has taken on a bit of water."

Goldberg nodded. "No problem. A little fresh air should take care of that."

Gripping Maggie by the elbow, he led her out to the terrace. "There now. Easy does it."

Leaning hard on a redwood planter, Maggie struggled to clear her head. Her eyes blurred, and her legs threatened to buckle. Had she really had that much champagne? She was sure the bottle was still more than half full. And Mitch had definitely downed his share.

"I'm not usually so susceptible." Her tongue was thick. The words oozed out slowly like toothpaste from a near-empty tube.

Goldberg looked grave. "I'd say you need to get more food into that stomach. I'll heat up the rest of the pizza. Be back in a minute."

An eerie feeling was overtaking her. Maggie didn't want Mitch to leave her alone. But she was operating in slow motion. By the time she found the necessary words, he'd gone inside and slid the terrace door shut behind him.

A bizarre sensation was creeping up her legs. Advancing army of electric spiders. Maybe there really was something wrong with her.

"Mitch?"

Her voice was forceless, thin as a breeze.

"Mitch!"

The darkness was thick and heavy. Standing, she inhaled deeply and shook her head to try to clear it.

The charged flush scaled her legs. It spread across her abdomen and chest and seeped up her neck. Her cheeks were ablaze.

Suddenly, her mind sharpened to startling clarity. A heavy pulse throbbed inside her.

Looking around, Maggie noticed that someone had pushed aside the super's temporary barricade, exposing the wide break in the terrace rail.

With purposeful strides, Maggie moved to set the barrier back in place. But as she neared the edge, the urge for safety was displaced by a stronger pull.

Her mind was frenzied. She could climb onto the remnants of the railing. Dance on the breeze. Conquer the sky.

Maggie slipped out of her shoes. Her heart was thundering now. Approaching the rail, she ran her hands over the iron uprights. She had no doubt that they would hold her. She was beyond danger.

Gripping the top rail, she lifted a foot. A sound from behind stalled her: the door sliding open again.

Maggie called over her shoulder: "Hey, Doc. You're just in time for the big show. Watch this."

"I'm watching, Maggie."

Maggie was caught by the voice. Turning, she was shocked to see that it wasn't the face she expected.

CHAPTER

52

Bannister sped toward Maggie's address. Leaning on the horn, he busted the scattered traffic clots and cleared the streets of stray pedestrians. They had to get to her.

Price clutched the dashboard and stomped an imaginary brake.

"Geez, Sammy. Take it easy. You're going to get us killed."

"Maggie told me she's having dinner tonight with that scum Goldberg. She's in danger, Lenny."

"Maybe so, but we'll be more help to her in one piece."

"He must've monkeyed with the phones. That's why I got that out-of-order recording when I tried to call. Son of a bitch!"

"All right, Sammy. Easy now. We'll be there in a couple of minutes. For Chrissakes, you almost hit that bus!"

They turned east at Times Square and headed up First Avenue. Bannister veered around a stalled truck, circled a wedge of construction horses, dodged a weaving drunk.

The way looked clearer as they neared Fifty-seventh Street. Bannister stomped the gas, urging the Camaro to its limits.

"This is crazy, Sam. Slow down. You're going to get a—"

As if in response, a cop car appeared out of nowhere. It wailed up behind them, cap light shooting blue and crimson sparks. Bannister's desperate eye veered from the rearview mirror to Price and back again. He set his jaw.

"Don't even think about it, Sam."

317

"I'll only stop if you promise you'll take care of it."

"How can I promise? What if it's someone I don't have a line to?"

Bannister pressed harder on the gas. The trailing siren grew more insistent.

Price sucked a breath. "All right. Okay. Now for god-sakes pull over before they start shooting."

Bannister did.

"Maybe they can help, Sam."

"Forget it, Lenny. We've got no time for explanations. Besides, these guys are in a traffic ticket mode. You know what it would take to shift them to murder-in-progress?"

Price nodded. "You could be right."

"I know I am."

At the curb, Bannister pressed Price to get out and approach the squad car, badge in hand. The move was risky, he knew, but nowhere near the danger Maggie was facing. They had to get to her immediately. They couldn't afford the time it would take for the cops to run a computer check of the Camaro's plates or anything else.

Bannister's nerves were jangling as he watched his partner at the squad car. Price was leaning in at the window. The two stiffs on patrol were nodding up and down.

Come on, already! We've got to get there.

Under three minutes later, Price waved a hand at the departing cop car and returned to the Camaro.

"Damnedest thing, Sammy. The younger one was Rick Devaney's son. Remember Rick? He used to play on the league basketball team I coached at the Y."

"Sure, Lenny. It's all I think about."

Bannister pulled out and barreled north, desperate to make up for lost time. Seemed an eternity before they turned onto Maggie's street, a dead end abutting the East River.

They ditched the car and raced toward the building's entrance. The lobby was deserted. No one at the door. Bannister found Maggie's name on the posted directory.

"Nine C, Lenny. Hurry."

The elevator opened as they approached. Bannister raced inside, pulling the reluctant Price behind him, and pressed nine. Price was paling, but Bannister couldn't worry about the guy's dread of elevators or anything else. All he cared about was Maggie, about getting to her before it was too late.

Or was it too late already?

Price was panting like an overheated dog. Damned elevator was taking forever. Watching the numbers, Bannister saw that they'd stopped moving.

He pressed all the buttons and pounded the emergency switch. Nothing.

"Hey! Move, goddamnit!" He thumped the elevator wall. "Move!"

"We're stuck?" Price could barely get the words out. His face was chalk.

"Forget it, Lenny. How the hell do we get out of here?"

Price struggled with his shirt collar. "I can't breathe."

"Think, Lenny. Goddamnit. You know everything about everything. How do I get this thing moving?"

Price wiped the sweat pearls from his forehead and swallowed hard. Clenching his eyes, he pointed up. "I don't know. But you can get out through the maintenance hatch."

Bannister saw the metal panel propped in the roof of the car. Standing on the handrail, he was able to reach up and work the square free. Pushing it aside, he hefted himself out of the stranded car. He pressured open the doors to the next floor and slipped through.

"Hold tight, Lenny. I'll send someone."

Price was slumped against the wall. "Yeah, Sammy. Thanks. I'd really like it if you would do that."

CHAPTER

53

Maggie's mind was reeling. "Henry? What's going on? What are you doing here?"

"Watching you, Maggie. Go on. Climb the rail. Don't let me interrupt."

Something in his voice pierced her like a blade. Dropping her foot to the terrace floor, Maggie clutched the iron uprights.

"Where's Mitch?"

"Dr. Goldberg is inside. I told him I needed to speak to you alone for a moment."

"Why? What's wrong?"

The heat had become intense, unbearable. Maggie's skin was on fire.

Henry appeared oblivious. A curious smile stained his expression.

"Nothing's wrong. In fact, I've finally made everything right so Mother can rest easy."

"I don't understand."

"Of course not. You never did. If you had a grain of understanding, you would have allowed me to remain myself. I was fine. Perfectly contented. Mother and I had a wonderful life until you and your damned clinic destroyed everything."

Maggie struggled to think past the stifling heat and her overwhelming desire to slip through the yawning break in the rail.

"That's crazy," she said.

320

"You murdered my mother. You killed her as surely as if you'd pushed her down those stairs yourself."

"She fell. It was an accident."

He was coming at her. "No, Maggie. *You* were the accident. *You* ruined everything I was. Everything I had."

"No, Henry. That's not true. Mitch? Mitch!"

Her voice rode the bloodless trill of Henry's demonic laugh. "He can't help you now, Maggie. Your young friend looked so tired, I put him down for a nice long nap. So many sleepy people here. I left the doorman napping in the storage room. Poor man couldn't keep his eyes open."

Henry was near enough to reach out and push her through the break in the rail. His brow peaked in amusement.

"Go now, Maggie. Give in to it."

"What? What did you do to me?"

"I discovered a chemical door through the fear, an experimental drug developed by one of your young patients. Just what you've always dreamed of, isn't it? A way to steal the fear from me and everyone. You *stole* my fear, you see. It belonged to me, and you took it away."

Maggie's own fear was returning. She felt the looming vastness behind her. The danger gripped her like a vise. She could fall like Lizzie. Plummet to her death like her sister.

She forced her gaze over Henry's shoulder. "Oh, Mitch. Thank God!"

Henry turned his head just long enough for Maggie to grab her mother's prize coleus and toss it at his head. But he ducked, and the pot shattered on the terrace floor. Lifting an elephant's-ear plant, she tried again, but he feinted out of the way at the last instant, and the clay pot smashed against the redwood planter. On the third try, she set him off balance with a false start. When he regained his center, she bashed a prayer plant hard against the side of his head. A startled sound escaped him, and he staggered back.

Trapped, Maggie watched, waiting for him to topple. He sank to his knees. She stepped around him, anxious to get to a safer place. But as she passed, superhuman hands gripped her by the ankles. Hands nudged her toward the broken space in the rail. She was at the edge. Through.

In a desperate rush, Maggie lunged for one of the remaining uprights. She caught it and held fast. Dangling from the terrace ledge, she heard her terrified breath rasp in the void.

Where was he? She had to pull herself up and get past him.

A sudden breeze buffeted her. Her arms ached, and there was a burning in her strained fingers. Not a sound came from the terrace above her. At any moment, he would lean over and spot her. He would pry open her grip and send her tumbling to her death.

Maggie forced away the tightening grip of terror. Groping for the crucial distraction, she thought of her lost twin. Lazy Lizzie. *Lazy bit.* Lost Lizzie across the room. Maggie kneeling on the rug beside her bed. Maggie saying her prayers.

Now I lay me down to sleep.

She saw Lizzie giggling as she pushed the window up. It slid open, smooth as glass. There was Lizzie at the edge, peering out.

I pray the Lord my soul to keep.

Slowly, Maggie pulled herself up until she could see over the concrete terrace floor. Henry was kneeling over the sprawl of broken clay shards and lumps of soil. Henry the neat nut, compelled to clean up the mess, even now.

If I should die before I wake . . .

Maggie raised herself higher, until her forearms were resting on the terrace. Straining, she brought her upper arms onto the concrete floor. Splinters of cracked clay raked her skin, but the pain didn't penetrate. She was too intent on the vivid memory of Lizzie at the window.

"Maggie, look!"

It was Lizzie's voice, small and sweet. Lizzie's tiny form worked to an awkward stance on the far bed. Maggie only half watched. She was concentrating on saying the prayer. The prayer was very, very important, Mommy said. The prayer could keep you safe.

I pray the Lord my soul to take.

Maggie had a knee on the terrace now. Both knees. On all fours, she crawled toward Henry. He was heedless, too busy tidying up.

"Look, Maggie!"

With sickening clarity, Maggie saw her twin disappear out the window. In a breathless rush, she was at the window herself, staring out in horrified amazement, watching her sister's dizzy descent on the hawk's back. The memory played on relentlessly, though she struggled with all her will to shut it out. Lizzie falling. Circling. Spiraling down until she hit the distant pavement with a harsh crack like a clay pot dashed against the terrace floor.

Henry stirred.

Finally, she knew the truth. She hadn't killed Lizzie. All these years, she'd been blamed. Shielded from the haunting facts. All these years, she'd been made to suffer that awful, endless nightmare.

Maggie allowed the rage to claim her. Lifting a pot of salvia high overhead, she brought the full strength of her fury down on Henry's bowed head.

He crumpled slowly, like ice cream melting on a torrid day.

"How many times do I have to kill you, you silly bitch?" he said. His voice wound down like a recorder with spent batteries. "You know I can never repay you, Maggie. You know I will never, never forget."

CHAPTER

54

Bannister bolted up the seven flights of stairs. His lungs were blazing, heart thwacking like a pickax.

Please let her be all right. Please!

He couldn't stem the flood of feelings. Damn it, he cared about the woman. She'd invaded a piece of him he'd declared closed to the public years ago. A place he'd had locked and condemned.

So maybe it was another mistake in the making. Maybe it would come to nothing. Or worse than nothing. That didn't matter. Nothing mattered but seeing her safe and whole.

"Hang on, Maggie. I'm almost there."

Bursting through the fire door on nine, he raced down the hall. The door to 9C was locked. Bannister backed into a running start and bashed it open with his right shoulder. There was a sharp pain in his freshly sewn mid-section, and he felt a warm, sticky rush.

Ignoring it, he raced in through the foyer and started groping his way around the dark apartment. *Where are you, Maggie? Where the hell are you?*

"Who's there?"

Turning, he tracked the voice to the kitchen. Maggie was on the floor. Her hair was a matted mess. Dirt streaked her face, and a rash of angry scratches covered her arms. A purple bruise was rising on the knee visible through the rip in her jeans. Woman was a total wreck. Best sight he'd seen in years. Goldberg was laid out on the floor. Jerk was muttering incoherently.

Bannister grabbed the guy's wrists and urged Maggie away. "Call the cops, Maggie. Goldberg's the one who killed Macklin and Gail Weider. He got his hands on this formula Jason Childs concocted. Makes people do crazy things."

"No, Sam." Her voice was strained but steady. "It wasn't Mitch. It was Henry."

"Henry?"

Maggie shivered, still battling her own disbelief. "He's out on the terrace. I knocked him out with a plant. I locked the door."

Bannister tried to absorb the impossible twist. His mind had already tried and convicted Goldberg and delivered the creep to Rikers Island. Henry? Guy looked like a Good Humor man.

"We'd better call the cops."

"I already did. Henry cut the phone wires, so I went next door and called the police and an ambulance for Mitch. I think he has a concussion."

Bannister deflected a hard stab of envy. "Hope it's not serious."

Maggie caught his meaning and bit back a grin. "It's not, Sam. Mitch is just a friend. I'm worried about Tony the doorman, too. Henry said he knocked Tony out and left him in the storeroom."

"I'll check on him."

His face was chalk pale. Maggie's eyes drifted to his midsection. "What happened to you? You're bleeding."

Eyeing the seeping wound, he winced. "Just a scratch."

Her green eyes went liquid. "I can't believe it was Henry. He hated me for curing his phobia. He blamed me for his mother's death. It's so crazy."

Bannister nodded. "Good diagnosis."

Maggie was staring at his abdomen. "That looks nasty. Sit down. Let me take a look at it."

"Really. It's okay. Everything's okay now."

Their eyes caught and held. Bannister felt a warm rush as if someone had filled his veins with chicken soup. Nice feeling. He hated to have to let it go, even temporarily.

"Will you be okay here alone for a couple of minutes?

My partner's stuck in the elevator. I'll check on the doorman, too."

"Sure, go ahead. Henry's locked out, and the police are
on the way."

"It's just that poor Lenny's phobic about elevators,"
Bannister said. He caught her eye again, and his mind
started dancing like a drunken fool. "Thanks, Maggie.
Really."

"For what?" she said.

Bannister didn't bother casting around for a logical response. None of this made sense, but some of the best
things didn't.

Time to get Price out of the elevator. Time to get his
whole stalled life unstuck and back in motion.

CHAPTER

55

"I'll pay it. I'll pay it not."

Bannister was in his office, sorting the bills. Despite the growing stack of unpaids, he remained curiously at peace. Things felt more sure and settled than they had in years.

His ex-wife, Lila, had a new man in her life, and the acquisition had softened her second row of teeth. The witch had become almost agreeable in their necessary dealings, giving him freer, less regimented access to his little girl. For that or whatever reason, Chloe seemed to be back to her regular self. Now Bannister could speak to his kid without having to don protective gear, and he had a reasonable idea of what to expect when they got together.

His financial situation remained catastrophic, but at least, the uncertainty was over. After several months of wheedling and discussions, Leona Rafferty had given them a definite answer about the reward on Theodore Macklin.

And the answer was no.

No matter how Bannister painted it, he and Price had not proven Macklin's guilt in Martha Rafferty's murder. The best Bannister had been able to squeeze out of Mrs. Rafferty was partial coverage of the mountain of expenses he'd incurred during the chase.

The Macklin case would go down in the Bannister annals as second only to the Schildhauer debacle. Or was it first? Adding up his part of the cost of the rental tenement, the alleged "meals" at Sergio's, and the parking tickets, Bannister figured he'd be paying for that assignment for quite some time. Still, the only thing he really resented was the medical expense. Once he admitted to running up the seven flights to Maggie's apartment and using his shoulder as a battering ram, his insurance company had refused to cover the restitching job. So much for the value of honesty.

So much for his fantasy Caribbean cruise, too. The way things were going, the closest he'd ever come to that was riding the duck boats downtown, something he and Chloe did from time to time on their days out. Thinking of that made him want to see his daughter. Maybe he'd give her a call and find out what she was doing this afternoon. And maybe he'd call and see what the other woman in his life was doing tonight.

On balance, the whole thing had been worth it. More than worth it, he thought, and felt that silly grin he'd been sporting for months spreading over his face.

The phone rang. Bannister expected a cranky creditor, but it was Price. Guy was his usual self, Mary Sunshine in drag.

"Hey, Lenny. Long time no speak. What's up?"

"I've got good news and amazing news, Sammy. You sitting down?"

Bannister made space for himself between the bill hills. "Now I am. Shoot."

Price had the most astonishing tale to tell. After their return from New York, they'd agreed to give up on the Macklin case. All their leads had been squeezed to the limit and found lacking.

But Price, ever the curious one, hadn't been able to resist dabbling with the loose pieces they'd picked up along the way. For the last six months, he'd continued to collect information on the Winslow-Gray Gallery and Nemichev and Sons Jewelers and the Alter Ego costume company and Fern Compton Harlow.

"I finally cracked it last night. Turns out Macklin was part of a money-laundering operation that involved Nemichev, Alter Ego, and the Winslow-Gray. They were turning Colombian drug profits into diamonds and art, selling those, and running the proceeds through a series of dummy corporations. Given the parties involved, there was also some predictable hanky-panky going on with counterfeit gems and fake art works. Very convoluted deal. Took long legs to follow it."

"Where did Macklin fit in?" Bannister said.

"The principals needed to make a lot of big money wire transfers. Because of his investment business, Macklin's company was the ideal front. He zapped the laundered cash to banks in the Caymans and abroad."

Bannister scratched his head. "Can I ask you one question, Lenny?"

"Sure. What?"

"Who cares?"

Price chuckled. "We do. That's where the amazing news comes in. You remember the reward we didn't get for solving the Rafferty murder?"

"Vaguely."

"Well, guess how much the state of Rhode Island had posted for information leading to the successful recovery of the state funds impounded in the Macklin investigation?"

"Are you saying what I think you're saying, Lenny?"

Price was laughing in earnest now. "Can you believe it, Sammy?"

Bannister sighed contentedly. His half of the Rhode Island reward would be just enough to melt the debt mountain with a smidgen left over for a down payment on some more reliable wheels. That happened to be doubly critical now, given his frequent drives to New York City.

"That's great, Lenny. Really terrific."

"We can go to Providence any time to get the check."

"Sign me up."

"Consider yourself signed."

Bannister was about to hang up, but something occurred to him. "What was that singer's place in the scam?"

"Fern Compton Harlow? Funny you should ask. That was the one piece I couldn't work out for the life of me. Held me up for weeks. Turns out, she wasn't part of the money-laundering deal at all. Ms. Harlow's a high-price hooker. Singing's just a sideline and a cover she uses to keep the IRS off her busy back. In reality, the diva travels the world to keep the smiles on rich guys like Ted Macklin and Howard the Frog from the costume company."

Bannister enjoyed a moment of pure, personal satisfaction. From the time he laid eyes on the diva, he'd sensed that she was way out of his price range. Nice to know his instincts were still in decent working order. When all else failed, he'd always had his gut feelings to fall back on.

"Bye, Lenny. And thanks."

"My pleasure, partner."

Bannister hung up and put in a call to his daughter.

CHAPTER

56

The closing reception had been scheduled to end at six, but at six-thirty, the crowd showed no signs of thinning. The symposium had been successful beyond Maggie's most optimistic imaginings. More than five hundred professionals from across the country and several foreign countries had attended. The press coverage was considerable. And the presented papers had generated tremendous enthusiasm and several important fresh insights about approaches to treating anxiety disorders.

Maggie's diabolical high moment was when petite president Alex Ivy strutted to the microphone to offer a few words before the keynote speaker at yesterday's luncheon.

"East End Hospital is proud of its part in this memorable event," he began. "We'd like to thank you all for coming. And we'd especially like to commend our esteemed colleague, Dr. Margaret Lyons, for her considerable efforts in making this conference a reality."

Maggie had sat at the podium, biting her lip to trap the sarcastic laugh. A single thought reeled through her mind as the minimonster finished flinging the bull and left the packed room: *You little shit. I showed you.*

Maggie took a sip of wine. With the conference over, she could relax and enjoy the praise and congratulations of her colleagues. Best of all, she could enjoy the results.

The clinic was secure. They could continue working their small miracles with clients like Jason Childs and Daisy Tyler. Both had worked as conference volunteers.

Jason had arrived wearing an M.I.T. sweatshirt, proud

331

emblem of the school he would start attending in the spring term. Jason had received a full scholarship after the college learned of the young man's outstanding scientific abilities. Turned out that Sam Bannister's partner, Lenny Price, had an old friend in the admissions office.

Daisy had rearranged her job schedule to help with conference registration and assorted other details. She'd been working for the past three months in the hospital gift shop. It wasn't a Madison Avenue boutique, but Daisy had developed a fondness for East End. And working in the gift shop made it convenient for the woman to fulfill her occasional duties as a therapy aide.

The horror with Henry was fading by slow degrees. At the trial, he'd been found not guilty by reason of insanity and placed in a hospital for the criminally insane. Maggie couldn't entirely forget, but most of the time, her mind was aimed in much more pleasant directions.

A hand looped through her arm. Turning, she smiled up at Sam.

"Hey, Doc. Almost ready?" he said with a wink.

"Almost."

He leaned closer, his breath tickling her ear. "I missed you."

"That's nice," she said, commenting on far more than the sentimental words.

So he was a fellow hothead. So he lived three hours away, and they only got to see each other on weekends. These days, Maggie had learned to be more accepting of the things that couldn't be changed. It still felt a little funny, but she was even getting used to the idea of Tina as her dad's new wife. So her stepmother was twenty-seven. Stranger things had certainly happened.

Now if only her mother would reclaim her life as well. Shedding the stifling secret of Lizzie's death had helped a little. Mom had signed up for an advanced horticulture class at the botanical gardens. The professor in charge, a charming Ichabod Crane clone named Nelson Long, had taken quite an interest in the fetching Francine Lyons. Maggie had done everything in her meager power to help the relationship bloom. But Mom was still a stubborn hybrid, highly resistant to the threat of happiness.

But that was her problem, Maggie reminded herself. When Mom decided to surrender to contentment, Maggie would be there to cheer the woman on. Meantime, she had some contentment of her own to enjoy.

She felt Sam's eyes on her. "I'm so happy for you, Maggie," he said in a conspiratorial whisper.

"You'll show me later."

"Whenever you say."

"I say, let's hit the road."

Looping a hand through his elbow, Maggie led him through the crowd toward the exit.

ABOUT THE AUTHOR

If I Should Die is Judith Kelman's seventh novel. In addition, she's written articles for major magazines, including *Redbook, Glamour, Ladies' Home Journal,* and *McCall's,* and for the *New York Times.* Judith Kelman lives in Connecticut with her husband and two sons.